ACKNOWLEDGMENTS

When writing a book, there are many people involved behind the scenes. Special thanks go to my husband, Matt, for his help learning about Indie Publishing and for helping me wade through all of the technology. His passion to see me published is second only to my own.

Ryan Murdock has influenced my writing over the last several years. The extent of his impact became obvious as editing for Chasing began and seven years' worth of material showed my growth as a writer. Thanks Ryan. You're a good friend, and I'm proud of you for making your dreams reality and inspiring me to do the same.

Michael Blankowski, Matthew Funk, Matt Wigdahl, Sandi Leonard, Melissa Green, Jeanne Gostnell, Judi Smedra, Cristi Kimrey, and Lenny Roberts all helped immensely with their feedback on story and cover. Thanks guys!

Lastly, while this book is a work of fiction, I want to thank my own "Oscar" for seeing in me more than I could. He taught me that life is to be lived and not merely survived. Rest well, old man. Rest well.

Kathryn J. Woodall

CHASING

Kathryn J. Woodall

For more information on Kathryn Woodall, Please contact:

A Comfortable Soul Publishing
P.O. Box 1055
Mission, KS 66222

Website: www.acomfortablesoul.com

Chasing is written by Kathryn J. Woodall and published by A Comfortable Soul Publishing

ISBN-10: 098279312X
ISBN-13: 978-0-9827931-2-1

CHAPTER 1

The rain fell softly outside the window. Though Ottum couldn't feel the drops, she knew their cold splash was starkly contrasted to the warm air inside the cozy cabin. The rain's gentle rhythm brought an old song to mind, and the old song brought memories of friends and other places. She smiled.

It had been a few months, but the wave was unmistakable. It passed over and through her, stopping the concert of rain and memory. There was a familiar danger out there in the cold, but familiarity made it no less evil. It would leave a trail of destruction in its wake if left unchallenged. And like all evil, it would not stop coming just because Ottum willed it to stop. Goosebumps formed on her slender, muscular arms while a shiver ran down her spine.

With the wave came restlessness and the knowledge that tonight was her last night in this cabin. Tomorrow she would move on, but for now, this place was hidden from the danger that loomed somewhere in the distance. The wave told her of its approach, but it was not yet so close that it would find her here.

It doesn't matter anyway, she thought to herself. She was a Chaser and therefore was never content to rest for long.

Last spring it occurred to Ottum that she could have a small reprieve from the chase. Something simply told her to take a break. She sometimes laughed about that and how asinine it sounded. *I'm going to take a break from fighting evil.*

It made her seem like a heroine in an epic tale who was having a crisis. Ottum envisioned herself with a perfect body and powers that made her win all her battles. She laughed as hard at this thought as she had at the idea of a break. She didn't feel like a heroine. Right now she simply felt relief that she wasn't out there in the cold rain.

Last spring was the first time since beginning her path that Ottum let the chase drop. She may have decided to take a break to allow herself and her Companion to heal, but Ottum remained mindful of the danger. Evil didn't cease to exist just because she stopped chasing it, and she didn't want to be caught off guard should an Avil engage them in battle.

Every Chaser she had ever known hoped to initiate the fight instead of reacting to an Avil's attack — every Chaser except one. Ottum did not feel that way. She wasn't afraid of the fight, but she held a quiet hope that one day evil would lay down its sword and take a different path. Until that day, she would fight to the death if need be. It was her path and she would walk it to the end.

Kai lifted himself and walked across the cabin to stand with her. He had also felt the wave and knew as well as Ottum that it would be time to go in the morning. He would miss this place but appreciated the bounty of food and the luxury of shelter it had given them for a few months. He leaned against her and she lifted a hand to run it through the thick hair on his head.

He had grown to love this woman. No. It was more than love he felt for her. The Path had pulled them together and there was a sense of destiny in their pairing. He would willingly give his life to see that she continue.

Ottum was more than a Chaser, and Kai knew it even if she wasn't ready to know. She would join the Greybeards, of this he had no doubt. But tonight, they were friends and not just Chaser and Companion. Kai kissed her hand and turned for the bed. Ottum didn't follow, and although he thought that she was wasting the last peaceful night of sleep she would know for what could be a long time, he knew it was pointless to convince her otherwise.

For Ottum, sleep had already been less than peaceful for several weeks now. She enjoyed the cabin and the break as much as Kai, but other things filled her mind with concern. Long after Kai and found sleep, Ottum stood there and watched the rain through flashes of lightening as she planned the next day.

She envied him sometimes. Kai seemed to have chosen this life while it felt to Ottum that this life had chosen her. She had reflexes and thought patterns that suited her well in her tracking and the battles that followed, but they were not things she worked to develop. They simply were. As a child, there were times when she had wished to just shut down her mind for a moment the way she felt the others did. Oscar had told her that it was impossible to do.

"Shut down your mind? Child, you cannot turn off who you are!" he had said, and then he had roared with laughter as though it was the most impossible thing he'd ever heard. When a tear escaped one eye and ran down Ottum's pretty face, Oscar had looked at her through eyes that were not quite blue but not quite gray, eyes with intelligence that was undeniable, and his laughter passed. Those eyes turned thoughtful, and he placed an arm about her. "But I suppose that sometimes it's hard to be who we are. One day you'll know yourself, and that will be enough. You'll come to understand that you're never as alone as you currently believe you are."

Ottum remembered the moment as though it was yesterday. She remembered it as though Oscar was still alive and she could smell the scent that was uniquely him and hear the voice that warmed her heart. It was one of the few things he had told her that still escaped her grasp. Kai might be here with her, and for his company she was extremely grateful, but his presence did not stop the horrible aloneness that washed over her at times.

There were people who knew the evil behind the wave existed, and yet they never felt its effects or desired to change things. There were people who would be content to stay in this cabin for the rest of their lives, to ignore the driving force that turned in her gut and would ultimately push her out the door tomorrow morning. She may not know herself so well that it was enough just to be, but she did know that she was not someone who could ignore all the signs and pretend everything was okay. Because of that, she knew that she should get sleep now while she still could.

Kai woke only slightly as Ottum slid onto the pallet beside him. She placed an arm around him and willed her mind to slow. Details were planned as well as they could be and beginning a journey without sleep would not help things go more smoothly.

Oscar had laughed when Ottum told him she wanted to shut down her mind, but he had somehow understood that it was almost too much for her to handle. So he had taught her a way to slow it.

"Concentrate on just this: I am," Oscar had instructed.

Now she began the chant that would slow her mind and carry her to sleep. *I am, I am, I am, I am*…until sleep took over and Ottum's chant faded to dreams.

CHAPTER 2

Saul topped the mountain with lungs that felt on fire. He'd pushed hard because he felt he was getting close. Once, he even thought the clouds cloaking the trail above him where also cloaking the wretch he had been pursuing. Saul's eyes had convinced him that he might be seeing the shadow of an outline, but he couldn't be certain. He hadn't realized just how close to the summit he'd been at the time, but now that he was here, Saul scanned below him hoping to have a closer look. To his great frustration, the clouds still obscured his view.

"Best not to chase shadows and be spent when the solid is found," he murmured.

He scouted the area and determined that there were no suitable hiding spots that could lead to a second ambush. Then he released his pack and sat upon a large rock to eat and drink. The air was thin here and someone with less endurance would be in trouble at this height, but not Saul.

Being in places like this was one of his favorite parts of being a Chaser. He didn't much care for the things that needed done when an Avil was caught, but Saul loved the journey between those gruesome moments.

Saul's stomach growled to remind him that he was hungry and thirsty. Saul took his knife from its sheath on his waist and cut a piece of jerky. He ate the meat slowly and surveyed what little he could see in front of him.

Saul was still hoping the clouds would burn off and let him know if it was only a shadow he had seen, or if the Avil was within distance of catching today. Begrudgingly, Saul realized that if the Avil was close enough for catching, it wouldn't be known about from here.

Saul took as little water as he could to keep his body functioning until the next stop. It was hard to know when water would be found again, but the snow all around him made it likely that there was a stream further down the mountain. As long as the Avil went down instead of crossing to the next mountain and heading up again, Saul would be able to drink freely within a day. He figured he still had a good four to five hours before sunset, and that meant he could sleep now and not be vulnerable at night. The Avil would expect him to sleep, but Saul knew he could force himself to travel through the night. The idea exhilarated Saul.

"I might even happen on the repulsive creature sleeping and have an easy go of it." This thought led to a much darker one.

"Damn, I miss her," he hissed.

The events of yesterday played out in Saul's memory...

Saul and Eyota were returning from a visit with his family who lived a three-week's journey from the Chaser camp Saul and Eyota called home. The mountain base they now walked along was not on the direct route home, but Saul loved the area enough to add a few days to their return trip. He'd not been here in years, but it was as stunning as he remembered.

Eyota groaned in pain as the wave passed through her. Its agony was in sharp contrast to the beauty surrounding them. The sunlight caught the aspen leaves, and each soft breeze turned the mountains to shimmering gold. But each torturous act that created a wave caused her blue eyes to blink in pained empathy. Eyota didn't need her eyes to find the cause. Instinct led her through the valley in search of the evil that caused the waves, and Saul followed with his sword ready to seek justice. As the pair approached, the sound of the Avil's laughter and its victims' terror guided them. The sight that met Saul and Eyota's eyes sent rage through both of them.

A band of wild horses milled below them, trapped on one side by a steep rock wall and on the other by the strong currents of the river. The horses were panicked, screaming, and pawing at the air as well as each other. The scent of blood only further increased the chaos. Some jumped into the swirling water and made it to freedom on the other side, but many of those that entered the river were overcome by the strong currents and drowned. Those who decided to back track received an arrow aimed as such that it would not kill them but would maim or cause extensive pain. The Avil was hidden from the horses' sight, but it loosed arrows anytime one of the herd crossed an imaginary line that might have carried it to freedom and away from the nightmare.

The sight sickened Eyota. It was all she could do to not howl in rage, but she knew any noise would only further scare the poor horses. There was nothing they could do for those who were injured or dead, but Saul and Eyota wasted no time finding and engaging the Avil. It had trapped the horses, but its own escape route was intact.

Saul and Eyota chased it up the mountain. The Avil stopped to loose arrows at first, but the pair was trained to hunt together. They were agile and powerful, and neither stopped even when an arrow whistled too close for comfort. Trapped and terrorized horses were easy targets; the Chaser and his Companion were skilled warriors. The Avil quickly realized that stopping only decreased the time it would remain alive.

The evil creature they chased was familiar with the territory, so it had an advantage. Compared with most of its kind, it also displayed impressive stamina. Saul and Eyota got close several times, but as daylight faded, the Avil continued to remain elusive.

"We should rest," Eyota said.

"If we lose it in the dark, we may have to hunt it for days," Saul protested. "Mountains make it easier to hide."

"We left before sunrise this morning and have had nothing to eat and very little to drink. We're ascending rapidly, Saul, and the air is thinning. We'd be fools to run low on food, water, and air when a few hours would refresh us," Eyota insisted.

Saul frowned. He hated stopping in the middle of a chase. The absolute injustice of the Avil's actions infuriated him. But his Companion was right, and she was stubborn. Her blue eyes said more than words could. Saul sighed, "Let's find a more sheltered spot, and we'll rest."

They climbed further up to a ledge that made Saul feel better about stopping. The Avil wouldn't be able to descend for as far as the eye could see without crossing this ledge. That meant that the only direction it could go was up. It was likely that the Avil was as tired, thirsty, and hungry as Saul and Eyota. That meant it would probably also stop when it realized the hunters were resting.

Saul and Eyota slipped out of their packs just as evening descended. The air cooled quickly once the sun slipped below the mountain top. Saul built a small fire that offered a little warmth as they ate and drank.

"This one is crafty," Eyota said.

Saul nodded. He'd agreed to stop because he knew Eyota would have it no other way, but his mind raced ahead.

"Do you notice anything different about this one?" Eyota asked.

Saul shrugged. "It's an Avil. How different can it be?"

"I don't know," Eyota replied. "Something just feels different this time. Did you notice how it stopped and looked back when it gained some distance?"

"It was probably just hoping it'd lost us," Saul replied as he finished his food.

Eyota didn't argue, but she silently disagreed. She loved this man, but the intensity of his focus often allowed him to miss important details. Visiting his family made it worse.

Saul's brother had been a Chaser. An Avil's sword ended Jachob's life, and Saul had left to take his place at the camp near his family's home the day after the burial. Saul had been young, but not so young that his parents' objections could prevent his leaving. When they increased their visits and protestations, Saul had transferred to a new camp much further away.

Time had mended the relationship with his parents, but each visit to see them meant that Saul also visited Jachob's final resting site. When Eyota woke on the last day of their visit with Saul's side of the pallet empty, she knew where she'd find him.

Saul had looked so peaceful in his sleep — his bedroll laid out beside Jachob's grave with his hand resting on the cool stones his parents used as a tribute to the strength of their son's honor. Eyota had imagined Saul and Jachob as young boys. Had they laid awake and whispered their dreams to each other? Did Saul fall asleep that night while talking to a brother who could no longer answer?

Eyota looked at Saul across the fire he'd just added more wood to. His rugged frame hid the tenderness she knew existed in his heart. Jachob's death had created a far fiercer Chaser than Saul would have been capable of had his brother lived. When an Avil was being hunted, Saul's focus was intense and ultimately deadly. Saul hated the kills, though. Had Jachob lived, Saul would never have become a Chaser. His father was an artist, and Saul's appreciation for beauty would have easily allowed him to follow in his father's footsteps. Saul couldn't admit to wishing for a different life, but Eyota knew it was true.

"You get some sleep. I'll take the first watch," she said. "And don't argue. You might slay every Avil we find, but you know I'll always win when you and I fight," she continued before he could object.

Saul grinned. "Yes, my lady." Saul settled into the bedroll. Despite his restless thoughts, he was asleep within minutes.

Eyota alternated between watching the fire and scanning her surroundings. She suspected that the Avil had stopped shortly after it realized she and Saul were no longer following. She was exhausted and would have preferred to have slept first, but if she had slept, Saul would have pressed on when she woke instead of taking a turn. She closed her eyes to rest them for a few seconds...

Saul jolted awake to the impossible sound of Eyota screaming as the Avil's blade separated her head and body. The Avil fled immediately, and Saul pursued. However, a man was dead this high on a mountain without his gear, and the Avil knew it. Even with the maddening anger and grief that filled Saul and pushed him to follow further than any other Chaser would have, the Avil was right. Saul abandoned the chase and returned for his gear.

Eyota usually woke him after taking the first watch. But they had pushed hard that day, and she must have drifted off. Life was a horrible price to pay for such a simple mistake. If Saul and Eyota hadn't become so used to each other, they would have known danger was near even in their sleep. Their closeness led to a trust that in turn led to her death.

Saul had gathered his gear and began the hunt again without her. He'd chased the Avil throughout the rest of the night and most of today. But now he sat on the cold top of a mountain. Eyota was dead, he was alone, and he missed her. Once again, an Avil had killed someone he loved. Anger filled Saul, and it occurred to him that he might just enjoy this kill.

There was still something about the whole thing that bothered Saul, though. The Avil had killed Eyota and not him. She didn't wield the sword that would end its existence, so why did it pick her and leave him sleeping when it could have just as easily taken his head first? As he was burying Eyota, this had come to him, and it bothered him still.

But daylight was moving on, and if Saul wanted sleep, he was going to take it now or not have it at all. Eyota wouldn't be here to take the first shift, or any shift, and he couldn't risk the dark alone and asleep. Worse than the dark in this region was the cold. Sleep too long and one might never awaken. Saul unrolled his bag and placed the water in it with him to prevent it from freezing while he slept. Then he programmed his mind to awaken him if danger neared or his body cooled too much. With his sword in hand, Saul drifted to sleep.

CHAPTER 3

Morning came, and though her brain had slowed and allowed sleep, it seemed to Ottum that this dawn had come faster than any since finding the cabin. She could tell by Kai's breathing that he was awake but waiting for her, giving her as much sleep as possible before their small vacation ended and The Path led them back out and into the world. The two of them had become quite close and knew each other in a way only time allowed. It was comforting for Ottum that Kai was a Companion who knew her desires with little outward communication. She had experienced that with very few. He nudged her now and she planted a kiss on his cheek as she rolled over him and onto the floor.

"Time to go," Ottum said.

Kai nodded, and in that comfortable silence they often shared, they gathered their gear were out the door. Each went about their morning routines outside before meeting by the stream. They drank deeply and hoped their journey would keep them close to water for several days.

After checking the fit of the water skins to Kai's back and shoulders, Ottum went to their food stores and gathered as much as she could into her pack. It was a hard thing for her to do, but she removed the remaining food and left it lying on the ground. Leaving it in storage was not likely to help another traveller, and perhaps it would be a pleasant treat for some of the other beings living near the cabin.

Kai was looking at it with the same guilt she felt. It was a hard thing to waste food when it was likely their stomachs would be screaming for it in a few weeks.

Ottum had worked on their food stores without thinking of the possibility they would be on The Path and need food. They'd never known how long they were staying, but she had begun to think it would be through the winter.

The wave last night signaled their departure before winter had even sat in and long before spring, so now they must make the best of it. She hoped her lack of planning wouldn't leave them somewhere on the mountains and dead. With each of them cursing themselves for the mistake, Ottum and Kai slipped out of their packs and sat to eat at least one more non-rationed meal.

When both were satisfied and another trip to the stream had quenched their thirsts, they slipped back into their packs. She and Kai each looked around them one last time. Ottum felt the mental shift happening and the drive taking over. She nodded a humble thank you to the cabin for the shelter and to the surrounding area for its abundance. Then without another glance, her feet turned and started the journey toward the mountains. Kai gave his own nod of thanks and matched her pace.

They had hunted the area near the cabin enough that the land here was still familiar to them. Leaves formed a carpet over ground that would have otherwise been left muddy by last night's rain, and it muffled their footsteps enough they occasionally startled a squirrel as it gathered food for the coming winter. Kai noted the abundance of small animals and was happy that there would still be fresh meat tonight when they camped. Now was not the time to hunt though.

The air warmed as the sun neared mid-sky, and they walked at a brisk clip which left the cabin and all sentiments of it behind them. Kai looked up and noticed what a beautiful blue the sky was——the light blue that only comes in late fall and early winter. He had definitely enjoyed the break, but being back at the hunt with Ottum thrilled him. His right shoulder had healed well and the feel of his muscles against his pack reminded him of how glorious life and hunting is.

He thought back to the wave of last night. There was either great evil involved or he and Ottum were not far from the Avil that caused the wave. He wondered if a Chaser had fallen at its hands. Kai only felt the wave, but he knew that Ottum would have known where it came from and that the trail they were walking led them toward it.

Ottum and Kai had been together for several years now and it was uncanny how she sometimes just knew things. He had known no other like her and yet felt a comfort with her that grounded him. He saw it in others too. They would be drawn to her and then almost unsettled by the depth of understanding she possessed. Yet despite the fear that in knowing them she would hurt them worse than any other, they trusted her and opened themselves further. It was as though she saw inside them the best they could be and then taught them to see it too. He wasn't sure if it was a gift or a skill she had acquired, but he knew it was a difficult thing for her to bear sometimes. Kai could understand that difficulty. It would be a delight to help someone see a better version of his or herself into being, but it would be a sad thing indeed to watch someone turn away from it and choose the lesser self.

Kai didn't know much about the Avils. He knew their scent, their appearance, and their ways, but he didn't want to believe what he had been taught about how they came to be. Mostly they appeared human in form, and yet, they were so evil that it was hard to imagine them being human at all. He wondered if that was how they got their name. Perhaps 'all evil' had been shortened to 'Avil.'

Avil's didn't beg for their lives to be spared when engaged and obviously losing. When they knew they were beaten, most of them would laugh the laugh that always made Kai feel sick to his stomach. The last one they engaged had simply fallen to its knees and placed its broken sword on the ground while laughing at them. But Ottum didn't take it that way. To Kai's horror, she had stepped away and lowered her sword. The Avil had run, and so they chased it again before catching it and repeating the fight. It didn't run the second time, but the broken end of the Avil's sword sliced into Kai's shoulder before Ottum managed to take the Avil's head. Kai asked Ottum about her actions later, because he could not understand them.

Ottum had shrugged her shoulders and replied, "I would've always wondered if the Avil regretted its life and decided to do better just as I took its head. I gave the Avil a chance, but I couldn't allow it to kill a being as good and just as you."

And that had been the end of it. Kai found it hard to understand how she had shown kindness in a moment that he, and he imagined most others in similar circumstances, had found consuming. He knew he would have killed without a second thought, but Ottum had given the Avil a second chance. Even though her decision was the reason his shoulder ached now, he didn't complain. He shifted the pack on his back, marveled again at the beauty of the sky, and thanked the universe that he was so lucky as to still be walking through the vast land of Nohnah with this delightful creature beside him.

CHAPTER 4

Ottum had been watching Kai and wondered what was running through his mind. He'd blocked her out of his thoughts and because it was so rare, she became curious as to why. As companions, they shared everything and kept few secrets from each other. It was usually she who shut him out to think through things that were troubling her or to reflect on something that involved him, but Kai mostly allowed her completely into his world. Ottum noticed that his gait had changed slightly and wondered if his shoulder was causing him pain. It was her fault the Avil had cut him, and she felt guilty about it. Still, in her heart she had so hoped that just once one of those creatures would make a good choice. She knew she wished it for selfish reasons, but it didn't stop the wishing.

Kai opened back up at that moment, so she did too. Speaking without opening her mouth was delightful for Ottum. It was something those who shared The Path could do. It was hard to get used to at first, but she eventually preferred it to using her voice.

"How's the shoulder?" Ottum asked.

"It is fine. It got lazy while we rested, and it is complaining a touch. But it will learn to work again," he said with a toss of his head. He shot her a look that dared her to baby him, but she knew better.

Ottum had watched his fierceness in battle and understood that, although it was in some ways her fault, it was Kai's injury. His decisions had led to it as much as hers had. She knew he would allow her to help soothe it tonight, but for now, he would bear its pain alone, and she would respect that.

"You'd better not expect extra rations tonight because of it," she teased. "Well, perhaps an extra crumb or two if you can sing for it."

Kai threw back his head and howled loudly as Ottum burst into a fit of laughter.

"What? Not what you had in mind?" he asked.

"Much more of that and we won't be eating fresh meat tonight," she laughed as the squirrels and rabbits anywhere within hearing distance scrambled to safety.

Kai watched them scamper away but knew he and Ottum would be far enough by the time they camped that his outburst wouldn't be a factor. "Perhaps you should let me worry about the fresh meat while you sing tonight."

"Perhaps," she said, merriment still playing across her face.

Kai loved to hear her sing. Oscar had taught her some of the old songs, and she had become quite good at singing them. She tried to teach Kai, but he preferred to listen and didn't try very hard to learn. He suspected she knew this and was gracious enough to let it be. To his delight, Ottum started to sing as they walked.

"Oh I once was a river of water. My path followed the earth's twists and turns. I may have followed the land but I left behind something grand. You'd be surprised what sure and steady can do.

Oh I once was a cone on a pine tree. I fell off and was buried by earth. But I reached for the sky, and the earth, water, and I made a tree that is bigger than you.

We are all made of fire, earth, and water. And we all have metal and wood too. Forget not from what you are made. You will return to them one day whether a wise man, a man, or a fool."

As she finished the verse Ottum closed her thoughts to him, and Kai knew it would be awhile before they spoke again. He had enjoyed the song and hummed silently to himself as they walked.

The song she had sung reminded Ottum of Oscar. Lots of things reminded her of Oscar lately, but she wasn't sure why. He had certainly taught her much about life, and she dearly loved him, but Oscar had been dead for a while now. Ottum wasn't one to hang on to the past, so it frustrated her that sometimes she could almost feel him with her or hear him in her thoughts. The worst were the dreams she had been having lately. In them she was standing with Oscar by a camp fire, and he would tell her to come to him when it was obvious she was standing right there.

He would reply to her, "No, you are only here in thought. Come to me."

The first night it was just a strange dream and since she had been thinking of him, Ottum dismissed it as nothing. But the dream occurred each night now, and Oscar was getting more urgent in his request to come to him. The dream was beginning to feel like one of her moments of knowing, but those always involved living people. Oscar was not alive.

It occurred to Ottum that perhaps she was going mad. Maybe the constant stress of chasing and striving to be better had caused something to snap in her, and each day she would become less grounded and more unstable. Perhaps that was what had happened to her brother. When she heard that Leon had become an Avil, she thought maybe he'd made bad choices for so long he no longer knew right from wrong. But perhaps he had just gone mad. This thought troubled her greatly.

She didn't feel like she was going mad with the exception of the strong sense that Oscar was near her and asking her to meet him. *If I am going mad, would I really know it or would I just find a way to rationalize the irrational thoughts?* She wasn't sure, but she did know that even if she weren't going mad, thinking this way would cause her to do so.

Ottum thought back through the many times she and Oscar had spent together. She remembered his lessons and the love he'd shown her. As her mind wandered, her feet stayed on course as though she had split herself into two creatures—one that had a clear purpose and destination which was never questioned, and one that struggled to make sense of the side that had no questions. Ottum finally settled her mind and thought through the dream. She tried to remember details that might be hints from the part of her capable of sensing what she couldn't yet see. *Maybe there's a lesson I need to learn before engaging this Avil, and perhaps Oscar's likeness is only being used because he was my mentor.* If the dream came again tonight, she would try to let it play out instead of waking herself to escape the discomfort.

As the thought of night came to her, she looked around and realized that dusk was upon them. They had made good time today, and it was reasonable to rest instead of pushing on through the dark. Kai's shoulder needed attention, and they needed food. Ottum opened her thoughts again.

"Welcome back. Shall I hunt now or are we pushing on a bit longer?" Kai asked.

"Hunt," was her only reply. Though she sent a weak smile his way, Ottum had already closed her thoughts to him again and was lost in them.

Because she'd been shutting him out more than usual lately, Kai knew Ottum was troubled about something. No good would come from asking her about it though. She would either talk when she was ready, or she would solve the problem and be done with it. Asking her would just result in her shutting him out even more. He supposed he could feel angry or hurt by this, but he'd been with her long enough to know it was just her way and that it had nothing to do with her trust of him. So Kai shrugged out of his pack and left Ottum making camp while he went to hunt their meat for the night.

Damp leaves provided a carpet to soften his steps, and shadows formed by the fading daylight helped hide him. Kai walked quickly until he was far enough from Ottum and camp that any noise she made was gone. Having decided that he was far enough away, he slowed his pace and primed his senses for the hunt.

Up ahead he saw a small group of trees with squirrels busily gathering nuts at their bases. Kai walked as softly as he could and placed each step with caution until he was standing beside one of the trees. Then he waited patiently for the opportunity he needed. His shoulder was sore from the first day of use in a long time, and he hoped it would not bother him now. One of the squirrels started toward the tree. Kai moved so quickly he had grabbed and shook the squirrel before any of the others even realized he was there. While the other creatures scrambled for their lives, the one Kai was holding lay dead without even the chance to react to its assailant. The others scolded after Kai as he turned toward camp with his and Ottum's dinner secured. He was proud of how easily he'd succeeded in the hunt.

Ottum had a fire started by the time Kai returned, and a real smile spread across her face when she saw the squirrel he carried. She took it from him and set about preparing their dinner. Kai noticed she had opened her thoughts again, and he felt pleased that the evening would be filled with conversation.

When dinner was prepared, they sat and ate together. The fire kept the chill of the night at their backs. As they ate they watched the flames dance, throwing light in seemingly random patterns about the fire. The aspen were blended with pine trees here, and the pine branches caused sparks to jump as it burned.

"Do you feel we were pulled away from the cabin before we were ready?" Kai asked.

"No," Ottum said with a shake of her head. "You're mostly healed, and I had rested. The Path is our destiny, and we can't turn that off or on at will. It was time or we wouldn't be here."

It was then Ottum realized that Kai was wondering what she had been thinking about all afternoon. It wasn't Kai's way to ask her or push if she didn't offer an explanation, but he would continue asking questions full of concern until she reassured him she was comfortable with where they were going.

"I suspect we'll run into an Avil about half way up the mountain we're headed for. It'll probably take us a couple of days to reach it, though. The Avil doesn't bother me, but I suspect there is something more to this chase…something different," Ottum paused. "The Avil feels somehow familiar and yet dangerous. But I can't figure out why."

That was as much as she would say, and Kai knew it. He stretched his shoulder and Ottum moved close to begin work. First she made sure the shoulder joint was moving properly, and then she started to work on his sore muscles.

It was hard to not move away from the pain, but Kai knew when she was done it would feel good again, so he breathed deeply and allowed Ottum to continue. She worked on him for the better part of an hour, and when she was done, Kai's shoulder felt healthy again. He kissed her cheek in thanks and then headed to the water for a drink. She followed and was grateful his vision at night was better than hers. In so many ways they complimented each other.

Back at camp, Ottum added more wood to the fire and unrolled their bag while Kai checked their perimeter. Then they both settled into the bag for sleep. There was no need for a guard yet, but they both set their minds to awaken if there was danger near. Ottum wrapped her hand about her sword before closing her eyes.

Kai was asleep almost immediately, but Ottum chanted her way there slowly. She looked forward to sleep, but at the same time, she held trepidation. Finally her mind allowed her to drift into slumber.

* * *

Oscar was sitting by the fire tonight instead of standing. He turned his head toward her as Ottum became aware of him.

Ottum struggled to control and analyze this dream. It was hard for her to see Oscar, and she wanted to retreat and force herself awake. He'd been a father to her and was the only person she'd ever completely trusted. Oscar was part of her in a way no one else was, and his death took a part of Ottum with him. So despite the growing desire to either embrace him or to force herself awake, she simply stood still in the dream.

Oscar sat there quietly and watched Ottum as she stood and surveyed him. He was dressed in a heavy winter coat, leather gloves, and warm leather boots. The fur-lined hood rested on his shoulders instead of atop the thinning grey hair on his head. Ottum knew the craftsmanship of every item of clothing he wore to be Oscar's. She also knew he would have used every part of the animals he killed, not just those parts necessary to make his clothes. She watched him reach out with his left hand to pick up a stick to push a log further into the fire.

He was the Oscar she had always known except he had a beard now. She loved beards and had asked him to grow one when he was alive, but his reply was that it always grew in gray and he wasn't ready for that yet.

"I see you like my beard. It took you long enough to notice it. Are you slipping since I left you?" Oscar asked as a wry smile played across his face.

Ottum forced herself to stay in the dream. She might have added a beard to his image, but this was definitely Oscar. He would so often taunt her as he was teaching.

"My child," he said as he shook his head side to side ever so slightly, "you still don't understand what's going on, do you?" Without giving her time to reply, he added, "But at least you're on your way to me now."

Ottum figured she had nothing much to lose except her mind, and it might be slipping away a little more each time she had this dream anyway. "What *is* going on here?"

Oscar laughed at her. "Now when did I ever give you a straight answer if there was something important to learn?"

Ottum considered this and realized she couldn't remember even one instance when he had. Oscar had loved her without question, and she trusted him fully. Some piece of her wanted desperately to believe that the man here with her now was somehow going to continue to come to her in her dreams to teach her as he had when he was alive—that he would always be with her. *Well, that's just crap,* another part of her interjected. *This is just a dream I made up because I trust Oscar, and there's a lesson I need to learn before facing the Avil further up the mountain. His image is simply the fastest way for me to learn because it's an established way.*

"You never did," Ottum said to Oscar. "So how do I go about answering your question?"

"You'll figure it out. Continue your journey to me. See you tomorrow," he said with a grin.

And then Oscar was gone. Ottum looked around her but there was nothing left of the dream scene except her. She was not awake and she had not ended the dream, but everything about the dream had ended like a curtain falling after the last act of the plays she'd watched during her time in Mandolia.

Ottum forced herself awake, and her eyes were met with blackness similar to her dream world, except that stars showed through the trees as the wind blew. Kai was still asleep, so she got up and added some wood to the fire as extra caution that there would still be at least a few embers burning come morning. Then she settled back into the roll beside Kai. The stars' position indicated she had only been asleep for an hour or two. Hoping for another glimpse of Oscar, Ottum lightly grasped her sword and willed herself back to sleep. Though sleep came, the dream with Oscar did not return. Instead, her dreams carried her up the mountain to a laughing Avil kneeling by a stream.

* * *

Kai woke Ottum the next morning and nodded to the squirrel on the ground near the fire. It was evidence of a successful early morning hunt.

Ottum watched Kai moved and knew that his shoulder felt better today than it had since being injured. The use followed by her work seemed to be speeding his improvement.

"I see you enjoyed the hunt so much last night that you had to repeat it this morning," she said, her speech still sounding sleepy even in Path.

"I actually repeated it twice, but was so hungry that one of them disappeared into my stomach while you slept," Kai said with pride.

Ottum smiled and roused herself from the bag. Kai had pulled the skin off of the squirrel for her. She laid it in the remaining embers of the fire to cook while she went about her morning routine and packed up camp. She was anxious for the day to get on so she could see if the dream with Oscar returned tonight.

"You are certainly in a good mood this morning. It is good to see you less distracted than you have been of late," Kai said.

Ottum knew he hoped she'd worked through that which had occupied her thoughts yesterday. She guessed that he wanted her to share the entire process, but she wasn't ready to share her dream yet.

"Great tasting squirrel! Thanks for getting breakfast," Ottum said as a means of changing the subject.

"I figure it will be the easiest hunt we have for a while. Once we're higher up the mountains, it will be the occasional rabbit, and if we are really lucky, a deer. But they are both faster than the squirrels and harder to surprise. So enjoy it, my lady."

Kai turned to head to the water when Ottum remembered her dream.

"Not today, Kai. We'll drink from the skins today," Ottum said.

"But there is fresh water right there, and we may need what is in the skins later," Kai almost whined at her.

"Not today," Ottum said with a sharp shake of her head. "I saw something last night and would rather be safe."

Kai's golden brown eyes looked questioning at her before he said with a toss of his head, "It is hard to argue with something that makes my pack lighter."

She filled a cup with water from the skin and sat it beside him. When he was done she finished it off. Then they slid into their gear and started on their way.

* * *

The terrain allowed them to cover a good distance. Ottum was pleased that they would begin the sharpest assent tomorrow. She was also anxious to return to sleep that night, so she rushed through the evening chores.

Kai felt he had caught the squirrels a little too easily, so they ate and drank from the supplies they had packed.

"What did you see last night?" Kai asked.

"I don't know if it was anything more than a dream, but there was an Avil bent over a stream. It was laughing," Ottum added.

"Those laughs are sickening. That was not a dream; it was a nightmare," Kai said while shaking his head as though he could hear the Avil's laugh. "What could be used to poison a stream to the extent that it is harming the creatures this far from the source?"

"Who said something was dumped in? I said that in a dream an Avil was bending over the water," Ottum replied with irritation in her voice. She hated it when others assumed her dreams or thoughts were reality when there was no way to know for sure. Just because they were sometimes accurate did not mean they always were. Then, softening some because it was Kai, she continued, "I would guess that if the stream is poisoned, it's with something I'm not familiar with. We need to get higher up the mountain and find that Avil, though. It's up to something more than the typical trickery, and it makes me uncomfortable not knowing what."

"Shall we push on?" Kai asked.

"No. We stay here tonight," Ottum said with a gentle shake of her head.

Her reply surprised Kai. He wondered if she was fighting her call to The Path, but then it occurred to him that perhaps she was hoping for another glimpse of the Avil in her dreams. He'd heard the irritation in her voice earlier, but he also knew Ottum trusted those dreams and flashes of pictures more than she let on. She just didn't like it when others did.

"If we are staying, can I get those magical hands of yours on my shoulder again?" Kai asked.

"Come here," she said patting the ground beside her. As she said it, the memory of Oscar telling her to come to him ran through her mind. Knowing it would distract her too much, she pushed the memory aside and concentrated on Kai. His shoulder was almost completely healed, and she realized that now she was mostly taking away soreness instead of helping him heal.

Ottum worked silently, and Kai was content to trade her touch for her thoughts. Ottum's hands were skillful, and the soreness of the day melted beneath her fingers. There was something else to her touch that was more than just knowledge of his body, but he didn't have a name for it and figured names didn't really matter when whatever it was worked so well. He was disappointed when she pulled away and declared her work done. Kai knew she had taken care of his shoulder adequately, but he'd hoped for a little extra work just because it felt good. Tomorrow would bring them close enough to the Avil that any relaxation would be tinged with vigilance.

While Kai was wondering why she had stopped so soon, Ottum was already starting her chant and preparing the campsite for sleep. She hoped it would slow her mind enough to find sleep quickly tonight. The chant worked well, as it always did, and she was drifting toward Oscar before Kai had even settled in the bag with her.

* * *

Saul awoke with a start and made ready with his sword. His senses screamed that something was wrong, but his eyes could see nothing. The clouds had thickened and daylight faded while he slept. The combination impaired his view to only that which was just a few feet in front of him.

Knowing his eyes would be of no help, Saul shut them again while willing his heart rate and breathing to slow. Using every resource available, he could still sense nothing around him. After several minutes of this, he opened his eyes and chanced to move out of his bag. Feeling an attack was imminent, he was clear of the bag and on his feet quickly. Saul's eyes were open again and trying valiantly to adapt to the sub-optimal conditions. He saw nothing except the gray mist of the cloud surrounding him. Even the mist was darkening as the sun slid below the edge of the unseen horizon. Only rocks with the appearance of solidified fog broke the white of the snow on the ground around him. The feeling of imminent danger was receding, but the sensation of something very wrong was not. It didn't make sense. However, unable to confront an unknown danger, Saul sheathed his sword and gathered his supplies to resume the chase.

When he had the bag rolled and all of his supplies strapped to him, Saul paused to drink from his skin. The thought occurred to him that he could fill this partially empty skin with snow for later. The snow here seemed pure enough, and water was always something to have handy. But he was in a rush to catch the wretched Avil and decided it would be a waste of time when there was bound to be a stream somewhere down the mountain.

The sensation that something was wrong lingered with him as he started his journey into what was rapidly becoming the black of night. All of Saul's senses were alert, but as he made his way down the mountain, no attack came. After a couple of hours of walking without so much as a hint of the Avil or any visible signs of a trap, Saul allowed himself to relax. By keeping his mind and body constantly alert for danger, he was causing fatigue and not allowing his instincts to do their jobs. He had never felt such a strong sense of danger without actually having had danger near, so it was difficult for Saul to let it go. But in the end, he shifted from being on guard to the task at hand. As his vigilance dissipated, his tracking skills came to the forefront again.

The clear, cold smell of mountain air filled his lungs and nose, and for the first time since waking, Saul was aware of the beauty of the night. The clouds had cleared and a full moon lit the way. Its light caught patches of scenery and painted the landscape into a living version of his father's craft.

It was bitterly cold, but Saul barely noticed. He loved the mountains, and thought he would live on one if the day ever came when he stopped chasing. Small shrubs and pine trees that were twisted as a result of surviving years of wind and harsh climate started to show themselves more often. He wondered if he would look as gnarled as those trees when he was old. Trying to imagine himself several years down the road and failing, he wondered if he would even become old.

A chill passed through him, and suddenly Saul was ready to be somewhere warmer. In another hour or so he would cross the timberline and there would be some shelter from the icy wind. There was no real comfort in that knowledge, as there would also be more shelter and more hiding places for the Avil. Still, he was tired of zigzagging back and forth across the rock, ice, and snow that made his descent slow. The timber would at least be a change of landscape, so he walked on.

Clouds moved in and covered the moon. Saul had barely made it to the timber line and into the thickening pines when snow started falling. It took longer than he had estimated to reach the timber, and the extra time in the icy wind made the shelter of the trees a welcome relief. He paused to take a sip of water from its skin. The effects of such a hard push during the last few days of hunting were taking their toll. Saul wasn't in trouble yet, but he could feel the hunger, thirst, and general achiness building. He promised himself he would care for himself as soon as he caught and destroyed the Avil. Until then, Eyota's memory would be enough to keep him going.

There hadn't been a single trace of the Avil since Saul started down the mountain. Perhaps that shouldn't have surprised him, but he hoped for at least a hint that he was on its trail. A large gust of wind swirled already fallen snow around Saul's feet. Looking back at where he had come from, only the most recent prints were still viewable. The Avil's tracks would be covered too. There were other ways to track a creature, a broken branch here or there, but Saul saw none of them. There was a lot of mountain, and it was impossible to know if he had entered the timber anywhere near the same spot as the Avil. Saul was frustrated with the lack of certainty, but he decided to continue making his way down the mountain because it was the most likely route the creature had taken. Come morning, he would stop to see if he could feel or find the Avil's presence on the mountain.

It seemed to Saul an eternity passed before morning finally cast daylight into his world. He had walked for hours through the cold of night. With each step he wished he could slice around the trees and down the mountain as easily as the icy wind. In areas where the trees thinned slightly, the wind tossed snow about on the ground as though it was searching for something or someone beneath it.

Saul was no longer aware of being cold or sore. He held no thought but that of finding the Avil, and his mind willed his feet to continue going forward even though his body was begging for shelter, rest, and care. But Saul's single-minded focus on the hunt forced him through his body's increasing protests. He continued on until his body was so in need of food and water that the pain could no longer be ignored. Once the signals became so persistent that Saul finally recognized them, his hunger and thirst were almost overwhelming. The babbling of a nearby stream settled the decision of which to satisfy first.

Saul sat his pack down on the bank and removed the skin that served as both a cup and a bowl. Lying down on the snowy bank, he reached beyond the icy edge and filled his cup as full as he could before sitting back on his knees and lifting it to his lips. His body was so dehydrated and tired that he couldn't distinguish the thirst, hunger, and pain sensations from the instinctual danger warning his mind tried to communicate. He drank the entire bowl, filled another, and drank it completely before he recognized the warning for what it was.

Saul immediately forced himself to vomit, but it was too late. He had been so in need of water that his body had greedily taken in some of what he had given it despite the poison the water contained. Now in addition to the other pains he had been feeling, he could feel the poison spreading through him.

What Saul had considered pain a moment before was now a small ache in comparison. His vessels burned as the fiery poison spread through them, and his muscles felt as though they might shred away from his bones. His vision altered, tilting his surroundings and altering his balance. Saul had pushed through the last several days because he knew his body could take the abuse. He'd pushed excessively on many occasions in the past and never regretted his actions. It seldom mattered how tired, hungry, or dehydrated he was when he engaged an Avil. Training and instinct always took over and carried him through the fight. Saul realized with sudden concern that he had no training or instinct to carry him through this fight.

Poison doesn't think or swing a sword. I just need to keep my head and I'll be fine, Saul lectured himself.

He reached for his pack, removed the skin of water, and drank deeply. Saul's aim was to dilute the poison that cursed through him, but his body would have none of it. He hadn't protected it, and now it would protect itself. With more force than when Saul had induced it, the contents of his stomach once again were hurled out and onto the ground.

This is the danger I sensed on the mountaintop. I shouldn't have let my guard down!

Saul knew he needed to get away from the stream and to find someplace safe to wait out the effects of the poison. If the poison didn't kill him, and the Avil wasn't watching for this moment so as to come out from hiding and take his head, Saul would surely pass out and freeze to death. Though he might regret prolonging his agony if he were to die anyway, Saul's will to live urged him to find shelter.

He tried to stand, but his legs would not hold his muscular frame. Complicating his plight, Saul's vision was distorting even more. The earth rolled about him and the snowy land waved every time he dared open his eyes. Saul grabbed for his pack again and tried to put it on his back, but gravity held it firmly to the ground. The poison had turned the strength of a warrior to that of a small child. Realizing he had no other choice, Saul hooked one of pack's leather straps so it lay in the crook of his elbow. He then closed his eyes to force the land to stop moving as he inched toward shelter.

It took every reserve of mental and physical strength Saul had, but he managed to move himself away from the babbling water. After making it a few meters, he realized that just leaving the stream wasn't going to help him. He opened his eyes and was greeted with a horrendous roll that left him heaving again. The effects of the poison were increasing so that it was becoming more difficult to think with each passing minute. His mind scrambled through his memory to find any piece of information that might help him. Then he remembered.

There had been scratches on several of the trees not far from the stream. Getting there would only be part of the problem, but he started angling that direction. Having a goal to focus on, his body again gave way to his mind so that his hands and feet slowly pulled and pushed him where he wanted to go. The fire coursing through him would occasionally distract him so much that he wanted to stop and let the cold freeze him just to make the burning go away. However, that was a more permanent solution than he was looking for. He took a mouthful of snow as a consolation and started moving again. The snow eased the throb in his tongue and seemed to give his mind a touch of peace. Saul knew better than to swallow the snow even when it melted. Holding it in his mouth to ease the pain of his tongue would have to be enough.

Saul wasn't sure how far he had gone and hoped it was further than it felt. Not wanting the effects of doing so, but knowing there was only one way to find out, he spit out what was left of the snow and opened his eyes again. The rolling was immediate, but his stomach did not lurch this time. He tried to figure out where he was, but in addition to the rolling, there was now at least two of each object he saw. Trying to make out scratch marks well over a yard high on scaly-barked tree trunks was challenging enough. But when the trees were also rolling and doubled, the task was even harder for a poisoned mind to accomplish. Saul wasn't sure if there were no scratches here or if he simply couldn't discern them, but he decided to try going further. So he closed his eyes, took another bite of snow, and willed his body to allow him to continue.

Stopping to rest Saul decided to attempt looking at the trees for scratches again. The fire coursing through him wasn't burning as hot, but his vision was worsening. His muscles felt as though every one of them had been pummeled and left barely attached to his bones. But he justified the muscle pain by reminding himself of how hard he had pushed recently and how dehydrated he was. He looked up and did his best to focus on the trees as they danced and confused him. Finally he saw what appeared to be a group of firs with scratches on them. Or at least he thought they were a group. It was possible it was just one tree his vision multiplied into a group. Regardless, he was fairly certain it was marked.

Now the difficult part began. Any shelter here was buried in snow, and he would have to dig to find it. Reaching deeply into his memory and training, he remembered the openings often faced north and were in the center of the markings. He crawled to the group with the markings and looked around again. He spotted another group of trees almost straight across from this one. He estimated where the center would be, crawled there, and began digging.

If Saul could have accessed his humor, he would have found it amusing that he had eight hands digging in front of him in four different holes. But not one of them found an opening. Knowing there was no other way, he moved a slight amount to his right and started digging through the snow again. As his eight hands found ground time after time, Saul's will started to fade.

I have to survive. I owe it to Eyota to kill the bastard that did this.

Deciding there were worse things to experience, Saul swallowed the snow that had melted in his mouth. Although his stomach clenched, it accepted the moisture this time. He took another mouthful to let it melt and moved to dig again.

It took nine attempts but finally his hands dug through snow and found the air he was looking for. He again swallowed the mouthful of melting snow and took one last handful of the cold powder before heading into the tunnel.

Although Saul knew what he wanted to do, there were at least four openings in front of him. It made choosing the right one challenging. No matter which opening he picked, his pack was not going to fit. Realizing where he was going, he decided it was best to leave it outside anyway. The scent of food would serve him better if it wasn't on his body. He blindly pulled the water skins off and attached them to his belt. Finally he gave up trying to pick the right entrance and just started crawling forward.

Saul had crawled only a short distance before it was too dark to see anything. He sighed in relief that his poisoned vision tolerated the dimness. The risk now was not in dying from the outside elements as much as it was of dying from the inside inhabitant or inhabitants. His training had taught him that hibernating bears either run or fight when unexpectedly awoken. He hoped that if there was a bear at the end of this tunnel, it would be the kind that wanted to run. He also hoped he'd be able to get out of its way. The poison was affecting his entire body now and he knew he was not going to make it much further. To his great relief, his hands felt the tunnel widen. He listened closely until he was fairly certain that the bear was on his right. Then he followed the left curve until his feet were out of the tunnel and in the den. Finally he swallowed the last mouth of snow, rolled to his back on the cool earth, tucked his water skins under his coat, and gave in to the sweet release of unconsciousness.

* * *

Fire! He had made it into the bear's den and had managed to survive the poison, but now the Avil had found him and lit a fire in the den.

Saul felt his flesh blister as the flames licked at him, and his lungs burned as they took in the putrid, smoke-filled air. The stench was nauseating.

My eyes! Why can't I open them? I've got to get out of this fire!

No matter what direction Saul moved, he couldn't escape the flames.

Are my parents to lose another son? Will they even know I died, or will they be left to wonder what happened to me for the rest of their lives? I can't do that to them.

The bear awoke and growled its displeasure at having its long nap so rudely interrupted. In anger, the mighty creature flailed a paw at Saul.

The claws sliced through Saul's gut. He felt them rip through his skin, tear his muscles, and slice into organs as easily as Saul's finest hunting knife would have. Saul screamed in agony, and the bear's answering roar nearly deafened him.

No! I've got to get out of here. I'm not ready to die.

Tears ran down Saul's cheeks. He fought against the panic and tried to find a way to escape. All that came to mind were a jumble of questions. Should he roll to put out the fire that was consuming him or would he just be rolling around in his own blood? Was there any chance he would live with the extensive burns he already had all over his body and the gaping tear in his gut? Should he just crawl out of the den and let the Avil take his head? Could he even make it to the opening of the den?

Saul had lived his entire adult life fighting Avils. Now he would die at the hands—no not even at the hands of—but in a fire started in a bear's den by an Avil.

What a mess I've gotten myself into! he thought as his frustration mounted by the second. Even if he could find his way out, the Avil would be waiting with sword in hand to take his head or feet as he emerged. But if he stayed, the next swipe of the bear's claw might save the Avil the trouble.

Suddenly the fire solved Saul's dilemma as it engulfed his legs in flame. The pain made it impossible to do anything but rock from side to side and scream. Saul shrieked with horror as the bear faced a similar plight and started to fall. Saul watched the bear's body floating toward his own head as though time was distorted and all actions were slowed. Then the bear was upon him, and Saul's head could take the pressure no more.

Saul's last thought was that if there were a hell, he would find this Avil in it and make sure it was well compensated for the evil it had performed here.

CHAPTER 5

The fire was burning low as Ottum entered into its dancing light. She marveled at the beauty of a fire completely encircled by snow. A log settled, and sparks flittered into the air. One tiny ember soared toward Oscar's cheek, but faded to ash and drifted away to his side. Oscar smiled at her, and for a moment, she forgot she was dreaming. She guessed that his face was not especially handsome, but as was always the case with love, Ottum saw him with her heart more than with her eyes. She felt a flood of emotion coming and surrendered to it.

"I miss you, Oscar." Ottum's voice carried both longing and loss.

"I'm right here," he said with a shrug of his shoulders and a gentle smile.

"No," Ottum said with a sad shake of her head. "You're a dream. You were my teacher and a father to me. When you were alive, I never told you how much I love you. But this," she pointed at him, "is not you. This is an image of you my mind has animated for a dream. Telling you here will mean nothing."

"I know you love me, child. You told me in hundreds of ways if not by words. And things that happen here *are* just as important as those that happen when you're in a more wakeful state. Although you're not quite awake here, you're also not quite asleep," Oscar said.

Ottum considered his words. Oscar had taught her to control her dreams when she was much younger. It was something she'd become quite skilled at doing. She decided to add a little flair to the dream and turned her fur lined leather coat to a dressy blue jacket. Oscar looked at her with amusement, so she decided to get rid of the gray beard that surrounded his smirk. But the beard didn't disappear. The silly wig she tried to place on his head wouldn't appear either. Confused, she turned to the fire and tried to put it out, but the flames defied her. Then Ottum altered her coat back to its original fur-lined leather.

"There's no time for you to play dress-up now, Ottum. You have work to do. Unless I'm mistaken, there's a Chaser on the mountain that's going to need your help soon. As you have glimpsed in your dreams, the Avil he is after is very crafty."

"I saw the Avil doing something by a stream," she said.

"No," Oscar said very firmly.

"Yes, I did," Ottum replied just as firmly.

"No," Oscar said. "What did you see?"

Ottum remembered the glint in Oscar's eyes. It was a look that was usually dangerous for her because it meant he was about to tell her something she didn't want to hear. It was also a look that meant he wouldn't back down and would do what was necessary for her to see things his way. Though she knew she would lose, she set her jaw and glared at him.

"I saw an Avil laughing by a stream," she said between clenched teeth. Now it was her eyes that were flashing.

"Stop the bullshit, Ottum," Oscar nearly growled. "You have run from who you are for long enough. It's time to stop the whining and crying about how life is unfair because you have talents others don't—talents you feel set you apart and cause loneliness. It's *you* who causes the loneliness, not your talents. People open their hearts and souls to you, and although you are very kind to them, you keep your own tightly closed. You fight to control everything and everyone around you, but that isn't the way life works. You're the only person you can control. Stop taking responsibility for things you aren't responsible for, and stop using those things to hide from what you really are responsible for. Now tell me, what did you see?"

Ottum's cheeks and ears were crimson. She was angrier than she could remember being in years. Who in the hell did he think he was, chiding her like she was some child? She was climbing a mountain, sleeping in snow, and about to risk her life by hunting and engaging an Avil. How was that hiding from her responsibility? Oscar didn't have her "talents" so he had no idea what it was like, and he certainly didn't know anything about her anymore. She'd opened up to him and what had it gotten her? He'd died and left her. Fuck him! He wasn't even real. She was getting out of this dream.

"Leave now and you'll regret it for the rest of your life," Oscar threatened.

Ottum heard his words and paused before she was fully awake. She wanted to leave, but there was something in his tone, something in the soft drawl of his voice that stopped her. She hovered between the dream and being awake, trying to calm her temper enough to make a decision that wasn't pure emotion. She might regret going back and she might be angry with him, but if she never dreamed of Oscar again, she didn't want this dream to end as it would if she woke now. The fire came back into view, and Ottum saw him still standing there.

Oscar watched her with his blue-grey eyes still declaring that he was right. "You'll have to deal with what was said later. For now, there's something more urgent." Very dryly he continued, "As you know, the stream was poisoned by the Avil." His eyes flashed, daring Ottum to argue but continuing without giving her the opportunity. "Though Saul is chasing the Avil on the mountain, it's you this particular Avil wants. It will use Saul to get to you, and if it possibly can, it'll get Saul to drink the poison."

Ottum's temper was fading despite the taunt. "An Avil is after me? Why? Who is Saul?"

"You'll find all of that out for yourself. But Ottum, this is a very dangerous Avil. You must embrace who you are or there will be much lost," Oscar stopped and stared deeply at her face, as though he searched for a long-lost treasure. "Now, wake up Kai and make your way further up the mountain."

Oscar turned, and Ottum realized that he was going to walk away and leave her with the curtain falling again.

"Wait! How will I know where to go?" she asked.

"Embrace who you are, child. Embrace who you are." Then Oscar turned again and the curtain of blackness fell.

* * *

Ottum woke herself and took a deep breath while trying to regain control. But that only served to remind her of Oscar's comments about how she tried to control everything. Her temper flared again. She wanted to take time to sort out all he had said, but she knew that now was not the time. With that in mind, she reached out and woke her Companion.

Kai looked at her and then up at the stars. "No sleep for the weary?" he asked with sleep still clinging to his voice.

"No," she said tersely.

Kai looked at Ottum for an explanation, but she gave none. He sensed her anger and knew her well enough to know it was best to just follow her lead until she had calmed enough to talk about it. He stood, walked to his pack, and slipped into it. She had the bag rolled before he had his own pack on, and he realized it was going to be a brisk pace they kept tonight. Ottum put out the fire, put on her pack, and set off up the mountain without casting a single look behind them.

"Be on guard," was all she said before closing her mind to Kai.

Ottum was so angry that her thoughts couldn't maintain a constant direction even as her feet carried her up the mountain. After a few miles, the cold air and vigorous pace calmed her temper. She tried to remember how long it had been since she had last been this angry and realized with a start that it had been when Oscar was still alive. He had been right then, and although she knew he was right now, she wasn't ready to admit it to herself. As a delay tactic, she focused not on the conversation about herself but on the portion of it that dealt with the Avil and Saul.

Ottum wondered who Saul was and why an Avil would be using him to get to her. She'd never heard of an Avil hunting a Chaser before unless the Chaser started the hunt or just happened to be in the way of something it wanted to do. In her time on The Path, Ottum had never engaged or ran across an Avil she hadn't ultimately slayed. It puzzled her greatly to think one was hunting her. She wished Oscar hadn't left her dream so quickly.

Ottum's emotions finally settled enough to think about what Oscar had said about her. Before she delved into Oscar's words, she decided to open up to Kai. *I should at least let Kai know where we're going,* she thought to herself. *If only I knew!*

"*Embrace who you are,*" floated through Ottum's mind, and she realized she did know where they were going. It occurred to her she could be going mad just as easily as she could be coming to terms with herself. Either way, it was time for Kai to know what might lay ahead.

"Sorry about waking you so abruptly," she said.

Kai just looked at her and nodded, so she continued.

"I've been having dreams with Oscar in them for a while now. They don't exactly seem like dreams, but I don't know a better way to describe them," Ottum paused. "He talks with me and is even trying to teach me in the dreams."

"Is that how you knew about the Avil and why we avoided drinking from the stream?" Kai asked.

"No, that was just a dream. Well, perhaps not *just* a dream. But I don't interact in those dreams." She paused to give him a chance to ask more questions or to comment, but Kai continued walking quietly beside her. Struggling to find the words, she was quiet for a time too. "Oscar said some things tonight that were difficult for me to hear. I need more time to think through part of them before, or if, I talk with you about them. But he also told me that there's an Avil higher on this mountain, and he thinks it's using someone named Saul in order to get to me."

Kai's head turned swiftly at her last comment. He had never heard her speak so freely about a dream or to offer that she might talk more about it later. But it disturbed him to think she was being targeted. "An Avil is hunting us?"

Ottum saw the surprise in Kai's expression and decided it was best to continue before she lost her momentum. "Oscar mentioned that this Avil is very dangerous but wouldn't tell me more about Saul," Ottum said before stopping. She bit her lip, closer her eyes, and shifted as though there was a weight on her shoulders she wasn't sure she could continue to carry. With a deep sigh she continued, "Kai, I'm not sure if any of this can be trusted and think it's very possible I'm simply losing my mind. Oscar seems so real to me in these dreams that I want to question his death. Is Saul someone you know?"

Kai thought for a moment. "No, my lady."

Her thoughts raced as she tried to figure out why a complete stranger would be used to get to her and why an Avil would hunt her in the first place.

Kai felt her retreating and decided to intrude before she was gone. "Ottum, I have never heard of an Avil hunting a Chaser. Has it ever happened before?"

"No. Well, I don't know that for sure, but I've not heard of it either. It puzzles me greatly," she said.

"How could an Avil use someone else to get to you—someone that you do not even know?"

"I don't know, Kai. I simply don't know," Ottum said as she shook her head and shrugged her shoulders. Not knowing what else to say, she closed off and they continued their climb with no sound but the crunching snow beneath their feet.

Ottum mentally returned to wrestle with the comments Oscar had made. Now that some time and her temper had passed, she realized her reaction to his comments might have said more than the words he'd spoken. She was angry, so angry it had taken her a fair amount of time to cool off even with other things to accomplish. Ottum hated it, but she knew there must be some truth to the comments Oscar made or she wouldn't have reacted so strongly.

Was she hiding from responsibility? She was a Chaser and she was on The Path doing her job well. How was that hiding? She knew she didn't let most people very far into her world. Most people would think some of her natural skills were reason to avoid spending time around her. Was it possible that if she let people in more often they would be more accepting than she thought? The idea scared her, and the imagined rejection hurt.

Oscar always had a way of getting her to examine her life. And that look of his always meant trouble for her. Ottum knew there was truth in what he'd said, but she wasn't sure why it was truth. Frankly, she really didn't want to deal with it now. She'd been enjoying the time at the cabin and had looked forward to having the winter off from chasing. Kai was such a delightful creature, and she had envisioned them spending the winter in comfort. She couldn't remember now what had made her think the break would last that long. *No sense in lamenting what's already gone,* she thought to herself. Knowing it wasn't what Oscar would've wanted her to do, she turned away from examining herself and went to the seemingly easier task of trying to figure out why an Avil would be hunting her.

After a fair amount of mental searching, Ottum concluded she didn't know anyone named Saul. He wasn't someone from her childhood or her days of training. It occurred to her that Saul might also be a Chaser, but that realization led her to no useful conclusion. All Chasers thought of other Chasers as Pack, but Pack or not, Saul was a stranger to her.

Why would it use a stranger when it could hunt me directly? she wondered. An Avil trying to get to her through someone else just made no sense, and it didn't explain the extent of deviousness she sensed lay ahead.

Ottum didn't fully understand Avils, but she was almost certain that Avil's considered no others friend, family, or pack. While a Chaser would lay down his or her life to save another Chaser, she was confident that the same was not true of Avils.

Occasionally the other part of Oscar's conversation worked its way into her thoughts, but she continued to push it aside. Saving Saul was more important than figuring out why Oscar's comments angered her. Ottum realized it was an excuse even as she thought it. But she wasn't ready to make all of the changes that would come with facing that particular knowledge head on. So she walked on; her thoughts going down one fruitless trail after another.

Ottum had been so lost in her own musings that she'd left it to Kai to keep watch for trouble as they walked. He suddenly stopped beside her, and all of her mental chatter ceased. With her hand on her sword she closed her eyes to better sense their surroundings. When she felt no obvious danger, she sent a puzzled look his way.

"While you might know where we are going, I do not. We have been going mostly straight up this mountain for a few hours now. I am wondering if you have any idea of how much further we are going or a better sense of what we might find when we get there," Kai said.

He reached for a mouthful of snow and Ottum realized they hadn't kept themselves as well hydrated as they should have. To buy time before answering him, she took the cup and some water from Kai's pack and offered him some as well. She then added enough fresh snow back to the pouches to keep their water supply as hearty as possible. The heat from Kai's body would keep the skins warm enough to melt the snow she added. She thought it safer to trust snow than the water in the stream she could sense was ahead. She also pulled some food from their supplies and shared it with him. They ate silently but with gratefulness.

"I don't know the exact location we're going to, but we're getting closer. I believe the stream from my dreams is ahead of us and that it's where we'll find Saul. Oscar mentioned that the Avil would try to get Saul to drink poison. I'm not certain what we'll find when we get there or what we should be looking for, but we are getting closer. While I'd like to offer us a longer break, I feel we should push ahead. I can sense danger and would like to arrive before anyone is unnecessarily harmed," Ottum said.

Ottum never liked seeing another be hurt, but Kai knew she would like it even less if it somehow had to do with her. "Where you lead I will follow, my lady," Kai said, his curiosity about their path satiated.

Ottum wrapped a hand around the cold steel of her sword as she and Kai hiked on through the snow. The night had given way to morning but heavily falling snow made their way no clearer than it had been in the darkness. Her senses were now too aroused for her to not be fully present, and she was aware there was indeed an Avil ahead of them. Ottum had never felt an Avil like this before. It was evil, but she couldn't shake the feeling that there was something familiar to it. She shivered.

"There's an Avil ahead, Kai. Though we seldom communicate any other way, if there's something you want me to see or know, point it out in Path," Ottum warned.

Kai simply nodded. He didn't share Ottum's keen senses for what lay ahead, but he could sense her. Kai knew Ottum as well as any being he had ever known, and everything about her said she was ready for battle. Until her sword was drawn he wouldn't set his mind to high alert, but the warrior in him was ready.

"Do you hear that?" Ottum asked.

Kai listened and then caught the sound. "Yes. It is a stream, and it is close."

The snow fell around and on them in large, wet flakes as they angled toward the stream. Ottum pulled her sword from its sheath in one graceful motion.

Kai admired the beauty of the sword and its wielder as his senses switched to high alert. He flexed his shoulder slightly and tested the injured area, but he found no weakness. Kai's memory flashed back to the Avil's sword slicing through his shoulder. He flinched and tried to shake off the sensation so he could focus on the current hunt. However, uncertainty filled him when he realized that this Avil was hunting them.

Ottum felt his hesitation and reached out to Kai. Her touch pulled him out of the past and into the moment. Fear was not a valuable thing in battle, and he wouldn't have her harmed because of it. Sensing he had gained control, Ottum pulled her hand away and continued with no further thought of his hesitation. They were now extremely close to the Avil, and there was no time to question ability. Skill acquired from past training and experience would carry them.

The stream was on their left. They walked closely enough that the babbling water served as a guide, but not so near that they could easily be pushed in. Kai thought he saw a figure move behind a pine tree ahead and on their right. When Ottum stopped and looked right at the tree with her sword held at the ready, the sickening laughter of an Avil began.

The creature stepped from its hiding spot but didn't charge them. After a moment the Avil's laughter faded, but it still did not move. In Path, Ottum requested Kai to only engage if the Avil attacked.

Realizing the Avil didn't have its sword drawn, Kai looked around for signs of a trap.

The Avil saw him look, and the dreadful laughter started again.

Kai hated the nauseating laugh of Avils and wished the creature would just engage them, but it didn't. Even when the laughter stopped, it made no move. Instead, the Avil stood silently and watched them as though it was highly amused that Ottum and Kai were standing there. Then behind it came the muffled sound of a creature in great pain. Still, none of them moved or spoke.

Finally the Avil, looking disgusted, spoke. "Aren't you going to rush to rescue your Pack? He's a Chaser, you know."

"I'm aware of that," Ottum said in a flat tone.

"So why aren't you slicing off my head and saving him? He's being tortured! Not really by anyone other than himself, but tortured none-the-less." Another laugh escaped the Avil. "Don't you care that he's in pain?"

"I care, but there's nothing I can do about it right now," Ottum replied.

"Ah, yes. You don't really know what's wrong with him or what's going on here do you?" The Avil mocked her and obviously took pleasure in the control it had of the situation. "Thirsty?" Another wave of laughter filled the air while more sounds of anguish rose behind the Avil.

"What game are you playing here?" Ottum asked. She was concerned for the Chaser, but there was still a lot of force in those cries. The Chaser wasn't as near death as the Avil would have her believe.

"What game? What *game*? This is no game, Ottum," the Avil replied.

The Avil thought that would somehow set her off her guard—hearing it use her name—but she only slightly tilted her head and narrowed her eyes.

Kai noted that the Avil was becoming increasingly agitated because Ottum wasn't reacting to its efforts. It wasn't moving toward them, but it was rocking ever so slightly and its voice was losing the hint of pleasure it held at first. Another round of cries emitted from behind the Avil

"Poor little Saul. Poor little, lost Saul. Seems his Companion was killed in her sleep and then he drank from a bad spring." Laughter followed the remarks, but it didn't hold the awful, nauseating sound Kai was familiar with. As Ottum stood silent and still after its comments, the laughter was replaced with something that sounded closer to an enraged roar.

"Aren't you going to take my head?" bellowed the Avil. It was now so enraged that it paced between two trees, rocking its body as it walked. "Saul is *dying* in that bear's den and you're just standing there as though he has all the time in the world. One can only take so much torture." Shooting her a wicked look it added, "Even a Chaser can be broken."

Ottum remained still. There was something familiar about this Avil, but she couldn't define what it was. It knew her name, and it'd planned something it thought she would react to. Once she would have went running at the sound of someone crying out like Saul, but she felt that with the exception of what a bear might do to him if woken, he wasn't in mortal danger. He was unquestionably in pain, but pain by itself is usually not lethal. Ottum realized her inaction was provoking the Avil more than any action could. So she stood, watching to see what it would do next.

The Avil muttered to itself as it paced, but Saul's almost constant cries prohibited Kai or Ottum from discerning the words. Finally it spun and faced them squarely. It was shaking with rage, but its voice was oddly calm.

"If you won't take my life, let's see if you can save Saul's."

With that, the Avil started backing away. Ottum was wary of its intent and followed slowly, but once it was beyond the location of Saul's cries, she ceased following. Kai wanted to pursue and to end its miserable life, but Ottum requested he stop. Unwilling to turn down her request, Kai stayed by her side. The Avil realized they were more interested in helping Saul than chasing it, and it turned to walk more easily amongst the trees. It cast a few glances over its shoulder but eventually disappeared among the trees and snow.

CHAPTER 6

Kai looked into the entrance of the bear's den. He'd volunteered to get Saul while Ottum stood guard, ensuring the Avil couldn't trap them if it returned. Kai moved beyond the snow Saul had dragged in earlier, and the hearty scent of earth filled his nose. The tunnel wasn't very wide and the sudden change in incline made him think it wasn't very long either. As Kai cautiously moved deeper into the earthen tunnel, he realized the man at the other end may try to kill him just as easily as he would accept help. The stick of fire Kai carried in his mouth served to light his way, but it would hopefully also keep any awakened bear at bay until he could get Saul out of the den. The opening was ahead and Kai tried to ready himself for what he would find. As the opening widened, his first reaction was relief that the true owner seemed absent. By the tracks present on the floor, it seemed likely that Saul had woken the bear, and it had fled. Then Kai took a longer look at the man he had come to rescue.

Saul was drenched in sweat despite the cold. His breathing was labored and even though he was being quiet, his body writhed from the torture his mind was providing. Kai placed the fire on the ground away from Saul, wishing for a way to save both the man and the fire, but he could see no safe way to get them both out. So he left the fire behind, grabbed Saul, and started backing out of the den. Kai had him in the tunnel before Saul started fighting. Saul slowed the process down by digging in his heals and thrashing about as much as the narrow tunnel would allow, but the ill man was no match for Kai's strength.

After helping Kai pull him clear, Ottum looked down at the Chaser who was being used by the Avil. He was indeed a stranger to her. She judged him to be over 6 feet tall and as well muscled as any Chaser would be. The fur inside his coat was made from multiple rabbit hides while the tooled leather of his pants was deer. Ottum liked that he let no piece of his meals go unused. His wet, dark blond hair was rapidly freezing, but it was obvious he was consumed in fever. Free from the confines of the tunnel Saul thrashed about in the snow, not conscious but apparently caught in a dream-like state.

Ottum decided to allow him to thrash for a while. She hoped the snow would cool his fever, and it was the safest thing she and Kai could do. Saul might be mostly unaware of what he was doing, but he was still a powerful man. Ottum suspected that he was delusional. Delusional or not, she didn't want to hurt another Chaser just to keep her and Kai safe.

"Any idea what is going on now that you've seen him?" Kai asked with a gesture toward Saul.

"No," she said, her brows creased with intense scrutiny. "This man is a stranger to me. However, the Avil seemed familiar. We've have never encountered one that wasn't ultimately slain, so I'm not sure how it could be familiar. But it is."

"So, what are we going to do with him?" Kai asked as he looked at the still thrashing Saul.

"We're going to help him the best we can."

They stood and watched Saul thrash about while keeping all senses aware for the Avil who could return at any moment. The fever abated, releasing more sweat to freeze in Saul's hair. Ottum watched his breathing become shallow and noticed he was moving less. She reached into the inner pockets of Kai's pack and found the small vial she was looking for.

"Watch him." She pulled the lid off and approached as quietly as possible. In one swift motion she knelt, lifted Saul's head, entered the contents into his mouth, and then prepared for the struggle.

But Saul didn't fight. He also didn't swallow. Suddenly aware she hadn't taken Saul's sword, Ottum realized she was in danger.

* * *

Saul awoke in the den with the bear's body mysteriously removed. In fact, he couldn't feel the bear anywhere within reach. He knew he was drenched in blood because he could feel it trickling around his head. He could also feel the blisters left by the fire and knew he'd been deeply burned.

The Avil must have put out the fire just in time and removed the bear. It doesn't want to kill me; it wants to torture me, Saul thought with exhausted despair.

Blood trickled from his forehead into his ear. He moved to shake the liquid out and pain seared through him. Saul's anger flared and the desire to kill the Avil came rushing back. He was pleased to be alive and to have the chance to still finish off the Avil, but right now he was at a disadvantage. He still couldn't exit the den or the Avil would take his feet or head as he came out. He could hear the Avil at the entrance and knew it was muttering, but he couldn't hear what was being said. Saul decided to see if the Avil could be lured in for a fight.

"Hey! Come and get me you wretched piece of shit!" He meant it as a challenging shout, but Saul's voice sounded small.

There was no reply, but he heard the Avil laugh. He hated those laughs. They made him sick to his stomach, or was it that something was wrong with his stomach? Suddenly Saul remembered that the bear had clawed through his mid-section. When he yelled the wound must have broken open. Pain consumed him again. The slash couldn't have been as bad as he had originally thought, but it was definitely not good. He reached to assess the damage. His fingers moved over his slick abdomen easily but they found no gashing wound. *Perhaps the bear just hit me so hard that it damaged my organs without tearing my skin, but where did all this blood come from?*

Saul struggled to make sense of everything he felt as the pain in his abdomen raged. He had been following the Avil, he drank from a stream which contained poison, and then he made his way into this bear den. The Avil had set a fire, and Saul and the bear had succumbed to the smoke and flame.

Saul's memory wasn't clear about what happened prior to starting down the mountain after the Avil, but he felt a great sense of loss.

Things don't add up.

The bear was gone and there was no scent of a fire. Perhaps he had adapted to the smell and could no longer sense it? Saul's mind raced. A part of him realized that logic was absent from the events he had been part of, but his senses didn't care about logic.

Suddenly he heard the Avil. The evil creature was mumbling, but he couldn't understand what it was saying. Then he heard another voice that sounded far away. His ears strained for a recognizable sound. The voice was muffled by distance and the den itself, but Saul picked up the quality of the voice and realized it was a female.

"Eyota…" She was the reason Saul felt such loss. He wondered if she could still be alive and whole. Could he have somehow only dreamt the rest of it?

The Avil was laughing again. If Eyota was still alive, the Avil was torturing her too. He *had* to get to her. Saul rolled to his stomach and couldn't contain the scream that escaped as pain pushed all other thought from his mind. While the challenge he had tried to elicit had sounded small, the scream echoed through the den and his mind and multiplied itself a hundred fold. His body turned itself over as the pain continued to consume him. The screams slowly gave way to moans, and then his mind graciously allowed him to lose consciousness.

* * *

Saul didn't know how long he'd been out, but he smelled the fire as he came to. He could hear something or someone coming into the den and wasn't sure if he hoped it was the bear or the Avil. Then, through closed eyes that would not open despite his best efforts, he saw a flicker of light that could only be fire. *"A wild bear can't carry fire."* He felt the flames lapping at him and the heat consuming him, but he was unable to move. Then the Avil had him and was dragging him out of the den and away from the fire. For some unexplained reason Saul knew its intent was to dump him in the stream. He tried to dig in his heels and to reach out for something he could grab that might slow him, but the Avil had bound him. Then the icy water started to flow over him. Saul struggled to open his eyes and to move, but his lids would not cooperate, and his arms were bound too tightly. The water wasn't going over his face and was really pretty shallow.

Freezing me after the fire is just part of the torture. It'll probably put me back in the den to recover enough to torture with fire again.

At least that explained why he'd felt like he was soaked in blood. The blood was really just water, and the den kept him just warm enough that it didn't freeze or evaporate. Freezing to death was better than burning to death, but he'd rather live.

Saul wasn't getting anywhere by struggling so he stopped. The cold was at least numbing the pain. He felt himself slipping away, and he found it increasingly hard to fight the voice in his head telling him it would be easier to simply let go and call it a life.

Just as he started thinking that maybe the voice was right, the Avil grabbed his head and dumped something in his mouth. While lifting Saul's head, it had very carelessly moved his sword. Until that point Saul assumed it had long ago been removed. Did the Avil really think a Chaser would just swallow more poison and die without a fight, especially when his sword was still on him? Saul attempted one more time to move his hands and found them to finally be free.

He moved a hand to his sword and made ready to draw.

* * *

"Saul, stay your hand and swallow. I don't want to hurt you, but I will to ensure my safety and that of my Companion. Stay your hand and swallow," Ottum commanded.

Saul stopped moving, but Ottum didn't have the feeling he understood or intended to stay still. His knuckles whitened as they gripped the sword more tightly.

"Stay your hand, Saul. I am Pack and the liquid in your mouth is herbal. It's the only vial I have. If you don't swallow it, the poison from the Avil will have tortured you longer than needed," Ottum said in an effort to reason with him.

The Avil was talking to him but Saul couldn't understand it. He could tell by the change in pressure on his head that the Avil was aware he had his hand on his sword. Saul wanted to laugh that he was finally in a position more equal with the beast. Saul hoped it realized if there was enough strength left in his tortured body that its head was as good as off. Saul edged his sword out the smallest amount more.

"Saul." Ottum said it in spoken word this time and the change of demeanor was pronounced. She felt silly for not realizing how altered the poison made his senses. "Stay your hand. I'm Pack and the liquid may help."

Saul realized it wasn't the Avil holding his head. *Not Eyota, but definitely female.* Whoever this was, she knew his name and claimed to be Pack. He worked to determine if it really was someone helping or if it was just the Avil up to more trickery. Then he felt a familiar touch on his leg that caused him to swallow. "Eyota." Saul released his sword along with his consciousness.

Ottum and Kai each looked at the other, but neither knew the meaning behind the single word he had spoken. Both were relieved there would be no fight with Saul for the time being and that he had swallowed the herbal mixture. It would take time to see if it helped, but at least there was a chance.

CHAPTER 7

Kai stayed near Saul and kept watch while Ottum went to the stream to search for and remove the poison. They had quickly removed Saul's sword and searched for other weapons he might have, but found only a knife.

Ottum had to give Saul credit for thinking to hunt for a bear den to provide shelter. He had to have been severely poisoned to risk being mauled, but it was the best option Saul could have picked given his circumstances.

It took diligent searching, but Ottum finally spotted the small satchel of poison and removed it from the cold waters of the stream. Unsure of how to repair the stream, she hoped that as nature often did, it would repair itself. She returned to Kai and placed the poison in another skin to take with them. She thought it might come in handy if Saul had lingering effects. He had remained unconscious, but since his fever hadn't returned, Ottum hoped the herbal mixture was helping.

The bear, angry at having its den stolen, had pulled some of the lower branches off the trees nearby before leaving the area. Ottum decided to use them along with some bindings from her pack to create a makeshift sled. Once finished, she stepped back to look at her work. The sled wasn't pretty, but it seemed likely it would do its job. She placed their bed roll on the sled and Kai helped load Saul on to it. Saul would need the added warmth given how wet his clothes were. She bundled him in the roll, and then tied him to the sled. It went against her nature to secure a Pack member away from his sword, but without knowing the state he would wake in, it seemed the only logical thing to do. Kai would carry the knife while she added the sword to her own gear.

Ottum picked up the sled, and they began their journey again. Saul wasn't a light load, but Ottum was a Chaser and was used to hard work. Kai had protested, but she didn't want Kai to use his shoulder more than needed just yet. Besides, she had the suspicion it was Kai who had stilled Saul and not her. She wanted him free to do so again should the need arise.

The snow made it easier for her to drag the sled. Still, it was still not an easy task and it required frequent breaks. They were still very much on alert for the Avil, but Ottum felt it had moved on. She didn't understand why it would go to so much trouble to poison Saul and challenge her. She wondered if there were more clues hidden in the conversation she and Oscar had shared.

"Can you keep guard while I think through something?" she asked Kai during their next rest.

"Anything particular I am looking for? And should I be concerned with where we are going or will you still lead the way?" he asked.

"Keep aware for any danger. I will lead the way; I just want the freedom to think without needing full awareness of our surroundings," she replied.

"Where you go, my lady, I will follow as your ever faithful bodyguard."

Ottum smiled at Kai's flair and then closed her thoughts to him.

The snow had stopped falling and the world they walked through was beautifully brilliant. Even the cover of the trees only slightly dimmed the sun's reflection off their surroundings. Saul remained quiet and still except for the occasional head roll as the sled slid off a slight snow ridge. Ottum stopped to check on him and to rest her arms. As she looked at his unconscious form, she realized he was a rugged but handsome man despite the effects of the poison. She didn't know why their paths had been drawn together, but she longed for him to recover so that they might make some sense of it.

The Avil had seemed so familiar to her. Something about it tickled her memory the way a lost word sometimes tickles the tongue. She replayed the meeting again in her mind, hunting for details that might give her a clue. It was as though the Avil had wanted her to end its life even though it hadn't quite expected her to. It wanted to teach her a lesson, though. That was obvious. It wanted to teach her something almost as badly as Oscar did.

Oh, yes. I'm supposed to be figuring out what I am and aren't responsible for, and embracing who I am…whatever that means. It crossed her mind again that she could be going crazy. But then again, there was a man named Saul who she had found because Oscar had bid her to in a dream. If she was crazy, she was certainly experiencing very realist delusions. *Although, I suppose all delusions feel realist.*

Ottum thought back on her life. She'd felt lonely so often that it had become familiar. Loneliness had become familiar enough to feel comfortable. It wasn't that people were always absent from her life. It was that she never felt she could truly relax and just be herself. Her childhood friends hadn't minded that she sometimes just knew things, but even they thought it increasingly strange as they all grew towards adulthood. And her family certainly didn't help matters. It wasn't until she left to become a Chaser that she felt there were others even a little like her in the world. Some of those she even called friends. But still, she couldn't relax and let them fully in. She'd let Kai in more than anyone other than Oscar, but he was her Companion. Their lives were deeply intertwined because their mutual survival depended on it. She doubted she would have let him see and know as much as he did if that weren't the case. *Perhaps I should change that.* Yes, she decided she could work at letting him in more without it being only for the needs of survival.

Ottum wondered if it was possible that she really didn't know what she was and wasn't responsible for. She felt the weight of the world on her shoulders at times. If anything, she was often frustrated by how little responsibility others took. There was so much that could be done if everyone would only realize their part and do it. But most people turned from doing their part and pretended to have no idea that in turning, they were part of the problem. Willfully ignorant. She'd heard someone else use the term, but she liked it. Too many of Nohnah's inhabitants were willfully ignorant.

Ottum had learned early that she had skills others didn't seem to share. In very little time, she could see inside someone and know what they were capable of. How ironic that she was being asked to do that to herself and couldn't. Was she turning from helping each person become the most he or she could be? She used to strive to help them, but some would refuse to believe their lives could be richer and more rewarding. Those fell into the 'willfully ignorant' category too. *No, she thought. I can't be held accountable for other's choices.* She decided that figuring out what she was and wasn't responsible for would have to wait for another day.

Her mind went back to the encounter with the Avil. She could clearly see it pacing and shaking, remembered the calmness of its voice before it turned to leave, and watched it walk away.

The blood drained from Ottum's face, and she stopped walking. She lowered the sled to the ground and moved away from Saul. Then she dropped to her knees and heaved the contents of her stomach into the snow.

Kai had been ready for danger but saw none. His first thought was that Ottum had been poisoned by the satchel she removed from the stream earlier. He moved toward her, but she held out her hand to stop him and shook her head. He remained alert while she cleaned her mouth and face with snow. When she stood and turned to look at Kai, he saw tears streaming down her face. She didn't look well, and his concern escalated. "Ottum, what is wrong?"

"It's my brother," she said, a sob catching in her throat.

Kai looked to where Ottum's eyes were fixed and saw no one there. It occurred to him that if she was hallucinating, things were going to get very difficult. But then he wondered if perhaps she meant Saul. "Saul is your brother?" he tentatively asked.

"No," she said, pausing to control the sobbing. "The Avil... The Avil is my brother." Ottum looked as though she might be sick again, but fought it off with rapid swallowing.

Kai didn't know what to say. He certainly understood her nausea. In all the years of chasing Avils with Ottum, he had never considered that an Avil had family. He had often thought of Avils as so evil that the human appearance seemed merely coincidence. To imagine them as one would any other human seemed surreal. But that the one who had poisoned the stream and Saul could in any way be Ottum's brother? That was unfathomable. Suddenly aware that she was watching him and reading his thoughts, he realized Ottum was currently something he had never seen her be before. She was vulnerable. Desperately searching for a way to ease her pain he asked, "How do you know?"

"I replayed the encounter to see if I could find any hints as to why an Avil would use someone to get to me. The familiarity haunted me, and I couldn't place it until I remembered the way it walked. It had bothered me at the time, but we had to protect Saul. What I saw hadn't quite sunk in as anything but familiar. But when I replayed it in my head, why it was familiar came to me and all of it fell into place," Ottum closed her eyes and swallowed rapidly again. "I heard he had turned, but I didn't want to believe it. I wasn't even fully sure that it was possible for an Avil to have once seemed normal. I thought maybe Leon had just gone crazy. Kai, I am so sorry."

"Sorry? Why would you be sorry?" he asked.

"He's my brother." Ottum said it as though it was an explanation.

Kai stood watched her for a moment before it sank in that she thought the Avil's actions were in some way her fault—thought that she should take responsibility for her brother's actions. "I don't understand why you should be sorry for its behavior. You do not make its choices."

"But he's my *brother*, Kai! If it weren't for me, Saul wouldn't be poisoned, and you wouldn't be in danger," she said. Sadness coated her words.

"If it were not for you, my lady, many things might indeed be different. But that does not mean your brother would have made different choices. There are many Avils that are not brothers of yours; I might have still been the Companion of a Chaser; and Saul might have still been harmed while hunting an Avil. I do not understand how you can feel responsible for what has happened recently when it is in no way your fault," Kai said as he walked closer to her.

Ottum looked at him with bewildered eyes. *Is he addle-brained? Why can't he see that it's my fault?*

But Kai stood there looking at her as though she was wrong to think it her responsibility.

"We need to keep moving. We have to find a safe place to camp and get Saul warm. Once he is well enough, I will go after my brother on my own," Ottum said, wiping the remnants of her tears away.

Kai wanted to tell her he wouldn't allow it, but he knew his words would fall on deaf ears if he spoke them now. Ottum had set her mind, and there would be no changing it for now. However, Kai had also made up his mind, and there was no way he would willingly allow her to go after her brother alone. The knowledge that she had a brother who was an Avil still shocked him, and he wondered how two beings with the same parents could end up so extremely different. But he would have to ponder those thoughts later. Ottum had set a brisk clip, and he wanted to make sure there were no surprise attacks. He wistfully hoped it would be days before the Avil was spotted again. *If they meet sooner, the meeting will be what it will be,* Kai thought. *Besides, there is no way for me to guess how the meeting will play out even if I try.*

With the exception of stopping to take care of necessities or to check on Saul, Ottum didn't break pace for hours. Saul remained unconscious but alive, and Ottum pulled him as though he were a feather on a string instead of the strapping man he was. As the day waned, Kai wondered if they were going somewhere planned or if the brisk clip was Ottum's way of attempting to leave behind a past that seemed to have found her when she least expected it. Knowing her mood had improved little, he was unwilling to ask which it was.

So they marched on through the cold snow and the trees. The further they went, the more questions Kai wanted to ask. How were they going to stay warm tonight with Saul in their bed roll? Were they going to try to walk throughout the night? What would he do if Ottum realized the true task in front of her and was unable to see it to its end?

It was these questions that were running through his mind when his eyes fell on the back of a cabin. Smoke billowed from its chimney, carried away from their direction by the wind. Ottum saw it at the same time and slowed their pace.

"Are we going to go around, or shall I go ahead to see if we are welcome for a night?" Kai asked.

"If Saul were not still so ill we would push on, but he needs a warm fire and the shelter. My brother could be staying in this cabin just as easily as a helpful stranger. For safety, you come in from that side," she said pointing east. "I will wait a moment and will then come around from the other."

They walked in silence toward the cabin, snow crunching below their feet and the sled. When they reached the point of separation, Kai slipped from his pack and left Ottum's side. She watched and waited until he reached the side of the cabin, and then she started toward the other side. She wished she could just leave Saul behind, but she didn't feel it would be safe to do so. It was hard to use stealth while dragging a large man on a sled. Just as she reached the edge of the cabin she heard Kai call for her.

"Ottum!" His voice warned of danger.

Ottum released Saul and pulled her sword from its sheath. She rounded the corner expecting to see her brother, but an entirely different sight met her eyes.

"Stop!" She said it out loud, but the man, standing with his back to her, didn't flinch or change the hold he had on the arrow he was aiming at Kai. "Lower your weapon!"

"Perhaps you cannot see the wolf that is standing in front of me?" replied the man in a much quieter tone.

"Kai is my Companion and he means you no harm. Harm him, and you will lose your head to my sword," Ottum threatened.

The stranger dared a glance over his shoulder at Ottum, but he didn't lower his bow. Instead he started sidling away from the cabin while turning so that he could keep them both in sight.

"Your companion is a wolf?" he asked incredulously.

"Yes. I am a Chaser," Ottum said.

"What, exactly, is a Chaser?" he asked, glancing from Ottum to Kai.

Ottum was exasperated. "We hunt Avils."

"Avils?"

Ottum lowered her sword slightly. She saw the look on his face that said he thought she was very possibly crazy. Explaining to him that Chasers could speak Path and therefore talk with their Companions would not help her and Kai's plight at the moment. At least the arrow in his bow was now between them and no longer aimed at Kai. Ottum looked at Kai with an apologetic look, and then spoke to the man between them.

"Kai is like a pet. I hunt people who have done horrible things and try to prevent them from doing further harm. Kai helps to keep me safe," she offered as an explanation that he might more easily grasp.

"You have a wolf as a pet. That would scare me enough all by itself to not do anything bad." The stranger paused for a moment before tilting his head slightly. "Are you hunting me?"

Ottum couldn't stop the slight hint of a smile that formed on her lips. "No. We are not hunting you. But I have another Chaser on the other side of the cabin who is very ill. We engaged an Avil earlier today, and since we didn't know who or what would be occupying this cabin, we split up in order to minimize the risk of harm."

"Oh." The stranger stood, trying to determine if the pair in front of him was sane and safe. "Is the other Chaser a wolf?"

"No. Wolves are our Companions but all Chasers are human. I will go get Saul if I have your word that Kai is safe," Ottum said.

"As long as he doesn't move, he's safe," the stranger said as he angled the arrow more in Kai's direction again.

Ottum retrieved the still unconscious Saul and brought him with her to the front of the cabin. While she kept her sword unsheathed, she didn't have it raised any longer. Carrying it and the sled was cumbersome at best.

One look at Saul and the man lowered his bow. "Let's get him inside before he freezes to death," he said with alarm.

Ottum headed toward the cabin door and the man rushed to open it for her. He tried to help her lift the sled, but Ottum had Saul inside before he could help. Kai had left his spot and was standing just outside the door.

"Um, will your wolf stay inside also?" the stranger asked.

"He is my Companion. If he is not welcome, then I will also stay outside as long as you do not mind me entering to check on Saul several times throughout the night."

Kai turned away from the door and moved out of sight.

The man looked from Saul to the spot where Kai had just stood to Ottum and back to the empty doorway again. "I'm not familiar with Chasers and their Companions so I don't know your ways. If the wolf is a being you trust, he is welcome. Now that I know he doesn't consider me dinner, and you and I have lowered our weapons, my name is Will."

"I'm Ottum and my Companion is Kai," Ottum said as she sat Saul's sled down near the fire. "And this is Saul," she said as she reached to feel his forehead for fever.

"Did I offend Kai and cause him to leave?" Will asked, trying to figure out if he should shut the door or wait.

"No. He went to retrieve his pack. It's hard to offend Kai," Ottum said with a smile.

As if on cue, Kai reappeared outside the door, but he didn't enter.

Feeling rather sheepish, Will patted his leg and made a clicking sound while looking at the wolf. Kai stood completely still except to roll his eyes toward Ottum.

"Come in Kai. This is Will and he said you are welcome."

Kai entered the cabin and shut the door behind him. He nodded to Will and enjoyed the surprised look that greeted the nod.

"You understand what we say, don't you?" he asked Kai.

"Yes." Then Kai realized that while he could understand Will, it didn't work the other way around. So he nodded again.

"My apologies for thinking you were going to eat me, but you are a rather large wolf and you were walking straight at me," Will said in Kai's general direction.

Kai simply nodded again before he slipped out of his pack.

Ottum watched their exchange out of the corner of her eye as she removed the bed roll from Saul and hung it near the fire to dry. Saul had gone still shortly after swallowing the herbal mixture, but with the exception of a small reprieve, his body had continued to alternate between fevered and drenched with sweat. At least in the cabin he would be able to stay warm despite the wetness. Still uncertain of how he might be when he awoke, Ottum decided to keep Saul's arms bound for the time being.

"So is he a Chaser turned bad guy?" Will asked as he saw her hesitate over the bindings.

"I don't think so. He was poisoned and was delusional when we first found him. I gave him some herbs to help counter the poison, but there is no way to know how effective they were until he awakens. Although he's sick, he's still a Chaser, and I don't want to have to battle him."

"I have never heard of Chasers or…what did you call the bad guys?" Will asked.

"Avils."

"Avils," Will said with a nod. "I've not heard of either before today. While I am familiar with the word 'companion,' it doesn't mean a wolf to me. How is it that I've not heard of your, um, group before? I believe my schooling was good, and I have lived in towns before. Are you some sort of secret society?" Will's eyebrows lifted as he asked the last question.

"When we speak of a group of us, we refer to ourselves as Pack. We're not a secret," she smiled. "Do you remember when you were a child and there were things you didn't know of because you were simply not ready to know?" Ottum asked.

"Are you saying you are superior to me, so I don't know about you?" Will asked, more amused than offended.

"No. When you were a toddler you might have seen letters, but you didn't know what they were. Then you learned your alphabet and recognized letters in many places, but you still didn't know how to read. Next you learned how to read, but there were always new words you still didn't know the meaning of. Eventually you also realized that some words had more than one meaning. Finally you learned of other languages and that you could spend a lifetime learning them if you chose to. Pack isn't superior; we simply have made choices that led us to learn a language you're not familiar with," Ottum offered as explanation.

"You may not be speaking literally, but is that how you communicate with Kai?" Will asked.

"Kai and I can speak because we both know how to speak Path." Seeing the questioning look Will gave her, Ottum continued, "Path is a form of silent communication. We can hear each other internally without making any external noise. However, I wasn't speaking literally with the language analogy. It was just an example of how some might consider Pack secret when really it's simply that they haven't grown enough to realize it exists or to understand it. If you choose to, you can learn to speak Path," she told Will.

A smile slowly spread across Will's face and a sparkle ignited in his green eyes. "I can learn to speak with a wolf."

Ottum was impressed at how easily he was adapting to the new information she shared with him. Most unfamiliars would have refused to believe Chasers, Companions, and Avils existed, and they certainly wouldn't have taken to the idea that they could communicate in Path. Will seemed intrigued and excited by the idea.

With the immediate threat of danger removed, Ottum studied their host in more detail. He was easily over 6'2" with almost black hair and green eyes. She could see the intelligence in his eyes and knew by the way he had held his bow that he was strong. He wore tooled leather, but it was made with a finer craftsmanship than Saul's. She glanced at the bow he had hung by the door and realized that it was also well made and cared for. As her eyes wandered the rest of the cabin, she noted detail after detail that increased her curiosity regarding Will.

Ottum hadn't interacted with unfamiliars in quite some time unless they happened to be the victim of an Avil. While she knew some unfamiliars emotionally and mentally grew more once they were fully adults, many of them didn't. It was hard for her to remain among the willfully ignorant. Will seemed like he was willing to grow. She decided it possible that he would become a Chaser if he chose to stay with her and Kai for a while and learn their ways.

"How?"

Will's question pulled her from her musings. "How what?" Ottum asked.

"How do I learn to speak Path? Will I be able to communicate with more than wolves and Chasers if I learn it?"

Now it was Ottum who was smiling. Will definitely wasn't a willfully ignorant unfamiliar. "You will also be able to communicate with any other being who is on The Path."

"What is The Path?" he asked.

"You sure ask a lot of questions!" Ottum said with a chuckle.

Will blushed, and Ottum was immediately sorry for the comment.

"That's a good thing, Will, but I need to discuss a few things with you and tend to Saul. We can talk more later, and I will attempt to answer as many questions as you can ask. In an attempt to change the mood, she gave him a playful wink and added, "I may even ask you a few."

Ottum hoped her smile eased his embarrassment. Typically it was she who was being told about how many questions she asked. Had things been different, she would have been delighted to sit and exchange information with him. But he needed to know that he had placed himself in danger by helping them. An Avil meant them harm and could be near. *Not just any Avil,* Ottum thought to herself.

Will watched her face change. Ottum's smile faded and an imaginary weight descended on to her shoulders. It was as though time suddenly fast-forwarded its effects on her body so that Will was looking at someone far older than the woman who had just been standing in front of him. He wasn't sure he understood or believed all she had told him, but he had no doubt that whatever Ottum might believe, she felt very alone.

"I'll help you tend to Saul. Why don't you go ahead and begin telling me what needs said. Shall I start on some food for all of us while you talk?" Will offered.

"Yes, thank you," Ottum said as she mentally closed the door on thoughts of her brother.

Will went to his wood supply and loaded the stove with enough wood to cook dinner. He expected Ottum to talk to him as he stoked the small cooking stove, so he was puzzled when she remained quiet. He looked up and realized that based upon the way they were looking at each other, she and Kai were talking. It greatly intrigued him that they could communicate, and he looked forward to being able to ask more questions soon.

After closing the stove's door, Will returned to the wood pile and placed another log on the fire by Saul. The man still lay unconscious, but his clothes were drying. Instinctively Will reached out and felt his forehead. No fever was present and Will took that as encouragement. Will wondered what it meant to be trained as a Chaser, and he hoped if Saul did awake delusional that all in his cabin would remain safe. He looked up from Saul and was caught in Ottum and Kai's watchful gazes.

"No fever and his clothes and hair are drying," he said.

"That's a good sign," Ottum replied.

Will smiled in reply. He wondered what Kai and Ottum had spoken of but felt he should contain that question until later. "I'm going to make some soup. Does everyone here eat soup?"

Kai knew that by "everyone," Will meant him. He had disliked being called a pet and disliked even more the look that had come to Ottum's eyes as she realized Will was an intelligent and open unfamiliar. Now was not the best time for her to take on a new student. Kai was glad she would be distracted by Will this evening so that he could have some time to figure out how to handle Ottum and her brother, but he was concerned they would endanger Will more than was necessary if he learned too much and wanted to participate.

"Tell him that soup will be fine," Kai told Ottum. "I would take some additional meat if he has it to spare, but not if it will decrease his supplies excessively."

"Kai will eat soup. Do you have enough meat in your stores for him to have some extra?" she asked. "We'll hunt and replace anything we use while we're here."

"Sure, and that isn't necessary. I've stocked my supplies well. Does Kai want the meat cooked or raw? I have preserved some of it and have some that is frozen." Will said this while looking at Kai. He truly wanted to be able to speak with the wolf but felt helpless to even try.

"He prefers it raw, thanks," Ottum translated. "If you set some by the fire it will probably be thawed enough for him to eat it when we eat soup. He also said to thank you for addressing him even though you can't understand his replies."

The two nodded to each other before Kai moved to sit near Saul.

"Do you need help with the soup?" Ottum asked.

"No, but you can retrieve a squirrel from my cold box and set it by the fire, please," will said as he pointed to the floor in the back corner of the cabin. He grabbed a candle, lit it from the stove, and handed it to her.

Ottum moved to the location he had indicated, saw a door in the floor, and opened it to find a cellar. By placing it on the north side of the cabin in the opposite corner from the stove and fireplace, it was possible to keep food cool all year long and protected from creatures with a strong sense of smell. Not finding any squirrels, Ottum moved deeper into the cellar. At the back there was a small door. She opened the door to find layers of meat alternating with layers of ice. The floor of the box angled such that any melt would be directed away from the cellar. She realized Will must have cut ice from a source nearby and carried it in once winter started. The cold box would be useless in summer, but it was a perfect way to maintain uncured meat during the winter when hunting yielded less fresh food. *What an intriguing man,* she thought as she climbed back out of the cellar and into the cabin.

After sitting the squirrel by the fire on a plate that Will handed her, Ottum turned and prepared to tell Will what he needed to know. The words were difficult for her to find, but Will continued preparing food as though he could be as patient as she needed him to be.

"I don't know how much to tell you and how much to leave out, but I'll try to tell you everything you need to know in order to make a decision," she said.

Will looked intently at Ottum and half smiled. "Given the day, this could be interesting."

Ottum couldn't tell if he was joking or serious, and decided it didn't matter. "Chasers choose to hunt Avils. Most Pack engage and then kill Avils when they are found. Sometimes during the hunt an Avil will be aware of the Chaser first and will engage instead of fleeing, but sometimes they flee. Avils may be evil, but they still want to live so they most often engage in the hopes of destroying the Chaser before he or she has a chance to destroy it. Many of us chose to be aware enough as young people that we attract a teacher into our lives, but some of the Pack were adults who grew enough to attract a teacher later in life. The younger Chasers typically do not engage Avils but will spend their time learning to speak Path and building skills that will be necessary when it's time to hunt. Some will decide to have a Companion such as Kai, while others will hunt alone or in pairs with another Chaser."

Will seemed like he was following her conversation well enough, so she continued, "Avils are sort of human, but they're selfish beings who do only for themselves. Over time the choices they make become more and more evil and less and less part of society until even their physical bodies change to reflect the habits and mind within."

Will watched the heaviness descend upon her again as he stirred spices and meat into a pot he had filled with water and placed on the stove.

"I have been hunting for many years and knew I was a Chaser even as a child. You might say The Path called to me. It brought me a teacher long before I could leave for a camp and formal training. Though there have been many injuries, I've always succeeded at defeating all of the Avils I engaged or that engaged me."

Will noticed that there wasn't any pride in her voice over that fact. Forgetting that he was to leave his questions for later, he asked, "If you've been so successful before, why do you seem so concerned about it this time?"

Ottum looked at him, and Will thought he saw pain flash across her face as she prepared to answer.

"This time the Avil didn't just try to engage me," Ottum paused. "It's hunting me, and for a reason I don't yet understand, it poisoned Saul as part of that hunt. I've not figured out why it would do that and then leave, but that's what happened." Ottum paused and Will watched her physically brace herself before continuing. "This time the Avil is my brother."

Ottum hung her head and closed her eyes briefly before she glanced up again. Will tried to determine if it was shame or guilt he saw in her golden brown eyes and guarded stance. Neither emotion seemed to fit her well, and by the look Kai casted her way, Will decided he wasn't wrong to think that both were mostly foreign to her.

"By allowing us into your cabin you're placing yourself in danger. If there were any other way, I would have moved on and left you out of it. Kai and I could have continued our journey through the night, but Saul might not have made it. He needs the warmth and shelter. Leaving Saul here while we journey on may still leave you in danger because I don't understand his true role in this yet," Ottum said as she looked toward Saul.

"Living by myself in this cabin comes with the knowledge that I might face danger. You, Kai, and Saul are welcome to stay tonight or as long as necessary to get Saul recovered enough to at least deal with the elements," Will said.

Ottum looked at Will and decided that he had a good soul. "Do you know how to wield a sword?" she asked.

"Not extremely well," he said with a shake of his head. "But I don't have one to wield even if I were skilled with it."

Ottum removed Saul's sword and handed it to Will. "You have one until Saul awakens and proves to have a mind at peace. If that happens, you'll return it to him."

"Of course," he replied, even though he knew that she was telling him how it would be and not asking. A mind at peace... Will didn't say anything to Ottum or Kai, but he doubted Saul would wake filled with peace. His eyes moved almost constantly beneath the lids covering them. Eyes moved like that when dreaming of things one didn't want to be dreaming about. Considering it was poison that induced the dreams, Saul was probably having great difficulty sorting truth from fiction within that world and this. *No," Will thought to himself. "Saul will not likely awaken with a mind at peace.*

To Ottum, he continued, "You should know I will kill for three reasons only. One is to eat, one is to protect myself, and the last is if someone innocent is being attacked. With the exception of the first, and if there is no other way, I will still try to harm enough to safely get away before I will purposely kill."

Ottum looked at him with an unreadable expression. "If killing is necessary, it will be by my hand."

"That's fine by me," Will said with a shrug. Will saw Kai shift uncomfortably, and he knew that Kai had no intention of allowing Ottum to kill her brother. Will preferred that no killing would happen at all. Sensing there was nowhere further for that thread of conversation to go, he turned his attention back to the soup on the stove.

"Do you have some water and a rag I might use for Saul?" Ottum asked.

With Will's nod to their respective places, Ottum retrieved both and went to Saul's side.

"He has not thrashed about since you gave him the herbal mixture, but his eye motion would indicate his mind is far from still," Kai said as Ottum settled by his side.

"Yes. I can see that. All we can do is keep him as comfortable as possible until he regains consciousness." Dismissing Kai from her thoughts, Ottum dipped the rag into the water, opened Saul's mouth, and dripped the water onto his tongue. Making sure he swallowed before she repeated the process, Ottum continued until she was satisfied he had obtained enough water. She would later do the same with the soup so that his body could have nourishment beyond the water, but for now, he needed the water more. Ottum checked his forehead with the back of her hand and was pleased he still remained free from fever or chill. His clothes were drying and she turned the sled so the other side of his body would be closer to the fire.

"Dinner will take some time to cook?" Ottum asked Will.

"Yes. But it won't be too long before it's ready. If you need something sooner, I have some dried berries and nuts in my stores," he said, pointing to the cellar.

"No, thank you. I'll wait until the soup is ready, but I'm going outside until then. Have Kai call me when it's done, please," Ottum said.

Ottum headed to the door, but Kai interrupted her.

"He will have to call for you himself, as I am going out also." Kai knew she wouldn't like it, but he was ready for her protest.

Ottum turned and raised an eyebrow at him as if to say, "*Oh really?*" She said nothing but stood waiting for him to comment further.

"It did not take long for me to adapt to the cold weather and sitting with Saul by the fire has me too warm. I figured you would not mind the company…unless you want me to continue to act like your pet and not your companion." Kai said it for effect, but the barb bounced off Ottum without as much as a cringe.

"Don't play games with me, Kai. You're my Companion and I know you too well for that. You've been watching me like a hawk since the moment I told you the Avil is my brother. If you think I'm not capable of going outside by myself, then you should just say so. You don't need to make excuses. Did you really think I'd fall for it?" she asked.

"Not really," Kai replied. "I am concerned about you, and you are very strong willed sometimes. It is not that you are incapable of going outside by yourself, it is that I do not feel you should face it by yourself when the time comes."

"Not 'it,' Kai. Avil or not, Leon is a 'he.' You don't believe I should face him when the time comes. I'll take your concerns into consideration, but I make no promises to ensure we're together at that moment. For now, I'm not going outside because I believe he is here. To the contrary, it feels as though his presence is getting further away instead of closer. I just want some fresh air and time to clear my thoughts before dinner and an evening of conversation that's likely to be directed away from today's events. If you'd like to join me, I'd enjoy your company. Saul seems nowhere near regaining consciousness, but even if he does, Will is likely to tell us immediately. Will is a very unusual unfamiliar, but he seems adequately wary of what Saul will be like upon awakening."

Kai was surprised at her reply and felt ashamed for not trusting her to be reasonable, but she was usually very set in her ideas. "Thank you, Ottum. I would like to join you. One of us should tell Will what is going on as he looks like he feels left out. Since he cannot understand me, I will leave that task to you."

Ottum turned to Will who was looking from one to the other with a look of concentration so intense it almost seemed painful. She realized that not only was he with beings who were speaking in a language he couldn't use, he was trying to decipher a language he couldn't hear or see.

"I'm sorry," Ottum said. "It's rude of us to speak in a foreign language with you present, but Kai and I have limited communication if not speaking in Path. I suppose that I could speak out loud at all times, but then you would still only be hearing half of what gets said. Kai has decided he would like to join me outside if you don't mind both of us being gone for a short time. Please let us know if dinner is done, if you need help, or if Saul awakens. We'll not be far away."

"That's Okay. I do really want to learn how to communicate the way you and Kai do, but I understand that sometimes it's necessary for you to leave me out for now. It would be nice if you could give me a signal so I know you're talking and not listening for some sound of danger when you both get quiet like that," Will said.

Ottum hadn't thought their silence might concern him in that way. Will was an intelligent and open unfamiliar, but he was still an unfamiliar with none of the reflexes that come so naturally to her. "Rather than create a signal, I'll try to tell you when Kai and I will be speaking for a moment. I'll let you know when we are done talking too. Will that suffice?"

"Yes. Thank you, Ottum. I'll let you know if there's anything happening inside that you needs your attention," Will said as he flashed a smile their way and went back to tending the soup.

Kai and Ottum stepped into the cold night air. They had stayed in a cabin a mere few nights ago, but things felt very different in this place. Both realized it had nothing to do with the place, but there was no going back to life as it had been before the latest turn of events. For quite some time they simply stood near the cabin door, content to contemplate their own thoughts and to enjoy the night air.

"Kai, who am I?" Ottum asked with furrowed brows.

It was a most unusual question and Kai wasn't sure how to answer it. So instead, he asked one of his own. "What do you mean by that?"

"In one of the dreams with Oscar he told me to embrace who I am. I've tried to figure out what he meant by that, but the more I think about it, the more puzzling it becomes, she said as she rubbed her chin. "Until the dream, I would have said I knew without a doubt who I am and what my purpose in life is. But now, well, I'm not sure I have even the slightest idea."

Kai sat down beside the front steps as Ottum found a seat on a log lying nearby.

"Ottum, I do not believe that is a question I can answer for you. I can give you my opinion of who you are to me, but that would still not be an accurate assessment of who you are. Is it possible that you will see Oscar in another dream and be able to speak with him about it?" Kai asked.

"I don't know," she sighed, sending an eddy of frozen breath through the air. "Even when Oscar was alive he didn't give me straight answers. He seems to think it's better when I answer my own questions with the help of the 'riddles' he provides." Ottum smiled in spite of the remnants of anger she felt toward the last dream conversation she and Oscar had shared.

"What else did Oscar tell you in the dream?" Kai asked as nonchalantly as he could.

Ottum was surprised by the question. It was unlike Kai to pry. But she couldn't think of a good reason to avoid answering him while remaining true to her self-promise of allowing him in for more than survival needs.

"It wasn't a very pleasant conversation for me. He said I use my talents to keep people away and that in doing so, I create my own loneliness. He also said I try to take responsibility for things I can't control and then hide behind those things so that I don't have to take responsibility for the things I have real control over. Oh yes," Ottum said dryly, "I believe he also mentioned that I try to control everyone and everything around me. Given your most recent behavior, I will assume you feel at least that part is true." Ottum looked at him with her eyebrows raised in question and defiance. She was still irritated Kai had tried to play games with her, but she was perhaps more irritated that Oscar had been right about any of the things he'd said about her.

"It seems we're being more open with each other. Do you really want my opinion on the rest of what Oscar told you?" Kai asked.

"Yes."

Kai sat for a moment, giving her time to change her mind. But Ottum didn't waver.

"I think Oscar is right about all of it," Kai said flatly.

It was a slap in the face and Ottum felt her temper rising. She knew Kai could tell, but he sat still and watched her.

"I am sorry you do not like to hear it, Ottum. However, that does not make any of it less true. You are one of the most intelligent, kind, sympathetic, and wise beings I know. But when it comes to your own life, you do not apply the same guidelines you do to everyone else's life. You could be so much more than what you are," Kai paused. "Having said that, I will also tell you that you are already the best being I know. But I do believe you are capable of more, and it is as much a waste for you to not achieve what you are capable of as it is for anyone else to fail to do so."

Ottum wasn't sure if she liked the new level of openness Kai felt they had reached. Though anger threatened to surface, she no longer had the energy for it. Kai moved to stand before her, and she wrapped her arms around him and buried her face in his hair.

"I love you, Kai," Ottum whispered.

"I love you too, my lady," he said as he leaned his large head against hers.

Ottum looked up as Will opened the cabin door and announced that dinner was ready. He also told them he had set some water aside if they wanted to wash before eating. Neither Ottum nor Kai was ready to go inside, but they didn't want to insult their host with rudeness.

"We can talk more tonight, my lady."

And with that Kai pulled away and headed toward the door and the delightful smell that was coming from their temporary residence. Ottum followed closely behind.

* * *

Saul knew he had felt Eyota touch him. He had felt it right before he swallowed the other Chaser's herbs. She had said he had been poisoned and she wanted to help him, but he was bound and unable to open his eyes despite his best efforts to do so. It seemed he had been tricked again, but he was too tired to fight any longer. Within seconds, he drifted to sleep.

Saul didn't know how many days it had been or if it had been months. The Avil continued to alternate between burning him with fire and dipping him in the freezing mountain stream. Saul called for Eyota, but she never answered. The Avil would laugh at him as he called for her and would tell him it was hard for her to answer when her head was no longer attached to her body.

Saul thought once that he'd heard other voices, and he had screamed for them to help him. But it seemed he was too deep within the bear cave for them to hear or else they were too far away. His arms had been broken or he would have crawled out of the cave to attract their attention.

* * *

Saul didn't know how it was that he had not either starved to death or died of dehydration, but the Avil was doing something that kept him barely alive. The fire and stream sessions had finally ended, but the latest form of torture was no better. He was buried with only his head above ground. It appeared he had been moved off of the mountain because it was not as cold, but his eyes were still held shut. He wondered if it was possible they had been removed, but he could not free his hands to touch them and know.

* * *

Saul was starving while the Avil was preparing a feast. Saul knew he would taste none of it, but he no longer cared. The torture had lasted weeks and broken him so that he didn't even want revenge. The smell was alluring to a man who had gone without food for so long, and his stomach started cramping in response to it. The cramping gave way to pain, but pain was familiar now and Saul made no attempt to get away from it. His body lay there listless and his mind eased him into oblivion again.

* * *

The hearty aroma of soup filled the cabin air and made for a truly inviting atmosphere. As Ottum washed, she realized that prior to announcing that dinner was ready, Will had already filled bowls so their food could cool enough to enjoy. To her pleasure, he'd filled one for Kai and Saul also. She didn't know his story yet, but their host intrigued her.

"Shall we all sit together?" Will asked as he motioned toward the fireplace and picked up two of the bowls.

Ottum picked up the other two and placed both down near the fire before checking on Saul. He still remained free of fever, but she was worried about how long he was going to remain trapped within his mind's poisoned delusions. Knowing there was nothing more she could do for him, she retrieved one of the bowls and sat on a chair Will had placed beside his own. The chairs were nothing more than leather mounted to a wooden frame. The seat sat just inches from the floor, but the back extended above Ottum's head so that she could fully relax as she sat.

"There are arm rests that can be added if you want them," Will said. "I tend to only use them when I'm writing or on those rare occasions when I have a new set of books to read."

"No, thank you," Ottum said. "The chair is quite comfortable as it is."

Both Kai and Will had waited on her before beginning, but once she was seated, Kai began eating his squirrel. Ottum said a silent thank you for the meal and moved a spoon full of soup to her mouth.

Will watched her for a reaction and smiled as she savored the flavor.

"Kai, I believe we have a chef on our hands!" Ottum exclaimed in approval.

Will laughed but was obviously pleased with her approval.

"Perhaps we can trade instruction. I would like to know what herbs you used to season this soup and you'd like to learn to speak Path. Kai might never eat my cooking again after tasting your soup," Ottum teased.

Will's deep laughter filled the cabin. "Kai looks like he's done okay with your cooking so far, so it can't be that bad," he winked.

"Personally, I think you are both missing the glory of bloody, raw meat and the delight of crunching through a tasty bone," Kai told Ottum.

She laughed and repeated his comment to Will.

"Indeed? Well, I will just have to take your word for it, Kai, as I won't be trying that anytime soon," Will said with a chuckle and shake of his head. "Seriously though, trading sounds like a very good deal to me. I can show you what herbs I favor in my cooking, but what can I offer Kai in exchange for his help in learning your language?"

Though he didn't want to admit it, Kai could see why Ottum was so intrigued by Will and why she would want him as a student. "Please tell him his willingness to share his food and shelter is plenty for me. So that you do not constantly have to repeat what I say, let him know it is okay to leave me out of the conversation for now."

Ottum performed her role as translator and Will smiled in Kai's direction. Will and Ottum then engaged in light conversation while they all finished their dinner. When Ottum was done with her bowl, she picked up the other and moved to Saul's side. Using the same cloth she'd used to give Saul water, she dipped it into the broth and began feeding Saul. Will set his own bowl aside and lifted Saul slightly so that the unconscious Chaser was at a better angle and less likely to choke.

In this manner, they fed Saul as best they could. When the bowl of broth was empty, Ottum spoke in Path to Saul. He didn't reply, but she felt she needed to at least try. Will gathered another rag and placed it along with some fresh water near Saul's sled so they could give it to him later. Then they both cleaned the dishes and placed what remained of the soup in the cold box.

With the evening's duties completed, they sat down to ask and answer questions. Kai excused himself from the conversation again by stating that he was going to keep Saul company.

Saul was only a few feet away, so Ottum suspected that Kai had also guessed it was his touch that had gained Saul's cooperation earlier in the day. Kai was her Companion and was loyal to her above all others, but duty and honor ran deep within him. She knew he would do everything in his power to take away the pain of any Chaser.

* * *

"What is it that you would like to ask first?" Ottum asked Will.

Will considered his options for a moment before answering. There was much he wanted to know, and while it wasn't something he expected to be able to do overnight, he felt learning the language Ottum and Kai shared would be something that was of deep value to him. "What's the first skill I should practice in order to learn to speak with Kai?"

This one aims high, Ottum thought to herself. To Will she said, "The first step is to learn to clear your mind. Once you've mastered that skill, the other steps will come more easily."

Will thoughtfully scratched the goatee on his chin. "What does it mean to clear my mind?" he asked.

"Stop all of the activity that goes on in the background so that there are no thoughts running through your awareness. Although you'll eventually learn to do both at the same time just as you do while speaking your current language, at first you want to learn to stop your thoughts and know complete silence."

"That sounds simple enough," he said with a slight shrug of his muscular shoulders.

Ottum smiled at his comment. It had taken her a week to be able to clear her mind even for a few minutes at a time. Even then, she would realize she had succeeded and become excited about it so that she failed over her own success.

"Once you have acquired that skill, you then direct your attention at the being you wish to speak with, and you think to them—you silently speak just one thought at a time to them. Path is easier to learn to speak than it is to hear and understand. While you're thinking a sentence, the person you're talking to will be experiencing your thought. Therefore, the sight, smell, feel, and sound involved in your thought will also be transmitted. In that manner, each being has its own voice which will become familiar to you over time as you learn his or her nuances." Ottum stopped because Will had closed his eyes and looked as though he were asleep.

Will remained this way for several minutes while Ottum watched with mixed amusement and admiration. She hadn't expected him to attempt to learn right then and there, but after several minutes passed with Will remaining still and silent, Ottum decided to check on Saul.

She quietly moved to Saul and dipped the rag in the water before placing it in his mouth. She repeated this a few times, checked his forehead, and decided she would interrupt Will's practice so that they could continue with their questions and answers. It was then she realized Kai was looking at Will and that Will was smiling. She touched Kai's shoulder softly, and he shifted his gaze.

With admiration filling his voice, Kai said, "He is a fast learner."

Ottum was stunned. "What?"

"He is a fast learner," Kai repeated. "I am not sure how well he understands what I am saying, but he is definitely speaking to me."

Ottum looked back at Will and caught him smiling at the two of them with a look she couldn't define. Still disbelieving it was possible, she spoke to Will in Path. "Can you understand Kai?"

"Yes."

It was a single word he spoke, although no sound came from his mouth. While he enjoyed the look of surprise on her face, Ottum stood staring at him completely speechless.

When she didn't reply to him Will asked, "Can you understand me?"

"Yes." She paused and then continued. "How did you do that?"

"I did exactly what you said. You're right. It's much harder to hear than it is to speak," Will said.

"No," Ottum said with a confused shake of her head. "I understand how you're doing it; I just don't understand *how* you're doing it?"

Will thought he knew what she was asking. "I learned to still my mind years ago with meditation, and I practice it daily. Until today, I didn't know that The Path even existed, so I didn't know it held its own language. Therefore, even though I was skilled at stilling my mind, I didn't know to attempt to merge it with other skills to be able to speak without moving my mouth."

"Well, it appears you had no problems once you realized it was possible," Ottum said, still miffed.

"How is it that when Kai spoke to you I could hear him, but I couldn't hear you speak to him? I know you spoke, because he replied to you. But I didn't hear what you said. Why is that?" Will asked.

Not only had he learned to speak Path in a few minutes, he had learned to listen for more than one voice! Ottum was so caught up in her thoughts that she wasn't replying to him so Kai spoke for her.

"It is possible to direct your thoughts to as many beings as you would like. It is also possible to choose to speak to only one at a time. Ottum was directing her conversation to me only, because at that moment, she didn't realize you would be able to understand her."

"That makes sense. Can you both understand what I am saying?" Will could sense the mirth coming from Kai. He also realized that, for some reason, it was difficult for Ottum that he had learned to speak her language in one evening. Both of them nodded to him. "While it's incredible to be able to speak your language, it's rather tiring for me to do so," Will said out loud. "I'm not used to experiencing other's thoughts in such detail. Is it possible for me to continue communicating with Kai in this manner while using my voice with Ottum?" He looked from one to the other as he asked.

"You may speak with me anytime you would like," Kai stated. "However, I want to return my attention to Saul if neither of you have objections. Should I need to speak with you and you are not listening to me, I will find a way to get your attention."

"It's good for me to use my voice sometimes," Ottum said, "so I would prefer it for now. Do you have other questions for me?" Ottum asked.

"Yes," Will smiled. "I have lots of them. But since you taught me to communicate with both of you, I think it's your turn to ask me a question. What would you like to know?" Will asked, settling back into his chair.

I'd like to know how an unfamiliar learned to speak Path in a few minutes, Ottum thought to herself. But she realized Will wouldn't have an answer beyond the explanation he'd already provided. Instead she decided to find out what she could about her host. "How is it that you came to be living here, or staying here if this isn't your home?"

Will smiled and paused to gather his thoughts. "I thought that might be one of your first questions for me. This is my home, but the story about how I came to live here isn't a short one."

"I like stories," Ottum said as she smiled at him. "Please continue." It was easy for Ottum to listen to other's stories. It was her own story she found hard to tell. She knew that sooner or later this man was going to ask for hers, and she also knew that because of the dreams with Oscar, Will would hear more about her than many of her friends had heard.

"I guess I'll start at the very beginning. I was born in a small town and spent the first few years living there with my parents. My parents, well, I guess you could say that they had a few problems. Another couple offered to take me into their school, and my parents happily agreed. The couple, Sasha and Adin, allowed me to live with them in their camp and took care of all of my schooling," Will said with fondness.

"Once my schooling was completed there, I moved to a larger town to seek out further education. I found that in many ways, the education I had at the camp was better. Innovation is something I appreciate, but too much of what is being called innovative is just destructive."

Will sat quietly, a sad look on his face. Ottum felt unsure of what to say, but with what looked like a shiver, Will snapped out of his silence.

"I've always enjoyed spending time in nature, but a few years ago I took a trip and when I returned, I realized I had lost my taste for living a modern life. So I packed what I thought I would need, sold the rest of my belongings, and headed off into the wilderness," Will said with a smile playing across his face. "I was very naïve about my skill at co-existing with unsettled lands. But I built a cabin and learned a lot of lessons the hard way."

Ottum nodded. "People often have a distorted idea of what it really takes to live from the land. They're used to co-existing with others and are more interdependent than they want to think they are."

"Indeed," Will agreed. "My first cabin was too close to Sasha and Adin's camp. On horse-back, it wasn't even a day's ride. There were too many visitors and I still felt too close to the camp. While it was hard to do after all the work I had put into it, I left it and moved much further away. I also took my horse back to camp after I was done with the second cabin. It forced me to be more independent."

"I stayed at the second cabin for a couple years until the spring that was my main source of water went dry. A cave-in further up the mountain was the cause and there was no reasonable fix. I discovered this area while hunting, and by then I'd spent enough time living on my own to realize that it would meet my needs better than either of the previous two. So once again, I found myself building a cabin. There's another cabin about a day's walk from here that I stay in sometimes while travelling to visit Sasha and Adin, or occasionally to hunt a different area. The original owners left it in great shape, but it's been abandoned for as long as I've been aware of its existence. I made some modifications to it in order to be comfortable when I do stay there, but this is the place I call home," he said as he gestured about the cabin.

Will sat smiling at her while Ottum wished he would fill in more of the gaps. His story left her with just as many questions as it had given answers. She was used to people opening up to her and really telling her about their lives. Will hinted at the larger story behind what he told, but he didn't share any of the details. Most people loved to share their details. Just as she was thinking that it was almost rude for him to leave so much out, Oscar's words drifted into her head... *"People open their hearts and souls to you, and although you are very kind to them, you keep your own tightly closed."* Perhaps it served her right to experience her own version of sharing. She smiled at Will to buy a few more seconds, but Kai saved her from replying.

"Ottum..." Kai said. He was sitting beside Saul with his right front foot on Saul's leg.

"Is he awake?" Ottum and Will asked at the same time.

"Yes and no. I have been attempting to speak with him. Sometimes his replies are coherent, but at others, he either misunderstands or simply cannot hear me. His is a very tortured mind and soul." Kai paused, trying to shake the pain he felt when he had connected with Saul. "It is his belief that his eyes are either removed or held shut. I would like for you to open his lids while I speak with him to see if we can break the illusion for him."

Ottum moved to Saul's side while Will remained seated where he was. She looked at Kai to make sure he was ready and then gently lifted Saul's eye lids. At first his eyes continued to move as though they couldn't see. Ottum held them for almost a minute with no change before she released and then lifted them again. Not wanting them to dry, she started counting to twenty and then closing and opening them again. This continued for several minutes with no change in Saul. Kai had not let her in on the conversation he was having with Saul, so she didn't know if they were any closer to Saul understanding his eyes were okay. But she continued her routine of closing, opening, counting to twenty, and repeating the cycle.

"Sing," Will directed Ottum.

His request startled her out of the rhythm she and Kai had settled into. She wanted to tell Will that now was not an appropriate time, but one look at him told her he had been extensively more involved than she realized. Ottum looked at Kai, and he nodded for her to proceed. Ottum picked one of the old songs and sang softy to Saul. She matched the opening and closing of Saul's eyes with the gentle rhythm of the song. Saul's body began to shake, and he attempted to snap his own lids closed, but Ottum maintained both the song and the rhythm. She continued until his eyes started trying to focus. It was then that she released Saul's lids and allowed him to blink for himself. Ottum also stopped singing, but Will bid her to continue, so she did.

Saul looked at Ottum, Kai, and then Will. It was with Will that Saul's gaze stayed. Tears streamed out of his eyes, and though he didn't speak, he didn't look away from Will either. After a few short moments, Will moved to the side of the sled. He took Saul's hand and gave it a gentle squeeze.

"Sleep well and enjoy peaceful sleep. You are among friends," Will spoke aloud.

At Will's words, Saul's eyes closed again. Ottum and Kai watched as Saul's body relaxed into sleep—real sleep instead of the tortured unconsciousness he had experienced all day. His eyes were still, his breathing was deep, and he was truly asleep.

"You may stop singing now. Your voice is quite beautiful though, and I hope to hear it again sometime soon. Perhaps you will teach me the song you were singing? I have not heard it before." Will smiled at Ottum as though they had been standing there discussing the weather and nothing significant had happened.

Ottum stopped and stared at Will. Thoughts raced through her head as she replayed what had just happened. This man, this *unfamiliar*, had reached someone who was Pack in a way she had no comprehension of with a language he had learned to speak in a matter of minutes. All evening she had thought of him as a potential student. For the first time ever, it occurred to Ottum that there might be those outside of Pack who could teach her more than she could teach them.

"I'll teach you the song." Ottum felt she should apologize for not realizing his level of skill and knowledge, and for thinking she was going to be the teacher. But the words failed to form. Suddenly she was extremely tired from the events of the day as well as the long hike through the previous night. So while questions abounded, what she most wanted to know was when she could sleep.

"Why don't you and Kai get some rest?" Will pointed to a pallet in the corner of the cabin. "I'll stay awake for a while, and when I am tired, I'll wake one of you to take my place watching over Saul. Please, use my bed."

Kai expected Ottum to argue, but uncharacteristically, she didn't. She excused herself to go outside, and Kai followed.

The cold air surrounded Ottum and awoke her senses. She was still tired, but her head felt slightly clearer. She and Kai had come upon a cabin occupied by a master who was also an unfamiliar on a day when she felt she'd forgotten who she was. It was as though she were so on track that The Path was no longer just a way of life; it was a vibrating stream of life that beckoned her to follow and be part of it.

Having taken care of their respective needs, Ottum and Kai returned to the cabin. Will was stoking the fire as they walked in and closed the door. He asked them to wait by the door for a moment as he finished placing the poker in its spot. He walked to the door and showed them how to use the lock he had created so they would be able to enter and exit if needed in the night.

While Will returned to Saul's side, Ottum and Kai headed to the pallet. Ottum removed her boots, lay down, wrapped her arm around Kai, and was asleep within seconds without even thinking about her chant.

* * *

Oscar was waiting for her by the fire again.

"I might be dreaming, but I'm still very tired," Ottum said through a yawn. "You could have warned me about my brother and told me about Will so that I wouldn't feel like a fool."

"Warning you still wouldn't have prepared you for meeting Leon," Oscar said as he stirred the fire. "Will is delightful though, isn't he? You'll learn much from him if you can put aside that ego of yours." Oscar flashed a grin at her.

Ottum glared at him but didn't have the spirit to argue. "It appears you were right about me. I still don't know what to do about all of it, but when I've slept some, I'll try to figure it all out." She looked into his eyes and love filled her. I don't understand how it is that we're talking, but I have missed you terribly and am glad you're in my life again."

"Child, I never left you!" Oscar exclaimed. "I'm in the songs you sing, the lessons you learned, and the memories you carry."

Tears rolled down Ottum's cheeks, and the look on Oscar's face was that of a parent wanting to take away pain, but knowing that the lesson would also be lost if he did.

"Will you tell me how to get through this?" Ottum asked.

"I cannot do that, Ottum," he said, his voice low and tinged with regret.

"Why?" She was whining now and knew it. "I've always worked hard to learn the lessons you teach and to do what is right. Leon is an Avil, Oscar. What am I supposed to do about that? Why can't you this one time just tell me what to do instead of making me go through the struggle of figuring it out?"

"If I tell you my way, then it isn't your life you're living but an imitation of mine. Those who do nothing to earn a place in this world will eventually feel dis-ease. There isn't one way to live, but many, so doing something my way might ultimately be a lie for who you are. You could then try repeatedly to convince yourself that the lie is truth, but you'd spend valuable energy in the deception and use time that could be better spent." Oscar looked deeply into her eyes. "Do you understand?"

Ottum stopped crying and wiped the tears from her face. "Yes. I don't like it, but I get your point."

Oscar smiled at her and his eyes twinkled. Ottum loved that twinkle.

"Will is a good man. Learn what he has to teach you, and share with him the things you know." Oscar turned to walk away, and Ottum felt the scene withdrawing as it had each time they talked.

"Oscar!" she yelled.

He paused for a moment and looked back at her. "Yes?"

"I love you."

"I love you too, Ottum. Now rest, my child. You have much work ahead of you."

Then he was gone.

CHAPTER 8

Will woke Kai part way through the night with a gentle touch and by softly saying his name in Path. Kai was sleepy, but he was pleased Will had woken him instead of Ottum.

"How is Saul?" Kai asked as he stood and stretched.

"He's still sleeping, and he seems to be peaceful enough."

"Good." Kai looked at Ottum who was also still sleeping. "It is hard for her, you know."

"What is?" Will asked.

"That you are such a natural. She grew up feeling alone because she always achieved everything more easily than those around her. While she felt isolated, there was also a sense of pride about her skills. You are the first she has met who can match if not out-perform her. It will be hard for her, so be gentle when you can," Kai said.

"What makes you think I can out-perform her?" Will said before yawning.

"Will, I may be a wolf, but I have been Ottum's Companion for several years. I have learned to hear what isn't being said by her as well as what is, but I have also learned to judge those we come into contact with quickly. It is my duty to protect her, and I will do so for as long as she allows it, but I no longer protect out of duty. If you have not noticed, but I believe that you have, Ottum does not exactly open up easily. I know more about her than any other living being does. You mean neither of us harm, but I will not take kindly to you hurting her whether it is meant or not." Kai stood there looking into Will's eyes. When he was sure they understood each other, Kai lumbered off to sit with Saul.

Realizing it might be awkward, Will looked about his cabin for another place to sleep but found only the floor.

"Sleep with her," Kai said. "It will be good for her to be close to a human. I will stay with Saul until morning unless I simply cannot stay awake any longer. If that happens, I prefer to wake you."

"Of course. Wake me if you need to," Will said.

Will walked to the pallet, removed his boots, and quietly lay down beside Ottum. She moved, and for a moment he thought he had woken her, but she placed an arm around him and continued sleeping. *She thinks I'm Kai,* he thought, but he didn't move her arm off of him.

As Will drifted to sleep, he marveled that he'd just had a big-brother talking to from a wolf. He wasn't sure whether to be more intrigued by that or by the fact that he could actually talk with a wolf. He smiled to himself. There was a beautiful woman on his pallet with her arm wrapped around him, and he was preoccupied with her wolf. *It is indeed strange how knowledge changes one's perspective of life.*

* * *

Saul was the first to wake that morning. Only coals remained of the fire that had burned most of the night. They shed very little light, so Saul only saw shadows as he craned his head for a look at his surroundings. He stretched and quickly realized that he was still bound to the sled.

Kai sat quietly and waited for Saul to spot him. When the Chaser's eyes fell on him, Kai spoke.

"Good morning, Saul. Your sleep last night seemed to be more peaceful than yesterday's unconsciousness."

"Yesterday!" Saul exclaimed. "The Avil had me for at least a few weeks, but it seemed more like several months. I have not had sleep such as last night's in a very long time."

Kai realized that whatever Will and Saul had spoken about, it hadn't included the reality of the time that had passed. He decided it would be best to allow Saul some space to reintegrate before that was addressed. It was enough for now that Saul had returned to the present world.

"I am glad you got some rest. Everyone else is still sleeping, and I cannot remove your bindings," Kai said with a slight shrug and a stretch.

"Oh," Saul nodded. "Why am I bound?"

Kai hesitated to find words that would explain enough without causing Saul excessive confusion. "When we found you, the Avil had poisoned you and you were hallucinating. We did not want to risk that you would mistake one of us for an enemy."

"Oh." After a moment Saul asked, "I didn't harm any of you, did I?"

"No," Kai said as he lay down beside Saul and yawned. "When we found you, it was just Ottum and I. This is Will's cabin, and he invited us to spend the night here last night so that we could be sheltered from the cold. You were soaked with sweat from a fever that came and went."

"Oh."

Kai noticed that "oh" seemed to be Saul's first response to almost everything.

"So Will and Ottum aren't mates?" Saul asked.

"Not as of yet," Kai replied, a wolfish grin showing his sharp teeth.

This time Saul didn't reply in any way except to raise an eyebrow.

Kai laughed. "I have been her Companion for many years, and he is new to speaking Path. It is not hard to see their interest in each other although both are attempting to pretend it does not exist at the moment."

Sadness crossed Saul's face when he heard the word Companion. It was then that Kai made the guess that Eyota had been Saul's. The sadness did not stay long though. By the time Kai glanced toward the pallet and back again, Saul was smiling.

"Will is an amazing person. He must be a most fearsome Chaser," Saul said with obvious admiration.

"He is not a Chaser."

"What?"

"He is not a Chaser," Kai repeated.

"No. I heard you. I meant how is that possible? He spoke in Path to me last night, and he knew how to help me. If he isn't a Chaser, what is he?"

"He is an unfamiliar. He learned to speak Path just last night. I do not know how it is that he helped you, but I can assure you that I find him to be most fascinating also."

"An unfamiliar and not a Chaser?" Saul said it mostly to himself.

"Yes. Will is truly a talented man." Kai returned to a seated position and looked at the shadowed forms of Will and Ottum. Seeing that they were both still soundly sleeping, he asked Saul, "How are you feeling today?"

Saul considered Kai's question. "Well, I'm thirsty and hungry and could stand to get up and move about some, but I believe I am okay."

"That is good. We were worried about you," Kai replied.

"Where's my sword?" Saul asked casually. "I remember it being on me for a while, but then I believe someone took it from me. Did you see it when you found me?"

"Yes. Your sword, knife, and water skins were still on you. We believe the Avil took your pack. Your weapons are in a safe place," Kai assured him.

"Where?" Saul asked.

"It does not matter at the moment. Your sword is safe, and you have no need of it right now," Kai said firmly.

"A Chaser doesn't like to be without his sword you know." Saul said with a smile.

"I know," Kai responded. Despite Saul's statement that he was okay, his behavior seemed strange to Kai.

Saul hid his anger at being denied his sword. After a few moments of tense silence, he asked, "When you found me, did you see my Companion?"

"We did not see a Companion or any trace of one. You called me Eyota once. Is that the name of your Companion?"

"Yes. For some reason my memory is a little fuzzy about all that happened to me over the last several weeks or months. I'm not certain if she's alive or dead," Saul said with sincere sadness.

"That must be difficult. I am sorry to tell you, but I believe it most likely that she is dead. There were no tracks, and the Avil was only interested in us. If it suspected that another Companion could be in the area, it would have been more vigilant with regard to its surroundings," Kai said.

"Oh." Saul turned his head away from Kai.

"While Avils are not to be trusted, the Avil that poisoned you said that your Companion had been killed. Truly Saul," Kai said as he placed his foot on Saul's leg, "I am sorry for your loss."

Saul looked into Kai's eyes and knew he was sincere. Companions could be counted on for their faithfulness and integrity. *But he's not my Companion,* Saul thought to himself. To Kai he said, "Thank you. I'm going to try to get more rest again now."

"Sleep peacefully." Kai meant it, but he was uneasy about Saul. It wasn't that the Chaser had made any attempt to escape the bindings or that he had acted menacing, but there was something that didn't feel right. Saul had tried to be casual about his interest, but Kai had noticed his anger at not being allowed to know where his sword was kept.

Saul's eyes were closed, but he had also closed his mind. Kai would make sure to share with Ottum and Will his uncertainty of Saul's condition.

Kai looked again at the pallet Will and Ottum shared. He wasn't sure why, but it pleased him that they were drawn to each other. He had the deep sense their pairing was a powerful and good thing.

CHAPTER 9

The first thing Will was aware of upon waking was that Ottum still had her arm wrapped around him. During the night they had moved so that her head was resting on his shoulder. His entire arm was numb, but he didn't want to move just yet. He lay there taking in the feel and smell of her. He'd been living alone for the last several years and waking up with a woman was something that had been absent during much of that time. His mind wandered to what it would be like to be with Ottum more intimately than they currently were.

Ottum awoke and her hand moved to her sword in the time it took Will to open his eyes.

"Whoa!" he said, placing his free hand on her arm that was closest to him.

Ottum lifted her head and looked around the dimly lit cabin. Then she looked at Will with slight confusion. She didn't speak, but it was obvious she was trying to find an explanation for something. Not finding it, she moved to allow space between them and lay down again. Her hand stayed on her sword.

"Was I thinking in Path?" Will asked her. Though he spoke that way now, he didn't think he had been earlier.

"No. Why?" Ottum cocked her head slightly to the side as she evaluated him.

Will really didn't know how to answer her question. He could feel the color creeping into his cheeks, but he hoped he might distract her from noticing in the dim light. "You woke up so quickly and went to your sword," he paused. "I was just trying to figure out why."

"Your breathing increased," she shrugged. "I thought you were Kai, and his breath would only have increased if there were danger." Ottum continued to look at him and noted his flushed face. Taking in the rest of him, she decided to be ornery. "What exactly were you thinking that justified me reaching for my sword?"

Knowing he was caught, that she already had a guess at what he had been thinking and was willing to tease about it, and that it was the only way he could be ornery in return, Will shared in Path exactly what he had been thinking.

Ottum's eyes flashed and Will wondered if he had gone too far. Her golden brown eyes searched his green ones for a moment as if looking for something specific. Will wasn't sure if she found it or decided it wasn't there, but her next sentence was a complete change of subject.

"I need to check in with Kai and see how Saul did last night." With that, she released her sword and in one smooth motion rolled away from him and off the pallet.

Kai had been watching the entire exchange and wondered what caused Ottum to go for her sword. When she made eye contact, Kai nodded, but he didn't ask questions.

"Things go well last night?" Ottum asked as she reached Kai's side and coaxed the fire to life with fresh wood and kindling.

"Yes. Saul was awake for a short while earlier. It is not that he acted strange or tried to get out of his bindings, but something does not feel right about him. I believe we should all use great caution when dealing with him until we know otherwise. He was asking for his sword, but I believe it best to not return it just yet. He will need to be unbound and allowed to go outside soon. He may not have had much to consume yesterday, but he did not make any of the stops we did." Then, closing Will out but glancing in his direction, Kai asked, "Everything okay, my lady?"

"Yes, Kai," she said with a smile. "Thanks for asking."

There was no indication of what had happened, and Kai realized Ottum wasn't going to share the experience with him. Will had remained on the pallet during their conversation but was now getting up and stretching.

"Shall we wake Saul?" Will was putting his boots on as he asked the question. He looked up and realized Ottum had been watching him, so he smiled at her. He thought he saw a slight sparkle in her eyes, but she didn't return his smile. *Maybe it was just a reflection from the fire,* Will thought.

"Yes," Ottum nodded. "Given the events of last night, perhaps it should be you who wakes Saul," she said.

Will moved to Saul's side. The fire was coming to life and the warmth was welcome. "Do I remove the bindings before or after he is awake?"

"After." Kai and Ottum said at the same time.

Will smiled to himself. They might not be the same species, but it was obvious the two had been together for some time. He reached out and placed a hand on Saul's shoulder. He noted that Ottum's hand lay almost unconsciously on her sword while Kai stood ready to spring to action.

"Saul." Will shook him slightly, but Saul didn't stir. "Saul. You need to wake up so that we can go outside." Puzzled that Saul wasn't waking, he looked to Ottum and Kai.

"He is not right," Kai said to himself as well as the other two. "You will have to use spoken word."

"Why will he be able to hear spoken word but not Path?" Will asked.

"Because," Ottum stated, "he's currently in a state that isn't aligned with the ways of the Path. Therefore, he can't access the tools which those on The Path can."

"But I didn't even know The Path existed until yesterday. How can I be aligned with the ways of The Path when I don't even understand what it is? I don't understand how someone who has been living his life much like you live yours could so easily not access tools which should be second nature to him by now," Will said, confusion on his face.

"There is much you have to learn, Will," Ottum paused, "and much you will teach as well. For now, it's important only to understand that Saul is playing something out in his mind that isn't in harmony with life. It isn't that he doesn't know that someone is speaking; it's that he can't understand what you're saying." Ottum half-smiled at him. "Try again with spoken word. He is bound and we're here to protect you."

"Saul," Will said aloud as he shook Saul's shoulder again. Instantly Saul's eyes flew open, and Will instinctively moved back. It was only there for a fraction of a second, but the look Will saw caused him to realize that Kai had every reason to be concerned about Saul's state of mind. Just as quickly, the look in Saul's eyes returned to that of a friendly man.

"How long was I out?" he asked almost cheerfully as he stretched against the bindings.

"Not long," Will replied, slightly guarded.

Saul moved his head so that he could see Kai. Once he spotted him, he smiled.

Kai nodded to him. "It was not very long at all. We are all going to go outside and thought you might like to join us."

"Yes. I'd love to be able to move. Is it safe to untie me now?" Saul asked the question with light-hearted ease as though there could be no thought of keeping him bound.

The question caused Will to shiver. If the man who was speaking with them at the moment remained, it was indeed very safe to unbind him. However, Will wasn't interested in experiencing the man he saw looking at him moments ago.

Saul's humor faded slightly as he watched Will look to Ottum and Kai for direction, and it faded completely when they didn't immediately indicate his release was warranted. "Why is my release being questioned?" Saul aimed this question at Ottum as it seemed that Will and Kai were looking to her.

"You are Pack, so I will speak openly with you," Ottum said. "The Avil poisoned you yesterday, and since then, you have not quite been yourself. A few moments ago you couldn't understand Path. While it may not fully be conscious, there are times when you're not functioning as a Chaser."

"Yesterday! The Avil tortured me for weeks if not months!" Saul said with barely restrained anger.

"No," Ottum shook her head. "It was only yesterday. I do not know what the poison was, but I know it was given to you yesterday. It's not likely you were in the possession of the Avil any longer than that. You wouldn't still be as well framed as you are if he had held you captive. Nor would the stream have become poisoned just two nights ago."

Saul looked at her in bewilderment. "But, I have *memories* of what happened!"

"While you probably have lots of memories that are accurate, the memories you have with the Avil aren't likely to be real," she said it firmly, but touched him to express her concern for him.

"Not real! How is that possible?" Saul asked as he moved away from Ottum's touch as much as his bindings would allow. "I could feel, see, hear, and smell everything going on around me," Saul argued. "You are wrong!"

"You told me yourself that your memory of recent events is a little fuzzy." Kai said with compassion. He knew that this was very difficult for Saul.

"I said it was *fuzzy*! I didn't say that it wasn't *real*," Saul glared at him.

The three of them stood looking at Saul, wishing they could help him process what had happened to him.

At last Saul turned to Will. "You helped me last night, and yet, Kai tells me you're an unfamiliar. Is that part right?" He asked with squinted eyes.

"Yes. At least it would be correct to say that I am not a Chaser," Will replied. "I can help you again if you'll allow me to. But the rest of the healing you need will take more time."

"How can I heal when I can't even remember what did and didn't happen to me?" Saul asked with unbridled frustration.

"It's possible," Will said. "Trauma is trauma regardless of how or when it occurred. There are techniques you can learn that will allow you to release it without you having to revisit the events." Will patted Saul's shoulder reassuringly. He looked into Saul's eyes and wondered if he'd really seen such a murderous look in them earlier. The confused man in front of him showed no signs of potential violence.

It was Ottum who broke the silence that ensued. "I believe it's possible for us to unbind you as long as you understand you may not yet have your sword back. We'll also use whatever force necessary to prevent you from harming yourself or us. Do you understand?"

Saul looked at Ottum with tears threatening to fall from his eyes. "I understand."

With that, Will set to work releasing the bindings that held Saul to the sled. Once the last rope was removed, Will took Saul's hand and helped to lift him to a seated position.

Saul's stomach lurched, and he wavered unsteadily. "I may not be myself at all times, but currently I think it would be very difficult for me to harm any of you." He sat there for a moment longer as he tried to regain his balance and hoped for the pain to go away.

"Where does it hurt?" Will asked.

"My stomach," Saul said, wrapping one arm about his midsection. "I remember that a bear…that is, I remember thinking that a bear had clawed through it. Every time I tried to move, it felt like my entire gut was being shredded."

Will motioned for Ottum to come support Saul. Once she had Saul held up, Will moved his own hands to two different points on Saul's body and just held pressure there.

"What are you doing?" Ottum asked.

"I'm trying to balance his life force," Will said. He continued holding pressure on the two points and closed his eyes in concentration.

"Life force?" Ottum asked.

"That must be one of the things I'll get to teach you," Will said with a quiet smile. Without opening his eyes, he continued, "I'll show you later. Suffice it to say that I'm trying to help him feel better."

"It's working," Saul said. He was almost sitting up by himself now and was no longer fighting to keep from heaving.

Will left his hands on Saul for a few moments longer and then pulled away. "When you're ready, I believe you'll be able to stand."

With Ottum behind him pushing and Will in front pulling, Saul slowly rose to his feet. He wobbled unsteadily for a few seconds with his feet straddling the sled, and then he found his footing. He swung one foot over the sled and almost tumbled over, but Will and Ottum caught him and waited for him to find stability again.

"I think I'll need to lean on one of you if I'm going to walk," he said sheepishly.

"Lean on me." Will instructed. Ottum almost argued with him, but Kai stopped her.

"It is best to let Will help him. If he is to heal, Saul needs to trust him," Kai said only to her.

Ottum hadn't really thought about it that way. She'd felt it was her job because she'd brought Saul here and he was Pack. She slowly released her hold of Saul and stepped away to allow he and Will to make their way across the cabin. When they were close, Ottum came forward and opened the door. She waited until they were all through and then closed the door behind them.

"I have a latrine built over here if you care to use it. I didn't think to tell you about it last night. Follow me and I'll show you where it is," Will said.

Ottum didn't see where Will had indicated, so she decided to simply follow along. Kai headed off in his own direction. Saul appeared to be growing stronger with each step. Once they were all done, they headed for the cabin again. Kai didn't return, and although Ottum was slightly concerned, she decided to give it a while longer before hunting for him. She reached out to him with her senses, and what she felt satisfied her.

"Should we be concerned Kai isn't back?" Will asked.

"No. Kai can take care of himself." Then she added just for Will, "and Saul looks like he is fading again. We should get him inside."

Saul looked pale, and he was leaning more on Will than he had been just a short while ago. Ottum opened the door and stood back to allow the other two to enter. Before she entered, she looked around the clearing.

Yesterday Ottum and Kai had been weary from travel and prepared for battle. Today, the sun was shining and the picture that greeted her was richer. The front of the cabin faced south and there were trees around it so that it would be sheltered from sun in the summer and wind in winter. The log she had sat upon last night was fashioned into a type of chair which explained why it had been so comfortable to her. There was a matching set on the porch that circled the front of the cabin. Off to the side of the porch, Will had a large stack of wood piled in neat rows. He kept some of it on the porch and under cover of the roof there, but the rest was piled on the ground. There was a box of kindling on the porch too. The contents of the box looked like it contained the remnants of arrow-making. Will had obviously put great thought into the layout of his cabin and wanted to use every resource he consumed without waste.

In addition to its practicality, Ottum noted that the area was extremely beautiful. She could hear the trickle of a stream in the distance and knew it would be a pleasure to sit in the chair and experience the sun setting in the summer. In her imagination she could hear the melodies of several birds singing and smell the delightful aroma of the woods around her. Yes, Will had definitely made this cabin and its surroundings into his home. *He's such an unusual unfamiliar,* she thought. In some ways he seemed very simple, but in others, Ottum could see him being her equal.

"Are you sure Kai is alright?" Will intruded into her thoughts.

"No. But I also have no reason to believe he is anything but safe," she said with a smile as she entered the cabin and closed the door. "He's a grown wolf. He's gone off by himself on more than one occasion and returned safely. If he isn't back soon, then I'll hunt for him."

Will didn't look satisfied with her answer, but he had his hands full trying to get Saul settled.

"Are you keeping my pack from me for safety reasons as well?" Saul asked.

"We did not see a pack when we found you, and we searched the area somewhat thoroughly. It's probable that my brother took it. Is there something you need from it that I might be able to share with you?" Ottum asked.

"Who's your brother?" Saul asked.

Ottum realized that they hadn't shared that piece of information with Saul yet. She closed her eyes and sighed deeply, the air blowing her dark hair off her forehead. *Might as well get this over with.* She opened her eyes, looked directly at Saul, and said, "my brother is the Avil who poisoned you. His given name is Leon."

Saul's gaze narrowed, but when Ottum didn't flinch or look away, he decided she was serious. He liked it better when he thought she was joking.

"Did you kill him," Saul asked.

Ottum shook her head. "I didn't realize who he was before he got away. By that time, you were too sick for us to hunt him."

"You realize that *your brother* didn't just poison me. He took my companion's head too," Saul said with malice.

"He mentioned that. Were you already chasing him when he killed her?" Ottum asked as she tried to remain calm.

Saul nodded.

"What had he done, or did your meeting seem unexpected?" Ottum asked.

"The Avil was shooting wild horses for sport. It wasn't even making sure it was a clean kill. Some of those horses had several arrows in them that would be painful, but not lethal. Others were drowning in the river he had trapped them with. Sound like your brother?" he mocked.

Ottum narrowed her eyes in anger and clenched her teeth. "He and I aren't close. I'd not seen Leon in years and didn't even recognize him yesterday. The boy I knew is obviously very different from the," Ottum paused, "from the Avil he has become. If you think that I in any way approve of his behavior, you can rest assured that I will treat him as I would any other Avil next time we meet."

"I'm sure all of us here have had a family member do something we didn't approve of or agree with," Will interjected. "Was there something in your pack that we can let you borrow until you're able to replace it, Saul?"

Saul and Ottum remained locked in a stare. Will cleared his throat and pulled Saul's attention to him.

"I suppose you're right. You realize I'll kill it the next time I see it, and that as soon as I'm well enough, I'll go hunting for it?" Saul asked.

"I'd expect no less. My intentions are the same," Ottum said, but it bothered her that Saul continued to refer to Leon as an "it."

Saul seemed to relax with her reply. He still wanted to question Ottum about her brother, though. He'd never known family members of an Avil and found it intriguing that one family had produced both an Avil and a Chaser. Even in his weakened state, he could tell it wasn't a conversation she would deal with well. The Avil might be her brother, but Ottum had saved Saul's life.

"There was nothing in my pack that can't be replaced. I was hoping to use my own bed roll. That's all," Saul said with a shrug.

"Please feel free to use the one Kai and I share," Ottum said. "The only reason we didn't try to place you in it last night was that it was still wet from the day's travels."

"Thanks. Will you please help me lay it out? I seem to be losing my strength again." Saul looked at them both with embarrassment visible on his face. He was as used to asking for help as Ottum.

"You're welcome to rest on my pallet," Will said.

"I prefer the floor, thanks," Saul said.

"Would you like it to be in about the same spot where you spent the night or will that be too warm for you?" Will asked.

"That'll be fine, thanks."

Ottum moved the sled, and Will placed the bedroll in its spot. She and Will then helped Saul settle on it. He was asleep within minutes of lying down.

"I think that getting food into him might help. Do you know what poison was used on him?" Will asked.

"No," Ottum replied. "I brought it with us in the event that it could be useful in his healing, but I didn't take the time to evaluate it yesterday."

"Perhaps we should look at it later?"

"Of course, but right now I think we should make breakfast. What can I do to help?" Ottum asked.

"I have a small amount of beans soaking over there," Will said as he pointed to a side cabinet. Will you drain and rinse them while I get the stove heating and the water in the pot?"

Ottum didn't answer except to head toward the cabinet.

"Are you sure Kai is okay?" Will asked with concern.

"Do you have reason to believe he isn't?" Ottum countered.

"I don't know," Will shrugged. "I'm just concerned by the amount of time he's been gone."

"Yesterday you believed he was going to eat you for dinner, and today you seem to be worried that he can't take care of himself for even a short time. Why do you believe he isn't capable of caring for himself?" Ottum asked, almost amused at the change.

"It isn't that," Will rubbed his chin. "Or perhaps it is. Yesterday Kai seemed like a very large wolf. While it would be unusual for a wolf to hunt a healthy human when winter has barely begun, it isn't impossible that circumstances could have caused me to look like an appealing meal. Now that I've spent an evening with him, it seems to me that he is more human than wolf. And a wolf who is more human than wolf seems vulnerable to me."

"Kai seems human to you?" Ottum asked.

It surprised Will that Ottum couldn't picture Kai as human when she spent so much time with him. He spoke with human inflections and speech patterns, he carried his own pack which he could get into and out of without assistance, he shared a bedroll with her, and he seemed about as wild as Will himself did. Rather than point out all of those things, he simply said, "Yes."

Ottum considered Will's point of view. She tilted her head a small amount to one side and then the other.

Will noticed that when she was deeply considering something she angled her head like that and pursed her lips slightly. His thoughts returned to this morning, and he wondered again what had been running through her mind right before she had changed the subject. Not wanting a repeat of that episode, he shifted his attention back to the present moment. Realizing she was still having some difficulty with the concept of Kai as human in nature, he decided to guide her.

"How old was Kai when you and he first met?"

"He was a pup. I attended a type of school for Chasers, and he was born to other Companions who lived on grounds. He was raised by his pack, but I spent time with him daily," Ottum said.

"Did he also live among the humans there and learn their ways?" Will asked.

"Of course. But I don't see how that makes him more human than wolf," Ottum said.

"Were all of the members of his pack also Companions?"

"Yes."

"So he was raised by other wolves who also communicated with humans and were Companions," Will said with both of his eyebrows raised in a, 'don't you think that's unusual' way.

Slowly Ottum started to understand where Will was leading her.

"Do you think Kai would easily communicate with another wolf who wasn't a Companion and didn't know their ways?" Will asked.

"I have seen him communicate with other animals, but he doesn't do it often. He prefers to communicate with other Companions or else humans."

Will watched her face change.

"We thought that Companions were more evolved wolves. They aren't, are they?" Ottum asked. Then she answered her own question, "They simply learned our ways."

"I believe Kai understands all of that. I'm not sure he understands his own culture, but he does seem to willingly choose to live in yours," Will stated.

"I've always viewed Kai as my Companion and a fierce warrior in battle. I know that he chose to live his life with me, but it never occurred to me that he didn't really understand what he was choosing between. I'm not sure I really understand what his other choice is, or perhaps even choices are." Ottum paused and looked deeply into Will's eyes. "What are you?"

"What do you mean?" Will asked as he looked up from stirring the fire in the stove.

"I am a Chaser, and it seemed that you were an unfamiliar. But you're more than that. As I've been discovering over the last several weeks, there are many things that aren't what I thought they were. Until now I thought people were either Chasers or unfamiliars. You're neither, so there must be something else. What are you?" she asked again.

Will considered her question. "Until you and I met, I'd heard of neither Chasers nor unfamiliars. I'm not sure I have an answer to your question about what I am that would be anything other than to say that I am human."

At that moment, the door opened and Kai entered the cabin. He carried with him one squirrel and one rabbit. He expected to see approval, but when Will and Ottum turned to look at him, he saw relief in both of their eyes.

"I decided to go for a hunt this morning. Did I miss something?" he asked, looking from one to the other.

"No. We were just making breakfast," Will said.

Ottum smiled at him, but Kai sensed that something was different, and he looked to Will for an explanation. He found none there. Will half smiled at him and then turned back to readying the stove to cook the beans Ottum had retrieved.

"Were these easy to catch?" Ottum asked.

"No, that is why I hunted a little longer and got the rabbit in addition to the squirrel. I did not eat either of them in case there was lingering poison, but the hunt was typical and none of the animals in the area showed signs of illness," Kai said.

"Why would they be easy to catch?" Will asked. "And what makes you think the animals have been poisoned? Concern laced his voice.

"It wasn't just Saul that was poisoned. The Avil poisoned the entire stream," Kai told him as he gave the squirrel and rabbit to Ottum.

"The stream that runs here is sourced by an underground spring. It's not likely to be the same stream that was poisoned where you found Saul, so the animals are probably safe to eat. Speaking of Saul," Will said with a look his way, "we didn't bind him this time when he went to sleep."

Ottum looked at Saul and saw him sleeping peacefully. "I'm aware we didn't bind him. He's a free man, and we can't keep binding him because in his sleep he varies from The Path."

"The man he was when his eyes first opened was not the one who appeared to be present after that. While the trauma occurred only in his dreams, he was none-the-less severely traumatized. Sooner or later he is likely to act based on that trauma," Will paused. "What do you think your brother is trying to accomplish?"

"I don't know," Ottum said, shaking her head.

"Saul is a stranger to us, and although he is pack, I don't believe Ottum's brother hand-picked him. It seems just as likely that any other Chaser would have worked," Kai said.

Will and Ottum looked at Kai with great interest.

"You know what my brother has in mind?" Ottum asked with raised eyebrows.

"Not absolutely. But before he left us, your brother said something about seeing if you could save Saul's life since you wouldn't take his. I have been pondering how it is that two people from the same family could be so different, and it is my guess that your brother wonders the same thing. It seems at least a little likely that he feels something special happened to you, and you kept it a secret from him. Since he feels he is no longer your family, he wants to see if you will save someone from your current family," Kai said.

"Nothing special happened to me, and he should know that. He was there," Ottum said. "And I tried to help him repeatedly!"

"Ottum, he may have been there with you during your childhood, but he does not know why the two of you are different," Kai said. "It is much easier to assume it was something external that he missed than to explore the possibility that the difference is internal. As long as he was in the mindset that it was external, the only help he would have taken would have been to take your 'secret' from you and use it for himself."

"Kai is very likely correct," Will gently stated when Ottum turned to him with a bemused look.

"Every time I tried to help Leon he always acted like I was belittling him, and he would be mean afterward." Ottum's eyes gazed into memories of the past. "You think he believed I was keeping something from him?"

Kai nodded.

"If that was truly how he felt, then he would've misinterpreted anything I said or did." Ottum paused for a moment before continuing. "I couldn't help him because he was unwilling to see that the answer was to help himself."

Ottum had never thought about Leon that way. When she was younger she would spend hours, if not entire days, trying to figure out ways to help him. Each attempt always ended so poorly that one day she stopped trying. She'd never stopped feeling like she had failed though, and there were always moments when she would wonder if something new she had learned could be taught to him. She felt there had to be some way to help change his life. Suddenly she remembered Oscar's comments.

"I was trying to be responsible for something that wasn't my responsibility," she said as she ran her hand through her black hair and then tucked a ringlet behind her ear.

Kai nodded. "Oscar was right about what he said. You did not like to hear the words, but that made them no less true."

"Who's Oscar?" Will asked.

Kai considered answering but decided he would prefer to hear Ottum's description.

"He's a good friend and a teacher. He was also a father to me. He died a few years ago," she said sadly.

Will noticed that Ottum spoke aloud instead of in Path and that she used mix tenses when speaking of Oscar. He wondered if there was meaning in her speech or purely grammatical error.

"There is," Kai said. "You are doing well, Will, but it would be wise to remember that when you are speaking in Path and don't close your attention afterward, we still hear your thoughts."

Ottum realized by Will's expression that he didn't know what to say. "It's okay, Kai. Oscar was also right that it's time I open myself to others." She paused for a moment to gather her thoughts. "Oscar is physically dead. However, as of late, it seems I can somehow communicate with him through my dreams. I'm uncertain of how real the communication is because I realize it might just be my mind attempting to fill in a portion of my life that feels like it's missing."

"Does it matter?" Will asked.

"What do you mean?" she said as she tilted her head and pursed her lips again.

"Does it matter whether the communication is real or simply occurring in your mind?" Will asked again.

"Why do you ask?"

"Because it seems to me that regardless of which way it is, you're growing as a result of it. I have teachers who live on inside of me and the others whose lives they have touched. One day, I hope to live on that way in others as well," Will said.

"You're mostly right, I guess. But I want at least part of it to be real," Ottum said with a sad smile.

"Why?" Will asked as he stirred the pot of beans.

Ottum looked at Will for a moment. Her first instinct was to tell him it was none of his concern, but that was the voice of fear speaking to her. If she was going to be more open with others, she needed to learn that she wasn't the voice telling her it wasn't safe.

"Because I want him to have heard me tell him I love him," Ottum said softly before should could lose her courage.

A smile spread across Will's face. "Ottum, did you speak Path with Oscar?" he asked.

"Of course! He taught me much of what I know," she replied.

"Then how can you think he didn't know of your love for him even if you didn't say the words?" Will was having a hard time not laughing now.

"I never told him while he was alive." Ottum wasn't smiling, and she was more than a little irritated at Will's barely contained laughter. Her golden brown eyes looked as though they might burst into flame.

"Ottum, I'm new to speaking this way, but I think it's safe to say that if you spoke to Oscar at all in Path, he knew of your love long before he died," Will said.

"What you do mean? How could he have known when I didn't tell him?" she asked, irritated at the thought that Will might be trying to make her feel better by making up an excuse.

"One of the first things I noticed was that more than words come through when speaking in Path. I not only hear what you're thinking, I also see, feel, and experience it as you do. You told me I'd notice those things, and I do," Will paused and looked at each of them before continuing. "Your emotions are part of what I feel when we talk. Am I alone in that experience?"

Ottum looked surprised and was instantly alarmed. Knowing that he experienced her emotions left her feeling exposed in an extremely uncomfortable way.

"My apologies for talking about you, Ottum," Kai said as he cast a sympathetic look her direction. "Will, Ottum does not identify well with emotion. She has difficulty identifying what she is feeling, so while we all experience emotions, she does not define it as well as you or I might."

"What exactly do you mean that I don't identify with emotion?" Ottum asked.

Kai noted the quietness with which Ottum spoke and knew it was in deep contrast to what she was feeling, so he chose his words carefully.

"It means that while you can alter your voice and your posture, when you speak to me in Path, I know you are angry and feeling betrayed because I told Will something about you that you consider to be private. It means I have felt the love you have for me thousands of times even though you first said it very recently. It means that if you allowed yourself to feel, you would open up an entirely different world for yourself to experience, and it would stop some of the miscommunication that occurs when you are with others," Kai said. He braced for retaliation.

Ottum glared at him. She closed her mind and fought to remain calm. There was no calm. She needed some air and a few minutes to clear her head.

In spoken word she said, "I'm going out for a bit."

"Ottum. I didn't realize…" Will said. "I wouldn't have laughed at you if I had understood. I'm sorry." Will reached a hand toward her that she brushed off as she walked past him.

"It's Okay. I just need some air." Ottum crossed to the door and was outside before more could be said.

Will started after her, but Kai stepped in his way. For a few seconds Will couldn't believe he had ever thought Kai couldn't protect himself.

"Leave her be," Kai commanded.

"Shouldn't one of us be with her?" Will asked.

"No," Kai shook his head slightly.

Will looked at the door again before looking back to Kai and deciding to trust his judgment.

"I'm going to continue preparing some food for us then," Will said, still feeling like Ottum shouldn't be alone. "Do you want me to cook the squirrel and rabbit as an extra precaution against the poison?"

"Cook them only if you want to eat some of the meat yourself. Otherwise, if you will please skin them, I will eat them as they are," Kai said, walking to where Saul slept.

Will picked up Kai's prey and carried them to the counter. He very deftly removed the firs and placed them in a bucket that Kai hadn't noticed before. Before Will replaced the lid, the aroma that filled the cabin was not nearly as pleasant as the soup had been the night before.

"What is that?" Kai asked.

"It's a solution to treat the skin and fur until I have time to work with it."

Kai smiled as well as a wolf can. The more he saw of Will, the more he liked him. "I am going to take a nap until your food is ready. Please wake me then, or if needed you may wake me before." Kai said as he lay down near the fire. Then he added, "Ottum will be fine. She's a fast learner, but she does best when she has time alone to think through new ideas."

Will nodded and continued making breakfast. Once it was ready, he woke Kai and Saul. Ottum hadn't returned, but Kai suggested they eat anyway. Saul sat in the short chairs Will had built, and he was as interested in them as Ottum had been. It was an enjoyable meal, and the three of them visited easily throughout it.

"Thanks for the chow!" Saul said, rubbing his belly. "It's still hard for me to believe I was with the Avil for only a day. My appetite apparently thought it was longer too, but my stomach seems to know better." Saul grinned a touch sheepishly as he looked at the food left in his bowl compared to Will's empty bowl and Kai's empty plate. "I'm still hungry, but my stomach won't hold anymore."

"The food will still be here later," Will said as he carried their dishes back to the counter to be washed. It's probably best you eat small amounts frequently for the next few days. Your body's still trying to clear the poison. While you need the food to heal, it would be easy to over work your digestion with larger amounts."

"Thanks, Will," Saul said quietly.

Kai watched Will continue to glance at the door from time to time as though he could will Ottum through it. The changes that had occurred in the last few days were truly remarkable. He and Ottum had never been this open with each other, and although it was difficult for her, Kai enjoyed it. He wished the experience could be easier for her, but growing isn't always an easy thing to do.

"I think I could stand to visit the latrine again. However, I think that it might still be best if I don't make the trip alone." Saul looked at both of them before continuing, "Hopefully soon I'll be able to be less of a burden."

"You're not a burden," Will said as he glanced at Kai who was already at the door fumbling with the handle. He just about rushed over to help when he realized that Kai hadn't had any trouble with the door last night or this morning. Will shook his head and laughed to himself. He'd been so worried that Ottum would let her emotions carry her far enough away they couldn't hear her if she needed help, but Kai acted as though she was sitting just outside the door. *She's a most unusual woman,* Will thought. For that matter, the entire party sharing his cabin at the moment was unusual.

Kai opened the door and Will followed Saul out. He glanced around for Ottum, but saw no trace of her.

Saul walked toward the latrine on his own while Will and Kai stayed close enough to hear a call for help but far enough away to give him privacy.

"She's close, isn't she?" Will asked.

"Yes."

"Was she always just outside the cabin, and if so, how did you know?" Will asked.

"She is my Chaser. You don't spend years with someone and not know their tendencies," Kai replied. "And yes, she was always just outside the cabin."

"So do you know for sure that she's close now, or do you just believe she is because of her past behavior?"

"She is close." Kai said.

When he didn't elaborate, Will asked, "May I ask how you know?"

"You may ask," Kai said. "I spoke with her before we exited the cabin."

Will could feel the mirth in Kai's reply. "Well, I guess that means she still isn't ready to rejoin us. Is there anything I can do for her?"

Kai shook his head. Not to tell Will that there was nothing he could do but because he had never met anyone who asked as many questions as Ottum. Not until now. "You are more like her than I realized. While both of you might wish it to be so, you cannot fix everyone each time there is a challenge to work through."

"I don't think she's broken!" Will protested. "Emotions were difficult things for me once. It isn't that I want to fix her. I just thought I might be able to help her find her way through reconnecting to herself."

"You will have to figure out how to do that on your own," Kai said. "So that you have no reason to doubt me, if you look over there you can see her walking." Kai tossed his head to the woods on the east side of the cabin.

Will's eyes shifted in the direction Kai indicated, and he saw Ottum moving slowly through trees several yards away. The sunlight brought out copper highlights in her nearly black hair. Although she walked with sure steps, Ottum looked lost in her thoughts and weighed down with emotion. Will longed to go walk with her and talk to her, to let her know that she didn't have to feel as alone as she seemed to feel.

With snow crunching beneath his feet, Saul ran past Will and Kai. For a man who was uncertain of his ability to make a trip to the latrine by himself, he moved with amazing speed. Kai realized it before Will, but there was no doubt where he was running.

"Saul!" Will shouted. It seemed doubtful it would have an effect, but maybe hearing his name would at least slow him down.

Saul cast a look over his shoulder without altering his pace at all, and Will realized Saul's eyes looked like they had when he was difficult to awaken. The weakened Saul had been replaced by the vengeful and dangerous version of the man.

"Ottum is in danger," Will said to Kai before realizing Kai was no longer beside him.

"Ottum!" Kai called out in warning.

Ottum heard Kai's cry and immediately sensed danger. She spun to see Saul coming at her. The hatred in his eyes was undeniable and his intentions were evident. The warrior in her took over and drew her sword. She watched Saul's reaction and knew she was truly in danger.

Kai was gaining on Saul but was uncertain if he would reach him before Saul reached Ottum. With a final burst of speed Kai jumped and soared toward Saul. The impact was hard, and with the momentum that was already present with their efforts, both he and Saul went rolling. Ottum moved out of their way while never taking her eyes off Saul. Kai was the first to regain his feet, but Saul wasn't far behind. Kai growled fiercely as he moved to place himself between Saul and Ottum. Saul appeared to not even notice him.

The hatred seethed through Saul. He felt the fire of it charge his body and prime his skills. The Avil was standing there in front of him, and Saul had no doubt it was going to die today. He lunged but tripped over a log the Avil was standing behind.

Kai smashed into Saul's leg and sent him tumbling to the snow again. This time Kai kept himself upright. He turned as Saul righted himself and started at Ottum again. Saul cleared Kai with a tremendous leap, and he grabbed Ottum's sword with one gloved hand as his other hand went to her throat. They crashed to the ground. Saul's weight compressed her into the snow, but she was able to use the momentum to push Saul over her. Her sword sliced through Saul's glove as he slid over her. Both of them were on their feet immediately.

"Saul. Stand down!" Ottum commanded.

Saul's response was to lunge again. Kai was waiting for any opportunity to help, but realized he could hamper Ottum's efforts if he rushed in without good timing.

They were circling each other as Ottum spoke quietly, but firmly. "Saul. This is not who you are. You do not harm Pack!"

"I don't harm Pack, but I have no problem killing Avils. It's your day to die!" Saul sneered.

The realization that Saul thought she was the Avil created just enough distraction for Saul to lunge again. This time he ignored the sword and went straight for Ottum's throat with both hands. He lifted her off of the ground and started spinning in circles while continuing to squeeze his hands together.

Ottum felt her throat close and willed herself to stay calm. She struggled for a few seconds and then went limp. Saul continued squeezing and turning as she fought to maintain consciousness. "Kai!"

Kai heard the urgency in her cry and bolted forward. Saul used Ottum to bat him away.

Kai could feel Ottum slipping away as he turned toward them again. As they came into view, Saul appeared to have his feet pulled from under him. The impact caused him to release Ottum, and Kai wasted no time rushing between them.

"Take her to the cabin," Will directed.

Kai looked toward the voice and realized that Saul's fall hadn't been accidental. Will pulled Saul by the feet to give them a little more time, but Saul quickly realized his predicament and worked to unwind himself. Kai grabbed Ottum's coat and dragged her away. He didn't look back until he reached the front of the cabin. Once there, he released Ottum and raced back to Will.

While Kai dragged Ottum to safety, Saul managed to unwind from Will's whip and find his feet.

"Saul, I'm a friend and do not want to fight you," Will said as he gathered his whip to him.

"Any friend of an Avil is no friend of mine!" screamed Saul as he lunged. He slammed into Will so that they fell to the ground, but Will pushed and was standing again before Saul had finished sliding through the snow. Saul lunged again with the same effect.

Will glimpsed Kai's return and noted that Saul's back was turned toward him.

"Kai, please don't intervene unless I need your help," Will said in Path.

Kai considered taking Saul down despite Will's request. Saul was trained for battle, and given the way he had handled Ottum, it seemed the adrenaline created by the hallucination gave him even more strength. But it was Will who had freed Ottum, so Kai stood ready.

Saul lunged again and this time Will met him with a solid hit to the chest that not only stopped Saul's forward lunge, but lifted him slightly off of his feet and swung him backward. Saul landed hard on his back. The impact knocked the air out of him, but he paused only long enough to regain a breath. It might have caused him to lose his air, but it only fueled the rage within him. Saul's actions rapidly deteriorated to mere reactions with no thought involved. He sidled toward Will and kicked. Will grabbed his leg as though Saul moved in slow motion. Once again, Saul picked himself up from the snowy ground. He ran at Will only to have Will's hand strike his chest and knock him to the ground again.

Saul regained his air more slowly this time, and took more time to stand. He acted dazed and stumbled forward. Will stood as quietly as he had between each attack. Saul looked up at him, and both Kai and Will knew that the battle was over.

"What...?" Saul started to ask. He looked confused and in pain. Saul looked from Will to Kai for an explanation.

Kai turned in disgust and headed for Ottum. He knew Will was safe, and Kai felt no sympathy for Saul.

"Do you know what just happened?" Will asked Saul.

"No," Saul replied. "I feel weak and bruised. The last thing I remember was walking out of the latrine. I have no idea how I came to be here." Saul continued to look around in an attempt to re-orient himself.

"You attacked Ottum, and because of our attempt to save her, you fought Kai and me too," Will said.

"I *attacked*?" There was complete disbelief in Saul's voice. He continued to look around, and when he saw Kai beside a figure on the ground, Saul reacted as if he'd been hit again. "What did I do to Ottum? Is she okay?"

"I don't know," Will replied. "I need to go tend to her now, but for all of our safety, I'm going to bind you again."

Saul nodded slowly as though he were now in a different type of dream. Even the vision of his bloody glove failed to activate his memory. Will made quick work of using his whip to bind Saul's hands and creating a form of shackles for his feet.

"Once we're all safe inside the cabin, I'll replace this with rope," Will said he secured the last knot. "You can either stay here until I know Ottum's status and can return to you, or you can make your way to us. Don't expect Kai to be friendly, but I won't allow him to harm you." Will turned and left Saul standing there alone to make his decision.

Ottum lay quite still in the snow. Kai lay next to her with his head resting on her stomach. To Will's relief, Kai's head rose and fell rhythmically with each breath Ottum took.

Kai looked up as Will approached. His look went from Will to where Saul stood.

"I know you're angry with him, but the man standing there now isn't the one who did this or the one we were fighting." Will looked at Ottum as he spoke and then turned back to Kai. "He's bound, and I will not allow you to harm him anymore than I allowed him to harm either of you."

The hair bristled on Kai's back for a brief moment as he considered the damage he could do with Saul bound. Then he sighed deeply and looked back to Ottum. "Keep him bound, and I will leave him be."

"Thank you, Kai," Will said as he laid Ottum's sword beside her. "How is she?" Will examined the bruises forming on her neck as he waited for Kai's reply. The print wasn't fully clear yet, but he realized that the bruises formed an outline of Saul's gloved hands.

"I do not know. I can't seem to reach her, but she is breathing," Kai replied. His fur stood on end as he turned and looked again at Saul.

Will leaned down and felt Ottum's neck. It didn't appear to be broken, so he decided it would be best to take her inside. "Let's get her in the cabin. Will you get the door for me, please?" Not waiting for Kai's reply, he lifted Ottum gently.

As Will had suspected earlier, Kai had no difficulty with the door. Will carried Ottum in and placed her on his pallet. Kai stood close while Will removed Ottum's boots, coat, and sword sheath. Once she was made as comfortable as possible, Will stepped back.

"I'm going to go get Saul now. Watch over her and call to me if you need me before I've returned," Will instructed.

Kai nodded, but Will noted he'd bristled again. Will couldn't blame him. Ottum had been around for only two days, and Will was already protective of her. Kai had known her for years.

Will closed the door behind him and looked toward Saul. The Chaser sat with his back against a tree; the cold added a sense of desolation. Snow bowed the branches of the tree, but it was guilt that bowed the head of the man who sat below them.

Saul glanced up as Will approached. "Is she," Saul paused and then found the courage to continue, "alive?" The wind whirled snow around his legs and feet.

"She's breathing. Beyond that, I don't know what damage was done yet," Will replied.

"I'm so sorry." Saul's head hung again. There was much more he wanted to say, but none of it would be close to expressing what he felt, so he remained quiet.

"Let's get you back to the cabin. Do you think you can walk?" Will asked.

"You're going to take me to the cabin?" Saul asked in disbelief.

"Of course. I'm not going to leave you bound outside in this cold." Will leaned down to help lift Saul. "We need to get a look at your hand and see how badly it's damaged."

Saul turned his hand and stared in a non-reactive way at the blood there. "How is it possible that I attacked and received injuries but remember none of it? I was having difficulty just standing when I was in the latrine."

"It's possible because of what you experienced with the poison," Will replied.

"The poison is causing me to go mad? If that's the case, just leave me here," anger and regret dripped from Saul's voice as he pushed away Will's hand.

"No. It's not a permanent problem provided that you're willing to do something about it. I won't leave you here," Will said, shaking his head. "Now, can you walk or shall I carry you?"

"I'll walk." It was a brave statement coming from a man who could barely stand. While Saul tried to help, it was mostly Will's strength that got Saul to his feet.

With Saul using Will as a crutch, they slowly made their way to the cabin. Saul's energy was gone, and the burst he had experienced during the fight had left him even weaker. Will debated about carrying Saul the last several feet, but decided it would harm Saul's ego more than it would help his body.

"Kai, please open the door for us," Will requested.

Will had spoken in Path and directed it only to Kai, so Saul was surprised when the door swung open. Fearing that Kai was about to attack, Saul instinctively recoiled and nearly sent both he and Will tumbling backward. Will caught them and held Saul until he realized Kai meant no harm.

Kai had watched Saul recoil and the flash of enjoyment he felt quickly turned to sympathy. Saul looked horrible, and despite what had happened, Will was right. The man standing in front of him would never willingly have harmed any of them. In the only gesture he could provide, Kai sat down beside the open door so they could enter.

Saul had no energy left to be embarrassed. Though Saul was giving it his best effort, Will had to half drag him through the door and to the first chair available. Saul dropped to the seat with a thud as Kai closed the door behind them.

Saul glanced toward Ottum's still form. "I'm sorry." Even in Path, Saul's voice was weak.

"I know." Kai still wanted to hate someone for the attack on Ottum, but he decided the Avil was a better target than Saul.

Will retrieved a bedroll and placed it on the floor close to the chair where Saul barely sat upright. Will helped him to the floor and removed the bindings on his hands long enough to remove his coat and then replace the whip with rope. Once the bindings were secure again, he turned his attention to Ottum.

"How is she?" Will asked Kai.

"She still isn't responding," Kai said. Concern and anger were mixed in his voice.

"Has her breathing changed?" Will asked

"No. Why would it?" Kai asked.

"Sometimes a throat will swell after being squeezed that way," Will said. "Keep a close watch on her breathing, but as long as it doesn't change, I'm going to tend to Saul's hand first."

After grabbing a few supplies, Will removed the glove from Saul's non-injured hand and then from the injured one. The glove pulled the freshly formed scab from the cut and caused the wound to bleed again. Will placed a cloth under the hand and examined it. The cut was relatively deep, but the tendons seem to have been spared. The biggest concern was that the muscle in the web of Saul's hand was partially cut. Will washed the wound, placed the sides of the cut muscle close together, rubbed something on it that Kai thought smelled just terrible, and bound the hand so that the thumb couldn't move. Saul had lost consciousness within seconds of his head meeting the bedroll. Will considered for a moment, and then found a way to bind his hands to the shackles on his feet.

Kai was lying beside Ottum, touching her in such a way that he could feel her every breath. Will watched them for a short moment before the attention caught Kai's awareness.

"Her breath is stable," Kai said.

"I know you're her Companion and are aware of subtleties with her I can only imagine at this point, but I'd like very much to work on her," Will said.

"What would you do?" Kai asked. His love for Ottum made it difficult for him to even consider leaving her side when he didn't have to.

"Something similar to what I did with Saul."

"She is thirsty," Kai said. "Can we get her some water first?"

"Is she speaking with you in Path?" Will asked hopefully.

"No. But her body speaks for itself," Kai replied.

Will wasn't sure what he meant, but said, "I'll get some water."

Will retrieved a cup of water and a clean cloth to use as a delivery system. He moved to the side of the pallet opposite Kai and started squeezing small amounts of water into Ottum's mouth.

"Kai, what do you mean about her body speaking for itself?"

"Her tissue is not as supple as is typical. That is a sign of dehydration," Kai replied.

Will knew Kai was right but was still amazed that he knew the feel of Ottum so well as to know that she was thirsty. After a fair amount of the water was in Ottum, Will set aside the cup.

"I know you want to be with her, but neither she nor Saul should be left alone right now," Will said. "While giving Ottum a drink, we've already left Saul alone longer than he should be."

Kai kissed Ottum's hand softly and then moved from the pallet to sit with Saul. He took a position that would allow him to see Saul while maintaining a view of Ottum.

Will settled onto the pallet so that he could place his hands on Ottum. He looked briefly at Kai and then began his work.

* * *

Ottum saw only blackness at first, but she could hear Oscar calling her name softly. Finally, the blackness started receding as the brightness of a winter day pierced her vision. She turned her head to the side and realized that her throat was wickedly sore. Involuntarily she reached a hand to it but was stopped part way there.

"No child."

It was all Oscar said and she wondered if maybe it was the whisper of the wind instead of his voice she heard. She looked at him, wanting him to tell her what was happening.

"For now, it's enough to know that I'm here. Now rest."

Oscar placed his hand over her eyes, and just as slowly as the daylight had cleared the darkness, the darkness returned.

Ottum didn't know how long it had been, but once again she was aware of blackness fading. This time it was a star filled winter sky that met her opening eyes. There was also the flicker of a fire to her side providing both light and warmth. Her throat was still extremely sore.

"Oscar?" Ottum called for him with a scratchy voice.

"Yes, child. I'm here," he said, gently patting her shoulder.

Ottum relaxed as the soft drawl of his voice drew her eyes to his. She saw the concern mixed with relief in the grey-blue oceans of soul that were Oscar's eyes.

"My throat hurts." She couldn't seem to remember why it would be so sore.

"Yes. I'm sure it does," he nodded.

"Why?" she rasped.

"Always full of questions." A smile played across Oscar's face as he said it.

"Well?"

"You wouldn't be my Ottum without all of your questions, would you?" he smiled. "You know why, it's just buried in your memory." Oscar's face and tone lost all playfulness as he reached for Ottum's hand and placed both of theirs on her tummy.

The gesture made Ottum uneasy and for a moment she wasn't willing to remember. Instead she watched the flicker of the fire as the flames danced with the wind.

"I am here, and you are here," Oscar nudged.

She realized he wasn't going to let her go until the memory had played out, and that allowed Ottum to relax. When memories didn't start surfacing immediately, she tried to help them along by doing an analysis of her body. Rather than start with the area that held the most discomfort, she started with her feet and worked her way up from there. One of her ankles and the leg above it was sore. Beyond that, there was nothing that seemed unusual with the rest of her body until she got to her throat. It felt sore and bruised, but no memories surfaced as she analyzed the area.

"We feel with more than our bodies," Oscar offered.

Ottum raised an eyebrow as if to say, "We do?" but then the memories started surfacing. She remembered leaving the cabin earlier that morning because of a conversation she had shared with Will and Kai regarding emotion. Later, Kai had let her know that if she still needed her privacy she should vacate the immediate area of the cabin, so she had left the porch to go for a short walk. Nothing had been unusual about any of it.

She remembered Kai calling to her. The sound of his voice carried an urgent warning. The Avil, her brother, hadn't been near or she would have sensed him. Ottum tried to remember, but she could think of no other reason she would have been in danger. She wondered if maybe the warning in Kai's voice wasn't for her. Maybe it was a warning that something was wrong. Perhaps something had been wrong with Saul.

At the formation of his name in her mind, emotion and memory flowed freely. This time Oscar didn't stop the hand that moved to her throat. Ottum swallowed repeatedly. The memory of Saul's hands closing her throat was so vivid that she needed to assure herself she could still swallow and breathe. The pressure of her hand hurt, but she decided there was nothing major wrong with it.

"Saul thought I was my brother, didn't he?" she asked.

"Yes, he did." Oscar squeezed her hand gently.

"Saul meant to kill me," Ottum looked in Oscar's eyes and found the comfort she knew would be there. "I have no doubt of his intent, but I don't think he was aware he was fighting the wrong person."

Oscar shook his head slightly in agreement.

"What happened?" she asked.

"You passed out."

"No. What happened after that?" Ottum asked as she ran her hand through her black hair.

"I don't know," Oscar shrugged.

"What do you mean you don't know?" she asked incredulously.

"I don't know," Oscar repeated.

"How can I be here with you if you don't know?" Ottum glared at him as though he were being dense. Then a different thought crossed her mind. "Did he succeed?"

"Did who succeed?" Oscar asked.

"Saul. Did he succeed?"

"At what? I swear, child, you are making no sense," he said with a shake of his head.

"Did he succeed at killing me? Is that why I am here with you?"

At this, Oscar tipped back his head as he laughed to the night sky. When he managed to get his laughter under control, he shook his head at Ottum.

"No. He did not succeed." A few chuckles still escaped from him, and his grey-blue eyes sparkled.

"Well, that's a relief." Ottum meant it sarcastically but it sounded genuine. "So, why don't you know what happened after that?"

"It's not my concern." Oscar said with a shrug as he reached for a stick to stir the fire.

"It's not your concern whether Kai lives or dies? You certainly knew a lot about Will for him to not be your concern."

"Ah," Oscar said as though he had suddenly realized what she meant. "Those are different questions. Kai lives. Will doesn't concern me."

Frustration mounted within Ottum. "What do you mean when you say that Will doesn't concern you?" She wanted to pull the stick from Oscar's hand and threaten to poke him with it if he didn't give clearer answers soon.

"He doesn't concern me. He doesn't cause any anxiety or uneasiness in me. He doesn't require my attention." Oscar continued poking at the coals.

"That's not what I meant!" Ottum said in exasperation.

"Then you should have asked me what you did mean instead of taking up more of my time answering a question for which you didn't want to know the answer," Oscar chided.

Ottum stared at him in disbelief. When Oscar was alive, he spent most of his time either teaching or teasing her, but he always did both with a large supply of patience. As she watched him stir the coals, she realized that was no longer the case. "Is Will alive?"

"Yes, he is. Now wasn't that easy?" Oscar asked as he added the stirring stick to the top of the fire.

Ottum rolled her eyes. "Is Saul alive?"

"Yes."

Oscar smiled, but Ottum felt the sadness in his voice and saw it in his posture. "My brother wanted to know if I could save Saul. Is the poison he took causing him to go mad?

After the slightest pause, Oscar answered, "No."

Ottum noticed the pause. "No the poison isn't causing him to go mad, but something else is?"

"You always were a fast learner, but that's a question I cannot answer," Oscar said as he stood, stretched, and then strolled around the fire scratching his grey beard.

Ottum rolled to her side and grimaced when her throat shot a sharp pain through her. Once the pain passed, she asked, "Is it that you will not or that you cannot answer?"

"I cannot."

"Cannot because you don't know or cannot because you are forbidden to?" she continued.

Oscar stopped moving and sat down by Ottum's side again. "I cannot answer it because I don't know the answer. Saul hasn't decided yet." Then, before Ottum could ask what it was that Saul had to decide, Oscar asked his own question. "Who or what would forbid me?"

Ottum felt the warmth of a blush creep over her cheeks. "I don't know," she said as she traced imaginary lines in the blanket beneath her. "I'm not sure how the rules work here."

"The rules are the same regardless of where you are, Ottum. In your world there are those who choose to think they can create new ones, but the new rules they claim to create are not really *the* rules. In the end, the rules are all the same."

Ottum was tiring, but Oscar's answer intrigued her. "What are *the* rules?"

Oscar pulled off his glove and brushed back the tendril of Ottum's hair that had escaped from her hood. "You already know them. You live by them every day, and when you break them, you deal with the consequences."

Ottum sighed. "In other words, you aren't going to tell me."

"There is no need to tell you that which you already know," Oscar said with a shrug.

Silence fell between them. The fire crackled. The wind blew. Oscar shifted beside her, and Ottum dozed. When she awoke again, she couldn't tell if she'd slept minutes or hours. The scene around her hadn't changed at all. Oscar looked at her and winked.

"Why am I here, Oscar?"

"Now that is a deep question," Oscar said with a smirk. When he realized Ottum would just ask more questions, he continued, "You're here because you've made a decision that is going to take your life in a different direction."

"I would ask what direction that is, but since you said I made the decision, you'd probably just tell me that I already know," she said as she poked a finger gently into his side.

Oscar smiled and the sparkle in his eyes was no less irresistible to Ottum than it had ever been.

Ottum realized that her hand wasn't in a glove and that it had not been cold until she noticed it was bare. "Is this real, Oscar?"

"Yes, Ottum. It's very real. It may take you some time to understand it, but that makes it no less real."

"Will and Kai are concerned about me," she said, almost puzzled.

"Yes, they are," Oscar nodded.

"How do I know that when they aren't here?" she asked.

Oscar shrugged slightly inside his leather coat. "Because," he replied, "we are all connected. In many ways, we are all one."

"Are you going to get all metaphysical on me?" she said, her eyebrow raised to emphasize her skepticism.

Oscar frowned. "It's not metaphysical. It's literal. That's one of the rules you try to pretend you don't know, but that rule will be harder for you to ignore from now on."

Ottum sighed. "All of the rules will be harder to ignore, won't they?"

"Probably," he said as he stroked his beard. "Not probably. Yes, they will."

Ottum thought about Saul again. "What is it that Saul is deciding?"

"What do you believe he's deciding?"

Ottum considered. "I'll answer your question. But first, will you tell me if the other creatures poisoned by the stream are facing a similar fate to Saul?"

Oscar nodded. "The other creatures that survived the poisoning are now all just as healthy as they were prior to the poison."

"Will said something about the trauma being severe for Saul. If the other beings are all fine, then it must somehow be the trauma. But I would have thought that the other creatures also experienced trauma from being poisoned."

"They did."

"Well, then why are they healthy while Saul is not?" Ottum asked.

"They have not forgotten how to shake off traumatic experiences. Saul, like most humans, carries all of his past traumas around with him. Plus, they had a little help," Oscar said.

Ottum considered his answer and wondered what he meant about shaking off trauma. Remembering that she was to answer Oscar's question, she returned to that subject matter instead.

"I think that Saul is trying to decide if he wants to put forward the effort required to heal or if he will give up. Is that correct?" Ottum asked.

"That is, at least partially, correct," Oscar replied.

The sensation that Kai was worried about her increased, and Ottum didn't want her friend to be overly concerned. "Oscar, I want to let Kai know I'm okay. I also want to let Saul know I understand what happened. Well, not that I understand, but that I forgive him for what he did. How do I let them know?"

"You go to them." As Ottum's face contorted into a look of questioning, Oscar continued. "Let your attention go to them, and then draw yourself there."

"Will I be able to come back if I want to?" she asked.

"Of course," Oscar smiled and winked at her. "This is a new form of communication for you, so it may take some time to really understand. However, good practice is the best way to build a skill."

Ottum let her attention direct toward Kai, and the scene with Oscar slowly faded. At first she thought she had faded into blackness again, but then she realized her eyes were still closed. It took some effort, but slowly she was able to raise her lids and focus on the room.

* * *

Shadows from the flickering firelight danced on the ceiling and warmed the cabin air around Ottum. The light that met her eyes was matched by a rich aroma. A mix of fire, wood, food, spices, herbs, wolf, and man filtered through her nose and lit up her brain with images and feelings. One of the men was lying close beside her, and his warmth radiated softly into her side. Though he wasn't on the pallet with her, she was aware of Kai's presence close by. Saul lay awake on the floor near the pallet. His shallow breaths revealed the guilt he felt. Ottum had always thought of herself as aware, but her senses were now giving her more information than she knew was possible.

"Kai." Ottum spoke his name quietly in Path.

Kai came quickly to her side and looked into her eyes with deep concern. "My lady," he said.

The mix of relief and fear in his voice caused Ottum to know she'd been gone for longer than she realized.

"I am okay, Kai. I'm okay," she assured him.

He kissed her hand, and she smiled at the familiarity of his soft tongue as she rubbed the bottom of his chin affectionately.

"You scared us," he said.

Ottum could feel his fear. The intensity surprised her, and she realized Kai had been correct to say she didn't process emotion.

"How long was I out?" she asked.

"Since this morning, my lady," Kai replied. "It is well into the night now."

"Saul, are you okay?" Ottum asked in Path.

"You're awake!"

Again Ottum was amazed by the flood of emotion she could feel with Saul's words. *How did I miss that for so long?*

"Yes, I'm awake," she replied. "How are you?"

"Happy that you're awake. Are you…okay?" Saul asked.

"Yes, Saul. I'm okay."

"I'm so sorry."

The words were simple, but the pain Saul felt for his actions nearly took Ottum's breath away.

"It's okay, Saul. Really—I'm going to be fine, so please stop feeling guilty." Ottum paused, feeling the confusion coming from Saul. "It was most likely my walk that triggered it. Leon's walk was what caused me to figure out that the Avil and my brother are the same being. Regardless of our differences, he and I are family, so there will always be some similarities. It's likely that on some level you recognized the walk, and the tortured part of you took over and sought revenge."

"Maybe," Saul said, "but that doesn't change what I did to you."

"If that is true, then how is it that we are going to keep both of you safe?" Kai asked. "Ottum, you are not likely to change your walk even if you try. Saul, you don't want a repeat of this morning, but there is no way to know it will not happen again." Kai looked from one to the other.

"I'll remain bound until morning. You've done a lot for me, and I am grateful for it, but tomorrow morning I'll leave," Saul said.

Ottum disliked his idea. "You're still sick from the poison. I don't have a good answer that allows you to stay yet, but perhaps Will does."

"He is sleeping," Kai said. "However he does wake often to check on you."

Ottum felt how pleased that made Kai. She realized she'd missed so much for so many years by blocking out the emotions that were transmitted with Path. The warmth and closeness she had longed for would be the result of opening and sharing with others. She could see that now, but before, she had thought it would make her seem weak and vulnerable.

"We've interrupted his life immensely since our arrival. Unless either of you disagree, I'd like to let him sleep until he awakens," Ottum said. "I'm feeling a little tired myself."

Kai shrugged. "He will awaken soon to check on you. We can talk with him then or in the morning. I'll remain on watch, and the rest of you can get some sleep."

"Have you been on watch the entire time?" Ottum asked.

"Will allowed me to sleep today so it only made sense for me to watch tonight," Kai replied.

"Wake me if you need," Ottum instructed as she closed her eyes.

Kai nodded, but Ottum knew he wouldn't wake her unless she was in danger. She tried to ease into sleep but soon realized that she was thirsty and needed to visit the latrine. She started to get off of the pallet, but there was a hand on her hip almost instantly. She relaxed and rolled back onto the pallet. Ottum turned her head to look at Will. His eyes were so intense and such a striking color, but right now they were filled with concern.

"Going somewhere?" He asked with a smile.

However, Ottum noticed the pressure on her hip didn't release.

"Hi Will." She smiled softly before continuing. "I need to find some water and go outside. I didn't want to wake you. I was just going to go back to sleep, but then I realized that wasn't going to happen without going outside first."

"Kai has been at your side all day. I'm guessing he knows you're okay?" Will asked.

"Yes. I spoke with him first upon returning," she said.

Will narrowed his eyes. "Returning? Where did you go?"

Ottum chuckled quietly. "That's a slightly longer story, but I do realize my body remained here the entire time I was gone."

Will eyed her for a moment, but his expression was unreadable.

"I really do need to go outside," Ottum said. "Do you suppose you could let go of my hip and help me?"

Will released her and was on his feet and around the pallet before she had even rolled back to her side. He helped her to a seated position. Taking his hands, Ottum pulled herself to her feet. She felt weak and a little dizzy, but her full bladder was what she felt most. Will remained highly attentive, but he allowed her to move as she needed toward the door, into her coat, and then out the door to the latrine.

Ottum stepped into the cold air again, and it made her throat contract painfully.

"How bad is it?" she asked Will.

"Hmmm?"

"My throat," Ottum pointed. "How bad is it?"

Will hesitated only slightly before answering. "It's bruised. But the swelling has stayed down, and that was the biggest concern. That, and we didn't know if Saul had blocked your air long enough to do other damage. You appear to be walking and talking just fine, so it seems he didn't," Will said with a smile.

"Tomorrow, I want to hear what happened. I don't remember much after Saul had me by the throat and started spinning. Tonight, though, I want to drink a little water and get some sleep."

Will nodded as he opened the cabin door and lead her back to the pallet. "I'll get you a drink."

"Thanks." Ottum resisted the urge to lay back and close her eyes until Will returned with water. After a few sips, she could no longer resist, and Will helped her settle back onto the pallet.

Sleep came rapidly. Not so quickly that she wasn't aware Will had settled beside her on the pallet and placed his arm about her, but enough that her thoughts didn't require her chant to settle them.

Will lay with one arm about Ottum and his head propped up on his other so he could watch her. Her breath flowed smoothly in and out in a soft rhythm created by the billows that were her lungs. The real danger was likely to have passed, but he wanted to make sure the sting of the cold hadn't resulted in further irritation. He noticed the bruising on her neck was darkening, but that was to be expected. The black discoloration seemed so out of place on her. *I guess it doesn't matter how strong or beautiful someone is. Life is always delicate,* he thought as he watched her sleep.

Will knew it was a combination of infatuation and lust that he felt for her, because there was no way he knew her well enough for it to be anything else. That knowledge did nothing to dampen his attraction to her.

He'd known her for only two days, and she had already taught him so much. Will delighted in the newness she brought to his life. He also delighted in the way her dark hair curled into ringlets as it fell to her shoulders, the curves that were mostly hidden by her clothes until she lay down, and the golden brown of her eyes.

It had been over a year since Will had even seen a woman. To be lying with one he found highly attractive was intoxicating. But right now she was in no shape to explore the intoxication with him, and he needed to redirect his attention to keeping her safe. After one more check that her breathing was smooth and even, he dropped his hand and head to the pallet and joined her in sleep.

CHAPTER 10

Ottum awoke to the smell of food cooking. The aroma caused her to salivate almost instantly. She lifted her head and looked around the cabin. Saul and Will were both gone, but Kai was curled up by the fire.

"Morning, Ottum. How do you feel?" Kai asked.

"Better, thanks. Where are Will and Saul?"

"Saul needed to use the latrine. Given that Will left the food cooking, it is likely they will be back soon."

"Do you think Will is safe alone with him?" Ottum asked.

"He seemed to handle himself well enough yesterday."

Kai said it with a slight shrug of his shoulders as though it were no big deal, but Ottum could sense the respect he felt for Will. Ottum felt extremely curious about what had happened yesterday after she had lost consciousness, but she thought it best to wait.

"Do you think Saul still wants to leave?" Ottum asked as she stretched.

"I'm not sure it is a bad thing if he does," Kai said gruffly.

"Kai, he thought I was Leon."

"All the more reason it is not safe for him to remain. We saved him from the Avil and cared for him enough to get him through the fevers and chills, perhaps it is time for him to care for himself again."

Kai would give his life for her without thinking twice about it, but when it came to those he considered outsiders, he was very distant. Typically Pack and anyone under attack by an Avil were spared this distinction, but Saul's attack on Ottum had placed him outside of Kai's circle of concern.

"I feel responsible for what happened to him. I didn't personally harm him or send him after my brother, but still I feel..." Ottum searched to find the word she was looking for but failed. "I don't know what it is I feel or why, but I know I want to help Saul."

"You hope you can save him from your brother even though you could not save your brother from himself."

Ottum looked at Kai with surprise. *Could that be true?* she wondered.

Will and Saul returned from their walk just as Ottum was about to voice her question.

"Good morning, beautiful," Will said with a wink.

Ottum blushed slightly at his greeting while Kai raised an eye and cocked his ears at him. Will pretended to not notice either reaction and proceeded to tend to the food.

"G'morning. Did you two have a good walk?" Ottum asked.

Will and Saul glanced at each other for a fleeting moment before Saul nodded.

"It's a nice day out there. Sun's out and the wind isn't too sharp." Saul managed to look Ottum in the face as he spoke, but then his eyes fell on her throat, and he looked away.

"Anyone hungry?" Will asked.

"I need to head outside first, but I'm ravenous," Ottum replied.

"Saul, will you put the food into dishes to cool? I'll help Ottum outside and then we can all eat together," Will said.

"Sure."

Kai moved from his spot by the fire and placed himself between Saul and Ottum. He looked at Will as he changed location, but Ottum couldn't tell if the two of them spoke. Saul didn't notice Kai's move immediately because he was searching for dishes. Once he realized Kai's intent, Saul concentrated solely on the task in front of him.

"It's better than binding him," Will said as they stepped out the door and into the sunshine.

Ottum knew he was right and that Kai had every reason to want to protect her, but she disliked both things. Saul was Pack and guarding against him felt wrong.

Ottum needed less help from Will than she had last night. The cold air still burned her throat and tightened already sore muscles, but the beauty of the sun glistening on the snow took her mind away from the discomfort she felt. The cold would eventually grow old, and she would long for warmth and lush green grass, but there was a part of her that loved this frozen world just as much if not more. She felt an odd sense of happiness when she noticed Will taking in the snow covered trees and then tipping his head back to bask in the sun as he stepped off the porch. She felt sure he'd meant his greeting to be flirtatious this morning.

Too many emotions washed over her, and she wished she could have some time to think things through. Will enticed her, Saul concerned her, Kai wanted to protect her, and Leon confused her. Add in the strange meetings with Oscar and Ottum felt as though she had stepped into an alternate reality. She and Will reached the latrine without speaking to each other at all.

"I'll wait for you." He smiled at her and moved to sit on a fallen branch a few feet away.

"Do you think Kai has Saul backed into a corner yet?" Will said with a grin when she stepped out of the latrine.

Ottum heard the attempt at playfulness in his voice, but the remark bothered her.

"Saul is Pack. It's hard to see Kai defending me from him. I understand why he is, and I even get that it might be necessary, but I don't like it. Saul needs to heal. I don't know how to help him, but I think maybe you do. Did you talk about it this morning when the two of you went for a walk?" Ottum asked.

"Yes and no," Will said, stuffing his gloved hands into his pockets. "Saul would like to leave, and we discussed that."

"And…"

Will shrugged. "I don't know what he'll decide to do."

"But do you think you can help him?"

Will stopped walking and was thoughtful for a moment. "Did someone help you heal?"

"What?"

"Did someone help you heal?" he repeated.

Ottum shook her head slightly. Despite her best resolutions to let down her guard and let this man in, she could feel the walls of armor racing up and in place around her. "What makes you think I needed to heal?"

Will laughed as Ottum took an even more defensive posture.

Watching her brace, Will settled and said softly, "We all need to heal, Ottum. You and I didn't learn all we did about people and healing without needing to know some of it for ourselves. At least in my experience, the only thing that happened was that someone gave me a tool. Then I had to use it to get results. I shared things with Saul that he can use to help himself heal, but it's up to him to do the work."

Ottum's armor fell away slowly. The soft internal chink chink of it mentally dropping away relaxed her. "Apparently I need to work on accepting that even when a person is provided with everything they need to change, they may choose not to."

"Hmmm. That's a tough one to learn," Will nodded.

Ottum found herself wondering what it was Will had healed from as he smiled at her and gestured that they should head back to the cabin.

"I'd like to know you better. I know we entered your life rather suddenly and we may have to leave soon, but you intrigue me." Ottum said before she could talk herself out of the vulnerability of it.

Will slid his hand into hers and squeezed softly. "Good. I'd like to know you better too. However, Kai is likely to come looking for you if we don't get back soon."

"He's a good Companion." Ottum grinned. "What makes you think he hasn't already checked on me?"

Will just shook his head and grinned wider, but after a few more steps he asked, "Has he?"

"Yes."

Will chuckled.

CHAPTER 11

They ate with light conversation, stories, and laughter. An outsider would have thought the individuals gathered in the cabin were old friends. However, at the end of the meal, after dishes were washed and the remaining food put away, Saul gathered a backpack and water pouch Will gave him and began filling them with food and supplies. Ottum looked at Kai and Will for help in dissuading Saul from leaving, but found no signs that either would intervene.

"Will you walk with me outside for a moment, Ottum?" Kai asked.

Realizing she wasn't likely to sway Saul by herself and knowing Kai might be persuaded to help her do so, she moved toward the door. Ottum and Kai walked a short distance from the cabin before Kai spoke.

"As you noticed, Saul is packing to leave."

"I noticed, and I really feel it best he stay here longer. The poison is still affecting him, and he needs to heal from the trauma it caused. We should try to get him to realize that, don't you think?" Ottum asked.

"He and Will discussed that this morning, so I believe he is aware of both points. I realize you do not want him to go, but for all of our safety, he needs to. Though it is difficult for me to make this decision, I will be going with him," Kai said.

Disappointment showed on Ottum's face. "I was hoping to have a chance to spend more time with Will, but perhaps we'll come back after we've seen Saul safely to somewhere he can heal. Did Will tell him about a specific place?"

"Will did tell him of a place. But Ottum, you will not be going with us. I did not say that *we* will be going with Saul, I said I will. So you will have your opportunity to spend more time with Will, and I will return when it is possible to do so."

"We travel together," Ottum said firmly.

Kai shook his head. "After yesterday, you need at least a few days to rest. Saul should not travel alone given his condition. Will is not Pack, so he should not be asked to care for one of our own when there is another option. If you were to go, the risk is simply too great that Saul would have another episode like yesterday. He is not willing to risk that—nor am I. That leaves me to escort Saul. Besides, you said yourself you would like to spend more time with Will."

Ottum stood without speaking. She and Kai had not parted company for several years. She hated the thought of being separated from him regardless of how logical it was. "Does Saul know that you're going with him?"

"Yes. We discussed it while you and Will were outside this morning. I would prefer to remain with you as we have always been, but that would not be in the best interests of all involved. We are Pack and must consider that," Kai said.

Ottum searched for another solution as Kai gave her the time she needed to accept the plan.

"I'll walk with you for a short distance. The sunshine and activity will be good for me," Ottum forced a smile and hoped that she would find a better plan as they walked.

Kai was uncertain of the truth in her statement. However, her walking with them would delay their parting, and he wouldn't argue against that.

Turning, he said, "Saul is sure to be waiting on me by now. I should get my pack so we can leave."

Ottum and Kai returned to the cabin, both of them lost in their own thoughts. Saul was packed and waiting as Kai had suspected. He and Will had been speaking but stopped as the other two entered.

Kai went straight to his pack and was pleased Will and Saul hadn't taken the liberty of packing it. Ottum was grateful for that as well. She made herself busy topping the water bag and packing the food obviously left out for that purpose. She moved for the bedroll, but Kai stopped her just as she realized it was no longer there.

"Saul already has our bedroll on his back," Kai said.

She was momentarily confused and then realized Kai was right. Kai would be acting as Saul's Companion while he escorted him, and Saul's pack had been taken by her brother. The only bedroll available was the one she and Kai normally shared.

Kai slipped into his pack. "Shall we go?"

Without conversation, they filed out of the cabin. Will and Saul led the way as Ottum and Kai walked behind. Ottum realized there had been conversations going on between the others as she had readied Kai's pack, because Will hadn't questioned that they were all going part of the way together. She suspected he and Saul were talking even now.

"Will has assured me he will watch over you while I am gone."

Kai said it in Path and Ottum again was surprised by the depth of emotion she could feel as he spoke.

"I'm sure we'll watch out for each other. You're right that it's best for you to go with Saul," Ottum admitted sadly, "but I'll miss you. Do you know where you're going or how long it'll take before you come back?"

"Will has given Saul and me directions to a place where there are others who can help Saul deal with the trauma. He said it will take a couple weeks to get there, maybe more because Saul is still weak and will need to rest longer. If winter has worsened, I might stay a few months. That will also give Saul the opportunity to return with me should he desire to," Kai said.

"Why do you think he might want to come back with you?" Ottum asked, disappointed Kai was considering anything other than a prompt return. She realized too late that he would know. Part of her wished emotions weren't transmitted when they communicated, and part of her realized that in some ways it was much easier.

"Though I don't believe that it is possible, you would still like to help your brother. The only chance of that happening is to meet him with a healed Saul at our side. It is not that I want to stay away from you. It is very difficult for me to leave you, but I think you and Will have a lot to teach to and learn from each other."

Ottum sighed. "You're right."

Will and Saul started speaking so Ottum and Kai could also hear.

"It's a good day for a journey. The sky's clear and the sun takes some of the cold out of the air. If you keep this pace and follow the map, you should reach an empty cabin you can use for shelter tonight," Will said.

"You've made this trip recently?" Ottum asked.

"It's a route I'm familiar with," Will assured her.

"If you haven't been there recently, how can you be sure the cabin is empty?" Ottum asked.

"I can't. It's a place I stay during the fall when I'm hunting to stock up for winter. There haven't been signs of anyone other than myself there for years. If someone is there now, there will be plenty of indicators to warn Saul and Kai."

"What do you think will happen if you should run into my brother?" Ottum asked.

Saul and Kai looked at each other, but it was Kai who spoke.

"If your brother engages us, it is very likely Saul will react as he did when he thought you were Leon. I will act as his Companion and do what you and I have always done when we engage an Avil. However, since there has been no indication that your brother tracked us or has been hunting us, I believe it unlikely our paths will cross."

"What Kai is saying makes sense," Will said. "Saul and I discussed the possibility earlier and came to the same conclusion."

Ottum didn't want to admit it, but she was getting tired. They had barely walked a mile, and already she could feel herself wanting to slow the pace. For Kai and Saul to make the cabin by night, they needed to walk faster than a stroll. She forced herself to keep going.

Kai eyed her from time to time. "You might be fooling Will and Saul, but I know how tired you are, my lady."

"I know. Just a little further," she smiled at him before continuing, "and I promise to rest before Will and I return to the cabin."

Will and Saul began to angle slightly so that they walked toward the stream. They came to its banks and followed along it for a few more yards before the entire party stopped. There was a log lying between the banks that would serve as a bridge, and Ottum realized it was here the group would part.

Ottum kneeled in the snow and hugged Kai as he rubbed his head against her cheek.

"Take care of yourself," she said. *You've been my best friend and the only constant in my life these last several years. I don't know what I'd do if something happened to you. I love you.* She thought all of that to herself as she buried her face in his fur.

"You too." Kai kissed her cheek softly and then turned to Will. "Watch over her," he commanded.

"And you watch over him," Ottum directed Saul, "as well as yourself."

"I will." With a sheepish look at her neck he added, "you too."

Will removed Saul's sword from his own belt and handed it to its owner at the same time as Ottum removed Saul's knife from Kai's pack.

Once his sword and knife were in place, Saul nodded one last time, and then he and Kai began working their way across the log.

Kai suspected that Ottum and Will had continued to watch their departure. Just before he walked out of sight, Kai looked over his shoulder and said, "Goodbye, my lady."

"Come back safely, my friend." As she bid him a last farewell, Ottum realized her energy was leaving too.

"How are you?" Will asked.

"Tired." *...and still fighting back tears.*

"Let's head home then. I didn't want to delay Saul and Kai's departure, but there's a spot part way back that has a gorgeous view. If you don't mind, we can stop there for a bit," Will said.

Ottum wasn't sure if Will was trying to protect her ego or if there really was something to see, but a rest sounded like a perfect idea to her.

The pace was much slower, and they made small talk as they walked. There would be time for deeper conversation later, but neither of them was in a hurry today. Will led them back along the stream in a slightly different route, and as he had promised, there was indeed an amazing view.

The stream dropped over a small fall and opened up into a wider area so that the sunlight shining on the fall was turned into hundreds of little rainbows cascading down into the water. Set against the contrast of the snow and with the icicles formed by the moisture that clung to the exposed tree roots in the bank, it felt almost magical.

Will brushed the snow off of a log he'd turned into a chair and sat down, pulling Ottum with him. His arms encircled her waist, and she laid her head on his shoulder. Ottum wondered if life would allow them to know each other well enough to be as closely bonded as an onlooker might guess them to be at that moment. For now, she was happy to rest and to enjoy the experience.

CHAPTER 12

Saul required several rests as they made their way along the route mapped out by Will. The terrain changed little as they walked, but daylight slowly faded to moonlight as the hours passed.

"If Will hadn't given such detailed instructions, we'd never have found this cabin," Kai said.

"Looks pretty empty," Saul said as he looked around at what had once been a clearing. Saplings stuck their scrawny trunks up through the snow, reclaiming the land around the cabin.

"Yes, but we should still use caution," replied Kai.

Saul nodded and drew his sword as they neared. He waited as Kai went ahead and circled the exterior of the cabin.

"No signs of occupancy or of recent access." Kai missed Ottum. Saul was a Chaser so there were common behaviors, but there was not the familiarity that comes from years of working together. Familiarity, right or wrong, lends itself to predictable habits and a sense of comfort and trust. Had it been Ottum's sword that was drawn, Kai would have known their next action.

"You want to go first?" Saul asked.

I should think of this as an opportunity, Kai thought. In his early training days he was with a new Chaser at each session. It had allowed all involved to use and demonstrate their natural skills. Once that was achieved, they were then paired so as to compliment the other. By pairing in this manner and competing with each other as well as other pairs, it was possible to train necessary skills which were less developed. It was more than that, though. In the height of battle, when Chaser and Companion were most likely to revert back to their own instinctual skills, as a pair they were still balanced. However, that was training and what was in front of them now was real life.

With a nod of his head, Kai moved forward to the cabin door. He looked back at Saul to make sure he followed and was ready. Kai then released the latch and pushed opened the door while simultaneously crouching low so that Saul could clear him and attack any unknown ambushers. Except for the moonlight that poured in through the open door, the interior of the cabin was dark. Kai remained at the door and watched Saul work his way around the cabin.

As Saul moved about the cabin, he removed the boards which covered the windows so that more moonlight was allowed in to aid his search. The layout was similar to Will's cabin, making it easier to maneuver in the semi-darkness. Feeling reasonably certain they were alone, Saul moved to the fireplace, found the flint Will had told him about, and sent sparks flying into the firebox. Wood and kindling had been pre-stacked and left ready for the next traveler who reached the cabin. Once the flames blazed enough to replace the moonlight, Kai entered and closed the door.

Saul sheathed his sword and removed his pack as Kai slipped out of his as well. Everything was as Will had said, leaving them to believe no one had entered the cabin since he had last been here. Saul found a candle-lamp and lit it from the fire in the fireplace. He then searched the pantry area for food. He removed two stone pots which were each encased in a wire cage. After studying them, Saul realized the cages were meant to seal the pot in order to keep other creatures away from the contents. Once removed, he was delighted to find a mix of dried berries and vegetables in one and dried meat in the other. The meat looked more like leather than edible food. He removed one and looked doubtfully at it.

Kai had been watching Saul, and upon seeing the dried meat, he wished they'd made better time.

"We could eat from our packs," Saul suggested.

"Will said to put the meat in some water for a while before eating it," Kai said. "He also said he hadn't been here in over a year. If it isn't any good after the water, then we can eat from our packs."

Saul nodded but still looked highly doubtful. Since there was no better option, he found a bowl and poured some of their water supply in before adding the chunks of dried meat. He carried all of it over to the fireplace so that they could sit and eat in warmth. There he removed their bowls from their packs and poured them some drinking water too.

"We'll want to make sure to refill our packs tonight with snow," Saul said as he set Kai's bowl at his side.

Kai nodded. "We should leave wood and kindling too. Having them already in the firebox was a welcome treat at the end of a day of travel."

"Definitely," Saul said as he took a small handful of dried berries and vegetables. "Will seems like an interesting guy."

Kai nodded. "What do you know about where we are going?"

"Will said it's a small community with a school and a training hall. He seems to think there's a way to physically release the emotional trauma I experienced and that it will be a safe place for me to learn to do that," Saul said as a light shade of crimson flushed his cheeks.

"There is no embarrassment in the trauma you received, Saul. The Avil could have picked anyone."

Saul shrugged and reached for his water.

"Prior to the poison, did you have any other contact with the Avil?" Kai asked.

"I saw it a few days earlier and had been chasing it. While it's hard to tell which memories were induced by the poison and which are real, I think it killed Eyota. That memory seems to have taken place before the poisoning, but at the same time, it doesn't make sense." Saul paused as though lost in thought.

"Why not?"

"Well, we'd been chasing the Avil pretty hard and decided to rest for a few hours at night. She was the first watch and was to wake me in a couple of hours, but she must have fallen asleep." Saul recalled again waking up to that horrible scene. He shivered as he remembered her scream and watched the life fade from her eyes. "The thing is, it took her head and left me. I hold the sword that will kill it, so why did it kill her? None of it makes any more sense now than it did then. She wouldn't have abandoned me, and you said that you saw no traces of her. Therefore I have to assume my memory of that night is correct and she is dead. Do you think it is a poisoned memory instead of a real one?" Saul asked.

Kai considered. "Given what the Avil said when we met it, you are probably right to think it killed her. If this was just any Avil, then it would make no sense for it…" Kai paused and with great effort continued, "no sense for *him* to have taken her head and left you sleeping when you were such an easy target."

"No disrespect to Ottum, but Avils will always be 'it' to me," Saul gruffly stated. "Do you think taking Eyota makes sense because it's Ottum's brother?"

"Yes." Kai sat quietly as Saul waited for him to say more.

When Kai didn't speak, Saul said, "If you hadn't noticed, I'm waiting to hear why."

Kai waged an internal debate on the good or damage that could be done by sharing what he only guessed to be true. After a few moments, he looked at Saul and decided to share his thoughts.

"This could be just as wrong as it could be right, so please do not assume it is truth. I think it is highly possible it was no mere chance you came upon the Avil. It seems very likely to me that Leon had hunted Ottum for some time, and when he found her, he set off to find another Chaser who was close enough for her to feel. While the attack seems very personal to you," Kai paused, "I think that to him you are nothing more than a pawn. You happened to be close enough. He took Eyota's head because he needed you alive for his plan, and he suspected you would follow him relentlessly as a result. I do not know how he managed to get you to drink from the stream, but he wanted you poisoned to see if Ottum would save you.

Ottum's family life was not always a happy one. Her father was often cruel to both of his children. Her mother never interfered on their behalf. For reasons I do not understand, Ottum never lost the ability to trust those who were worthy. Her brother, based upon the things she has told me, lost his ability to trust even those who repeatedly proved they deserved it. So while he continued to become more embittered with life, she reached out to the people offering to help her. In his perception, and again this is just a guess, she found a way to be happy and kept it from him. Even if she tried to help him, Leon's distrust of everyone kept him from believing even the one person who shared the experiences of his childhood. So it seems possible that he believes she abandoned him and that it is her fault his life is in its current state. While Leon calls no one his family, he found out that Ottum became a Chaser. Since most Chasers consider others in the Pack to be family, he wanted to see if she would abandon her new family as easily as she had him."

"Hmmm," Saul said as he chewed. "She doesn't strike me as the abandoning type. If we hadn't left today, she probably would have put up even more of a fight about coming with us."

"Indeed," Kai said as he took a drink. He found the dried berries and vegetables acceptable food, but they weren't his preference. He peered into the bowl where the meat was soaking and decided it was time to try a piece. As his teeth sunk into the surprisingly supple jerky, multiple flavors met his senses. He expected only dried meat, but Will had obviously ground it and added several herbs and seasonings. Kai enjoyed a few of the flavors, but he still wished there had been time for a hunt tonight.

"How is it?" Saul asked with begrudged curiosity.

"It has Will's touch," Kai replied. After Saul raised one eyebrow in question, Kai continued, "He added other things to it so that it is not just deer. It makes it tender, and the taste is good. I would venture it has some form of healing property to it as well. However, I still prefer fresh meat."

That was good enough for Saul. As Saul chewed, he decided that while he didn't mind fresh meat, especially a piece seared by a hot fire, this was easily the best dried venison he'd tasted in his life. Will was one of the strangest men he'd ever met, and yet it seemed possible that he was also one of the most talented.

"What do you think he is?" Saul asked.

"Who?"

"Will. What do you think he is?" Saul repeated.

"I'm not sure I understand your question."

"He isn't a Chaser. He knows way too much to be an unfamiliar. He has skills I've never seen, is a damn fine cook, and knows a thing or two about healing." Saul paused to take another bite of deer and chew it before continuing. "I've never met another like him and have been wondering what he is," Saul said.

"As far as I can tell, he is a good man," Kai replied as though he still didn't fully understand Saul's question.

"Well, yeah. That seems obvious. I mean, well, I want to know what he's *called*. We are going to this community he recommended, and my bet is that there are more like him there. I wish I could know what he is so that I can know what to expect. That's what I am getting at." Saul shrugged and took another bite of meat.

Though he had lived among them all his life, Kai still found human behavior to be odd sometimes. Their desire to know something before having any experience with it puzzled him. Humans would often go out of their way to avoid an unknown experience when it was the experience itself that would give them the knowledge they sought. For him, the only question he felt when entering a new situation was whether he would live or die. Even then, he knew the answer to his question was 'yes.' Kai was more comfortable in familiar situations, but he understood that sometimes the unknown was necessary. If Will was sending them somewhere for Saul to heal, Saul would be a welcomed guest.

"It seems you will find out in good time. We will get there in a couple of weeks. I would venture a guess that as long as your weapon is not drawn, none will be drawn against you. It is the wolf at your side who may raise their caution," Kai stated.

"Will didn't seem to have a problem with you," Saul said dismissively.

"You were not awake when we first arrived."

"So what was his response?"

"He did not know of Chasers, Companions, or Avils. What he saw was a large wolf behaving in a way that might be threatening had I been a typical wolf. He drew an arrow-with amazing speed, I might add." Kai said with admiration. It didn't matter that the arrow had been aimed at him, Will was obviously skilled with a bow and Kai respected that skill. "As you may have guessed, he did not release it."

"Why not?"

"I did not attack, and Ottum intervened."

"You're lucky he wasn't a typical unfamiliar," Saul said. "You done?"

"Yes, thank you."

Saul returned the remaining food to its cages and cleaned up. Saul filled their water sacks with snow, and then they each settled in for the night.

The next morning, things were taken care of quickly and they started on their way just after daylight. Kai decided an earlier start might allow him to hunt that night.

As the morning progressed, Saul and Kai descended the last of the mountain's slope and entered the valley. The sun's bright glare was reduced by the variety of trees that also decreased the wind's chill. Winter had claimed the land here too, but a few birds still flitted about in the trees. Squirrels searched for missed remnants of food to be added to their winter stores. Kai watched as a mountain cat chased and caught a careless rabbit.

The two of them had walked without speaking since leaving the cabin. Saul broke the silence by asking, "Who's Oscar?"

"How do you know that name?" Kai asked, surprised by the question.

"I heard Ottum mention it," Saul shrugged. "Was he a past partner or Companion?"

"No." Kai offered no further explanation.

"I didn't mean to harm her," Saul said tersely.

Kai wondered what that had to do with the current conversation and why Saul's words were laced with anger.

"What do you mean, Saul?"

"You seem reluctant to share information with me regarding Ottum just because I hurt her. She is Pack, and I would not harm her in my right mind. When I attacked, it wasn't her I was trying to kill. She's not even here, so answering my question doesn't put her at risk," Saul glowered at Kai.

"I am protecting Ottum, but not from you. She is a very private being, and it is not my place to tell you her story."

"Oh." Saul didn't seem completely convinced.

"I did not know Oscar well. If there are things I can answer about him that do not have to do with Ottum's private life, I will be happy to do so," Kai offered.

"I knew an Oscar when I was a kid. He's part of why I became a Chaser, so I thought maybe he's the same person Ottum mentioned. Although she seemed fond of him, he often irritated me. Every question I asked was answered by a question," Saul frowned.

One look at Saul's furrowed eyebrows and Kai couldn't help but chuckle.

"It does sound like it might have been the same person," Kai said before Saul's narrowed glance turned to real anger.

"I heard he died some time ago," Saul said without emotion.

"He did," Kai confirmed.

"Hmmm. Is he a Greybeard now?" Saul said this casually, hoping that Kai wouldn't catch the curiosity in his question.

"I believe he might be." Kai observed Saul closely. "I do not mean to offend you, but you seem more intelligent than your language implies."

Saul shrugged. "Sometimes more is said when words aren't used."

"You have a point," Kai conceded. "How do you know about Greybeards?"

"One of the men who trained me mentioned them once. I thought he was off in the head a little. When Ottum spoke of interacting with Oscar in her dreams, it reminded me of the stories that guy used to tell," Saul said as he pushed a broken branch out of his path. "How do you know about them?"

"It is part of our training."

Saul's eyes narrowed again. "I've been a Chaser for years, and it was only mentioned once. None of the other Chasers I have spoken with about it have even heard of them. Who included it in the training you and Ottum had?"

"I did not say Ottum was trained regarding Greybeards. When I said 'our,' I meant Companions. Ottum is not familiar with the term even though she is interacting with Oscar."

"So you are trained regarding Greybeards?"

"Yes."

"Why? And what kind of training?"

"I am not at liberty to say."

Saul laughed at this. "Oh come on!"

"I am not joking, Saul. We promise to share the information we learn exclusively with our paired Chaser and only when asked. I am acting as though I am your Companion for this journey out of need, but I am not your paired Companion."

"So you're telling me that Eyota knew about Greybeards and never shared that knowledge with me because I didn't ask her to?"

"I cannot say for sure. But if her training was as mine, then yes," Kai answered.

"I find that hard to believe," Saul said as he stopped to mentally check their position with the map Will had described.

"We're still on course," Kai said. "Truth has little to do with what you do or don't believe, Saul. Truth simply is."

How does Ottum put up with his arrogance! Saul thought to himself. "So if I want to learn more about the Greybeards, I have to wait until I have a new Companion?"

"If you want to learn about them from a Companion, then you are correct," Kai nodded.

"You really aren't going to tell me, are you?" Saul's voice was laced with barely restrained anger.

"It is not my place to do so, Saul."

Snow continued to crunch beneath their feet, wind blew through tree branches above them, other creatures moved to safety or in search of food, and all of it was punctuated by the silence between Saul and Kai.

"I believe we are being followed," Kai said after covering significant territory without the sense that who or whatever was following them was either gaining or trailing behind.

"Seems so," Saul said.

Ottum would have checked her sword in a way only Kai would have seen, but Saul had given no indication that he knew of their company. Kai missed Ottum's awareness and the comfort that went with it.

"Can you tell if it is friend or foe?" asked Kai.

"No."

"Are you well enough to fight if we need to?"

Saul glanced briefly at Kai through veiled eyes. Then he replied, "I am well enough to do what needs done."

Saul's eyes might have attempted to mask his emotions, but there was no mistaking the feeling that was transmitted with that thought.

Kai had often felt Ottum held too much compassion for the Avils they hunted. She didn't fully compartmentalize any being she met, even an Avil. She formed an opinion quickly, but always left room for the possibility that she was wrong. There was no such room left by Saul, and Kai wondered if he'd been wrong to view it as a weakness in Ottum.

CHAPTER 13

"They know ol' Lolli is watching, but they don't know what he is. No. The man is dangerous. See how he walks, Lolli? Yes, he is dangerous. He would see me and assume things. Yes, he would. Lolli is not all that he seems to be, though." Lolli would have laughed to the sky, but he was not yet ready to face those he tracked.

CHAPTER 14

Ottum felt as though she could have slept right where she and Will had sat. But the cold and the angle of her head as it rested on Will's shoulder caused her throat to ache. The water falling was hypnotic, so she stayed as she was until the aching was greater than the pleasure of the experience. She stirred and stood.

"All ready to head home?" Will asked.

It was such a simple question, but the word 'home' created an odd stir in Ottum's emotions. She had lived many places, but it had been years since any of them had been called home. 'Home' to her had become Kai. His companionship warmed her heart, delighted her soul, and provided a source of stability. She wondered if other people ever thought of home as someone instead of a certain place. Knowing that Will had made his home with masterful skill and loving thought, she answered as simply as he had asked, "Yes. The warmth of a fire would be quite welcome now."

They strolled through the snow and the trees, enjoying the sunshine's brightness and the relative warmth it provided as it chased away some of the chill. Despite the fatigue, Ottum felt a growing curiosity about Will. How had he come to live in this place, was he who he was by decision or by example, and was the man she saw on the surface a true reflection of the man within?

"Are all Companions as open as Kai is?"

"What do you mean by 'open,' Will?"

"With rare exception, anytime I directed my attention to Kai, anything he was thinking was easily heard in Path. You tend to be the opposite. Saul was poisoned and still suffering with its effects, so I can't really use him as an example. I'm just curious if it's common for Companions to be more open, to leave their thoughts unguarded, while Chasers are less so?"

"I've never really thought about it before. Perhaps you should also ask Kai when he returns, but my opinion is that the openness has less to do with Companion or Chaser traits than it does with the amount of trust extended to those around." Ottum paused for a moment because she realized that she was not completely open to Kai at all times despite fully trusting him. So she added, "In addition to trust, there may be an element of certainty as well. If I'm considering different options, I'll often close off until I've decided on what I believe to be the best choice."

"Wouldn't it be more efficient to remain open so that Kai could know your reasoning process without you having to explain it to him when you decide?" Will asked. "It would also allow him to point out important fact you might not be considering but should be."

"Perhaps."

Will watched her closely. There was so much more said than her single-word answer implied, but as seemed to be the case more often than not, Ottum's thoughts were closed to him. It would be easy to consider her arrogant, but Will didn't think Kai would tolerate arrogance even if he was her assigned Companion. And the way he had seen the two of them interact dismissed any indicators of an imagined superiority. He switched to Path. "Why do you close Kai out?"

"I don't close Kai out when it's important and certain. There are times I close him out when I don't want the flow of my thoughts to be interrupted. As you said, when I remain open, Kai will sometimes point out things worth considering. Sometimes this is extremely useful, but sometimes it sidetracks a particular angle I want to consider. And sometimes I close Kai out because I want him to close me out."

"Why would you want that?" Will asked with more than a small amount of surprise in his voice.

Ottum chuckled before she answered. "Have you never reveled in a moment of silence? I suppose it isn't true silence, but to still your mind so as to hear the wind in the trees and the activity of life going on around and within you—I find it very peaceful."

Will stopped, closed his eyes, and breathed deeply before he said, "It is rather nice."

Then Ottum added, "Sometimes I close Kai out for other reasons too. There are thoughts I simply don't want to share with him. Maybe they don't apply to him or us, or perhaps I just want privacy," Ottum paused. "But to answer the question beneath the one you asked: regardless of any relationship you and I form, there will be times when I shut you out too."

Will blinked. He hadn't realized why he had asked, but she was right. He became suddenly aware that as Ottum sorted out the last few days, she relaxed into her real self. He might have been able to share ideas with her that she had not thought of before, but this woman was not a fool. She could read people as well as he could, was willing to question others and herself, had an unending curiosity, and had experienced things he had not even known about prior to meeting her. He looked with appreciation at her and saw a big smile on her face. He found himself thrilled at the concept of spending time with her and learning from her. And her smile thrilled him in a completely different way.

"You might want to remember that when you're speaking in Path and then continue to have thoughts without closing off, the other person hears what you're thinking," Ottum said with a wink.

He snapped closed and berated himself. He then realized that Ottum was right, and that there would always be times when he wanted to have private thoughts. It suddenly occurred to him that while he hadn't necessarily wanted to share those thoughts with her, the feelings sent with Ottum's words indicated that she'd enjoyed hearing them—even the last one.

"You're right," he said. "There are times I'll want to close off even to someone I deeply trust."

"Of course I'm right!" she said with mock arrogance. Then in a more serious tone, "Experience beats theory more often than not."

"Indeed, it does," he nodded. "And it's my experience that it's good to be home," Will said as they came into the clearing surrounding his cabin.

The cabin lay in front of them, and while her "home" was still walking through the snow with Saul, it was good to be with Will. Despite the sun's best efforts, the air was cold and the thought of a fire warmed her even before she stepped through the door.

Will tended the coals and added a couple of logs while Ottum ladled water for both of them to drink.

"Thank you, Ottum. I'll make some tea for us later this evening."

"You're welcome, and thanks for tending the fire. If there are tasks that can be shared, please feel free to let me know. It's been a long time since sharing a cabin with another human. With Kai, tasks are easy to define," Ottum said.

"Until you, there's never been another human here with me. There've been other people in other places, of course. Just not in quite some time. You're my guest, but please feel free to consider this your home while you're here. We'll learn to share the work and play as we go," Will smiled.

Ottum returned his smile and said, "Thank you." She wondered what other places Will had been to. She'd lived in the large city of Mandolia for a year at Oscar's request. He'd said it would be good for her to experience more culture, but all the people and socializing weren't for her. She pictured Will in a suit at a theatre and smiled. *He'd be handsome*, she thought. *Then again, he's just fine as he is.*

"Well then, the fire seems to be doing its job!" Will said as he removed his coat and warmer outside clothing. "I'm not sure what Chasers do, but I have a few things I prefer to practice daily. You're welcome to join me, engage in your own activity, watch, or ignore me. Regardless, I'm going to tend to my health now."

Ottum was intrigued to learn what he meant by that. Her training was always for battle, but she knew she had some healing of her own to do. She'd not gone through her own exercises for a couple of days, but she was too sore and tired after Saul's attack. "Chasers train daily so they remain healthy and capable. I'm interested in learning what your practice is, but at least for today, I believe I should rest. So I won't be attempting either your or my practice."

"Very well. I don't mind if you watch," Will said, "but I prefer to not speak until I'm done. It'll let me fully concentrate on what I'm doing. I'll let you know when I'm finished as long as you're still awake then."

Will moved to the center of the cabin and began 'tending his health.' Ottum watched in an off-handed manner as she removed her boots and other outside clothing. What Will was doing seemed very odd to her and didn't look anything like the training techniques she was used to. Her body longed to train while her mind longed to sleep and her intellect longed to learn. She compromised by lying on the pallet in such a way as to watch Will while she rested.

Ottum's training always centered on creating enough strength and endurance to do what was necessary during an extended encounter with an Avil as well as endurance for the long travels required. Other Chasers stayed in towns and cities, but she enjoyed the exploration of chasing in more scenic areas. That preference created a need for greater endurance.

Will's training looked more like he was having a good laugh while trying to shake off imaginary children who were tickling him and hanging on his arms and legs. Ottum longed to ask questions about what he was doing and what value there was in it. After a short while, he started moving his body in a way that was more familiar. Ottum realized he was putting himself through the ranges of movement Ottum used when she worked on fellow Pack or people Avil's had injured. It looked like Will was testing his own joints. This part of his training made instant sense to her, and she wondered why she'd never thought of it before. She'd be able to test her own function and maybe even improve some of the minor aches and pains she felt. She chided herself that she'd never thought to apply the same techniques used to heal others to someone already healthy. It was simple but brilliant.

Will finished moving his joints and began working his muscles. Although contact had been minimal in the conflict with Saul, the emotions of the last two days were lodged into his movement. It felt good to be freeing himself from their restrictions and finding balance between mind and body again. It had been some time since he'd interacted with new people, and the emotions it created were varied and strong. He'd left what others called civilization and felt little regret about leaving. He missed those he'd been close to, but he made the trek to see them once each year or two. That was enough for him most of the time.

If he were honest with himself, he missed female companionship as well. A few weeks of interaction once every year or two wasn't enough in that regard. But he had met no woman interested in living his lifestyle, although one occasionally tried to make him believe she would be enough for him to want to live hers. The woman on his pallet seemed to live an even less 'civilized' life than he did.

Losing his balance and nearly falling on his face, Will realized he had allowed his mind to wander from his practice. He could hear his teachers reminding him to be mindful of his breath, structure, and movement. They never told him to stop being emotional. They knew it would only cause him to focus more on the emotions and carry him further from the breathing, structure, and movement that was necessary to balance them. He knew his teachers were right, but Will was also aware that Ottum watched his every move. It bothered him that he'd nearly busted his head open while trying to push himself further to impress her. *Too much ego is a dangerous thing,* he reminded himself. He exhaled and returned to his practice.

It wasn't the smooth and flowing session Will was used to because thoughts of his recent guests kept interfering, but he got through his practice. He wondered what Ottum had thought about it and turned her direction only to find her sleeping.

He laughed to himself and shook his head. She was sound asleep and paying him no attention at all while he'd struggled to think of anything but her. At least one of them was able to shut down their thoughts and fully do what was needed. *I'll have to follow her example next time.*

Will would have found it ironic that Ottum forced her attention away from his practice and into sleep because she thought she was following his example. Before she stilled her mind, Ottum promised herself that she would learn to 'tend her health' as Will was doing.

* * *

Ottum opened her eyes and saw shadows that indicated daylight was already fading. Across the cabin, Will prepared their evening meal. The aromas drifting in the air caressed her senses and whet her appetite. She tested her throat and grimaced. *Saul apparently has a strong grip,* she thought. Despite the soreness, she felt refreshed from her nap.

"I didn't mean to sleep for so long," she said in Path.

Will didn't jump, but he was surprised at the sensation of hearing an unexpected voice in Path. It wasn't as though Ottum had intruded into his thoughts and surprised him; it was more that he was used to hearing with his ears and the absence of the actual sound felt odd when he wasn't expecting it.

"You've had an eventful few days. Even if you didn't mean to, extra sleep is something you need," he replied.

"I do feel better. I'd like to learn the practice you use to tend your health. Some of it instantly made sense as I watched you, but I obviously didn't see what you were doing as I slept. Will that be part of what Saul learns when he and Kai get to their destination?" Ottum asked.

So she was watching! The thought brought a smile to Will's face. "If Saul's willing to learn, the people there will teach him the things I was doing as well as other skills."

"I wish Saul didn't need to go there. But at the same time, I wish I could see where he's going. I'd like to know that he'll be at peace and well again by the time he leaves."

Will replied, "If Saul's willing to do the work, he can be both." Thinking of his teachers, he added, "Possibly even more so than before the poison."

"How do you know that for sure?" Ottum asked.

"It was my experience and everyone else I know who's been to the camp too," Will answered. "What we practice helps us heal and then stay healthy."

As with most things, Ottum was willing to believe it was possible but held some skepticism until she had more experience to guide her. "I'm looking forward to trying it."

"And I'm looking forward to hearing what your experience is," Will replied. "But for right now, I'm more interested in eating this food. Would you care to join me, dear lady?" he asked as he gestured at the table with flair. A large grin accompanied his request.

"Why thank you, dear sir. I would be delighted." Ottum curtsied after rising from the pallet, and they both laughed.

CHAPTER 15

"There are no longer any visible traces of Saul's attack," Will said as he watched Ottum working with an exercise he had taught her several weeks earlier. "Are there invisible traces?"

There had been much laughing and teasing over the last several weeks, but intimacy of any form had been avoided. They had even ceased to speak in Path. Therefore it surprised her that Will was prying into the unseen. "I miss Kai immensely. He's with Saul instead of here with me...does that count as invisible?" Ottum asked.

"That isn't what I had in mind, and you know it," Will said.

Ottum wasn't sure what had brought about the change, but it seemed that Will was ready to explore deeper than the surface information they had been sharing. The intensity with which he was watching her move suggested he was looking for clues in her body language as well as in her words, so she continued with the exercises as she answered. "Saul's attack on what he believed to be an Avil occurred after several other events. The attack itself is just a small piece of something that's been developing for much of my life. There are more than traces within me of those experiences, Will. Is there something specific you want to know?"

"Part of doing the exercises I have taught you is that it allows the release of emotions as well as returning suppleness to the body. When people begin to practice these exercises consistently, they sometimes experience an emotion or a memory that has been dormant. There are methods to work around the movement that causes the emotion or memory to surface in a way that makes it easier to deal with. I mostly asked because if you're experiencing lots of emotion, I want to teach you how to deal with it."

"And what's the other part of why you asked?" Ottum asked.

"What 'other part'?" Will said as he moved into a different exercise.

"You said that you *mostly* asked because you want to teach me how to deal with the emotions. There can't be a 'mostly' if there isn't also a 'partially.' I'm curious what the other part is." Ottum stopped moving and began watching Will just as intently as he had previously watched her.

Will performed the laughing shaking motions Ottum now knew decreased stress levels. He looked at Ottum, exhaled, and shook his head slightly as he began to talk. "You don't play games, do you?"

Ottum wasn't sure if he was trying to distract her instead of giving her an answer or if he was trying to ease himself into more openness between them. "I enjoy some games," she answered.

Will laughed and exhaled deeply again. "I meant social games. Things like asking one thing while really hoping to find out the answer to something completely different."

"Oh. No," Ottum said with furrowed brows. "I hate those types of games. I can see value in them on rare occasion, but the rest of the time I wish people would just spit it out and get it over with. If someone is capable of understanding what you're 'trying' to say, then there's no reason to avoid just saying it."

"The reason people do that sort of thing is to be able to say they weren't really saying a certain thing. If you take offense or don't feel what they were hoping for, they can convince themselves that it was you who misinterpreted them. Even though I know it's only to protect me from embarrassment, it's something I do from time to time. I've not seen you do it once, but you do try to find out things about people without directly asking." Will stated.

"What makes you say that?" Ottum asked as she started putting herself through various ranges of motion.

"I've watched you doing it over the last few weeks. We've both been watching and hoping the other will open up first." Will moved toward her as he spoke, and then sat down at her side while facing her, so he could still look into her eyes. "So the 'partially' I was trying to find out has to do with how you view the world in general. Do you hold a permanent grudge when someone harms you? Do you go to the other extreme and never hold them accountable for their actions? Can you see grey or is it all black and white? Do you learn from the experiences in your life? Do you deal with, avoid, or internalize problems? I've experienced how skilled your hands are at healing so it puzzles me that you picked a life of hunting and fighting. Why did you pick that life? How do you feel now that you know your brother is an Avil? And what will you do the next time the two of you meet?"

"That is an awful lot of 'partially.'" Ottum said with a raised eyebrow and a smile.

Will smiled back as he reached out and took her hand.

Ottum looked down at his hand covering hers and then back into his eyes. For the first time since the day Kai and Saul had left, Ottum spoke in Path.

"I only hold a grudge when the person who harmed is unwilling to take responsibility for what they did. We're all responsible for our actions. That doesn't mean that people don't make mistakes because they miscalculated, or perhaps didn't calculate at all, the effects those actions would have. But if I am to respect others, I expect them to learn from their mistakes. To the best of my ability, I apply that to myself as well. I can see the black and white of an issue, but the grey is typically closer to the truth." She paused while trying to remember the rest of his questions. "I'm also more likely to remember things I see than those I hear. What was the next thing you asked?

"I'm not sure if it was the next thing, but I did ask how you handle your problems." He replied.

"Ah, yes. You asked if I deal with, internalize, or avoid them. I think the answer to that is yes. In order to grow I know I have to deal with my problems, but sometimes I internalize them for a while or try to pretend they don't exist. As I'm sure you know, that doesn't work very well. So I almost always come back to dealing with them. Despite that, there are some issues I've struggled with for years and still don't have answers for." Ottum breathed deeply and found herself running her thumb along the edge of Will's hand. His skin was soft but the callous near his wrist left no doubt his hands were used to work. She was aware she'd left her thoughts open to him, and he knew she was searching for the words to answer the rest of his questions. "I'm not sure what I'll do when my brother and I meet again. He didn't raise his sword when I saw him last time, and I've never killed an Avil unless they were trying to kill us or someone else."

Will knew Ottum had left her thoughts open for him, but the rate of thinking with the depth of emotion made it almost painful for him to try to keep up and process all of it. He closed his mind and shook his head for a few seconds. He reopened to her when things had settled, but Ottum had closed off. Fearing she misunderstood why he had shut her out, he spoke out loud.

"Speaking Path is still new to me, and I haven't practiced since Kai and Saul left. I didn't close off because of what you were sharing. It was simply that I couldn't process all of it quickly enough. Trying to keep up was causing my head to hurt," Will said.

Using Path, she replied, "What I was thinking causes my head to hurt too."

"I'm sure it does." Will wanted to say more, to somehow comfort her, but he couldn't find words that seemed adequate. "I did ask a lot of questions today, but some of the answers could be saved for later."

"Would you go for a walk with me?" Ottum asked. "Being outside clears my head, and we have some time before it's dark. Perhaps after that I can finish answering your questions and ask a few of my own."

"That sounds fair enough," Will replied and squeezed her hand with his own.

Once outside, the cold air rushed into Ottum's lungs and distracted her thoughts. The cloud cover was thick and grey, filled with moisture that would soon fall in white puffs to join the blanket already covering the ground.

They walked in comfortable silence for a short time. The wind gusted through the protection of the trees and swirled around them, challenging the warmth their clothes provided.

"It looks like there's going to be a heavier snowfall this time, doesn't it?" asked Will.

"Yes. I love the silence before a storm and the smell of the air. There's apprehension and anticipation present in the same moment," Ottum said.

Will watched her tilt her head back and turn her free hand palm up as though she were taking in some unseen elixir from the very air around them. He was once again struck by the contrast of what seemed to be the essence of her nature and that which she chose to do with her life. "How can someone as beautiful and full of life as you spend her time chasing others and fighting?"

The turbulence of his emotions hit Ottum full force, but she didn't close off from him. He might not have practiced speaking in Path since Kai and Saul had left, but she'd not practiced experiencing more than just the words that were transmitted. It took some effort to feel the flood of his emotions without mixing them with hers and without being caught up in the undertow as he became aware of them and tried to dam their outflow.

"It's not the contrast for me that you seem to perceive," Ottum began. "Those I chase have no difficulty harming anyone who gets in their way. I don't like to see others suffer needlessly, so I try to prevent the damage instead of healing them after it's already done. Obviously it's not possible to always prevent damage, so I learned to heal too."

"I hadn't thought of it that way, but that doesn't change that you chose the fighting first," Will said.

"People don't like the idea of fighting. *I* don't like fighting. That doesn't change that there are times when it's necessary to do so." Ottum changed their route in an effort to return them to the cabin.

Will looked at the grey sky and said, "We probably still have some time before it begins to snow. You wanted a break from the conversation, and I started right back in on it. I'm sorry. If you want to walk more, we can."

Ottum smiled. "The conversation is fine as long as you don't mind that I can't easily put my answers into words."

"I don't mind. We're a bit alike when it comes to that." Will's eyes were warm as he smiled at her, but the intimacy momentarily caused him to look away before risking another look.

"Why I'm a Chaser is difficult to explain," Ottum said. "Frankly, it feels more like this life chose me than I chose it. I've considered doing other things, but there are so many who turn away from even recognizing how much danger exists that I always seem to come back to it in the end. If you know you can make a difference, how do you walk away from that?"

Will considered her question. "What if so many others are causing problems that the little bit of good you're doing doesn't really make a difference? Do you ever feel that way?"

"That thought has crossed my mind a few times," Ottum said as she nodded. "I suppose it's something most who are trying to make a difference feel at one point or another. As a Chaser, there are times when I may never know who my actions affect beyond the Avil that is being fought. But there are other times when I interact with those who were harmed, and I realize that if my actions stopped even one person from being hurt, it makes enough of a difference."

Ottum felt something from Will at that moment that she couldn't define, and she closed off. He was agreeing with what she said, and yet, there was something that felt somehow not quite right. She decided to come back to it later and reopened. If Will had noticed the few seconds she was closed, he didn't show it in any way. She decided to change the topic to see if it would rid the last traces of the emotion that bothered her.

As they neared the cabin, Ottum said, "It seems we made it back just in time."

"Just in time? Eh, we could have gone longer," he said with a wink as they stepped onto the porch.

Ottum looked at him with enough surprise that he turned as though to point at what he thought would make his comment obvious. Instead of illustrating his point, he looked with wonder upon the snowfall taking place beyond the cover of the porch.

"But…" he stammered, "How did you know?"

Ottum shrugged. "Kai and I have spent the majority of the last several years living outside." She offered the statement as a plausible excuse he could accept if he desired to. He didn't.

"I don't think you learned that by living outside. I've spent plenty of time outside myself. I know a storm is coming and I can judge it fairly closely, but you knew it was snowing before you had seen it. And *that*, I cannot do," Will said. He watched her reaction closely and searched her face for an answer.

Ottum wasn't blocking him out, but she was guarding her thoughts. "As I said, there are things that make it seem the life of a Chaser chose me more than I chose it."

Will looked back into the greyness as the rate of snowfall increased. "You're aware of subtleties others might be able to learn with a lot of practice, but you didn't have to learn them, did you?" he asked.

She reached out from under the cover of the porch and caught a few flakes in her gloved hand. "No. I didn't have to learn them," she answered.

"Sensing the weather is just one thing that's like that for you, isn't it?" Will asked.

Ottum didn't answer so he continued. "Why don't you want to talk about it?"

Ottum had been careful with her thoughts before, but there was even greater caution now. "Not everyone feels that what I do is learnable. It's been my experience that things which seem foreign to others are often met with fear…if not outright hatred."

"So, you just lock it all away inside," Will stated with disapproval.

Ottum looked off the porch as the storm increased in intensity. Finally she said, "No. I use it every day, and when what I experience can help someone, I find a way to share it with them in a manner that won't scare them."

"Or cause them to abandon you," Will added with a hint of challenge in his voice.

Ottum stood beside him, taking in slow and deep breaths. She hadn't closed Will out, but her mind was focused exclusively on her breathing. Any emotion that might have been present was lost in the concentration.

For Will, part of tending his health was learning to change his focus from anything else going on around him to his training. He was good at it, possibly better than most. Ottum, he realized, was a master. It would have taken grave danger for Will to have altered his focus so quickly. He wondered if she perceived his statement as a significant danger, or if she simply didn't want to share that part of her life with him. *Maybe she just hopes I'll take a hint and change the subject.*

"It comes from fighting," Ottum said quietly.

Will realized he had once again forgot to close his mind to her. "What does?"

"My ability to change my concentration comes from the many times I've faced Avils. Kai's and my life often depends on the ability to stay focused on what is happening now and to let go of all emotion. We train to improve it, of course, but it's the fighting that creates the difference between your and my skill level. After enough fights, it's habit. It doesn't require great danger to change focus as I did," Ottum said, "only the desire to do so."

"That doesn't mean that you didn't perceive my comment as dangerous," Will challenged.

"Perhaps, but it also doesn't mean I did. Regardless, it isn't something I want to keep talking about right now." Ottum closed her mind and verbally asked "Shall we go in and start dinner?"

Will watched her closely for a brief moment before he nodded. As he opened the door, he also closed his mind. After a few hours of speaking Path, he welcomed the relative quiet of hearing only his own thoughts.

Ottum was experiencing her own relief at not sharing so much with Will. Even though others had always known at least some of her emotions when she spoke in Path, she'd consistently worked to hide them from most people. She realized it was going to take some time to get used to letting others know how she felt.

"Shall we have squirrel or deer tonight?" Will asked.

"Deer sounds good, please." She removed a few dried greens from the storage area, added them and water to a pan, and set them to cooking. What would have been a comfortable silence before today was now filled with an edge of tension. Ottum found herself feeling irritated Will had asked her so many personal questions all at once. She knew that hours before she'd found it to be sweet, but that didn't change that right now she felt like he'd been pushy.

It was one thing to ask her all of the questions he had, but it was completely another that he thought he had the right to challenge her answers or to imply she wasn't being fully truthful. And while she was on the subject of truth, she wondered what it was about his identifying with her earlier comment that bothered her. It was as though he had twisted what she'd said and was using it to justify something. She'd spoken Path for years, but experiencing someone else's emotion was a completely different task. So many emotions had been transmitted in that moment with Will that she couldn't hold them all in sequence or accurately decipher the picture they painted. But she definitely felt he was using her answer to justify something.

"I'm sorry."

Will spoke it in Path and the genuine regret he felt was unmistakable. For a brief moment, Ottum wondered if she'd left her thoughts open to him. She realized she wouldn't have to open them now in order to answer if that were the case, but she had no idea what he was apologizing for. "Hmmm?"

"I felt like we'd been holding each other at a distance since Kai and Saul left. I wanted to change that, but not wanting to be the first to be vulnerable, I asked you a lot of questions. You answered most, if not all of them. Instead of realizing you'd gone where I'd been unwilling to and instead of accepting it was my turn to share with you, I decided to call you on one of your answers. I rudely pointed out something you might not have been aware of or that is so painful you didn't want to discuss it. I even managed to feel angry you weren't so delighted by my discovery that you felt compelled to discuss it at length with me. I behaved like an ass, and I'm sorry."

Will had just apologized for the very thing Ottum had been irritated about. The apology was sincere, but she still felt angry that he'd pushed. Holding on to her anger made it feel justified. However, Ottum realized she was being petty, so she did her best to let it drain away.

Ottum smiled at Will. "It did seem like we'd been holding each other at a distance, and I'm glad you began the process of changing that. Being vulnerable isn't something I'm good at anyway, so it didn't sit well that you pushed me even further when I was already pushing myself into uncomfortable territory. It might have been different if we'd both been sharing things, but we weren't."

"We'll have to change that," Will said with an almost shy look. "However, I feel compelled to admit that vulnerability isn't my strongest quality either."

"So you won't be terribly upset if I suggest we enjoy our evening and leave further questions until tomorrow?" Ottum asked.

"If I do a little happy-dance will you know my answer is yes?" he asked as Will broke into what could loosely be called a dance.

Ottum laughed. In answer to his question, she joined him in cavorting about the cabin.

The rest of the day passed with light conversation and the same easy playfulness they'd share earlier. When they went to bed, Ottum laid awake thinking through the day. She tried to decide if there was truth in the "so they won't abandon you" comment Will had made, and she wondered what it was that Will would want to justify.

All of that was fresh on her mind as she drifted to sleep, so it startled her to suddenly be aware of Oscar.

"You look surprised," Oscar said with a wry grin. "Just because I've been letting you decide when we meet doesn't mean that I can't visit you from time to time on my own whim, does it?"

"Something tells me it would be difficult to stop you even if I wanted to," Ottum shot back with an equal amount of orneriness. She didn't understand how it was possible, but she had accepted these meetings with Oscar as extremely enjoyable regardless of the status of their reality.

"However, I do prefer my setting to yours. Two in one bed seems plenty," he said.

She couldn't see his face, but there was no need to see his features to know that he had noted the intimate position she and Will lay in. The setting changed to an outdoor view. Large pine trees with snow caressing each branch surrounded a blazing fire ring.

"Those were some interesting questions Will asked you today, weren't they?" Oscar asked as he moved to sit down on a log beside the fire.

"I suppose 'interesting' is as good a word as any," Ottum said as she sat down beside him. Suddenly it occurred to her that Oscar might know what it was that had made her feel uncomfortable when Will had identified with her comments about making a difference. "Why didn't I like it when he got excited about my answer as to why I continue Chasing when it may only make a difference to a few people?"

"You are close in your thoughts that he is justifying something," Oscar replied.

"Okay. So what is it that he's justifying?" Ottum asked. "And why don't you just spit out the answer, because you know I'm going to keep asking questions until you do."

Oscar laughed. "My, you are getting bossy in your old age!"

"If I'm getting old, then you're already ancient!" she teased.

"Nonsense! My beauty is timeless." He struck a pose that was at least beautifully comical.

Ottum laughed but would not be swayed from getting her answer. "Seriously, Oscar, the change in Will didn't leave me with a warm and relaxed feeling."

"Will is brilliant, talented, and a truly amazing man, isn't he?" Oscar asked.

"Yes," Ottum answered as she wondered where Oscar was going with that statement.

"What is it that you like most about him?"

Ottum eyed Oscar to see if he was playing with her, but decided there was seriousness in his eyes, so she considered his question. "He sees things in a very unique way."

"Yes, he does," Oscar drawled. "He sees them in a unique way and very quickly. Would you agree?"

"Yes. He grasps difficult concepts as though they're simple," she nodded.

"But Will does have trouble with one particular concept. Can you guess what it is?" he asked.

"There are a lot of concepts, Oscar," Ottum said as she stretched her long legs toward the fire.

"Yes, but this particular concept is one that doesn't fit what he believes to be reality. He's aware something isn't right, but he can't seem to resolve it because he won't face that he might be wrong about the concept we're discussing. It's why he questioned you today and assumed it was a fear of being abandoned that keeps you from discussing your talents with others. What would make him think that?" Oscar asked.

"Well it isn't impossible that it's the truth," Ottum said, hoping Oscar would dismiss it.

"It's very possible that it's the truth," he said. "That's a question I'll leave you to answer on your own. But that isn't why Will made the assumption. How did he describe what you did when you knew it was snowing without even seeing it? Did he think it was magic, evil, or divine?"

"No," Ottum replied. "He said something to the effect that I'm aware of subtleties others can learn, but I didn't have to learn them."

"And what did you think of that?" Oscar asked.

"Well, at the time I didn't pay much attention to it. However, it's probably the best description I've ever heard. I'm not sure it would completely take away the reaction a lot of people seem to have to my ability to do those things, but it does explain what it is that I experience."

"Why wouldn't it take away the reaction some have when they find out how aware you are?" Oscar asked. He knew the answer and had experienced it himself at times, but he wanted to hear her say it.

"Well, because." When Oscar lifted his eyebrows as if to imply that she could do better than that, Ottum continued. "It seems that while it *is* possible for many people to learn to be aware of the subtleties that come naturally to me, not many people actually do. Because it's so rare, people are more likely to believe it's not possible than they are to think it's just sharply developed, normal skills. People tend to fear what they don't understand."

"And that perfectly illustrates the concept Will can't grasp," Oscar said.

Ottum watched him lean forward and stir the fire. "I think I missed something because I still don't know what we're talking about."

Oscar frowned at her. "Was Will scared when he realized you knew it was snowing without having seen the snow?"

"No," she said as she shook her head.

"If it's your experience that most people would have been, why wasn't he scared?" Oscar prodded.

Ottum considered this as she stared into the fire in front of them. "He was momentarily surprised, but then he found a way to explain it. He wasn't scared because it made sense to him. That brings us back to how quickly he can simplify complex ideas."

"So why do you think he would assume you falsely believed people would abandon you if they knew about your talents?"

"Are you saying that I do have a fear of being abandoned but that it's justified?" Ottum asked.

Oscar shook his head. "No, I'm asking why Will would assume your fear of being abandoned is false. I told you, the abandonment stuff is something you can work through on your own."

Ottum sighed and concentrated on his question. Finally she said, "He would believe my fear was false if he assumed that everyone else would understand and accept the explanation he gave for what I can do."

"But they wouldn't, would they?" Oscar asked.

"No." Ottum replied while shaking her head. Then she continued, "so Will can't grasp that other people don't see things as he does?"

"He can understand they might not agree with him for any number of reasons, but he doesn't realize that most people don't even glimpse what he believes to be blatantly obvious. He thinks they're being, um, what's the phrase that you like so much? Oh yes!" Oscar said with a grin. "He believes they're being willfully ignorant and just pretending certain problems don't exist. What he doesn't realize is that many of them are not capable of even seeing the problems he does, let alone the answers he has, without a significant amount of help."

"It wasn't my abandonment issues he wanted to talk through, was it?" she asked as she began to understand how it was that a man such as Will came to prefer life in an isolated cabin.

"No, Ottum, it wasn't. And it's good to hear that you have finally owned up to the fact that you have abandonment issues," Oscar added with a grin emphasized by a sparkle in his eyes.

Ottum shook her head at him and affectionately nudged her shoulder against his. "You know, I see a lot of irony in the fact that he went into hiding because he can't see he is different while I, at least emotionally, went into hiding because I knew I was."

They sat and watched the sparks flitter away from the fire. Each small ember turned to grey or black ash before being lost on the wind. Ottum's thoughts raced and returned again to the questions Will had asked her earlier.

"Oscar, why do you suppose it is that I'm a Chaser?" Ottum asked. "Will can't seem to fathom why I would choose this life, and I can't help but feel it chose me."

For the first time since Oscar had started appearing in her dreams, Ottum saw him look uncertain. He was watching her, and she had the distinct impression that what he was wrestling with had nothing to do with whether or not he knew the answer. No, she was certain he was struggling with how much to tell her. Oscar looked away while biting his lip and bouncing his leg up and down. Finally he made his decision and turned back to her.

The Oscar facing her seemed different. Ottum couldn't describe exactly what the change was, but it was the first time she fully accepted that the man sitting beside her was the one she'd known in life and that he was not just a figment of her imagination. Something in her face must have given away her thoughts because Oscar's expression softened, and he reached out and stroked her cheek with a soft smile that contained a depth of love that momentarily took her breath. He dropped his hand, looked at the fire one more time, and then he spoke.

"Chasing is what we all do. We believe we're on a path, or at least looking for a path. Some even talk about 'The Path.' We believe this path will contain exciting opportunities or end with an event that will define who we are. There are even those who believe it is divine intention that picks our path. We chase after the path or the events, most people never fully realizing it's not the exciting opportunities or a single event that defines us. Instead, it's the simple choices made each day of chasing. All of the things and behaviors we repeat are what we'll call upon when an exciting opportunity or event comes along. And because the thrill of something new opens our awareness, sometimes we suddenly see for the first time the skills we have been building for so long. We falsely believe it was the event or the opportunity that enabled or even granted new skills to help us triumph, but it was really the plodding we did all the days before. We are all Chasers," Oscar paused and gave Ottum a half-smile.

"You have been chasing Avils for many years now, Ottum. What do you get from it?" Oscar asked.

"I make a difference," she replied.

"You do make a difference," he nodded. "But tell me, how does chasing and killing an Avil make a difference?"

Ottum considered for a moment and then replied, "It decreases the amount of evil that is present in our world."

"If you really believe those words, why do you insist an Avil must be attacking you, Kai, or someone else before you kill it?" Oscar asked.

Ottum shifted on the log. The question made her stomach clench, and not having an instant answer made it worse. "I'm not completely sure why. It just seemed wrong before, but now there's the added knowledge that my brother is an Avil. There was something about seeing Leon myself, even having heard years ago he had changed…it was difficult to know without question what he is. He'd changed so much that I didn't even recognize him!"

"How does that make a difference?" Oscar asked.

The question was painful and Ottum didn't like having to say the answer. "Leon and I obviously aren't close. He's done some horrible things and lives his life in a way I can't fathom. I no longer love him or even like him, but because he's my brother I still want for there to be at least a chance for him to experience a happier life. I suppose in some ways, because we grew up together and share a family, I even feel like he's part of me and I of him. Perhaps it shouldn't make a difference, but I will not kill without an Avil attacking in the hopes that eventually one of them will choose better; I want one to justify my belief that, even now, there is still hope for my brother. I may not like what he's become, but I knew Leon before he made so many bad choices that he became an Avil. I knew him when it was easy to see how he could grow into a good man. Being honest, that means that I am being selfish by providing that opportunity to each Avil I encounter. It might also mean that I'm naïve, but it doesn't feel right to kill when I or someone innocent isn't being attacked. So it has become something I will not do."

"Why do you suppose that is, Ottum?" Oscar prodded.

She heard the softness in his voice. Oscar was once again teaching her. He was leading her to find the truth she needed by getting her to question the version of reality she'd created in her mind and unconsciously accepted as truth.

Oscar pushed with his words. "If you kill Avils to rid the world of a bit more evil, why can't you kill unless you're being attacked? If an Avil promises to change, is it no longer evil? How would you know if it spoke truth or if it only meant to deceive you for long enough to save its life?"

Ottum rubbed her forehead with her fingers while her thumbs made circles on her cheeks. "I hadn't thought about what would happen if one wouldn't attack. Even the ones that stop for a moment will try to attack again when I lower my sword," she said. She felt like a fool to have never thought through the possible actions required if an Avil actually ceased to attack.

"You might want to consider that because it says much more about what you have experienced as actual truth. Feel free to think out loud," Oscar said with a wry grin as he leaned back to stretch.

Ottum rolled her eyes but knew he was telling her more than asking her to share her thoughts. The heat from the fire started to feel too warm, so she drew her legs back in and hugged them to her chest.

"If an Avil wouldn't attack, I wouldn't kill it. But there isn't any way to trust that one would follow through on the promised change. At best, it would be a distrustful reprieve until we were no longer in each other's presence. At worst, it would be trickery aimed at the opportunity for my easy death. Either way, it's likely that as soon as the Avil was a safe distance from me, it would go right back to its old ways."

"So shouldn't you just kill it regardless?" Oscar asked. "Doing anything other than that is risking your and Kai's life as well as leaving opportunity for the Avil to harm others."

"No!" Ottum said emphatically. "It does risk our lives, but killing it regardless isn't right!"

"Why, Ottum? Why not kill something that is evil so that you and the world can forever be done with it?" Oscar asked.

"I don't know. I'm trying to find the reason but you keep talking and won't let me think!" Ottum shot back in exasperation.

"Perhaps that's because you're being a sentimental fool instead of thinking! Are you trying to save a childhood long since gone; a piece of yourself that doesn't even exist in your brother; or do you have a reason for your actions?" Oscar challenged.

Ottum's temper flared. She wanted to call him callous even though she knew Oscar was only prodding her and didn't honestly disapprove of her actions. As a child she always just played along and let the emotions pull her true thoughts out of her. Today she didn't want to play the games of a child. She cared deeply for this man. She'd learned to control her emotions enough that she could choose to stay calm and to find the answer he knew lay within her.

Oscar watched Ottum closely and saw the transition in her eyes as that thought went through her mind. She started to see the beginning of an answer to his questions, and he knew it.

"Avils," she paused as she cocked her head to one side, "are not evil?" Ottum's words were laced with wonder and the hint of a question.

"They aren't?" Oscar asked with mock surprise.

"No. At least they aren't innately or permanently so. I only kill when being attacked because the truth my experience has taught me is that things, including living beings, are not good or evil." Ottum searched to find words for all she had just realized.

"Go on. Remember, you can think out loud," Oscar encouraged.

"I'm trying. I got angry, and then I realized that I didn't have to be. Then I realized that I was angry at your words, words you don't even believe, and not at you. So I chose to let the anger go and to be the capable person you see me as. And then," Ottum hesitated, "well, I realized that the pause between us was the exact same thing as the pause between me and any Avil not attacking."

"And what is that pause?" Oscar asked.

"It's the moment between habit and choice," she replied.

"And why is that moment so important that you will risk your and Kai's life for it?"

"Because," Ottum rubbed her forehead again, "it's in that moment that the next action is decided. But it isn't *just* the next action being decided then. In that pause, we're defining who we are. We're no longer chasing what we *could be*. We're declaring what we *are* by choosing and following through with action."

Oscar sat quietly and allowed Ottum's discovery to settle. He knew it meant remapping a significant portion of her view on life.

"An Avil can choose to change in that pause between options and actions," Ottum said with a voice searching for a way to be comfortable with the new knowledge she had discovered.

"Yes. We all can," Oscar agreed.

"Have I needlessly killed Avils who were really just lost souls?" Ottum was mortified by this thought and felt nauseous at the possible truth. Her stomach clenched further, and she started rocking.

"Would you have killed if they had laid down their swords and walked away?" Oscar asked.

"No. It would be a comfort to believe it was always done in self-defense, but would they have picked up their swords in the first place if I didn't go hunting for them? Is it possible I could have taught the Avils I killed that there's a different way instead of engaging them in battle and taking their lives?" Ottum asked. She didn't say it to Oscar but she thought, *How am I any different than them if I killed when there was another way?*

"Some Avils would have listened and some wouldn't. You tried to help your brother for years, and he was unable to see anything other than the reality he had created and accepted as truth. You can't choose his actions or his beliefs. Nor can you choose those of any being other than yourself." Oscar looked at her for a moment before continuing, "And Ottum, they can't choose yours."

Ottum sighed and wondered why knowledge always seemed to weigh so much. "So those times when I have felt I was on The Path, when I could almost feel it humming and vibrating beneath my feet and around my body, was that all illusion?"

"What do you think?" Oscar asked.

"I don't know," she shook her head. "It seemed very real." Ottum paused, shifted her feet as though she were restless, and then continued, "You may not be able to choose my beliefs, but does that mean you'll withhold your opinion?"

"A relatively short time ago you didn't even believe I could be real, and now you're asking my opinion?" Oscar mocked.

Ottum realized he had reason to goad her. "Can you blame me for questioning how real you are? You come to me only in dreams; I've stood by your grave and wept at your death; and I have a brother who is an Avil. For all I know, I could have lost my mind and be imagining all of this." She glared at Oscar, daring him to say otherwise. He didn't take the bait, so she continued, "When you were alive, you wouldn't have believed the current you could be real. However, since we create what we call our reality with our beliefs, it seems pretty likely that I need some. I'd like the beliefs I have to be as filled with as much truth as possible. You're so much like the man I knew in life that even if you aren't completely real and I'm just guessing at what you would say based upon your previous actions, yours is an opinion I desire."

Oscar nodded. "Since you believe it matters, I'll give my opinion." Oscar smiled softly, "You should know that I'm aware you no longer believe me to be a figment of your imagination."

Ottum saw the sparkle in his eyes and marveled at the complexity of feelings. The knowledge she had killed when there might have been better options weighed heavily on her. It weighed so heavily that she couldn't force herself to think about for more than a few seconds at time. And yet, her heart leapt with pleasure that her beloved Oscar was happy with her.

"Do you think what you experienced as The Path was illusion?" Oscar asked.

"It certainly felt real," Ottum sighed. "And there have been times when Kai felt something at the same time I did. He even mentioned it first a few times. So if it was completely illusion, then it was a shared one."

"Is it possible to have a shared illusion?" Oscar asked as he stood and walked around the fire.

Ottum bit her bottom lip as she considered his question. Finally she answered, "Yes, it's possible. Many people don't believe that our actions are having an effect on the world we live in while others believe they're having a profound effect. Both cannot be completely correct. Therefore, there's at least some illusion that is present and shared by those with the same beliefs."

"So does The Path exist, or is it a shared illusion?" he asked as he looked over the fire at her.

"I don't know, Oscar. I don't know." Ottum looked away from his gaze and into the flames. "So much of what I thought to be solid truth has changed in such a short time that it's becoming difficult to feel certain of almost anything. Everything I thought to be truth might as well be the logs being turned to ash in that fire."

Oscar walked back to the log and sat beside her. She looked at him again and asked, "Is it possible to know?"

"Why don't you think on it awhile, and we'll come back to it next time we get together."

Though his sentence appeared to be dismissive, Oscar remained seated on the log with Ottum. The fire crackled with warmth even as their breath swirled in a tornado of frozen mist that mingled with the cold air. Oscar placed his arm about Ottum's shoulders, and she laid her head on his.

"You said I make a difference. If Avils aren't inherently evil and if some of them are simply lost in a false reality, how do I make a difference as a Chaser?" Ottum asked without taking her eyes off of the fire or her head off his shoulder.

Oscar leaned his head so that it rested on hers for a moment and then answered, "I didn't say that you make a difference as a Chaser, only that you make a difference." As a father would, he kissed the top of her head before continuing, "No more questions today, Ottum."

"Thank you, Oscar."

"What for, child?"

"For not leaving when I pushed you away," came her quiet reply.

Ottum felt the soft rumble of Oscar's chuckle as he hugged her even closer.

"You learned more than the lessons I overtly taught you all these years. You bite your lower lip and narrow your eyes when you're thinking. You bounce your leg when something is wrong or you're restless. You yawn when there is an emotion you don't want to deal with or you want to buy time before you have to speak about it. Ottum, you are the closest thing to a child I have. The bond we share is likely to always pull me to you more strongly than you could ever push away," Oscar assured her.

She reached up to the hand resting on her shoulder and wrapped her fingers around his. "Good," she said.

"Good, indeed," Oscar agreed.

They continued to sit in the quiet, comfortable silence until Ottum slowly drifted away from him and fully to sleep.

CHAPTER 16

"Night is falling, and it seems we are interesting enough to be followed all day," Kai said.

"Yep," was Saul's only answer.

Kai changed pace just enough to watch Saul. Saul's posture said he was a fierce warrior, but his movements had slowed considerably. They had rested very little that day, and Kai suspected it was taking increasingly greater effort for Saul to maintain his posture and pace as the day progressed. If the being following them had any tracking skills at all, it would have noticed the change too.

"We should rest," Kai said.

"We're not to the next cabin yet. There's no time for rest," Saul tersely stated as he picked up his pace again.

Kai was used to stubbornness. Ottum had plenty of it, and he was even willing to admit there were times when he was capable of such silliness. However, Saul was being a fool if he believed he could travel throughout the night without rest. If Saul were fully healthy continued travel might be an option, but he was not. And if the being following them was malicious, it would know that Saul was not fully healthy. Humans didn't travel through such remote places in winter without being in exceptional health or at least very fit and moderately healthy. If it were not for the poison, Saul would fit that description. As it was, Saul was fit but unhealthy. A human in exceptional health wouldn't have slowed pace as often as Saul, and any creature capable of surviving in this cold climate would know that.

"Do you really believe our follower does not know you are ill? What good is exhausting yourself even further going to do?" Kai asked.

Saul turned his head sharply. "What do you mean?"

Kai sensed the challenge in Saul's question. Saul had been nothing but argumentative for most of the afternoon and Kai was tired of it. He considered turning around on the spot and beginning the journey back to Ottum, but his commitment prevented him from doing so. He'd given his word that he would see Saul safely to the end of this journey, and Kai would not lightly break his word over Saul's arrogant ignorance. He also wouldn't risk his life for it.

"Wanting to be recovered from the poison does not make it so. We are stopping here, and you will rest for a short time while I keep guard. Then we will continue to the cabin," Kai stated with authority that few would have argued with. As he suspected, Saul continued walking. "If you walk out of my sight, I will return to Ottum. I promised to accompany you on this journey because you are ill. If you choose to purposely lead us into unnecessary danger I cannot stop you, but I will not participate."

Saul breathed hard from the increased pace his anger inspired. In one corner of his mind a small version of his voice whispered that he was being foolish, but in another corner a booming voice was rattling off all of the reasons he shouldn't trust Kai. Each of those reasons urged his feet further away from the travelling companion the quiet voice knew he needed.

Kai sat and watched. Saul was letting the urgency of his ego push aside the importance of his journey as well as their survival. To Kai's disgust, it looked like the urgency was going to win. At the edge of his gaze, Kai saw that although it had angled away from him, the other being continued to follow Saul. Kai had no qualms about expecting Saul to be personally responsible for his decisions, but he also knew it broke Companion code to leave a Chaser when there was an Avil in pursuit. Kai's problem was that he couldn't be certain what was following Saul. Cursing Saul's arrogance and his own unwillingness to act outside of Pack rules, Kai stood and began following the creature.

Dusk gave way to night-fall. The pace remained rapid for longer than Kai expected, but eventually the creature began to vary its speed in a pattern similar to that which Saul had done throughout the day. The clouds suddenly cleared and a bright moon shown down. The lighting allowed Kai to see enough detail to know that the creature didn't like being between the two of them, but it didn't stop following. The creature matched Saul's pace, and Kai matched the creature's until it slowed enough that it was obvious that Saul's body was no longer able to respond to its ego's demands.

Kai realized it was time to close the gap. If there was malicious intent and Saul was unconscious, there wouldn't be enough time to prevent an attack on him. Kai moved quickly, and to his surprise, the creature changed course. Kai continued closing the gap between himself and the creature until he spotted erratic movement at the edge of his vision. He slowed enough to realize that it was Saul, and that they were actually moving away from him.

He stopped and so did the creature. Kai moved closer to Saul, and the creature angled toward them in a way that let it see both of them, but it only moved if one of them moved.

Kai moved close enough for Saul to easily see him. Saul stopped trying to walk and placed a hand on his sword.

"I doubt that you have the strength to use that, but if you do, save it in the event that our company is not friendly," Kai said.

Saul let his hand drop. "I thought you were returning to your beloved Ottum." Path only amplified the resentment Saul felt toward Kai.

"As a Companion, I cannot leave if an Avil is present." *Regardless of the irresponsible actions of the Chaser I am with,* he thought to himself.

Saul stopped and looked toward the creature. "So, it's an Avil chasing us?"

"I do not know what it is. When I stopped following you, it did not," Kai said. "Are you ready to rest now, or are you going to persist in this ignorance until you lose consciousness?"

"We're close to the cabin. There's no reason to stop now," Saul said.

Kai decided that anger would be a waste of energy. "If it is an Avil, we will lead it to Will's cabin."

Saul's internal chatter was again telling him that Kai was right, but the same voice that had encouraged him to keep walking earlier was still babbling. "It isn't like he has only one. Besides, Will told us to use the cabins. He knows that we can't be responsible for them."

It was times like these when Kai wished that he was human if for no other reason than to have fists. A well timed punch might not change Saul's mind, but it could knock him out so that Kai didn't have to listen to such obscenity. Saul was not going to listen to reason, but if Saul persisted, his body would shut down his mind's consciousness in order to save itself from the stupidity of its owner's ego. Kai decided to trust that would happen before they reached the cabin.

Kai followed in silence, watched the creature, and considered how he would keep an unconscious Saul safe and alive.

Kai could keep the Avil at bay, but keeping Saul warm enough to survive an unsheltered and fireless night in this cold was a more difficult challenge. As that thought ended, Saul dropped.

Kai's first concern was that their follower would attack, but it showed no signs of doing so. His second concern was that Saul had fallen face first into the snow and needed to be turned. There was no way to turn him without either putting Saul between himself and the creature or else turning his back on the creature. Turning his back was too much of a risk.

Never taking his eyes off the creature, Kai grabbed Saul's sleeve and pulled. Had Saul not collapsed as the result of his own arrogance, Kai would have fully turned him over. As it was, he freed Saul's face from the snow but left his lower body twisted; Saul's sword in its sheath pierced the snow leaving its handle in the air and bare. Kai considered removing Saul's sword — not for Saul's comfort, but for Kai's own safety.

The being that had followed them watched in still silence. Kai decided against removing the sword and settled on standing at Saul's feet. The creature stood where it had stopped when Saul fell. Kai was aware that neither of them had so much as glanced away from the other. Finally the other creature moved.

Kai watched with interest as the creature, always keeping an eye on Saul and Kai, gathered wood. Initially Kai thought that it was planning to build a fire or a make-shift shelter. It didn't take long to realize that he was wrong on both accounts. The creature was making a sled, much like Ottum had made a few days earlier. Kai still didn't know what their follower was or what intention it held, but he thought it was very likely that the sled was being built for Saul.

CHAPTER 17

"Let Lolli come over and he will help," Saul and Kai's follower said.

"You speak Path," was Kai's surprised reply. The creature had completed the sled and stood waiting for some assurance of safety if he approached.

"Yes, yes. Lolli speaks Path. Let Lolli come over, and he will help. Okay?" he paused only briefly. "Okay for Lolli to come over?"

When Kai didn't answer, Lolli took a cautious step towards them.

"How will you help?" Kai asked. It should have assured him that Lolli spoke Path, but it didn't. Kai was still uncertain of his intent and was used to the trickery of Avils. Speaking Path would be a new depth of unexplainable cunning, but Kai wasn't willing to deem it impossible.

"Lolli will put the man on this sled and pull him where you are going. The man will freeze and die if he is left there. Lolli knows he is not well," he said. "No, he is not well, and Lolli knows. But Lolli can pull him to where you are going. Okay? Okay for Lolli to help your Chaser?" Lolli cautiously stepped towards them again.

The use of the term caused Kai to be even more guarded. Few outside of Pack had any idea what a Chaser was. So he asked, "What do you know of Chasers?"

"Lolli knows much. Yes, Lolli knows about Chasers, and Companions, and Avils."

Kai noticed that Lolli continued to take cautious steps toward them. He wasn't willing to trust him, but he also knew Saul needed help. "What do you know about them?" Kai asked.

"Lolli knows enough. You do not need to know what Lolli knows for Lolli to help," he answered, and then he stopped moving.

It seemed they were at a stand-off. The creature didn't speak like a Chaser, and he certainly didn't look like a Chaser. There was something very

Avil-like about him and it bothered Kai. If Saul hadn't been so ego-driven, they wouldn't be in this situation. But Saul had been and now they needed help. Kai looked from Saul back to Lolli and growled to himself. Finally he said, "If your intention is only to help, you are welcome, and I will be grateful for the help." Kai didn't move from his position at Saul's feet, and he watched Lolli closely for any aggression.

Lolli looked from Kai to Saul and rocked slightly. Then he pulled the sled the remaining distance and lay it beside Saul. He stepped back a few feet and looked to Kai again.

"Lolli does not trust the Chaser." He glanced at Saul's sword and back to Kai. "You do not trust me, but Lolli does not trust the Chaser to be wearing a sword while Lolli pulls him behind his back. Lolli wants to help, but Lolli wants to live too. What do we do?" Lolli asked as he rocked slightly from one foot to the other.

Kai believed him to be sincere in his desire to help, and he couldn't fault Lolli for distrusting someone who acted foolish enough to push to unconsciousness in this climate. Kai found it odd that the creature asked what to do when it seemed there was really only one course of action that would be adequate to appease him.

"Remove the sword as well as his knife. I will carry his knife, and you may bind the sword to the sled in a way that will not allow Saul to draw it." Because the creature had not assumed he could remove them, Kai added, "Does that suit you?"

Lolli nodded, and again Kai was struck by the deep lines between his eyes, the grey-ish skin, the scar running along the underside of his jaw, and the subtle rocking from one foot to the other. Lolli looked like an Avil, and yet there were smile lines at the corners of Lolli's eyes and mouth, his scent was clean, his hair was wild and unruly but the hair on his chin was trimmed neatly, his shoulders were square on his tall and muscular frame, and the whites at the bottom of his eyes did not show. One arm had obviously been broken in the past, but Lolli didn't favor it in any way.

"Lolli really does not trust the Chaser. Lolli knows what Lolli looks like, and the Chaser would trust him less than his Companion does." As he spoke, Lolli's eyes darted from Saul's face down to his sword and then to Kai before beginning the sequence again.

"I will hold his sleeve while you remove the sword." Kai saw no other way to ease Lolli's fear that Saul would take his head if he happened to gain consciousness as his sword was being removed. *I'm not sure it will make a difference if Saul wakes up and thinks you're an Avil,* he thought. However, he thought it best to not share that thought with Lolli.

Lolli nodded again and stepped forward. Kai grabbed Saul's sleeve while never taking his eyes off of Lolli. The Avil-looking man made quick work of removing the knife, sword, and Saul's pack. As soon as the pack was free,

Lolli stepped away quickly. For a second Kai thought Lolli was going to take the weapons and run, but then he realized his new travelling comrade simply didn't want to be close to Saul.

Lolli attached the sword to the underside of the sled. He also made several unsuccessful attempts to pull it off of the sled and out of its sheath before seeming content that it was secure. Then he motioned for Kai to come to him.

Kai realized the two of them would be wary of each other for some time, but beyond following them all day, the creature had given no other reason to distrust him. Kai left Saul and walked to Lolli, presenting the side of his pack where the knife would go.

Lolli placed it in the sheath on Kai's pack and said, "I was wrong. He is not your Chaser." As Lolli said it, he looked around as though someone else might step from behind one of the trees.

"Why do you say that?" Kai asked as he moved back to Saul's feet.

"The sheath on your pack was not made for the Chaser's knife. Lolli thinks it was made for another Chaser's knife." Seeing no traces of another person Lolli's gaze settled upon Kai, and he continued, "That is strange."

Kai expected more questions, but if Lolli had them, he didn't ask. Instead, Lolli moved the sled to Saul's side. After watching Saul's breathing for signs of consciousness, Lolli hoisted him onto the sled. He removed the rope from Saul's pack and used it to secure him to the sled. Kai saw him consider doing otherwise, but Lolli left Saul's hands free and wound the rope under his arms instead. He also tied Saul's pack to the sled.

"Lolli is ready to go now," he said. "You lead."

Kai had debated the route to take even before he was given the lead. Although he wasn't sure exactly how far Lolli had followed them, it seemed likely he'd been walking at least as long as he and Saul had. Saul was still unconscious, but it was impossible to know how long he would remain that way, and he wasn't likely to be very happy when he did wake up. Kai hated the thought of leading a stranger to one of Will's cabins even if it wasn't his current home, but it was the last cabin they would have the luxury of resting in for several nights. With reluctance, Kai resumed the route Will had described.

After walking for a short while, Lolli said, "The Chaser is poisoned. He needs anti-poison and Adin."

"He was given an antidote," Kai said.

"Not the right one," Lolli said while looking back at Saul. "Lolli has the one the Chaser needs. How many days?"

"What do you mean? How many days of what?" Kai asked.

"Poison," Lolli replied.

"It has been four days," Kai said before adding, "and his name is Saul. Why does it make a difference how many days it has been, and what is Adin?"

Lolli shook his head and his wild hair hid a smile. "Adin is not a 'what.' Adin is Lolli's friend. She is very nice." Lolli looked uncomfortable and turned to look back the way they had come as though he were leaving something of importance behind. Then he looked at Kai and shrugged before changing his grip on the sled and continuing their journey. "Four days is not good. You sure it is four?"

Kai didn't like being questioned. "Yes, I am sure. I would not have said it if I were not."

"Hmmm, Lolli does not know if he can help," he said.

There was genuine concern in Lolli's comment. Kai wasn't used to a human using his own name so frequently, and it left him wondering if he was really being spoken to or if Lolli was talking to himself. Regardless of which it was, Kai wanted to know why four days made a difference. So he asked, "Why does it matter how long it has been since he was poisoned if you have an antidote?"

"Lolli's anti-poison will work, but the Chaser may not drink it. No," Lolli shook his head again. "Saul may not want the anti-poison. That is not good. Lolli wants to help, but the Chaser must be willing," he said as he switched from shaking his head to nodding.

Saul had been unreasonable in his behavior, but Kai didn't think he would refuse an antidote. "He will drink it as long as he understands what it is."

"Lolli is not sure," he said as he shifted the sled and moved his shoulders to relieve tension from carrying such a heavy load.

Kai tried to not let his frustration show as he said, "Please explain why you think that Saul will not drink it just because it has been four days."

"Because," Lolli shrugged. "The poison will only come out with the anti-poison. If it has been more than 3 days, the poison is part of the Chaser, and it takes more drinks of the anti-poison to get it all out," Lolli paused and looked directly into Kai's eyes. "Lolli does not understand how it becomes part of the Chaser, but it does. It's not the poison that makes him stink. It is what the poison makes," Lolli said as he wrinkled his nose in distaste.

Kai was aware of the scent, but he assumed it was the poison blended with Saul's sweat. "What does the poison make?"

"It makes a new poison," Lolli shrugged. "Saul will want what he wants more."

"He will want what he wants?" Kai asked.

"More," Lolli nodded vigorously causing his hair to go flying about.

Lolli suddenly spun, switching his hands so as to be facing the top of Saul's head. Kai guessed Saul had found consciousness.

"You are bound to keep you on the sled, Kai explained as he moved to be in Saul's line of sight.

Saul looked down at his bound body before turning his gaze to Kai. "I will walk now. Untie me."

"You need an antidote. It is not safe to untie you," Kai stated.

"There's nothing wrong with me. Untie me." Saul hadn't regained enough awareness to realize that Kai couldn't have built the sled he was tied to.

"You will need to drink the antidote first," Kai said.

"You will need to drink the antidote first," Saul mocked, rocking his head from shoulder to shoulder. "Since when did you become the one in charge? Now untie me from this fucking contraption!" he bellowed.

Kai didn't think Saul was hallucinating. It was as though he were so focused on being untied that he was unaware of anything else. Kai watched as Saul searched in vain for a knot that would release him. Though Kai hadn't noticed it while Saul was being bound, it was now apparent that Lolli had made a special effort to keep every release just out of Saul's reach. In his frustration at not being able to untie himself, Saul finally noticed that he and Kai weren't alone.

Lolli stood quite still as Saul flailed about and tried to reach him.

"You let a damned Avil tie me up?" Saul bellowed. "You worthless piece of shit. Was it not good enough for you that one tortured me? You had to find a new one to finish the job? Untie me from this fucking sled now!" Saul thrashed without result.

"Get his attention and walk to Lolli," Lolli said in Path and with complete calmness.

Kai couldn't see how that was going to help. He reasoned that Lolli hadn't tried to harm either of them despite ample opportunity, so he complied. Kai grabbed Saul's leg and clamped his jaws enough to get the desired attention. With Saul cursing him, Kai nipped at his hand, adding further fuel to Saul's fury. Deciding his actions were adequate to hold Saul's attention, he walked to the top of the sled. As he did, Lolli stepped toward Saul's turning head. He released the right handle and simultaneously threw a right punch that landed with precision upon the point of Saul's chin. Lolli then caught the handle with his leg before scooping it back into his hand. The bottom of the sled never touched the ground, but Saul's dangling arm and the bob of his head as Lolli caught the handle was ample evidence that Saul would not be yelling obscenities for at least a while.

Kai looked at Lolli with admiration. As a warrior, he couldn't help himself. What Lolli had done was beautiful.

"Lolli is sorry to have hit, but now you see. Saul wants what he wants more," Lolli said with an over-exaggerated nod of his head.

Kai was beginning to understand why Lolli didn't think Saul would take the antidote. "The extreme focus without awareness – he wants what he wants more," Kai said.

"Yes!" Lolli said with excitement. "You understand! Lolli didn't know what else to do," he said as he looked at Saul again.

"If I had hands, I might have hit him earlier. Perhaps it wasn't ideal, but it was effective. I can appreciate that you did not do it earlier, but now would be a good time to bind Saul's hands to the sled too. As much as we might want to, knocking him out again should be avoided if possible," Kai said.

Lolli showed his agreement by lowering the sled and quickly binding Saul's hands to the sled. When he was done, he picked up the sled and began walking. "Follow Lolli."

Since they were still going in the general direction of the cabin, Kai didn't argue. He was no longer as wary of Lolli, but he was very curious. "I understand how the antidote can help Saul, but what can your friend, Adin, do for him?"

Lolli smiled and didn't try to hide it this time. "Adin will show Saul how to be free."

"Free?" Kai questioned. "I am going to assume you are not just talking about his current situation. The antidote will free Saul of the poison, and in all other ways, Saul is already free. I don't understand what you mean."

Saul shook his head with fervor, his black locks of hair tossing about in the air. "The poison is from," Lolli paused a moment as though the words had to find their way over an unseen chunk of rotten food in his mouth," an Avil?"

"Yes." Kai answered.

"Then Saul was not free," Lolli said with a shrug.

"What do you mean?" Kai asked.

"Why does Saul have poison?" Lolli questioned in return.

"He told us he drank from a stream that had been poisoned." Kai stopped walking and his eyes widened with concern. "All of the other beings…"

Lolli shook his head again and said, "All others are fine."

"Why are the other creatures fine while Saul is not?" Kai asked.

"All creatures drink," Lolli said with another shrug as he started walking again.

Kai was frustrated with the short replies that didn't really answer his questions. "Of course all beings drink. What does that have to do with why Saul is still poisoned when you are saying the other being are not?"

"All beings drink," repeated Lolli. "After the poison, anti-poison would be used. Saul did not drink again, but the others had no choice."

Kai understood this time. The Avil needed to eat and drink. In order to safely do so, he watched and waited for Saul to drink. Then Leon added the antidote. Kai understood, but it did nothing to alleviate his concern for the other creatures. "Ottum removed what she thought was the poison from the stream.

Lolli slanted his eyes and asked, "How many?"

"One. I'm sure Ottum searched the area well and would have seen if there were others," Kai stated.

"Maybe. Lolli thinks there were more. Not right," he said pointing at his head with a tapping motion, "to risk. There were more. Other creatures are fine."

"How can you be so sure?" Kai asked.

Lolli looked at Kai, looked away, and replied, "Lolli knows."

The scent of smoke wafted to Kai's nose and diverted his attention. Given the direction, it was unlikely to be coming from anywhere except the cabin Will had directed him and Saul to. *If I lead Lolli away from the cabin, there is no way to know when we will find shelter. I am no stranger to long nights, but Saul is eventually going to wake up again. He is likely to be nothing but trouble. Lolli is walking directly toward the cabin anyway, so perhaps he knows who lit the fire I smell.* To Lolli he said, "There is a fire ahead."

"Yes. It's Adin's fire," Lolli said. "We are close."

"Adin lives close?" Kai asked.

"No," Lolli said shaking his head. "Adin's friend lives close. Adin is just visiting. Adin will take care of Saul." The thought seemed to spur Lolli to greater speed.

"I still don't understand why you said that Saul was not free when he drank from the stream," Kai said. He hoped to understand what Lolli meant before they reached the cabin. He also wondered if Adin was really Will's friend, or if someone else had occupied the cabin since Will's last visit.

"Was Saul's water empty?" Lolli asked.

Kai considered this and remembered that it hadn't been. "No, but he might have been trying to conserve the water he carried," Kai replied.

"Poison tastes bad. Saul should have tasted it and stopped. Saul was not free," Lolli said with another shrug and a toss of his wild hair.

As all of his conversations with Lolli had done so far, the answer left Kai with more questions. But a better answer would have to wait because they had arrived at the cabin.

The moon shown down, illuminating the smoke that drifted out and rolled through the air. The sheer volume of it indicated that the fire inside had recently been stoked. As they neared the front of the cabin, Will's touch was easy to see, albeit a less masterful touch with this cabin than the one where Will and Ottum were currently staying. It sat at an angle that wouldn't keep as much of the winter wind out; there was no porch to keep snow and rain off the door; and the cabin itself didn't fit as smoothly with its surroundings. Will had learned things from living here, and Kai liked that. He wondered how Will and Ottum were getting along.

"Adin does not know about Companions. Lolli will explain, Okay?" Lolli asked.

Remembering his first meeting with Will, Kai had no objections to that plan. He did, however, wonder how it was that Adin didn't know of Companions when Lolli seemed to know so much.

Lolli propped Saul against the side of the cabin and then knocked on the door. His head rocked forward and back with each knock making it difficult to see if it was his fist or his head that caused the booming knock.

"Hello Adin!" Lolli called out. "It is Lolli! Lolli is back with guests! Hello Adin!" Lolli banged on the door a few more times before once again shouting, "Hello Adin! Lolli is back. Hello!" He then turned to Kai and said in Path, "Adin might be sleeping. Lolli will wake her up."

Kai thought to himself that anyone who could sleep through the racket Lolli was making was either deaf or wearing a very thick hat.

Just as Lolli moved his hand to begin knocking again, they heard the inner locks being slid to allow entry. Lolli reached to embrace her before Adin had fully opened the door.

"Hello Adin! Lolli is back!" he said again.

"So I heard," Adin said through laughter. "Welcome back, my friend! What is this you said about guests?" she asked as she looked past Lolli. Her eyes fell upon Kai sitting beside the bound Saul.

"This is Saul and Saul's wolf," Lolli explained.

As though it were the most natural thing in the world to have a bound man and a wolf as guests, Adin stepped back and motioned for them to come in to the warm cabin.

Lolli grabbed the sled and pulled the still unconscious Saul through the door. After lowering the sled to the floor, he made several rapid hand movements beckoning for Kai to come in. In Path he said, "See, Companion. Adin will help!"

Kai entered, swept the room with his gaze, and then rested his eyes on Adin. She was slightly older than Lolli. Adin's long, dark brown hair was streaked with grey while years of smiles had etched their lines upon her face. Her eyes were golden brown and held warmth and intelligence. Her hands were strong and Kai guessed them to be equally capable of providing comfort or doing hard work. He also noticed that she was evaluating him as much as he was evaluating her.

"It would appear that you do not trust Saul," Adin said as she shifted her gaze to the bound man.

"Saul drank poison, but Saul did not drink anti-poison," Lolli raised his cupped hand to his mouth to illustrate his point. "Saul does not like Lolli. It was best to tie Saul," he said with a reassuring nod.

"Saul does not like *me*," Adin said with a wink. "Did you forget our language lessons in only two days?"

"Lolli...*I* is still learning," he said with a bashful grin and shrug of his shoulders.

"Very good try, but it would be 'I am' instead of 'I is'. None-the-less, why doesn't Saul like you?" Adin asked.

"Saul does not like the old Lolli," he said while shaking his head and looking at Saul.

It was slight, but Kai watched embarrassment and guilt cross Lolli's face.

"Lolli, were you an Avil?" Kai asked in Path.

Lolli and Kai locked eyes. Both of them breathed harder as the air thickened with tension. Lolli slipped his hand to the handle of the knife at his waist as he watched Kai's every movement.

"Yes, but no more." Unlike his usual answers that were accompanied by the fervent tossing of his head, Lolli stood nearly motionless as he answered.

Kai couldn't say he was surprised. Much about Lolli reminded him of an Avil. Almost everything except his behavior had hinted at the possibility.

Kai chose his words carefully. "My Chaser and I have never faced an Avil without killing it." Seeing Lolli's grip close more firmly about his knife Kai continued, "However, she chose to never kill without it attacking us or another being. Your actions have not been that of an Avil, so I will honor Ottum's choice. Please ask Adin to lower her weapon."

Lolli had been so caught up in the possible fight that he hadn't noticed Adin move toward her sword. He was still concerned about Kai, but he was also impressed that Kai had kept Lolli in his sights while he remained aware of Adin.

"Adin does not need a sword," Lolli said. "Saul is dangerous, but the wolf is not."

"You didn't seem to be as certain of that just a moment ago," Adin said with her sword still held ready.

"Lolli was mistaken," Lolli said.

Adin set down her sword, and Kai sat his haunches upon the cabin floor.

"Saul knew you previously?" Adin asked.

"No. Saul knew someone like Lolli. I mean, like *me*," Lolli said.

Kai could tell that it wasn't just him who felt as though every question Lolli answered came with several more questions in tow.

"When we've taken care of Saul, you'll have to tell me more about your new friends. He may not be dangerous, but I will venture that this wolf is very protective of Saul." Adin continued to stare at Kai like a child trying to see the secret behind a jester's trick. "Do you know what poisoned Saul?" she asked Lolli.

"Yes. Lolli has the anti-poison here." Lolli took off his pack and quickly found a pouch he handed to Adin as her gaze finally left Kai.

"You had it with you?" Kai asked in Path.

"The poison has a strong hold. Lolli could not risk what Saul would do without someone to help him," Lolli replied out loud. "Saul would think Lolli dangerous even without the poison."

Kai had to admit that Lolli was right, but he disliked that the poison had taken an even deeper hold. Still, Lolli couldn't have forced Saul to swallow the antidote, and given Saul's temperament for most of the day, no amount of logic would have convinced him to do so on his own. "He might not have taken it on his own, but you could have given him some once he was unconscious."

"Lolli did not think of giving it to Saul while he was unconscious," was all he said out loud, but in Path he continued to just Kai, "I will not make a Chaser do anything against his will."

"Even if it saves his life?" Kai asked angrily.

"Lolli does not know what is best for everyone. You are," Lolli paused while trying to find the right word, "arrogant to believe you do."

"So says an Avil who took other's lives because it suited his needs!" Kai challenged.

"So says a Companion who has done the same!" Lolli shot back without backing down at all.

Kai was taken aback by Lolli's retort. Had he not caught Adin watching them closely again and noticed what she had been doing, the next words would have been very different ones. But her watchful eye brought him back to the situation at hand.

"It looks like Adin is not afraid to save a man's life," Kai huffed.

Adin had taken the pouch and gathered a cup and some hot water from a kettle over the fire.

"How do I prepare the antidote, Lolli?" she asked.

"A swipe mixed in water to make it go down. Saul will need more," he said.

"He will need more than a swipe or more than one dose?" Adin asked.

"More than one dose, Adin. Just one swipe. Do you want Lolli to do it?" he asked.

Adin answered by moving to make room for Lolli to join her. She watched closely as he prepared the solution and noted the ratio he used.

"How do you know this is the antidote?" she asked.

"Lolli knows," he said without looking up.

"I have never seen you behave so peculiarly. Are you okay, Lolli?" Adin asked.

She doesn't know the half of it! Kai thought to himself.

"Lolli is okay. He is at war. That is all," he said as a weak smile tried to form a measure of reassurance.

"At war?" Adin couldn't hide the concern in her voice. "I don't understand. Are you at war with Saul or perhaps his people?" Her posture changed, and she looked around the cabin as though others might have come in unseen.

"No, Adin." Again Lolli tried to smile at her. "Lolli is at war with Lolli. Saul is like a…" the frustration at not being able to find the word creased his brow. "Saul is like a picture? Not right word, but like that," he said with a frown.

Kai had thought that Lolli might be mixing poison instead of antidote when he heard Lolli's war comment, but now he thought he understood. In Path he said, "I think 'symbol' is the word you are looking for."

Lolli's head bobbed up and down. "Symbol. Yes! That is the right word. Saul is a symbol of the old Lolli. He carries many strong emotions with him," Lolli said pointing to his own shoulders as though the emotions were physically stacked there. "Who Lolli used to be and who Lolli has become have different ideas about Saul. Lolli wants to be only who he has become, but who he was is still part of Lolli. So Lolli must fight to help the old part be a better man."

Ottum must meet this man, turned Avil, who once again chose to be a man, Kai thought to himself. They might disagree extensively on multiple subjects, but Kai would not begrudge any being truly trying to make positive changes. Kai couldn't fully trust that Lolli would succeed in helping the Avil Lolli once was to be a good and just man, but Kai would not hinder his progress if possible.

Adin didn't know of Avils, but she understood personal growth and guessed that Lolli had grown more than most. She also thought he would continue to better himself for the rest of his life. Both she and Kai watched Lolli as the weight of the emotions seemed to double and visibly drop his shoulders.

"Lolli needs help. He cannot talk the old Lolli into forcing Saul to take the anti-poison. He will not prevent Saul from having it, but because he does not know Saul, Lolli cannot be sure that Saul would not refuse it." It was Adin he spoke to, but Lolli's gaze turned with a sad look to Kai.

It occurred to Kai that choice was very important to Lolli. Realizing that choice existed at all times might very well have been what caused Lolli to leave behind the life of an Avil. It still angered Kai that his behavior was compared to that of an Avil, but that was something he could deal with later.

Lolli was right that even though Saul was poisoned and unconscious, the choice he would make as a healthy man should be considered. Kai didn't know Saul much better than Lolli did, and the only version of Saul Kai had ever known was the poisoned one. Still, Kai saw the look of regret and felt the anguish Saul had experienced when he learned he had harmed Ottum. Kai couldn't be certain that Saul would want to live or die, but he could be mostly sure that Saul wouldn't want to be transformed into someone so selfish that most of his actions harmed others.

"Lolli, I think I understand your problem with forcing Saul to do anything you cannot be sure he would want. Before the poison took as strong a hold as it had when you began following us, Saul made it very clear that he did not like to cause harm to others. If he does not get the antidote, he will become selfish and destructive. I am certain he would not want to do that," Kai said.

Lolli and Kai's eyes held for a moment before Kai nodded subtlety and moved to Saul's side. Saul appeared to still be unconscious.

"Lolli will hold Saul if Adin will get the anti-poison in him," Lolli told her.

Adin seemed surprised by his willingness to do all but actually put the antidote in Saul's mouth. She didn't understand it, but it was clear that Saul needed to swallow the antidote.

"If he awakens, will he cooperate with us?" she asked.

"Lolli does not know," he said with a shrug. And it was true. The poison accentuated all of Saul's desires. What he desired with Lolli and Kai were not necessarily the same things he would desire with Adin. Lolli was concerned about what Saul would desire once he saw Adin.

"Hopefully he will cooperate, but I guess he'll be what he is." With that, Adin gathered the antidote and a spoon and walked over to Saul. She directed Lolli to lift Saul and hold him at an angle. Lolli did as instructed, but his expression remained a combination of dislike and wariness.

The antidote disappeared one spoonful at a time into Saul. About half of the mixture was gone when Kai became aware of a change. "He is awake, Lolli."

The warning was heeded but unnecessary. Saul's eyes snapped open. The fierce look in them made Adin glad that he was still bound. As he looked her over, the fierce look melted rapidly into one of unrestrained desire. His interest was so intense that he failed to notice either Lolli or Kai.

"Hello," Adin greeted him quietly.

"Hello," Saul replied, his voice heavy with suggestion as his eyes continued to rove over her body. He paused while staring at her chest and when he could not reach out to touch her, he realized he was bound. Then he remembered Kai and the Avil.

Adin watched Saul look with anger at Lolli. She didn't know what caused his anger, but she knew things would be much easier if Saul cooperated. She decided that hope was not going to get them very far.

"Don't mind him," Adin said. "Your wolf and my sword will assure that he does as we say. You'll have to accept my apologies for leaving you bound, but seeing as how I am merely one woman, two strangers in my home seemed a bigger gamble than I was willing to take." She motioned for Lolli to prop Saul's sled at an angle on the pallet and for Kai to guard him.

Kai and Lolli caught on immediately while Saul watched all of them with seething anger.

"Last I knew, Kai was aiding the wretched creature. Perhaps you should untie me," Saul said. His voice was thick and husky while his anger and lust were barely contained.

"That was just a bluff to get him to lead you here to me," Adin quickly countered. "Besides," she continued with a surprisingly playful and slightly suggestive lilt to her voice, "I think I rather enjoy having you bound. How else will I be able to be certain I can have my way with you?"

The smile that spread across Saul's face and the glint in his eyes were almost too much for Lolli, but Adin maintained her composure, so he held his too.

"You must be hungry and thirsty," she said as she patted his shoulder. "I'll gladly share my tea with you if you don't mind drinking from a cup my lips have already touched." Adin licked her lips as she moved the cup to Saul's mouth.

Much to Kai's surprise, there was no resistance from Saul. The rest of the cup was gone quickly.

"Now that my thirst is satisfied, why don't you untie me so that my hunger is equally sated?" Saul said with a flirtatious lilt.

"My dear man," Adin smiled, "this is my home, and it is I who will have my way with you, not the other way around. Have no fear, though. When I'm through with you, you'll feel better than you can imagine right now."

Kai found great humor at the truth in Adin's words but was fully aware that if he were not bound, Saul would stop at nothing to get what he wanted. "How many doses will it take before this nonsense can be stopped?" Kai asked.

"Too many," Lolli replied, disgusted at the way Adin was being ogled. "Saul is a big man, so it may take as many as 10, but maybe two will decrease his want."

Adin moved away and began preparing food while pretending to not hear Saul's many, and increasingly graphic, comments.

"The knots you tied are secure?" Kai asked.

"Yes. Lolli can tie a good knot," Lolli replied in Path.

Saul remained obsessed with Adin, and while she continued to ignore his comments, she would occasionally move in such a way as to accentuate the various aspects of her that Saul was most interested in. It kept his attention and desires focused and decreased the risk that he would decide she was working with Lolli instead of against him. It was a dangerous game she played, but she saw no other way to maintain his cooperation.

So it was that when she returned to Saul's side with food, each spoonful she lifted to his mouth lifted her breasts. If he refused to eat, she sat the bowl down and crossed her arms until he asked for more. After the bowl was empty, she fed him another cup of antidote.

Kai's admiration for Adin grew as he watched the entire exchange. She continued to maintain the fine line between keeping Saul interested while giving him what he needed. Kai was surprised when Saul yawned. One look said that Saul's desires hadn't changed. Kai remembered that an Avil's victim several years ago had started yawning before she lost consciousness and died after being hit.

"He just yawned," Kai directed to Lolli. "How hard did you hit him earlier?"

"Hard enough for Saul not to be awake," Lolli replied.

Kai wanted to tell Lolli that his reply was obvious. But Kai's concern grew as Saul yawned again and actually shut his eyes for a brief moment before making yet another lewd comment. "He yawned again, Lolli."

"Adin is not concerned," Lolli said with a shrug.

Kai looked at her and saw that she appeared to be very calm. But considering how direct Saul had been since he awoke, Kai wasn't sure that Adin would understand the full implications of Saul going to sleep. He wished he could communicate directly with her. Instead, Kai observed Saul closely. Despite Saul's state of arousal, his breathing was slowing. The depth of each breath was still there, but the rate was less. Saul's eyes were open an equal amount to each other, and while the comments were still just as vulgar as they had been, Saul was speaking coherently. If Saul was suffering ill-effects from Lolli's hit, the obvious signs were not showing.

"Could the antidote cause him to sleep?" Kai asked.

"No," was Lolli's only reply.

Saul's entire body went limp quickly which alarmed Kai further.

"Well, he's something else, isn't he?" Adin asked quietly. "He should sleep quite nicely and give us all a break for a few hours." It was the first that Adin gave any sign of how much she disliked Saul's behavior.

Lolli giggled as he realized that the food Saul had consumed was laced with a sleeping powder. "He slept because of Adin, not Lolli," he told Kai in Path. To Adin, he continued, "Lolli does not like Saul's behavior, but it is the poison making Saul want what he wants. He needs more anti-poison."

"We will have to feed it to him while he sleeps. I enjoy helping others, but I've had more than enough of Saul for the time being," Adin said.

Kai moved to her and ran his head under her hand. She looked startled at first, but when he repeated the action, she began to stroke his head and back.

"Apparently even the wolf approves," she said to Lolli.

Lolli watched as each stroke of Adin's hand over Kai's head shaved away at the tension on Adin's face. Lolli smiled at Adin and nodded. "The wolf approves.

CHAPTER 18

The sun shining through the window caused Saul to awaken, but the effort to lift his eyelids seemed too much. *I'm sleeping more each night than I used to sleep in two, and still I don't want to get out of bed,* Saul thought as he worked to force his weary lids open. The room was bright and warm, and he knew he should be thankful for it, but he missed waking up with fresh air filling his lungs.

"Are you going to lay in bed all day?" Kai asked gruffly.

"Don't tempt me," Saul moaned.

"I'll leave that to Adin," Kai quipped.

"Ha, ha," Saul said without any humor. "The prior effects of the poison seem to be a constant source of entertainment for all of you."

"'Entertainment' is not the word I would use. You were insufferable. I would think you would be happy that Adin teases you about it instead of retaliating in some other way," Kai replied.

"Adin, I can tolerate. I don't even overly mind it coming from you. It's the Avil I don't care for."

"There is no Avil in this camp, Saul."

"You know what I mean," the Chaser said tersely.

The antidote had removed the effects of the poison, but Saul continued to be bitter, stubborn, and angry about the entire experience. No one in the community felt the brunt of those emotions more than Lolli. Adin kept Saul's weapons locked away, and she kept a close eye on Saul every time he was near Lolli. But Saul found moments when only Lolli's ears could hear the hateful things Saul felt toward him. It didn't matter that Lolli wasn't the Avil who had killed Eyota or harmed Saul, it only mattered that Lolli was once an Avil.

Despite Saul's nasty disposition, Lolli worked to be kind to him. Saul's behavior limited that kindness, and occasionally Lolli would strike back at

Saul. Lolli always felt bad for those moments, but Saul never showed remorse for his own behavior. It saddened Kai greatly that a past Avil showed greater strength of character than a Chaser. However, it also gave Kai hope for Ottum's brother. Kai didn't care about Leon, of course, but he cared deeply for Ottum. And Ottum wanted to save her brother from the life he'd chosen.

"I know what you mean," Kai said, "but I will not tolerate it. Lolli has chosen a different life. He treats you as he does because of how you treat him…as do I."

"Now there's irony. You're punishing me for mistreating an Avil. How many of them have you killed in your life time?" Saul asked haughtily.

"I do not know how many Avils Ottum and I have killed. However, you are mistreating a man, not an Avil. Lolli chose to change, and as far as I can tell, he strives to be a better man every day. Can you say the same about yourself?"

Saul's temper exploded. "I wouldn't need to improve if an Avil hadn't poisoned me! I wouldn't have attacked Ottum, I wouldn't have offended Adin, and I sure as hell wouldn't be sitting here listening to your condescending tone if a god-damned Avil wasn't involved!"

"Really?" Kai asked as he raised his hackles. "I find it interesting, and sad, that you feel you played no role in any of this. Tell me Saul, who drank the poison?"

"Don't you dare try to make this my fault!" Saul threatened.

"Look at you, Saul! You are sitting there with your emotions raging out of control — knowing that it is harming your body and slowing your recovery — and you are doing nothing to change it. The Avil did not make you drink the poison. Your own stubbornness, your unwillingness to vary from what you want, and your own carelessness led you to drink it."

"Shut-up!" Saul screamed. His voice bounced off the wooden walls of his cabin. The veins at his temples throbbed, and he clenched his fists.

Kai continued as though he'd paused only to draw a new breath, "Your actions with the poison were only an intensification of your habits and desires. You pushed harder than you should during the hunt, were too intent on your desires to pay attention to your needs, and you drank from the stream instead of from the skin of fresh water you carried with you. That is how it happened, right? Did your actions lead to Eyota's death too?" Kai asked.

Anger emanated from Saul like steam from a boiling pot as he sat on his pallet and glared a murderous look at Kai.

"You can blame whoever or whatever you want, but the only thing that is going to save you now is your own hard work. What you have done over the last several weeks is nothing compared to what you need to do. When it comes to improvement, the only things that matter are your actions. You can have the best teachers, the best healers, and the best knowledge, but it will do nothing for you if you will not apply it and do the work necessary to get you from where you are to somewhere better. It does not matter who you were, Saul. It does not matter who you want to be or who you think you will be. It matters only who you are right now and what you are doing about it today. Do you have any idea who you are?" Kai asked. "Do you ever apply yourself to the exercises being taught or do you just wallow in self-pity?" Kai looked at Saul with disgust.

Saul didn't move, and he didn't speak.

Kai shook his head and walked toward the door. "I am leaving tomorrow to return to Ottum. I will share my opinion with Lolli before I leave."

"And what opinion is it that you're going to share with the stinking Avil?" Saul spat at Kai.

"That you are wasting their time and energy because you see yourself as the center of the world instead of as a tiny piece of it. You could stay here for years and never improve if you continue to feel sorry for yourself. You feel something out of your control changed you, but you played a large role in that change. You have greatness within you, Saul. Stop wasting everyone's time and make something of yourself." Kai opened the door and looked back at Saul one last time. "Goodbye, Saul," he said as he stepped out and closed the door behind him.

Saul wanted to scream. He wanted to punish someone or something for all that was wrong in his life, but he was too tired to do either. "Good riddance," he whispered as he lay back and succumbed to the exhaustion his emotional outbreak had caused.

* * *

"You should watch yourself when around him," Kai cautioned.

"Lolli has escaped Chasers before," Lolli said with a wink and grin.

"I am being serious, Lolli," Kai said. "You are not an Avil, but Saul is struggling with that knowledge. If he acknowledges that you changed, then he has fewer excuses about how hard it is for him to change. The road in front of him is a difficult one. I do not know how he will react to what I told him. It might be that he will ignore it and neither improve or get worse. It might be that he will retreat further into denial to the point that he becomes mentally unstable. That is the part you must be most careful of. The most unlikely outcome is that he will see the truth in what I said and will work to improve.

"Lolli will tell Adin, and we will be careful," Lolli said.

"Good," Kai said. As much as he wanted to return to Ottum, he realized he would miss Adin and Lolli. They made the last several weeks in this camp enjoyable. He was obligated to spend time with Saul, but he never looked forward to those times. The same was not true with Adin and Lolli. "It will be good to see Ottum again," he said to distract himself from the sadness of leaving new friends.

"Lolli would like to meet your Ottum. Do you think Ottum would like Lolli or would she be like Saul?" Lolli asked. He eagerly watched Kai for an answer.

Kai had thought through the scenario hundreds of times, so there was no hesitation in his reply. "She would like you," Kai said firmly. "In fact, she has been hunting for you for a long time."

Alarm crossed Lolli's face.

"Not that sort of hunting," Kai said, "or at least not directly. Hoping for you would be a better way to say it," Kai reassured him.

"Lolli does not understand," he said as he shook his head.

Kai was used to it now but part of him always laughed when Lolli's black hair flopped so wildly. The small amount of grey that was present added the illusion of even more motion. "For some time now, Ottum has refused to kill any Avil that was not attacking us or someone else. This scar is the result of one of the times," Kai said as he nodded toward his shoulder. "The Avil's sword broke. When the Avil dropped to its knees, Ottum lowered her own sword. It took that opportunity to slice my shoulder," Kai paused. "Until meeting you, I thought that Ottum was being naïve." Kai looked Lolli over from head to toe. The contrast of features no longer alarmed him. *I cannot tell if I am just used to it now or if there are less Avil traits.* To Lolli he said, "Yes, Ottum will enjoy meeting you."

"When?" Lolli asked in his ever exuberant way.

Kai considered. "I do not know. Will you be leaving here when the weather warms?"

"Lolli has not decided," he said with a glance toward Adin's cabin.

He means that Adin hasn't decided, Kai thought. Lolli wore his heart on his sleeve. Although Adin's feelings were less visible, Kai was certain that she was quite fond of Lolli. For reasons Kai didn't understand, the two never spent the night in the same cabin.

"There is much to discuss with Ottum when I return to her," Kai said. "She has never talked of taking a mate, but I think Will intrigues her more than any man she has ever met," Kai said as he again wondered how the two of them had gotten along since he left. "Then there is the problem of her brother. I would very much like her to meet you before she meets her brother again. However the meeting with Leon ends, I want her to know that he was capable of choosing. I will try to convince her to come here when we leave Will's cabin. That is, of course, if we leave."

Lolli smiled and nodded. "Adin sent Lolli to find Will. Saul needed help, so Lolli came back."

Upon arriving here, it had quickly become obvious that this camp was the one Will had intended for them to reach. But with Saul being as difficult as he had been, the question of why Adin had been staying in Will's other cabin never got asked. After so many months, Kai felt almost foolish asking now, but he wanted to know. "Why were you looking for Will?"

"Sasha died."

"Who is Sasha?"

"Sasha was Adin's," Lolli replied.

"Adin's what? Lolli, that does not explain who Sasha was," Kai said in frustration.

"Lolli is sorry," he said as he scrunched his face into an apology. "Sasha was Adin's mate and Will's teacher. Sasha left something for Will, so Lolli was helping Adin find him."

Kai thought back to the day he had met Lolli. "You followed us to protect Adin?" Kai asked.

Lolli smiled bashfully. "Adin didn't know which cabin Will would be in. She sent Lolli to find him when he wasn't in the first cabin. You and Saul were where Lolli was going next to look for Will and to sleep. Lolli slept outside. The next morning when Saul and Kai left, Lolli smelled the poison. When the poisoned Chaser started walking toward Adin, Lolli had to follow." Lolli rocked uncertainly from foot to foot.

"You did the right things, Lolli," Kai assured him. "If Saul had reached Adin, she would have been in great danger."

"Saul was in danger, too," Lolli said.

"Saul's still in danger, but only from himself," Kai said with a sigh. "I will let Will know Adin wants to see him. What is it that was left for Will? Is it something I can take to him?" Kai asked.

"Lolli does not know," he said with a shrug. "Adin would not say. Lolli was going to bring Will to Adin at the cabin."

"Adin did not or she would not say?" Kai asked.

"Lolli only asked once, but Adin would not say."

Will had been instantly fascinated with Path and quickly learned to speak it. Adin didn't believe it existed. At best, she thought that Lolli and Saul were just good with animals and that Kai was an unusually intelligent wolf. Kai was quite fond of her despite their lack of communication. At times like this though, he wished there was a way to speak directly with her. "Perhaps Adin's desire to tell Will of Sasha's gift will ensure that Ottum gets to meet you sooner than later."

A team of sled dogs directed by a young man approached.

"Kai's sled is here," Lolli said, beaming with pleasure. In spoken voice, he continued, "Hello! All ready? You remember Lolli's instructions?"

"Hello!" greeted the sandy haired young man. "I'm ready, and I remember *everything* you told me. We went over it so many times that I'm likely to remember it years from now!"

Kai had taken an instant liking to Sam. The lad had a gentle way about him, and he cared for his team of dogs with devotion. The dogs did as he bid them not because he commanded it, but because he had earned their respect. As Ottum would say, Sam was good Chaser material.

Lolli had been working with Sam to teach him Path. Kai had understood him twice, but Sam had yet to hear Kai. The intense look of concentration on his face let Kai know he was trying to communicate again, but Sam was too excited by the pending trip to still his mind.

"He will be a good travel partner, but why is it you feel I need a ride?" Kai asked Lolli.

Not knowing that Kai was speaking to Lolli, Sam interrupted. "Thanks for talking my folks into letting me go, Lolli! It will be good for the team to get some exercise on a longer run."

"Sam is welcome. Sam will make sure the new people do not see Kai. New people do not like wolves. Adin and Lolli tell them wolves are not bad, but they do not listen."

Lolli was shaking his head about in the comical way that Kai had grown to enjoy, but there was nothing comical about the emotion visible on his face. In the months that Kai had known Lolli, anger had never been present with such intensity.

"These new people…they are killing my kind on sight?" Kai asked.

Lolli nodded, his face looking more like an Avil than Kai cared for. A shadow crossed his face, his skin became mottled red and grey, and his nostrils flared. Even Sam noticed and involuntarily took a step away from Lolli. Gaining control of his anger, Lolli shook himself all over and then smiled at both of them. "Sam will keep Kai safe, and Kai will keep Sam safe."

"And we'll both keep the rest of the team safe too," Sam said, reassuring himself as much as anyone else.

"Not that she will believe you, but give Adin my regards," Kai told Lolli. "Remember to use caution with Saul. Sam may need some extra time since this is his first trip alone, so we need to be on our way. Please tell him that I am grateful for his companionship on the first leg of my return. Since he is young and may be tempted to extend his help, remind him that he is to return tomorrow."

Lolli did as asked while Kai went to the lead dog.

"I think it might be best if you rode on the sled until we are further along," Sam said as he went down the line checking gear one last time and making sure all was ready.

Kai didn't like the thought, but realized it was in his best interest to do so. Kai had thought Adin was trying to keep an eye on him when they came to the camp. Now he realized that she had been protecting him. He lightly leapt onto the sled and Sam placed a blanket over him. From a distance, Kai would look like Sam's prey.

Sam whistled and the dogs dug in, sending them on their way.

"Goodbye, my friend," Kai said to Lolli as the sled slid by, snow crunching beneath it and the feet of the dogs. The horses in the nearby pen pranced with jealousy that they weren't the ones heading out for a run.

"Goodbye, friend Kai! Goodbye Sam!" Lolli said waving to all of them. The anger of earlier had left and sadness took its place on Lolli's face. He watched until his friends and their sled were out of sight. *Lolli is Kai's friend.* The thought brought a smile that frequented Lolli's face throughout the rest of the day.

CHAPTER 19

Ottum awoke refreshed but with her mind already wrestling with parts of the conversation she and Oscar had shared. So much had changed in such a short time, and the things she had been made aware of last night brought with them even more change. She longed to escape somewhere alone to have time to sort it all out and to hear Kai's thoughts. *Is Kai really so much a part of me that I consider myself alone even when with him?* She had never really considered how much a part of her life Kai was until he was gone. But he was gone, and until they were together again, a piece of her would feel like it was missing.

Will slept peacefully beside her. His black hair was disheveled, and she was tempted to feel its silkiness between her fingers. She suspected she would wake him if she gave in to that temptation. Will was not a Chaser or an unfamiliar, but he spoke in Path and had an insatiable appetite for understanding the world around him. Ottum wasn't sure if she found his mind or his appearance to be more arousing. The combination caused her thoughts to wander down the road of an intoxicating fantasy.

I think the time is not far away when fantasy won't be necessary, but for today, I either need to stop or else follow through. She looked with longing at Will and decided that for today, distraction would be the path to take. *Path,* she thought, *If The Path is nothing more than a shared illusion, then what does it mean to speak in Path? How is it that communication of that sort is possible between Chasers and Companions but not with unfamiliars? How did Will learn it so quickly when he isn't Chaser or Companion? So many questions to answer and things to sort out...*

Will stirred as if sensing her stare, but his breathing deepened again in mere seconds.

This is doing me no good, Ottum chastised herself. *Will is too close for me to be focused for very long. I'm not answering any of the questions I have, and every trail of thought leads back to him.* She slipped out of bed, added wood to the fire, donned her gear, and headed outside to walk answers out of some of the questions she had.

The cold air slapped her face and sent a shiver rippling through her. Snow had stopped falling, but a deep layer of it now covered everything. She wound her scarf so as to more fully cover her face and set off toward the stream.

The sky remained grey despite the dawn. Whirling eddies of snow raced across the ground like ghosts of the leaves and needles beneath it. The trees whispered as the wind danced with them, but the world Ottum walked in was mostly silent. Even her thoughts stopped their previously constant questions and ponderings. She walked in complete but temporary peace. Ultimately the same questions she had awoke with returned.

By the time she reached the stream, Ottum's inner world was in turmoil again. The water babbled over rocks the way her thoughts tumbled over each other in her mind.

So much of what I know has changed in a very short time. She replayed the conversation she and Oscar had shared. *If Avils aren't inherently evil because they always have a choice, then it isn't likely that I'm inherently a Chaser without it having been my choice. It doesn't matter that I was unable to see other choices or that events shaped me so as to make this seem the only life to lead, I could have turned from it.* She stood staring at the flow of water within the banks of the stream. *I can still turn from it,* she realized. *I'm like this stream that has travelled the same path for so long that it seems the only option. It will take a lot of growth to flood beyond my self-made banks, but it's possible.*

Restless, she started walking again. Ottum wanted to find a way to create a new future, but instead, she retraced her past. Looking back with the thought that her life might not have been prearranged for her, she was aware for the first time of the choices she made along the way as well as why she made them. She found it to be similar to evaluating another's life when you know how it ends for them. It's much easier to see the 'why' and the 'how' when your perceptions and misconceptions aren't altering the view.

As she walked, she sorted through many of the questions Oscar had asked, and this time she found answers. It weighed heavily that she had killed Avils when there might have been other options. *It will take some time to forgive myself for not trying other things,* she sighed. As it was, nausea nearly overwhelmed her each time she thought about it. She knew she needed to think about it though. She knew it because her brother hadn't poisoned Saul and planned their meeting without also planning on seeing the end result of his actions. He would return, and when he did, Ottum would have to face him. *I don't want to cross that bridge without thinking through what might be on the other side. What will I do when Leon is standing in front of me?*

Ottum had walked in a large loop away from the stream and was now returning. She looked in front of her and shook her head. The log Kai and

Saul had used as a bridge lay within her view. She walked to it and looked across. *Now **that** is timing.*

"Goodbye, my lady," Kai had said that day. Ottum felt just as much heartache at his absence today as she did then.

"Kai, I wish you were here," she whispered to her surroundings. Knowing her wish would not be granted that day, she continued her walk to the cabin.

CHAPTER 20

Ottum felt a rush of warmth escape as she opened the cabin door and hurried in. The aroma of food filled her senses, and her stomach rumbled.

"Good morning for a walk?" Will asked as their eyes met. He stirred their breakfast and waited for a reply.

Ottum nodded. "Lots of snow from last night and a little cold, but it was peaceful." She continued freeing herself from the extra layering of clothes that had been needed outside. "It's nice to be back inside with a fire though."

"There's hot water for tea if you're interested," Will nodded to the pot on the stove.

"That sounds delicious! However, the fire is tempting me more at the moment. I'll warm up a touch and then get some." *I'm getting soft. A few months in a cabin with Kai and now time here with Will, and the cold from a little walk penetrates as deeply as being in it all day used to.*

Ottum moved to the fireplace and stood watching the flames lick against the logs. *It's strange,* she thought, *how perspective changes everything.* She turned to see Will sipping his tea and watching her. *I want him, but what will choosing him mean for my life? And will he choose me?*

"That's quite a look you're giving me. Care to share it in Path?" Will asked.

A slow smiled spread across her angular face. "Perhaps later."

"That must have been some walk you took," he said with a raised brow.

"What makes you say that?" she asked as she admired his handsome face.

"Last night I went to sleep beside the woman who showed up at my cabin nearly two months ago. This morning, the woman Kai pictures when he thinks of you walked through my door. While you are one and the same, the contrast is striking. So I'm thinking that must have been some walk," Will said.

"Which version of me do you prefer?" Ottum asked.

"I don't know yet."

Ottum expected there to be orneriness behind his comment, but Will appeared sincere.

"Which one do *you* prefer?" he asked.

There it is again, Ottum thought, *the ability to see from an angle that most people never even think of.* "Well, given that Kai always wants to see me as the best person I can be, I think I prefer this one."

"So what did you decide during your walk that caused the change?" Will asked.

"Multiple things," she paused and smiled at him. "Including that it's time, or maybe past time, to take a real bath."

Will burst into laughter. "I see. Somehow I doubt that particular revelation is at the heart of the change."

"Nonetheless," she grinned, "it's a revelation I intend to do something about today. You seem to be a highly resourceful man. Where might I get a good bath?"

Will realized she was serious when she continued to wait for an answer. "I have a bath of sorts by the stream that I use in warmer weather. Once it gets cold, well, if the stink gets bad enough I go outside with a couple kettles of heated water and some soap. It might not be a good bath, but that's as good as it's going to get if you want to get clean today," Will said.

"Hmmm. I'll start trying to convince myself it'll be refreshing. Care to join me?" she asked.

"Are you saying I stink?" he asked with mock offense.

"Not from this distance," Ottum replied with a wink.

She watched as her flirtation sunk in, and Will's eyes traveled over her body. Her cheeks flushed, but she caught and held his gaze as she waited for his response.

"Let's get those kettles heating!" Will exclaimed. "Had I known all it took to get you naked was a bath, I would have suggested it long ago!"

"It would have been a lot warmer if you had," she fired back.

He laughed and moved toward the kettles. "At least this version of you still has a good sense of humor."

They filled the kettles and hung them over the fire to heat.

"We'll need something to dry with, or at least I have no desire to air-dry in this weather," Ottum said.

"For my winter baths, I usually use a clean blanket. Towels seem smaller when you're standing in snow." He moved to the pallet, reached just under the edge of the mattress, and pulled out a drawer Ottum had never noticed before. He gathered two blankets and set them aside before grabbing several more. "If we're going to be clean, the bedding might as well be too."

Once the bedding was changed, they sat and drank tea until the water was warmed. There was an excited tension in the air that starkly contrasted with the casual conversation they shared.

"If we use a bowl to get wet and rinse with, we can probably both get clean without needing to heat more water. I realize you wanted a real bath, but given the cold, you might be more interested in a fast cleaning once we begin," Will said.

"Although I've worked to convince myself that the cold will be invigorating, I suspect you're right about wanting to be done quickly," Ottum replied.

"Shall we?" Will asked as he grabbed a couple bowls and headed toward the kettles of water.

Scooping up the blankets and soap first, Ottum grabbed the other kettle and followed Will to the door. The air had been cold when she was dressed for it. All of her fantasies of the leisurely undressing they might do for each other the first time evaporated with the blast of cold that greeted them when Will opened the door. There would be nothing leisurely about the race to get clean and get inside as fast as possible.

Will had stepped off the porch and was already stripping by the time Ottum closed the door and joined him. He paused long enough to hand her a bowl and to get soap from her.

He grinned and said, "The water is losing heat fast. I suggest you hurry." And then he turned his back to her and continued.

Feeling a bit let down, she stripped and bathed as quickly as she could. She used her breathing to help create internal heat, but it did little against the coldness of the air.

"Invigorating enough for you?" Will asked as he gathered his clothes and bathing supplies to head for the porch and a blanket.

"Yes, thank you. I'm surprised you didn't savor the experience more, Mr. Speedy," she said looking over her shoulder at him as she finished rinsing.

He laughed and met her eyes. "I'm not so fast with everything."

The sparkle in his eyes and suggestion in his voice drew her to the porch more quickly than the cold alone would have. He handed her a blanket as she approached and opened the door. Once inside, they headed straight to the fire to dry. Ottum noticed that despite his suggestive comment, Will still kept his eyes averted from her. Unsure of why, she decided to let him make the next move. Finally he looked away from the fire and at her.

"My cabin has been my refuge for many years now," Will said. "At most, I leave it once or twice a year to visit friends and get supplies I can't make myself."

Totally puzzled by the direction of conversation he picked, Ottum just nodded and waited to see where he was going.

"Most women don't care much for this life," he said as he pointed and looked around his cabin. "The ones who visited me in the other cabin did so hoping they could convince me to leave it. Once I built this cabin even further away, I became willing to accept that I might live the rest of my life alone except for those occasional visits I make to see others."

Will searched her face, but Ottum didn't know what it was he was looking for.

He continued, "There were times I met a woman who captured my interests, or at least my lust. If it became obvious that there was nothing more to it than that, I always just left. I could be completely open and vulnerable because if it didn't work, I didn't need it to. I have a life here." He turned back to the fire.

Ottum waited for him to say more, but there was nothing but the crackle of the fire and the occasional drip of water from one of them to the floor. Finally she said, "I'm not sure I understand what you're trying to tell me."

"The woman who walked through my door this morning is not the same as the one who has been staying here. I kept expecting you to change your mind about the bath, but you didn't. And now here we are. While part of me thinks I should save the questions for later and take advantage of what's being offered, another part wants to know what changed. Why have neither of us crossed this unspoken boundary despite our flirting? I don't know about you, but I've imagined what you're offering since the very first evening with you. What happened today that made you willing to cross that line?" Will asked. His green eyes searched her face for answers to other, unvoiced questions.

It was Ottum's turn to stare into the fire. "I went for a walk this morning because so many things have changed since realizing that it was my brother who poisoned Saul, and I have been avoiding dealing with them. I needed to answer some very difficult questions and to try to figure out who I am now that some of what I knew to be truth is, at best, questionable." She paused, seeking the right words to explain without going deeply into detail.

"I often felt my life had been chosen for me, and sometimes I disliked that I had no say. I now realize that feeling was just my perception. I think it's pretty likely that we have at least some choice in every decision we make and every action we take." Ottum half-laughed, half-choked, "Ironic that now that I know it was all my choice — even when I didn't realize I was choosing — I almost wish it wasn't." She glanced up to see Will nodding with a wry smile.

"But only almost?" he asked.

"Yes. Only almost," she said with a sigh. "I answered some of the more important questions and made progress at deciding who I want to be and what it will take to get me there. For other things," her voice lowered slightly, "it's going to take some time."

The fire crackled as they both stared into it. A small puddle had formed around their feet from the water the blankets didn't absorb.

"All of that makes sense as far as why you came back a different person," Will said. "However, it still doesn't answer my question about why we're standing here with nothing on but blankets."

"Well, I suppose it's like you said. I'm willing to leave if it doesn't work."

There was silence again.

"So we're only willing to be together if we can leave each other?" Will asked quietly.

"Is that really a bad thing?" Ottum countered.

"It doesn't seem to be a good thing, does it?" he asked.

"If we stay, it's out of want instead of need. That doesn't seem so bad to me. If we were to stay out of need, sooner or later one of us would begin to resent it. I would, at least. Wouldn't you?" Ottum asked.

"I don't know," Will said. "If we're both so independent that we don't need each other, what's the point of being together?"

"You think that two people can't benefit from each other's company without need being involved?" she asked with raised eyebrows.

"I didn't say that," Will shook his head. "I've just never been involved with someone who didn't need something from me. Then again, none of those ended up working."

"Look, Will, I don't know what will happen with us anymore than you do. But one of the things I decided while out walking this morning is that I'm willing to see where my desire to know you better will take me. If you're willing to do the same, then I don't see the harm to either of us," she said.

"Does that mean that my desire finally gets to," he paused for effect, "take you?"

Ottum laughed at the exaggerated "come hither" look on Will's face. "Well, this certainly isn't the romantic or even wildly passionate scene I imagined. Then again, life is seldom ever as I imagine it might be. Kai always chides me for trying to determine every possible scenario."

"Kai's a very smart Companion," Will said as he turned and closed most of the space between them with a single stride. With one hand holding his blanket about him, he lifted the other to stroke a drying ringlet of hair behind Ottum's ear. "And you're a very beautiful woman."

Ottum was faintly aware of the sound of his blanket landing against the floor as he hooked her chin with his finger and lowered his lips to hers. Her blanket fell to her ankles as her hands reached for his shoulders, found them and caressed their way up his neck until her fingers were entwined in his silky black hair. He pulled away, and she opened her eyes to see him searching her face, his eyes clearly showing the hunger in them.

"Will you open your thoughts to me?" he asked in Path as the hand not caressing her cheek stroked gently up and down her back sending shivers of thrill through her.

"It's all or nothing with you, isn't it?" she said. She felt intoxicated by his touch.

"Not always, but I want this to be," he smiled and stroked her back again.

"I've not experienced that before."

"Me either," he said as he leaned in to brush her lips and pulled away again. Then he continued in Path, "but I think that knowing what the other is thinking without having to say it might be rather enjoyable."

The images he sent with that thought broke through any resistance that lingered. "I'm all yours," she said in Path as she opened her mind to him and guided his head so that their lips met and locked in a passionate kiss.

"And I'm all yours," he replied as he lifted her and carried her to the pallet.

CHAPTER 21

"Did you get bored as a greybeard and decide that maybe you should be a shadow instead?" Kai asked.

"Good to see your awareness hasn't waned," Oscar said. "Ottum is occupied with Will at the moment, so I thought that you might enjoy some company."

"You are certainly better than some of the company I have kept over the last few months. But then again, you are not as good as some of them either," Kai teased.

Oscar roared with laughter. "Kai, you might have the best sense of humor of any wolf I know."

"I will take that as a compliment. Now why are you really here?" Kai said as he sat upon the snow.

"Such seriousness!" Oscar mocked before becoming more serious himself. "Please, Kai, walk with me."

They walked, the wind playing a soft symphony in the treetops. Kai watched Oscar. He had spent very little time with him, but Ottum had filled Kai's head with tales of Oscar's teachings and their experiences together. Tonight the man, if he could still be called that, was unreadable.

"He's coming, you know?" Oscar asked.

"Her brother?" Kai asked.

"Yes," Oscar nodded. "I've tried all that's within my power to prevent their meeting again, but it will happen."

"What do you want me to do, Oscar? If you cannot prevent it, do you expect me to do so?"

"No. That isn't why I've come to you tonight. No. I've come for a different reason," Oscar said.

"Then spit it out. For a greybeard, you certainly are a wordy one," Kai said.

Oscar laughed again. "You might have spent too much time around Ottum!"

"That is not possible," Kai replied with a slight wink.

"I'm inclined to agree with you on that one," Oscar chuckled. "I'm not sure she'd feel the same about me, but then again, she doesn't know I'm always there."

"Is she in danger?" Kai asked. Oscar's delay in getting to the point started to concern him.

"No. Well, not any more than is typical for her, and not at the moment."

"Then tell me why you're here, old man."

Oscar realized that Kai had definitely spent a lot of time around Ottum. He shared her sense of humor and her impatience. "I'm here because I can't save her this time, and I might not be able to save you either."

"If you are saying that you have to choose, pick Ottum," Kai said. Some Companions would have given his reply out of duty and honor. Kai said it out of love.

"That isn't what I'm saying," said Oscar as he shook his head slowly from side to side. "And although I know you would do it without a second thought, I'm not asking you to die for Ottum."

"You are almost as bad as Lolli when it comes to causing more questions than you answer," Kai said. "What *are* you asking?"

"I'm asking you to live for her," Oscar replied.

Kai knew that Oscar kept his face a mask for a reason. He tried to read what was being hidden, but couldn't get through Oscar's defenses. *He acts like living would be harder than dying for her. Greybeard, what are you up to?* he thought as he narrowed his eyes and watched Oscar.

"Will you do that, Kai? Will you live for her?" Oscar asked.

"Have I ever done anything else since I met her?" Kai countered.

"You've always been her faithful Companion, but Kai, I want to hear you promise," Oscar said.

"Oscar, I pledged my life to Ottum as her Companion. I have spent years willing to die that she might continue, and willing to fight for my life so that she need not continue alone. I do not understand your need to hear me affirm what I have already been living. But because it is you, I will." He looked into Oscar's eyes and said, "I promise that I will live for Ottum."

"Thank you," Oscar said with a sad smile. "Now I must leave. Be watchful, Kai. And if you have it in you, don't rest tonight. Go quickly to Ottum and Will," Oscar paused, "even when you think you shouldn't."

Just as suddenly as Oscar had appeared, he was gone. *Greybeards are a strange lot*, Kai thought as he continued walking alone. *Rest would have been nice. I'm not the young pup I once was.*

* * *

Kai walked alone for less than an hour. Then he heard a sound in the distance that seized his stomach and raised his coat. Oscar hadn't said just how soon it would be when he said Ottum's brother was coming. *If he is following me, I will lead him straight to Ottum.* "...*even when you think you shouldn't.*" *I have no idea what you are up to Oscar, but it had better be good.*

CHAPTER 22

Ottum awoke, instantly aware of Will. His breath caressed her shoulder and tickled her ear, reminding her of all they had shared earlier. Her head rested on his right upper arm, their hands intertwined. His left arm wrapped around her, his fingers rested on her chest and lightly touched the underside of her breast while his thumb rested on the soft inner mound. With each breath Will took, she felt the hair on his chest press softly against her shoulders and back. The front of his thighs and hips pressed against the back of hers and one of her feet rested atop his. Ottum breathed deeply and took in the scent of him and them. *He is so perfectly, delightfully male,* she thought. A contented smile spread across her face.

The fire burned low, and although she knew she should get out of bed and add some wood, Ottum couldn't bring herself to move. She sleepily watched the shadows from the fire dance on the cabin wall and listened to the gentle crackle of the remaining flames. *If the fire goes out before morning, there are other ways to stay warm,* she thought as she snuggled more firmly against Will. Wrapped securely in his arms and pressed against his body, she drifted to sleep again.

Ottum had her sword and was at the door before Will opened his eyes. Will had his bow before the door opened, but he was still surprised when Kai entered.

"My lady," Kai said with a tired, but happy nod. "Will."

"I felt him," Ottum said with a fierceness Kai admired and that alarmed Will. "Did he harm you?" she asked as she peered into cold, dark night.

"No. Leon never even engaged me. He caught my trail not long after night began, and followed me just at the edge of my senses the rest of the way. I would not have brought him here, except…" Kai paused. Oscar had not said that he should keep their meeting a secret, but he hadn't said to share the details either.

"Except what? Does he have Saul? Are you wounded? Kai, tell me!" Ottum begged.

I forgot just how many questions she can ask in a single breath! "He does not have Saul, and I am not wounded. Oscar is the reason I led him here."

"Oscar?" Ottum asked as she backed slightly away from the cold rushing through the open door. She lowered her sword slightly. "Can Oscar be in danger?" she asked herself as much as she asked Kai.

"I do not know if he can be, but he was not. Or at least he did not say that he was," Kai said.

Ottum tensed her body and closed her eyes. "He's leaving. We must hurry if we're going to catch him," she said as she headed toward the door.

"No. Not now," Kai said firmly.

"Kai, I told you that this would not be your fight," Ottum said.

"So you did, my lady. But I told you that you would not go alone, and I am too tired from travelling here to go out again now. The least you can do for an old friend is to offer him some food and water. Your brother will return, and you can face him another day," Kai said.

"He's right," Will said as he closed and locked the door.

Will's voice startled her. Yesterday afternoon and last night Will was all she could think about, but with Kai's return, she had forgotten Will was even there.

"Besides, the two of you might be a little cold if we were to leave this instant instead of waiting for the sun to rise," Kai said with a wolfish grin.

Ottum heard the teasing in his voice, and for the first time since his arrival, she realized that Kai had returned to her. She was reluctant to let her brother escape, but Kai and Will were right. Leon would return. "Come here old friend," she said as she dropped to circle him in her arms. "I've missed you!"

Will returned his bow to its spot and got clothes for himself and Ottum.

"Deer, squirrel, or rabbit?" Will asked as he dressed.

Kai felt the restraint of emotion from Will. *His Path has improved, but he's also learned some of Ottum's tricks.* "Rabbit, please."

Ottum forced herself to wait until Kai had drank water and eaten part of his food, but she had lots of questions to ask. "How's Saul?"

"Saul was given the antidote and his body is fine. What you pulled from the stream was actually the antidote and not the poison. If only we had known, it would have saved us all a lot of trouble," Kai said. "Adin has been taking good care of Saul," he said with a glance Will's direction.

"Does she know how to do anything but take care of others?" Will asked with a wink at Kai and a rumbling chuckle.

"Well, she doesn't seem too shabby at handling a sword or a bow," Kai retorted.

Will laughed. "You got to see that side of her, did you?"

"Adin is a good woman," Kai paused, "and a good warrior. She would like you to visit her as soon as the weather warms."

"She and Sasha always want me to visit," Will said with a chuckle. "The problem is, they also never want me to end the visit."

"Will, I am truly sorry you cannot hear this from Adin, but Sasha died."

Ottum and Kai watched the weight of the news slam into Will's chest and then bend his shoulders forward.

"You're sure?" Will asked with disbelief.

Kai nodded as the first drop of liquid sorrow spilled from Will's eyes.

"I am going to rest now. He needs you and some time to process the news he just received. As I understand it, Sasha was his teacher but the bond they held was similar to that shared by you and Oscar," Kai said just to Ottum. "We will talk more when I wake," he added as he made his way near the fire.

Ottum moved to Will. He sat there motionless, not looking at her and not, Ottum suspected, at anything anyone else in the cabin could see. She reached for him, kissed his forehead, and he collapsed against her, sobbing. They stayed like that, Ottum rocking him gently and stroking his hair as he clung to her, until the sun had fully risen.

CHAPTER 23

"Best sleep I have had since leaving here," Kai told Ottum in Path as he stretched and yawned. "Will sleeping?"

"Yes, and I think that the grief is likely to keep him asleep for a while longer. You need anything?" Ottum asked.

Kai knew it was her way of asking if the deluge of questions could begin. "It is good to be with you again," *even if I led danger and heartache to our door,* he continued to himself. "What would you like to know first?"

Ottum smiled. "It might be easier if you just start from when you and Saul left us."

"Still a fan of detail, I see," Kai teased. "It is good to know that you did not change too much while I was gone. Although with you, even when things appear the same on the surface, mass chaos could be occurring at a deeper level."

Ottum laughed quietly so as to not wake Will. "Mass chaos is accurate, my friend. I'll tell you my story when you're done with yours."

While Will slept, Kai told Ottum about Saul, Lolli, Adin, the camp, and his experiences since they parted. While he didn't omit his meeting with Oscar, he didn't elaborate either.

Ottum did her best to save her questions until the end. By the time Kai was done, there was a swarm of them in her mind.

"I hope I have not failed you by leaving Saul, but my staying was not aiding him," Kai said.

"Ah, Kai. You've not failed me in any way. I wish that things had been different with Saul, but you kept your promise to the best of your ability. I couldn't ask any more of you." Ottum was lost in her thoughts temporarily. "So, it really is possible."

Kai knew she was talking about Lolli, but he wondered what conclusions she would draw from it and how she would apply them to her brother. "Lolli is, well, he is like no one else I have ever met. He would really like to meet you, and I suspect you feel the same."

"Yes, indeed! Adin seems like someone I'd like to meet too," Ottum said.

They both turned as Will stirred on the pallet. His eyes were puffy, and despite his time asleep, he looked exhausted.

Amazing how much grief mimics aging, Ottum thought.

"I hate crying," Will said.

"Me too," Ottum said with a nod. "Although it doesn't seem to stop it from happening, does it?"

"No. It doesn't," Will replied. "I'm going to go for a walk to see if the air will clear my head."

Kai immediately looked at Ottum and said only to her, "We should join him."

"A walk does sound like a good idea," she said to Will.

"I was planning to go alone. I'm sure you two have plenty to talk about while I'm gone," Will said with a weary glance from Ottum to Kai.

"I understand your desire to have some time alone, but currently you aren't at your best. I can't sense him right now, but Leon is out there, and he could be near. It would be best if Kai and I go too. We'll give you some distance if you desire, but we will go with you," Ottum said.

Will was frustrated that she wasn't respecting his wishes, but he was too filled with grief to argue. He shrugged his shoulders before getting off the pallet and heading toward his coat.

Ottum joined him at the door. "Aren't you taking your bow?"

Will shook his head. "You're the warrior. I just want to take a walk."

Ottum never left the cabin without her sword. Wearing it was like wearing a shirt and pants. She couldn't comprehend going anywhere in a vulnerable state without taking a weapon. "But…"

Will opened the door and stepped out before Ottum could say more. He might not be able to prevent them from following, but he had no intention of taking his bow regardless of the chances of running into Ottum's brother. There had already been enough experience with death in his life today.

Ottum furrowed her brow in disapproval. "That doesn't seem like the smartest thing I've ever seen him do," she said in Path to only Kai.

"Will does not see life the way you do," Kai said.

"No. I suppose he doesn't," Ottum said as she shut the cabin door behind them.

Her reply surprised Kai. Ottum could often see another's perspective easily, but when it came to safety, her opinion was always the one she trusted most. *She has changed while I have been gone.* "I believe it is your turn, my lady," Kai said.

Ottum raised a questioning eyebrow his way, but realized what he was asking before he had time to answer. "Ah. You want to hear about my mass chaos."

Kai's eyes sparkled at her reference to his description. "Indeed," was his only reply.

They walked far enough behind Will to give him space with his thoughts. As they walked, Ottum told Kai about her meetings with Oscar, the self-discoveries she had made, her decision to see where things might go with Will, and the doubts she still held.

When Ottum was finished, Kai walked silently for a moment. He worked to let it all sink in as he kept an ever watchful eye on Will and their surroundings. Finally he said, "I am going to need some time to think through some of that conversation."

Ottum laughed out loud. Will startled at the sound, but after a quick glance, just kept walking. "I felt the same way every time I left Oscar," she said with a grin.

"It seems nearly impossible that The Path could be an illusion. It felt so real at times. What does Will think of all of this?" Kai asked.

Ottum looked away before resting her eyes on Will's back. "I've not exactly told him." From the corner of her vision, she saw Kai shake his head.

If they are to be mates, she will need to stop keeping secrets, Kai thought to himself. But to Ottum he said, "It might be useful to have an outsider's opinion."

"He's not exactly an outsider to me anymore, Kai," Ottum said.

"I meant someone outside of a Chaser/Companion point of view. Someone who does not carry a weapon with him everywhere he goes, and who does not understand why you chose to live your life as you did until meeting him," Kai explained.

Kai's words caused Ottum to watch the man walking in front of them. The weight of Will's grief was still obvious by the carry of his shoulders. His pace varied slightly with the intensity of his thoughts and emotions. But even lost in his own world, Will's was not the carriage of a man Ottum would fight without great need. "He calls me a warrior, but he's one too. We just fight different battles."

"Much has changed while I have been gone, Ottum. It will take us some time to catch up with what the other has learned," Kai paused, "and I have spent the majority of my life with you. It will take more than a few months for you and Will to truly know each other, and I suspect that during that process you will each come to know yourselves better too."

Ottum reached out and stroked Kai's head fondly. "Is that your way of telling me to back off and let Will grieve?"

"No, my lady. It is my way of telling you to go to him and let him grieve. Relate to him with a position of simplicity and kindness. A lot more can be accomplished if you strive to see how he might be right than if you consistently try to show him how he is wrong." Kai watched as Ottum stiffened and clenched her jaw. "Do not get defensive, my lady. I agree that you are both warriors and that you fight different battles, but it seems unlikely Will is in a mood that will allow him to see that now. In fact, I believe you have much in common. But I think that you view the differences you do have as negative things when they are not."

"What do you mean?" Ottum asked.

"You and I have been Chaser and Companion for a long time. I am a wolf and you are a woman. We are very different. Those differences serve to keep us safe and to make us better at what we do. What makes you think that the differences between you and Will will not serve you just as well?" Kai asked.

"I suppose I just hadn't thought of it that way." Ottum smiled at Kai. "I've missed you, my friend."

Ottum didn't know if it was on purpose or if it was just habit, but Will had made a large circle so that they were approaching the area he and Ottum had sat the day Kai and Saul had left.

"Go," Kai said with a toss of his head. "I will keep guard."

Ottum leaned over and hugged Kai before she picked up her pace to catch Will. He turned as she approached.

"May I join you?" she asked.

"Do I have any choice?" Will asked as he looked away from her and started walking again.

"Yes, of course."

Will glanced at her. "What changed?"

"My brother is still a risk, but Kai has offered to keep guard so that I might walk with my friend," Ottum said.

"So I'm your friend, am I?" Will asked as he stopped walking.

The anger in his voice confused Ottum. Had it not been for Kai's advice, she would have responded with her own anger. Instead she said, "I'm not trying to anger you or keep you from doing what you need to deal with the news of your friend's death. When Kai and Saul left, we sat here," Ottum gestured ahead, "and you comforted me. I thought perhaps I could return the favor for you."

Will closed his eyes and sighed. "Okay," was all he said. He started walking again.

Ottum looped her arm around his and squeezed as she leaned her head against his shoulder for a couple of steps. She pulled away to keep her balance, but let their arms remain linked until they arrived at the waterfall. Ottum dusted off the log that served as a seat and turned to find Will looking at her with tears welling in his eyes. She didn't know what to say or what had triggered them, so she stood, feeling torn about whether to embrace him or to wait for him to come to her.

"When do you leave?" Will asked.

The question caught her off guard. "I," she paused as her heart started racing, "I'm not sure I understand. Are you asking me to leave?"

Except for the tears that had escaped and were rolling down his cheeks, Will remained still. Finally in Path, he said, "Yesterday you went for a walk and came back a different person. Last night, I shared something with you I've never experienced before. But Kai returned before the night was even over, and you were ready to leave in search of your brother. When I found out about Sasha, you comforted me, but I could feel that you were itching to catch up with Kai. I'm guessing I wasn't asleep for long before you left my side and did just that." He paused as he wiped tears from his face. "While I've been walking to clear my head and see through some of my grief, the two of you have been talking and laughing as though he never left. I thought you had changed, but you haven't. You're a warrior, and one day you'll leave to hunt your brother or some other Avil," Will sniffed. "If you aren't going to change, you might as well leave now."

Ottum reeled. She tried to keep her thoughts open to him, but the emotions were so intense that it was painful. She suspected he had meant for it to happen that way.

Kai, who had apparently heard Will's comments, spoke softly to only her, "Simplicity and kindness, my lady. And stop keeping secrets."

She'd kept her thoughts open to Will as she stood there processing what he had said. She was sure he could feel her pain, confusion, and anger. She looked at him, and realized that he was getting something from her turmoil. That emotion was one she understood. "Fighting is easier, isn't it?" she asked.

This time it was Will who was confused. "What?"

"Fighting is easier," Ottum repeated. "It lets pain be turned to anger which channels your thoughts into a single focus. It's easier than living in a world of uncertainty where you can't control anyone but yourself, and even then, sometimes things happen to you that you can't stop."

Will glared at her, tears no longer falling.

The wind gusted around them and sent powder flying into the mist of the waterfall. The sun turned each piece of snow into a miniature rainbow. Neither of them noticed.

Ottum continued, "I remember the pain when Oscar died. I wanted someone or something to pay for it. At the same time, I was trying to figure out how to never get hurt like that again. Ironically, I hurt myself in a different way by trying to avoid it," she looked away from Will.

If I hadn't been caught up in what I thought was an honorable code and an unchangeable way of life; if I hadn't tried so hard to protect myself that I never let anyone in... Ottum looked at Will again. He continued to stand as still as the log behind her. He kept all other emotion firmly guarded behind a face of anger.

I've fought and defeated Avils that were larger than me, she reminded herself. *If I was able to overcome my fear to do that, I can tell this man how I feel.*

Ottum took a deep breath and said, "You're right, you know? I am a warrior. And you were right to think that I've been changing. I'm likely to always be a warrior, but the things I'm willing to fight against and for have changed. My walk yesterday was to help sort some of that out, but the reality is that I just don't have answers for all of the questions I have about my life at the moment.

Kai has been with me for long enough that sometimes I forget he wasn't always there. I was being selfish to want to talk with him instead of comforting you. I shouldn't have been that way, and I'm sorry." Ottum watched a little of the anger melt from Will's face. "At the same time, I love him dearly and wanted to make sure that he had been well during our time apart. Kai is my Companion, but if I no longer hunt Avils, I'm not sure what role he'll play in my life or I in his. That's something else I've been trying to figure out, but I haven't found a good answer. I can't imagine my life without him, but I think I might have already been unfair by asking him to be my Companion instead of taking a mate and having a life of his own.

To add to it, here I am talking about all of the things that have troubled me lately instead of listening to what's troubling you now. But before I stop my ramble, you should know that I don't know where things will end with you and me, but I don't want them to end here and now. I'd like to think that even if I one day leave to seek my brother that I might return to you again." Ottum paused and then said quietly, "Last night was new for me too."

Ottum looked to where Kai stood. "And as for Kai and I laughing and talking, you missed the tongue lashing he gave me for being self-absorbed. You also missed that it was his idea I come be with you, and that he pointed out that our differences could make us better for each other instead of being a bad thing. Kai is my Companion, but he and I will never share what you and I are capable of sharing together. Just because you and I talked about being willing to leave doesn't mean that I plan to leave at the first sign of difficulty." Ottum trembled as she finished speaking. She'd allowed Will to feel everything as she spoke. It left her feeling as though she were standing in front of him far more naked than she had been last night.

Will walked to the log and sat down. He reached for Ottum's hand and pulled her toward him and onto the seat beside him. They sat there for a few moments, watching the waterfall and letting some of the emotion in the air fade into the mist the fall created.

Finally Will spoke. "You scare me."

"What? Me? Why?" she asked.

"Well, for starters, just by the sheer number of questions you ask." Despite his tear weary eyes, a smile played on Will's lips. Then he continued, "For the first time in my life, I'm spending significant time with someone and instead of losing interest, every day ends with me wishing I knew more about you.

That's good except that you look like you're just going about day to day life on the surface while underneath you're questioning everything. How am I ever going to know if it's me you're questioning? What if I'm growing more interested day by day while you're growing less?" Will asked as he bit the corner of his lower lip.

"I don't know," Ottum replied. "If it makes you feel any better, I feel the same way you do about it. Then again, it could just be my abandonment issues. Not that I have any, of course," she said as she laid her head on his shoulder.

Will laughed softly, and Ottum felt its rumble. She pulled back to look at him again. His green eyes were puffy and red from the crying. They still glistened from the tears that fell earlier. His skin was paler than usual, but the cold kept his cheeks rosy.

"I have to admit that it feels a lot more rational when I'm the one experiencing the fear," Will said.

He placed his arm around her and they leaned their heads together.

After a few moments, Will said, "It isn't like I thought that death would never come to me or those I care about. But at the same time, Sasha was always so alive that it was hard to imagine him dying. He and Adin wanted me to visit more often and stay longer. Actually, they never wanted me to leave in the first place. Now that he's gone..." Will's voice caught in his throat. "Now that he's gone, I find myself questioning if I was being selfish. At the time I told myself that leaving was something I needed to do, but was it really? How do you know the difference?" Will asked.

Ottum shook her head. "I don't know. I've asked myself similar questions lately. I think that perhaps it comes down to there being no one right way. If you had stayed, your life would have been different. I don't know that it would have been better or worse, but it would have been different."

"I suppose," Will said.

"As a Chaser, we're taught that there's a path for each of us. We're led to believe we'll be happiest if we follow our path. It isn't completely predestined, but there are things that are unchangeable," Ottum said.

"Do you believe that now?" Will asked.

"There were times when Kai and I felt like we were on The Path. We both felt it without saying anything to the other. During those times, we felt that we had it right. Do you know what I mean?" Ottum asked.

"Do you mean 'right' like you were doing what something or someone greater than you wanted you to do?" Will asked.

"I might not have used those words, but yes. For instance, when you asked how to know the difference between something selfish and something you needed to do, it was very easy for me to think you were guided to leave. If you hadn't left, we wouldn't have met," Ottum said as she slipped her hand over his thigh.

"I do like having met you, or at least I like it most of the time," he chuckled.

"Hey!" Ottum said as she playfully poked him. Then she became serious and continued, "Yes, but six months from now we might have parted ways. One of us could even leave Nohnah for another land like Gizmania. So would the reason you left change, or would we have just misinterpreted what was happening earlier? I'm not really asking that question, and I hope that isn't how things end, but it brings me back to whether or not something like The Path exists. How do we know if it's something that's meant for us or something we created that we choose to enjoy…or sometimes endure? If there is no Path, then isn't all of it selfishness that sometimes benefits others and sometimes doesn't?"

With the hand that wasn't holding Ottum, Will reached under his hood and scratched his head. "That's quite the question, and I don't have an answer to it. I think that on another day when I've not been through quite as much, I'd like to talk about it more."

"Meanwhile, daylight is nearly gone, and we should return to the cabin. The fire will be in need of attention," Ottum said as she stood. "I'd like to hear more about Sasha and Adin if you feel like talking. Even though I believe that he might have listened to everything we said, I'm sure that Kai would be interested in actively joining our conversation."

Will initially looked alarmed that he had shared things with Kai he meant only for Ottum. *I might as well get used to it,* he decided. *If I'm going to be with this woman, I'll also be with Kai.*

CHAPTER 24

"Saul is leaving? Lolli doesn't think that's a good idea," Lolli said as the furrow between his brows deepened.

"I don't really care what you think," Saul said as he brushed past Lolli and handed Adin the bundle of supplies she had loaned him during his stay. "I've been here several months, and it is time for me to go," Saul said

"What will you do when you leave here, Saul?" Adin asked, her voice as calm and gentle as though he were going for a small stroll.

Saul turned to gaze upon her. "I don't know." He felt bad for lying to this woman who had done her best to help him.

"I see. Well, if your mind is set, then all we can do is wish you safe travels and see to it that your pack is full. Would you like us to accompany you a day's journey?" Adin asked.

"No, Adin. I'll go alone," Saul said as he loaded the food and water she had offered him. "All I need is my sword and knife, and I'll be on my way."

Lolli stiffened at the thought of Saul being armed again. After Kai had left, Saul had become better about practicing his healing rituals. Lolli wasn't sure that the increased practice had helped. Saul continued to be self-absorbed.

Adin seemed to share none of Lolli's concern. She removed Saul's weapons from the locked chest they had been in since the day Saul arrived at camp. With no hesitation, she handed them to their owner.

Saul pulled the sword from its sheath and saw that it had been well cared for. Next he did the same with the knife. "Thank you, Adin." With the knife tip still between his finger and thumb, he looked at Lolli. One motion and his knife could be planted in the Avil's head. Of course, Adin's sword would be through his neck a second later, but the Avil would be gone. He smiled and nodded at Lolli, *another day, then. Another day.*

189

Adin and Lolli both knew the smile wasn't friendly.

"Just for clarity, Saul," Adin said, "you are always welcome in our camp as long as your intentions are that of healing either yourself or others. Should you come for me or one of mine in any other way, be it in this camp or outside of it, you will be found and dealt with. Do I make myself clear?" Adin asked with authority ringing in her voice.

"Yes ma'am," Saul answered, but his eyes looked away as he said it. "I'll be on my way now. Thank you for the food and water and for the other stuff too," he said with a shrug. He'd been at the camp for months and still felt ashamed that he needed help healing.

Adin and Lolli walked out the door with Saul and watched him leave camp.

"Lolli does not like Saul leaving," Lolli said with an emphatic shake of his head.

Adin hooked her hand in the bend of Lolli's elbow and leaned her head upon his shoulder. "Sooner or later, we must all see what we can do on our own. Did you change overnight, Lolli? Or did it start slowly with a decision, and an action, and then another decision?"

"It started slowly," he replied.

"And did you make mistakes as you went?" Adin ask.

"Yes, Adin. Lolli made mistakes. Lolli still makes mistakes," he said with a sheepish grin.

"Lolli still needs to learn how to say "I" and "me" when talking about himself," Adin said with a laugh. In a more serious tone she continued, "Saul will make mistakes too. He thinks he lied when he said he doesn't know what he'll do after leaving here. I think that might be one of the most honest statements he's made the entire time here."

"Lolli, oops! Lolli means *I* don't understand."

Adin couldn't help but laugh at the way Lolli tried to correct himself. "Saul seeks the one who poisoned him. I hope he finds him before anyone else is harmed," she said.

"But Adin! Saul would not have been poisoned if Saul had not been who he is," Lolli said with alarm.

"My dear friend, I did not say that Saul would find it to be anyone other than himself at fault. Now, shall we pack and be on our way too?" Adin asked.

"Where are Lolli and Adin going?" Lolli said with a confused look on his face.

"We're going to let Will know that Saul is heading his way. Since we'll be on horseback, I think that we should have plenty of time to get there before Saul."

CHAPTER 25

Oscar sat on the seat by the waterfall that Ottum had come to think of as her and Will's spot. He watched the reflection of the moon shatter into thousands of pieces at the base of the fall. Every time he tried to form a plan to help Ottum through the coming meeting with her brother, it shattered as easily as the reflection he watched.

Ottum was young when Oscar first saw her. Something was different about her even then. Something he still couldn't define.

He and his wife, Mahree, were playing music at a summer celebration. During a break, Ottum had picked up his flute and played it very quietly. As she played, she lost herself in the music, and the flute came to life. Soon a small crowd had gathered and was making requests. She was singing when her father approached.

Oscar recognized his type at once, and not just because the life left Ottum's voice the moment she saw him.

I should have just taken her and never looked back, but that would have only taught her to run from her problems.

Oscar made an enemy that day and gained a daughter. He watched after Ottum from a distance, spent time with her every chance he could, and did his best to love her enough to counter all she experienced at home. He hoped that she would eventually feel safe exploring the world around her so that one day she could leave on her own.

Ottum had grown quickly. He marveled at how fast she had gone from child to woman. Ottum had indeed felt safe exploring the world around her, and one day she left.

Oscar was still a part of her life, but his influence lessened as she became an adult. He and his wife moved from their home in the small town of Onloh to the large city of Mandolia, and they invited her to stay with them.

Ottum agreed, but the highly social city wasn't comfortable for her. Oscar had done such a good job of teaching her that she could survive on her own, that she preferred it.

Ottum had made friends that she visited when she travelled through, but she was most at home in the wilderness. That was what made Oscar decide to introduce her to the leader of a Chaser community. He hoped the experience would make her comfortable enough with herself that she would want to be part of a community.

Ottum excelled as a Chaser, but she still seemed most at home on a mountain or in a forest. Initially she was even opposed to the idea of a Companion. She resisted until the day Kai was born. He was the runt and not expected to survive the night. Oscar's friend liked to say that Kai survived purely on Ottum's refusal to let him die. He grew from runt to Alpha at the Chaser camp. Although he held the respect of an Alpha, Kai felt his life was with Ottum. Once the two were fully trained, they paired as a Chaser-Companion pair and took off on their own to battle Avils.

In those days, Oscar had been battling a different beast. He'd said nothing to Ottum in the letters and messages they exchanged while she was with the Chaser community. He didn't want to worry her, but he knew he was ill.

When Ottum and Kai set out on their own, the first stop was to be at Oscar and Mahree's home. By the time they arrived, Oscar was dead.

I was so tired of fighting, but I left her without saying goodbye.

Ottum had grieved fiercely for Oscar. Any progress she had made at feeling the connection between herself and others was lost. Kai became her world. When the Avil wounded him last Fall, Ottum suddenly realized that Kai was a wolf and that love and her refusal to accept that he wouldn't live as long as she would could not make him immortal.

Oscar had risked coming to her in her dreams then. Kai would die so that Ottum could live, but Oscar feared that Kai's death might kill her anyway. Oscar had worked to help her thrive instead of just survive, and he simply couldn't stand thinking that his failure to warn her of his impending death caused her to be content with less than she deserved.

So he sat by the waterfall Ottum called her and Will's spot. Oscar's presence in her life confused her, but he knew she had finally accepted him. And now, he needed her to meet him here so that he wouldn't make the same mistake twice.

How do I tell her that death is coming? Oscar asked, but no one answered. *Might as well get it over with,* he said after sitting on the log for another hour without finding what he thought would be the right words.

"We've never met at a spot near where I was staying," Ottum said as she came into focus. They'd been meeting like this for months, and not once had Oscar picked somewhere close to Will's cabin.

"I'm never far," Oscar replied with a weary grin.

"You know what I meant," she tossed back.

Oscar changed the subject. "You have company approaching...company I think you'll find quite interesting."

Ottum watched him closely. He looked tired. And beneath his smile, she sensed he hid other emotions. The more she looked at him, the more she thought he looked like a man carrying a heavy burden. She reached out with her senses but failed to find her brother. "Who?"

"The much talked about Adin and Lolli are resting at the cabin Will sometimes uses when he hunts. They're less than a day's travel from here even as we speak. As you noticed, your brother is not that close."

"If they're the ones travelling, why is it you're the one carrying so much weight around with you?" she asked.

Oscar chuckled and temporarily looked away from her. "I can't seem to figure out how to pack lighter."

"Why don't you tell me what you're packing for, and maybe I can help carry some of it," she paused, "especially since I suspect you're carrying some of it for me."

"Once we're adults, we choose the loads we carry. I could set this down if I wanted to, but I don't." Oscar shook his head with a soft smile. "If I could carry someone else's load, there'd be nothing for you to carry now."

"What do you mean?" Ottum asked.

"I'd have taken care of things, and you'd not have to go through what I believe is coming," he replied.

"What's coming?" Ottum asked. "And if you believe it's coming, are you saying it's predestined and unstoppable?"

Oscar reached down, picked up a small twig that had fallen near his feet, and tossed it up in the air over the stream. "Is that stick going to land in the stream?"

"Of course," she replied as the stick splashed into the icy water and shattered the reflection of the moon that had been bubbling there.

"Was it predestined to do so?" Oscar asked.

"I don't know," Ottum shrugged.

"Once I tossed it in the air over the stream, was it predestined then?" he asked.

"So you're saying I've tossed my stick in the air?"

"It isn't that simple, Ottum." Oscar stroked his grey beard and sighed.

"Then why give the demonstration?" she asked.

Oscar bent over and picked up three more sticks. He tossed one in the air and then promptly threw the other two at it. One of them hit the first stick and both of those fell to the other side of the stream while the third stick fell in the water. "Leon tossed a stick in the air when he poisoned Saul. But now there are several more sticks that have been thrown by others in response to his, and it's hard to know where they'll all land. That doesn't stop me from guessing the paths they will take, but it stops me from knowing."

"You're saying that what is coming isn't predestined. It's just very likely," Ottum said.

He nodded.

"Oscar?"

"Yes, child?"

"Can I throw another stick that would knock all the others safely to the other side?"

"That would be a large stick, now wouldn't it? Where and how will it land even if it could succeed?" Oscar asked.

Ottum once again looked deeply at Oscar. She knew in that moment that he had ran through every possible scenario he could imagine, and he didn't like the ending to any of them. "You won't tell me how you think it's going to end, will you?"

"No." He realized that as much as he wanted to tell her, he couldn't warn her of impending death when he didn't know whose life was going to end.

Ottum nodded. She and Oscar stood with the sounds of the night slithering about them. Finally Ottum spoke. "Sometimes life isn't easy."

"Sometimes, child," he paused, "sometimes life is extremely hard." Oscar patted the log beside him and Ottum sat down with him.

"It's okay that you can't fix this, Oscar," she said. His sadness concerned her and she sought to ease it. "I wish that you could. Actually, I wish that there was nothing to fix. But it isn't your job to make things right."

"Hey! I'm supposed to be the consoler in this relationship," he said with mock offense.

They laughed lightly and then slid into silence again.

"I feel sorry for him," Ottum said with a large sigh.

"For Leon?"

"Yes," Ottum said. "The things he does are wrong, and I'm not trying to justify them in any way, but can you imagine how alone, scared, and angry he must feel all the time?"

"It's his choice to feel that way, Ottum."

"Oh, I know that. I'm not defending his behaviors or choices. It's just that, well, I don't know. I guess it's hard for me to understand how he and I share so much in common and yet are nothing alike. When did I start becoming a Chaser; when did he start becoming an Avil; and why did either of us choose those paths?"

"You each chose them because of how you believed the world saw you," Oscar replied. "You made each choice based upon those beliefs until it became a self-fulfilling cycle."

"But why did he and I see ourselves so differently even as kids?" Ottum asked.

Oscar smiled, but there was still great sadness in his eyes. "Do you really want to know?"

His question surprised her, but it didn't stop her reply. "Yes. I want to know."

"You misunderstood something that happened to you."

"Oh come on, Oscar! You're saying that Leon and I chose different lives because of a misunderstanding on my part?" Ottum asked with disbelief.

"Yes."

Ottum shook her head with doubt. "Well, go on then. Tell me what kind of misunderstanding made such a big difference."

"You once told me about a time when you were quite young. Your father hit you and knocked you unconscious. When you came to, your mother was threatening him with his life if he ever did it again," Oscar said.

"Yes. I remember that, of course. What was there to misunderstand about it?"

"I had the opportunity to talk to your mother after you told me the story." Oscar paused and searched Ottum's face. Reluctantly, he continued, "Your mother had a different version of what happened."

"Different how?" Ottum asked. She could feel her heart racing, and she was winding up as though something in the shadows was about to pounce on her.

"I had to piece together some of what comes next because she didn't remember that you were there. But she knew the phrase you said she told your father. 'Do that again and you won't live to regret it,' were words she definitely remembered saying, but not as a result of something done to you. So what I believe happened is that after you were knocked unconscious, your father took a swing at her too. That was why she was threatening him when you came to," Oscar said softly.

"No." It was barely a whisper. Suddenly Ottum became fierce. "Then why did he never hit me again? If she wasn't protecting me, tell me why he never hit me again?"

Oscar wished he didn't have to answer, but Ottum needed to know the truth. "He wasn't sure if she meant just her or both of you, and he wasn't willing to ask or risk it. You didn't know he had hit her too, so you naturally thought she was defending you. That's what a loving, well-adjusted parent would do."

Tears streamed down Ottum's face and she shook her head to un-hear what he had said. But Oscar didn't stop talking.

"That gave you an incredible sense of self-worth. You thought she loved you enough to risk her life by threatening someone bigger than either of you. From then on, no matter what form of abuse he sent your way, you thought she would keep you from any real harm. She never again interfered, though, did she?" Oscar asked gently.

Ottum sat on the log and clung to it. Her mind raced through memories and searched for something...anything that said he was wrong. But Oscar was right. Her mother never interfered again. Ottum always told herself that her mother didn't know about the things her father did and said to her and Leon, but now she realized that was impossible. Oscar's story explained so many things that had never quite made sense to her. "So it's all a lie?" she asked.

"What's a lie, child?" Oscar asked.

"My life," she said through tears. "Is my entire life the result of a lie I believed because of a misunderstanding? Is that the only difference between Leon and myself?" Ottum sobbed.

Oscar moved to wrap his arm around her shoulders, but she pushed him away.

"No! You don't get to tell me something like this and then think you can tuck me under your arm and make it all okay. You started this, so tell me," she demanded. "Is my entire life a lie?"

Oscar was very quiet. Had Ottum been less upset, she would have seen the pain on his face.

"What do you think?" Oscar asked.

"No! No games! No teaching me through questions! Tell me the truth and do it now!" she said through clenched teeth and tears.

"I can't, Ottum. You have to answer that question yourself," Oscar said.

"Fuck you! I don't have to do anything just because you want me to!" Ottum was furious, and sobbing, and furious that she was sobbing.

"No. You don't," Oscar said quietly as he looked again at the moonlight shattering at the base of the waterfall. "You've never had to do anything just because someone wanted you to, and neither have I. However, you're still going to have to answer that question for yourself." Oscar stood.

"Oh, so you're going to leave now? You tell me something that changes my entire world, and now you're just going to waltz away?" she seethed at him.

"I'm not waltzing. You asked me a question and then assured me that you really wanted to know the answer. I told you the answer. I wish it didn't hurt, and I wish I could answer your other question, but all I did was show you a truth you have been searching after for years. You are the only one who can answer if your life is a lie or the truth," Oscar sighed. "I was leaving to give you space to think. I can stay if you'd like."

Ottum placed her head in her hands and rocked her body forward and back. She didn't know what she wanted. She was angry and wanted Oscar to leave, but she was also confused and scared and wanted him to stay with her. She felt like she couldn't breathe and that her head was going to explode from the massive number of thoughts flying through her mind. She couldn't deal with any of it, so she rocked.

At some point Ottum became aware that Oscar had sat down beside her, but she didn't acknowledge or shun him. Time passed, and with its passing, the rocking slowed. Eventually Ottum realized that she was chanting 'I am' repeatedly to herself. As it always did, her mind slowed with the chant. Finally she felt she was able to take a breath, and she looked at Oscar. His head was bowed, and he was crying. In all her years with Oscar, Ottum had never seen him cry.

*Why is **he** crying?* Seeing someone she loved with tears streaming down his face pulled her out of her own misery.

She placed her hand on Oscar's leg, and he looked up at her. Their eyes met, and Ottum saw love, hope, and fear in them. As his blue-grey eyes looked into her golden brown ones, she learned another truth.

He took to me all those years ago because he recognized a reflection of himself in me and wanted to make it easier for me than it had been for him. All of the really big issues I have or had, he had too.

"So, is it all a lie?" Oscar asked almost timidly.

Ottum mentally ran through her life. She saw her achievements, her failures, the people in her life who mattered most to her, the Avils she had killed, the people and other beings she had saved, Leon and the rest of her family, her teachers, and Kai. She locked eyes with Oscar, blinked, and shook her head ever so gently back and forth.

"No, Oscar. It isn't all a lie." She watched relief wash over him and could almost feel love emanating toward her.

"And Leon? Is his life a lie?" Oscar asked.

Again Ottum shook her head, but this time with great sadness. "No. His life isn't a lie either. We both lived what we believed to be truth until it became actual truth for us. The beliefs that spurred our actions could have been truth or lie, but our actions and their results are true."

Oscar wrapped his hand over hers and squeezed softly. "I'm sorry."

"For telling me the truth?" she asked and then continued before he could answer. "Don't be. I shouldn't have been so upset with you. It was just too much change all at once."

"I know. I'm sorry it hurt so much," Oscar said.

"Me too," she said leaning into his shoulder with a gentle nudge. "Leon's life is more of a lie than mine, though," she said.

"How so?" Oscar asked.

"The things we were told as children that he believed — things about what we deserved and how good or bad we were — they weren't true. If nothing else, my life proves that those things were wrong. So while my self-worth stemmed from a misunderstanding, Leon's stemmed from actual lies," she said.

Oscar nodded.

A single tear escaped down Ottum's cheek. "That doesn't change anything for him though. Experience changes beliefs, and every experience he has only reinforces his beliefs because they spur his actions. It's why all the talking I tried to do to help him never helped. It's also why all of the things I did for him didn't help. He saw them through a completely different perspective.

I'm the only thing that doesn't make sense in Leon's world. He heard the same comments made about me that were made about him, and we come from the same 'material,' but my life doesn't reflect those comments. He thinks I'm somehow cheating to get more than I deserve, doesn't he? He poisoned Saul to prove that I'm a fake. He thinks that if I were really a good person I would have helped him too, all the while failing to see that I tried. Leon's trying to prove that to himself by seeing if I'll help Saul. But Saul may have similar perspective issues, and even if he doesn't, the only beings we can change are ourselves. Kai said something to that effect when we first realized that it was Leon who poisoned Saul, but I didn't understand what he meant then," Ottum looked like the weight of the knowledge she gained was never going to allow her to stand upright again.

"I think that's likely," Oscar said. "Now do you understand why I can't see an ending that works out for everyone?"

"Yes. But you know it won't stop me from looking for one that you might have missed." Ottum straightened, pushed the mental weight off her shoulders, and took a deep breath.

"I'm counting on it," he said with a not quite convincing smile.

"Oscar?"

"Yes?"

"Your childhood was a lot like mine, wasn't it?" Ottum asked.

This time there was surprise in Oscar's eyes. "What makes you ask?"

"It seems to be a night for learning the truth," she replied.

"Okay. Fair enough," Oscar nodded. "Yes, Ottum. Our childhoods were similar."

"Your sister that you never really talk about, she's a bit like Leon?" Ottum asked.

"Yes," he replied.

"Does she know about me?"

"What?" he asked.

"Does your sister know about me? Does she know that we bonded and that you saved me?" Ottum asked.

"I didn't save you!" Oscar protested.

"I know, but from her point of view…"

"No. I never told her about you." Oscar said.

"She would have hated you for saving me when you didn't save her, though, wouldn't she? And she would have hated me too," Ottum said.

Oscar briefly closed his eyes and nodded ever so slightly in answer.

A cloud passed over the moon and thrust the world around them into darkness. Ottum smiled. Despite the darkness of night, she could see her life more clearly than she ever had.

"You actually did save me, you know," Ottum said. "Not in the way either of us would like to save our siblings, but you saw in me someone even better than I could see. Part of who I am is because I didn't want to let you down. Oscar, do you know why you saw all those good things in me?"

The question seemed to catch him off guard, and he took some time to consider. "You don't think it was just because they were there?"

"Perhaps. But I think there was more to it than that." Ottum looked at the ground as though the twigs scattered in the snow were her thoughts, and she could gather them just by staring. "I think you needed to prove to yourself that what you did wasn't a fluke. You needed to know that someone could become more than they had been told they were, and even more than they thought themselves capable of being."

Oscar was thoughtful as he rubbed his fingers through his beard. "I suppose that's possible. But even if that's what caused me to reach out to you, it isn't why I stayed in touch with you."

"I know. All those years when I thought you were just being my mentor, I was helping you grow too, wasn't I?" Ottum asked.

Oscar chuckled an almost embarrassed laugh. "Yes. I always tried to make it so that you were getting more out of the relationship than I was, but you definitely kept me growing. Beyond that, I just enjoyed your company. You're one of the most curious creatures I've ever met, and that makes for some entertaining times," Oscar said.

"I've no idea if it's still night or not, but I am going now and hope to get some real sleep. If I'm to entertain company tomorrow, I need my rest."

Oscar chuckled. "You'll need all the rest you can get for those two. Sleep well, child. Sleep well," he said as he faded from her view.

CHAPTER 26

Since leaving the cabin that morning, Adin's horse was becoming increasingly high-spirited. Lolli suspected it was a reflection of the black stallion's rider's emotional state. Will was special to Adin, and whatever she carried to give him seemed to cause nervousness every time the subject was approached. Adin handled herself well on a horse, but Lolli was concerned that Midnight's prancing and jumping might lead to Adin being knocked off her mount or hit by a branch. "Adin?"

"Yes, Lolli?"

"Midnight would be a smoother ride if you weren't so nervous," Lolli said.

Adin knew he was right, but that didn't mean she liked hearing it. "Lolli, I love you because you nearly always just speak your mind, but it's more enjoyable when I'm not the one you're speaking about."

"Yes, Adin. Lolli is sorry," he said. He reached forward and patted the dappled mare he rode as thanks for ignoring her mate's many feigned attempts at alarm.

Adin laughed. "Don't be sorry. You're completely right, of course. It's just that I'm not sure if Will is ready for the gift I suspect Sasha left for him."

"Adin doesn't know what the gift is?" Lolli asked.

"No," Adin said as Midnight lurched sideways at the sound of a twig breaking under Thunder's hoof. "Sasha kept few secrets from me, but I don't know for certain what's in the letter I'm giving to Will." When she saw Lolli's eyebrows furrow, she continued, "Don't fret about it. Sasha had his reasons, and that's good enough for me."

Lolli harrumphed.

Adin reined Midnight in a tight semi-circle and to a sudden stop facing Lolli and Thunder, forcing them to pull up sharply. "Sasha was my friend, lover, mate, and a damn fine man. Were he still alive he would have been your friend and accepted you into our community as I have. You will not harrumph away his reasoning when you can't possibly know what it was and then expect me to be tolerant of your behavior." Just as suddenly as she had stopped, Adin turned Midnight and continued their journey.

Lolli didn't follow immediately. He and Adin had spent a significant amount of time together and had discussed a bounty of subjects, but Sasha had never been one of them. Lolli had been happy to leave Sasha out of their talks, but now he wondered if he had made a mistake. In all of the time with her, Lolli had never seen Adin show anger the way she just had. Having that anger directed at him resulted in a mixed reaction of guilt, confusion, despair, and a hint of his own anger.

Lolli squeezed his legs into his horse's sides, and Thunder started forward. For a while, Lolli allowed Thunder to follow but would not permit her to fully catch Adin and Midnight. Logs that could have easily been stepped over were steered around and avoided. Finally, after some time to work through his feelings, Lolli urged Thunder alongside Adin and Midnight. The horse had behaved extremely well following Adin's earlier outburst. It was as though Midnight had realized his rider was in a bad mood and wouldn't tolerate further misbehavior.

Adin turned her head to glance at Lolli as he rode up beside her. Fire still flashed in her eyes.

"Adin is still angry?" Lolli asked even though the answer was obvious.

Her only reply was another searing glance.

"Adin?"

"What?" she asked with exasperation.

"I am sorry. I shouldn't have harrumphed, and I should have asked you about Sasha before now."

Adin glanced at him again, realized he had referred to himself correctly, and just shook her head. "I wouldn't have talked about him even if you'd asked."

"Oh," Lolli said. He felt even more confused than when Adin had scolded him.

Adin laughed a frustrated laugh and shook her head. "Lolli, you are perhaps one of the most intriguing people I have ever met."

"Is that good?" he asked, his voice sounding more hopeful than he wished it did.

"It's mostly good except for when it's frustrating," Adin smiled at him.

Lolli smiled in return, but confusion soon furrowed his brow.

Adin slowed Midnight's pace and looked at her travelling companion.

Lolli had shown up at her camp just a few weeks after Sasha died. Jameson, their friend on the coast, had sent him to the camp thinking that they could use the help. Jameson knew of Sasha's illness, but couldn't close his fishing business to come himself. So he sent Lolli. Jameson was right that Lolli was a good worker despite the language barrier that had to be worked through.

It took a few months for Lolli to learn her language well enough to tell his story. He was scared that Adin would turn him away, but Lolli told her everything anyway. She was brave while he talked, but later that night when she was alone, Adin cried for him. Her Sasha had been a good and honorable man, but he'd not had to deal with even a fraction of the difficulties Lolli lived through.

As the months passed, Adin grew increasingly fond of Lolli. She knew he adored her, but she felt guilty every time she thought of allowing their friendship to blossom into anything more. She thought this trip was going to solve that problem for her, but Adin suddenly realized that she couldn't run from guilt any more than any of her students could. The only way to the other side was to work through it.

She took a deep breath and said, "Lolli, you and I have been flirting with each other for about a year now. The entire reason I set out on our last trip to see Will was because I had decided that before I could move forward with you, I needed to finish this last task Sasha had asked of me." She watched surprise and then pure happiness spread across Lolli's face. "I thought that once I had given Will his letter, I could box Sasha away and start a new life. But our trip was cut short, and now I realize that I was wrong to believe Sasha could be tucked away that easily," Adin said.

Lolli's face fell. "But maybe someday?"

"No Lolli," Adin said while shaking her head. "I don't think I can ever just box Sasha away. He was too much a part of my life and a part of me. I am partially who I am because of him."

"So there will be no Adin and Lolli?" Lolli asked sadly.

"I don't think there's an answer for that yet," she replied. "If there's to be an 'us,' then you have to understand that earning my affection isn't about how you compare to Sasha or how he compares to you."

"How does Lolli, how do I earn Adin's, Lolli means, I mean your affection?" Lolli stammered.

This time Adin's laugh was deep and genuine; all the angry fire of a few moments ago was replaced by affectionate warmth. "Adin would like it if Lolli would just be Lolli," she said with a wink.

Lolli gave her a sheepish smile. "Lolli can do that."

"And how do I go about earning your affection?" Adin asked.

"Oh! Adin already has all of Lolli's affection," he said with complete seriousness. "There is nothing she has to do!"

"I was teasing, Lolli," she said with another laugh. "But it's good to know where I stand."

Lolli blushed.

The horses snorted simultaneously, pulling Adin and Lolli's attention away from each other.

"Smoke," Lolli said.

"That has to be Will's cabin," Adin said, suddenly nervous again.

CHAPTER 27

"They're close," Ottum said. She, Will, and Kai were relaxing on the porch. Winter was not over yet, but today was a beautifully sunny day.

"Not that I doubt you, but how do you know?" Will asked as he lazily stretched his long, powerful legs in front of him.

"I don't know," Ottum shrugged. "I can just feel them."

"You've never even met them!" Will replied.

"She has met my interpretation of them," Kai interjected.

"Okay, but that still doesn't explain how she knows they're close," Will said.

"She knows because she is Ottum," Kai said with a wolfish grin. "And she is right. I can smell them," he paused with his nose in the air, "and their horses."

Moments later, Ottum and Kai's statements were confirmed as Adin and Lolli rode into the clearing surrounding Will's cabin.

"Showoffs," Will said so that only Ottum and Kai could hear him.

"You certainly don't make it easy for an old woman to find you!" Adin exclaimed as Will strode toward her and helped her dismount.

"Good thing you aren't an old woman then," Will replied before wrapping her in his arms.

Ottum's eyes shifted from them to Lolli, just as his moved from Kai to her.

"Ottum, meet Lolli. Lolli, meet Ottum," Kai said.

Kai lumbered toward Adin to say hello in the only way she would hear it from him, but Lolli and Ottum remained rooted where they stood.

"I'm so sorry about Sasha. I should have visited more often. I didn't know he was sick. I didn't know..." Will said quietly when they finally released each other.

Adin reached up and took his face in both hands. "Hush boy. There was no way you could have known, and neither Sasha nor I would have had you change your life for us. He loved you, and he knew you loved him. That is enough," she said as she pulled his head low enough to kiss his forehead.

They embraced again as both of them fought back tears.

"How did you know?" Adin asked as she suddenly realized she hadn't told Will about Sasha.

"Kai told me," he said as though it should have been obvious.

Adin looked at Kai and narrowed her eyes. "Who really told you William? And don't you be telling me more stories of talking wolves!" she said as she shook a warning finger at him.

"I am not sure that Lolli or Saul ever got her to believe it is possible to communicate with me. She just thought they were good with animals," Kai warned Will.

"Adin, it's a long story that I'll tell you later. Meanwhile, we should tether the horses and go inside for tea," he said as he reached for Midnight's reins. The black stallion tossed his head, but Will let him know with a firm tug of the reins that he would tolerate no games.

Adin stepped aside and saw Ottum for the first time. She looked curiously from her to Lolli as they stood staring at each other. "Where are my manners? For that matter, Will, where are yours, and who is this young lady?" she asked nodding her head Ottum's direction.

"Adin I would like you to meet Ottum," Will said.

Ottum reluctantly pulled her eyes from Lolli and reached out a hand as Adin approached. "It's very nice to meet you after hearing so much about you," she said with a smile.

Adin blushed. "I hope it was all, or at least mostly, good." And then turning toward him, "Lolli! Come here and say hello. Seriously!" she said to Ottum. "He brings a wolf to my cabin and thinks nothing of it, but then he acts terrified of the likes of you!"

Ottum walked slowly toward Lolli, their eyes locked the entire way. Lolli cautiously raised his hand, and she took it. They stood that way for a moment, each looking as though they wanted to read the other's soul. Then Ottum released Lolli's hand and pulled him into a bear hug.

"Something tells me that there's another long story," Adin said to Will as she nodded at Ottum and Lolli.

A long story, indeed, Kai thought to himself.

Will just nodded. "Do you have a tether or do I need to get one?"

CHAPTER 28

Ottum and Will sat on their log by the waterfall. The reprieve from winter hadn't lasted long, and there was fresh snow on the ground again.

Will had used the excuse of wanting to read Sasha's letter in private, and had invited Ottum to come with him. It was their first time alone since Adin and Lolli had arrived a few days ago. Their guests were a whirlwind of stories and questions, and although everyone was enjoying the visit, a little time apart seemed like a good idea too.

"Do you think Adin and Lolli are enjoying their time alone as much as we are?" Ottum asked.

"I think that you and I would have put our pallet and a lockable door to better use than they will," he replied with a smoldering look and a mental image.

In response, Ottum grabbed Will's head and kissed him deeply.

"The snow can't be that cold, right?" he asked when they reluctantly pulled apart.

Ottum laughed. "If we're going to be in the snow, I get to be on top." She watched Will consider and, despite the temptation, she decided it best to finish what they had come here for. "As much as I want you, I think that you should read Sasha's letter. Or at least read it first," she added with a wink and a teasing touch.

"I'd be less distracted if I read it second...and neither of us has to be on the ground," he said before kissing her again.

Would it really matter if he read the letter before or after? She thought. *It isn't like anyone but Kai would come looking for us if we take a bit longer alone.* Kai had walked out the door with them, but graciously decided to remain near the cabin. He and the horses had become friends and enjoyed chasing each other around in the snow as much as their tethers would allow.

Ottum felt the wave wash over her. *Avil!* She pulled away from Will and signaled for his silence. "The cabin. Leon's at the cabin!" Without another word, she stood and exploded into a full run.

Will followed, uncertain of what they would find, but willing to trust her urgency. "Kai is there, and Adin is skilled with weapons," he offered in Path as much to console himself as her.

"Hush!" was her only reply.

The distance wasn't great, but Ottum felt like every stride was one too many. She hadn't felt a wave like that since last fall when Leon had taken Eyota's head, and she would feel uneasy until she knew what had happened. *If he's harmed Kai...*

Will watched her pull her sword and slow as they neared the clearing. Both of them were breathing hard, but Ottum seemed to have no care if her approach was heard or not. The horses were making enough ruckus that Ottum and Will might not have been heard even panting or at a full run.

Ottum took time to note that Kai, Lolli, and Adin were safe before she spoke. The smell of blood was what was causing the horses to stomp, whiny, and pull at their leads. The stallion was pulling hard at his tether, but so far it held him. Ottum couldn't blame the horses for wanting to get away. "Leon. What have you done?" she asked as her eyes took in the sight in front of her.

Leon had Saul held with a knife to his throat. That wouldn't have bothered Ottum nearly as much as the patch of red that was expanding on the lower front of Saul's coat and down his pants or that Saul wasn't fighting to get away.

Leon laughed. "It looks like our poor, little, lost Saul found his way home. I'd think you'd be happy to see him again!"

"Let him go." It wasn't a fierce command or a plea. If anything, Ottum's voice was filled with weary sadness.

"Can't do that, Sis! Without your boy, here, it'd be an unfair fight," he said with a flick of his head toward the porch. "I hadn't counted on you having friends over when I came to visit."

Even now he refuses to take responsibility for his actions. He wants to believe that Saul's injuries are someone else's fault.

Lolli looked like he was living a nightmare while Adin was oddly quiet and still.

"What are we fighting over or about?" Ottum paused and checked the spot on Saul's stomach. "Whatever you want to say, Leon, you'd better make it quick if you're counting on Saul to protect you."

"Oh, he's still got some time. He'll eventually bleed out, but I made sure it won't happen too fast," Leon paused for effect. When Ottum didn't react, he pushed the knife a bit deeper into the skin at Saul's throat.

Saul didn't react at all which concerned Ottum greatly. She wondered how Leon had managed to injure Saul and if the wound was fatal. She tried to communicate with Saul in Path, but he didn't reply.

"Of course, I could change that," Leon said with anger.

"No, Leon. There's no need to do that," Ottum said. *Why isn't Saul responding?* She fretted.

Leon glowered at her for a bit longer before his face broke into a smile again. "So you *are* fond of my boy here, eh?"

"Saul isn't really the issue here. As you said, he's your way of keeping the fight fair. So, now that you have my full attention and a way to protect yourself, talk to me," Ottum said as she lowered her sword.

"'Cause that's what families do, right, Sis? We talk because we love each other. We don't fight," Leon squinted at her. "What the hell family did you grow up in, because that isn't how mine worked," he said as he spit to the side, the knife accidentally digging deep enough into Saul's throat to draw a faint line of blood.

Saul barely winced. He was pale, but still conscious. Leon was bigger than Saul, but Ottum knew that Saul would have no problem getting out of his hold if he really tried. But Saul didn't try. Ottum knew he heard her when she spoke to him in Path because he looked at her. She realized that the only reason Saul wouldn't fight or respond was because he knew he was dead regardless of what he tried. *Leon wasn't lying about the wound. Saul's being still so that I can take Leon out without anyone else getting hurt.*

Ottum didn't know how to answer Leon in a way that would keep from provoking him further. Saul's wound might be mortal, but she didn't want him to suffer any additional pain if it could be avoided. Ottum could feel Will planning to take action soon. Kai had told her the moment she came into the clearing that he would follow her lead and that he'd instructed Lolli to do the same.

They're all waiting on me, she thought to herself, *and I don't have any idea what to do next.* Ottum had spent days trying to figure out how to save Leon, and now he was standing in front of her holding a man who he had knifed in the gut. The reality of the scene pressed into her, preventing her from deciding on the best action to take. Finally she managed to say, "I keep trying to find a way for this to end well, and I can't. How do you see this ending, Leon? Is there a way for all of us to walk away and live happy lives?"

"Well, Saul here won't be walking far even if I let him go," Leon said with an Avil's nauseating chuckle.

Ottum ignored the malice in her brother's voice and the callousness of his laugh. She searched his face for any trace of the good man Leon could have become. His skin was grey, the whites at the bottom of his eyes showed, and every line on his face was the result of anger. The harder she looked for some clue that her once innocent brother still existed, the more Avil she saw. And that Avil was getting more impatient.

"I'm serious, Leon. I understand that Saul is mortally wounded, but I still want to know how you see this ending. Is there an ending that would make you happy?" Ottum asked.

"You and your happiness crap," Leon said with a huff while shaking his head.

In that moment Ottum realized that her brother had never been happy for more than fleeting minutes since he was a very small child. He wanted to feel it desperately, but didn't believe it was possible, or at least not for him. Even those moments of happiness he did experience, he viewed as punishment. They weren't a break from the harshness of his life. Instead, it was the world showing him what he couldn't have. For the first time in her life, Ottum realized there was absolutely nothing she could ever say or do that would save Leon. In that same moment she also realized that she would never be able to deny him the opportunity to save himself.

"I can't," she said as she turned to look at Kai, her eyes apologetic and filling with tears.

"You can't *what?*" Leon asked tersely.

Ottum shifted her attention back to Leon just in time to see a surprised look cross his face. He released Saul, who fell to the ground at Leon's feet. Then Leon looked toward the porch.

Ottum didn't have to look to know what Leon would see. She didn't know when Adin had sneaked away, but the woman Will considered his mother was not standing on the porch. Adin was standing behind Leon. "No," Ottum whispered as she started toward them, but Leon was dead before she arrived. "No," she said while shaking her head at Adin, her face full of disbelief.

"I'm sorry, lass. I made it as quick as I could," was all Adin said before moving to tend Saul's wounds.

Ottum looked at Leon lying motionless on the snow. She watched Will reach down to close his eyelids, saw the blood seeping into the snow beneath Leon's body, and was aware of Kai brushing against her side. Ottum still held her sword. She had killed many Avil's with it and had intended to kill this one with it too. Leon had deserved to feel it's cold steel end his life just as much as any other Avil, but as Ottum looked down at the Avil lying on the ground, all she could see was her brother — her brother who had never known happiness, had never felt loved, and who had died filled with as much anger as he had lived with. Ottum had seen death plenty of times, but as she looked at her dead brother lying in the red-stained snow, she realized that Leon had never known what it was to live.

Adin gently turned Saul over and tried to open his coat, but he feebly reached to stop her.

"There are some wounds even you can't heal," Saul said as he looked to his side at Leon and then back at her. "Does this mean I'm one of yours?" he whispered.

Adin gathered his hands in hers and smiled at him.

Saul shut his eyes briefly. "The day I left camp, you threatened to hunt me down if I ever harmed you or one of yours. Given his current state," he rolled his eyes toward Leon, "it makes me think that perhaps I'm one of yours."

Tears rolled down Adin's face. "Ah, hon, you became one of mine the day Lolli brought you to me."

"I'm sure it was all the sweet talking you did that day," Kai said in Path. He leaned against Ottum's leg to help support her, but Leon's death didn't affect Kai the way it did Ottum. Like her, Kai had realized that Saul knew his death was approaching. It pleased him that the man he had known to be so selfish had acted honorably today.

Saul's breathing shallowed further, but he managed a smile at Kai's teasing. If he hadn't been such a stubborn fool, he would have gotten along well with Kai. It was always good to have a friend who could make fun even in dire moments.

If I hadn't been such a stubborn fool, Saul thought, *I wouldn't have been poisoned, Leon would have fallen to my sword, my parents wouldn't have lost both son's to Avils, and I wouldn't be dying here now with a wound that should have been prevented. It's a bit late to realize it, but at least I kept him occupied so that no one else was hurt.*

With the last strength Saul had, he turned to where he'd heard Lolli approach. In Path to only him he said, "She's good people. You take care of her, and," he paused, "and..."

"And?" Lolli asked.

"And," Saul said so quietly that Lolli wasn't sure he even heard it. But then Saul closed his eyes and spoke no more.

CHAPTER 29

"How are you?" Oscar asked.

"It's been a touch of a long day," Ottum replied. Even in this dream world her eyes and head ached from crying. She looked around and realized that Oscar had brought her to one of her favorite places in all of Nohnah. The scent of pine wafted about her, the stars seemed close enough to reach out and touch, and a fire took the chill out of the mountain air.

"I imagine so," Oscar said as he patted the ground beside him.

"I'll say one thing though," she said as she sat on the blanket beside him.

When Ottum didn't continue, Oscar asked, "What's that?"

"Adin threw a stick I didn't expect."

Oscar nodded.

"Did you?" she asked him.

"Expect it? No," he said with a shake of his head.

Ottum reached for his hand and draped his arm about her shoulders. "Were there any possible scenarios where Leon and Saul both lived?" she asked wistfully.

"Yes, of course," Oscar replied as he squeezed her hand. "You know that based on your own evaluation. But none of them are what happened. We have to live our lives based on what actually happens, Ottum, not on what could have been."

Ottum sighed and remembered the sight of Leon lying in the scarlet-stained snow. "But still, I want to know. Is there any chance he would ever have changed?"

"I don't know," Oscar replied. "Saul was the first person Leon killed. He made life a living hell for some, but mostly he did it with manipulation, fear, and empty threats. As long as he didn't directly, physically harm them, he felt any suffering was their own fault and that they deserved it. As long as he didn't hit them with his hands, feet, or other physical weapons, he felt he had nothing to do with the trauma his victims experienced. Unlike some who are born without empathy and who will harm for pleasure, Leon started his life able to feel other's pain. With time, that part of him faded, but your brother didn't like to believe he ever hurt others."

"But he stabbed Saul, Ottum said. "That's pretty direct."

"And there's what he did to you," Oscar replied with a gentle, but very direct look.

Ottum met his eyes at first, but looked away to calm herself. She was very quiet for a few moments. Oscar hadn't defined what Leon had done to her all those years ago, but she remembered and knew without asking what he meant. Occasionally the memory found its way into her dreams and woke her with a panicked start. "He did it for power, you know," she said as she moved her view from the ground to Oscar. "As far as I know, there was no one else."

"That doesn't change that he did it to you," Oscar persisted.

"No," Ottum said quietly. "It doesn't change that he did it to me." Oscar had found out years ago and tried to get her to talk, but she never would. Apparently now he felt it was worth trying again.

"I know it's been a long day, but he's gone now," Oscar said. "Talking might help you grieve for him," Oscar paused, "and for what he took from you so long ago."

She had no will left to fight Oscar tonight, so she sighed and said, "We were just kids. I was the only person he could force to do anything, especially something that made him feel good. That doesn't make it right, but he was just a kid. Somebody should have stopped him when I told them what was happening, but his life as a child should never have been such that it was the only power he felt he had.

It was wrong, it hurt, and it's at least a small part of the abandonment issues I have. Maybe I should still be angry at him, but the things he did later in life seem far worse because he did them as an adult who was no longer powerless. I've no problem holding him accountable for those things, but for the other, to some degree it was a reaction to his environment. A very unfortunate reaction for me, but not one I was capable of stopping or changing at the time," Ottum said with another deep sigh.

"You forgave him long ago didn't you?" Oscar asked, surprised that he never realized it before now.

"Yes," she said quietly. She sat with her head down, staring into the past.

"Child," Oscar said.

Ottum looked up at him.

"I wish I'd been there to stop it, but I met you too late for that. Although you wouldn't have grown into the fierce and beautiful woman you are now, I wish I would have just taken you away that first day I met you," Oscar said as he brushed a ringlet behind her ear. "I wish that I hadn't hidden my illness from you. And I wish that I'd said goodbye, told you how much I love you, and made sure you knew how lovable you are."

Tears once again streamed down Ottum's face. With each sob that wracked through her, grief and anger were dislodged and allowed to melt away into nothingness. She cried for Leon, for Saul, for Oscar, and for herself. She cried until all the raw emotions were stripped away and all that remained was the need for time to heal her again.

The stars rotated in the sky, the fire burned low, and peace settled into Ottum's life.

"Oscar," Ottum finally said, "why did Leon stab Saul if hurting people felt wrong to him?"

"I wondered how long it would take for you to ask that question," Oscar said.

"I suppose that means you aren't going to answer?"

"I'll answer if you'll tell me what you think first," he replied

"Well, it's possible that he found a way to not feel guilty about it or thought that it wouldn't be a mortal wound. Another possibility is that Leon just totally snapped and knew Saul's wound would be fatal. And the only other reason I can think of is that Saul had changed, and it threatened Leon's entire perspective of the world in a way that made it easier to just get rid of Saul instead of looking at everything else differently. I'm just not sure which it is," Ottum said.

"It was a little of all three," Oscar said, "but more of the latter two. If Saul changed, and he had changed enough for Leon to notice even if it wasn't enough to avoid Leon's malice, it meant you had saved him. Leon's entire experiment had been set up to prove that you wouldn't. Having most of your beliefs disproven in one slice can rattle a soul."

"So I've heard," Ottum said sarcastically.

"Are you going to be okay?" Oscar asked.

"In what way?"

"In all ways, but specifically related to Leon's death, Adin's actions, Saul's death, and all the change that's been thrown your way lately," Oscar replied.

Ottum looked away and into the fire before answering. "In many ways, the Leon I'm grieving for died long ago. It's more permanent this time, but perhaps now I can let him go," Ottum paused. "I find it strange that I can grieve for who he could have been while being angry at who he chose to be."

Oscar listened quietly, but nodded to let her know he heard her.

"Adin's actions weren't that different than mine have been on many occasions in the past. Leon crossed a line. If you're willing to dole out violence and death, sooner or later someone is likely to return both to you. I want to be unhappy with her over it, but if Leon had lived and walked away, all of us would have been in danger from him for the rest of our lives. She did it with mercy and speed which is more than Leon gave Saul. It's not like I didn't kill Avil's that were brothers, sisters, sons, daughters, and even parents to someone else. But that doesn't change that Adin killed my brother at a time when I had recently realized that our lives are filled with choice. With time, Adin and I will get past it. For now, I can forgive her, but I'm not ready to be friends with her."

"That seems fair enough," Oscar said.

"When you first started communicating with me this way, you told me to stop taking responsibility for things I'm not responsible for, and to stop using those things to hide from what I really am responsible for. I was quite angry with you and thought that you were wrong about me. Since then, and there's no need for you to gloat over this," Ottum added, "I've come to realize that you were right."

Oscar chuckled and winked at her.

"There is a part of me that tries to feel responsible for Saul. Logically, I know that I'm not. But on some other level, it's a challenge to allow Saul and Leon to carry the responsibility that is theirs. At least I've realized that if I try to shoulder their stuff, it prevents me from doing, or at least takes energy I could use away from other things that only I can do."

"That's a start. Recognizing our weaknesses is the first step to making them strengths," Oscar said.

"As for all the change, well, something Kai said not that long ago has stuck with me. He was talking about how the differences between he and I made us better. Then he went on to point out that the differences between Will and I could work the same way. It might not be quite the same thing, but if I can embrace that which is different instead of fighting against it, my life might be better for it. So I've decided to do my best to look for the ways that understanding more than one point of view makes me stronger, wiser, better, etc.

Does all that mean I'm going to be okay enough for you to be satisfied?" she asked Oscar.

He smiled and nodded. "I believe it does."

"Oscar?"

"Yes, child?"

"What are you?" Ottum asked.

"Hmm?"

"What are you?" Ottum didn't elaborate because she knew he understood her question. She'd heard Kai call him a Greybeard and wondered if Oscar would elaborate.

"I'm just me," Oscar said with a shrug of his shoulders and a smile.

Ottum knew that was all she was going to get for an answer, at least for now.

CHAPTER 30

Will sat with Sasha's letter in his hands and Ottum at his side. The mood today was very different from the last time they had sat here at their waterfall.

Saul and Leon had been cremated because the frozen ground prevented burial, and Adin objected to the thought of their bodies being food for the creatures in the area. As the fire had burned low, Adin and Lolli started talking about returning to their home. Will knew they were waiting on him to read Sasha's letter before they left. Like Adin, he suspected he knew its contents. Unlike her, he thought he could do without knowing for certain at least for a while longer. But Will realized that the time had come, and he needed to read it now even if he didn't feel ready.

So with an uneasy feeling, he took Ottum's hand and began reading.

> *Hello Will,*
>
> *For much of your life, you and I have approached difficult topics in small chunks and sometimes from the side. We had time, after all, so there was no rush. However, with the exception of this letter, my time with you is done.*
>
> *I suppose I could use that as a reason to be direct, to outright tell you the things I only hinted at before, and to attempt to force you to see a few things you either didn't want to or just couldn't see. That wouldn't make the obvious any more obvious or that which you can't or won't see any more seeable.*
>
> *If I know you at all, you didn't read this the moment my sweet Adin handed it to you. Instead, you took some time to try to figure out what it might say and what sort of gift I'd leave to you in a letter. If*

time allowed, you probably even worked out your response to both. If I'm right, good! That saves me a lot of writing.

Shortly after you came of age, Adin and I added you as an owner for the camp and all of its land. We figured that you would at least find someone well qualified if you didn't want it when we were both gone. So while you may not have known before, you do now.

Don't think of that as a gift, though. We worked you hard when you were here, and you have consistently worked to improve yourself so we felt (and feel) that you deserve it. Besides, both of us think of you as our son.

Don't think of it as a burden either. You've always lived your own life and we would never ask you to permanently take on something you didn't want. Be a part of the camp if you want to be, or pass it on to someone capable if you don't.

The only gift I'm leaving you is this truth:

It doesn't matter how many years you get to be here, it will never seem like enough if you're really living your life and loving those you seek to keep close.

With that out of the way, I'd like to ask a favor of you. When Adin takes up with another man, assure her that I would have wanted her to. I'd be a damn fool to think someone as beautiful, intelligent, and talented as she is wouldn't attract another man. And any man who isn't attracted to the most magnificent creature I've ever known is a damn fool. I can't stand the thought of it, but that stays between you and me. She'll pick a good man who'll enrich her life, and my Adin deserves the best life has to offer. That's something I can stand the thought of and hope she gets. I'll be dead anyway, so my opinion doesn't really matter, but she'll still think it does. So let her know it's okay.

Now for the hard part. I'd hug you if I could; tell you again that I'm proud of you, and that I hope you are proud of yourself; and remind you to make sure that when you take a mate, she's a woman who loves deeply, fights fairly, and lives fully.

There's other stuff that matters when it comes to mates as well as life, but you'll figure that stuff out for yourself. Mistakes are some of the best teachers I've ever had.

There's more I'd like to say and so much more I'd have liked to do with you, but we do what we can in this life…no more and no less.

Goodbye, son.

Love,

Sasha

Will smiled despite his tears as he folded the letter and tucked it back inside his coat. *Goodbye, Sasha.*

"You're smiling and crying. Does that mean you like what you read?" Ottum asked as she gently squeezed his hand.

Will squeezed her hand in reply and nodded. When he could trust himself to speak without sobbing, he said, "It wasn't what I thought it would be, but it was what I should have expected." He smiled through his tears and said, "It was Sasha."

Ottum wanted to ask what the letter had said, but knew that sometimes curiosity needed to be contained.

"Walk with me?" Will asked.

"Of course," she replied, but she was surprised when he stood and turned away from the direction of the cabin.

"It's been an eventful few days, hasn't it?" he began.

"There's no arguing with that," Ottum said.

"Emotion has been running high," he paused, "and low. Multiple things have happened that create the possibility for change and that have allowed me to see things from a different view. Because of all of that, I don't think it's the best time to make major decisions. However, Adin and Lolli will be leaving soon...probably tomorrow, now that I have read Sasha's letter. I'd like to be able to tell Adin when I'll visit her, but I want to talk to you about a few things first."

Ottum nodded, uncertain of where the conversation was going. "Okay," she said.

"I'd like to go back to the camp for longer than a visit. I don't' know if I'll stay or eventually return to my cabin, but now that I see things differently, I want to go back to see if I was perhaps mistaken about some things," Will said.

Ottum nodded, but her heart was racing. It hadn't been that long ago that he had wanted to send her away because he thought she would eventually leave. Now here he was talking about leaving. Logical or not, fear that Will was leaving her began to build.

"You and I have a lot to learn about each other, and I'm not sure I've any right to ask this, but I'd like it if you would come with me. I mean you and Kai too, of course. If you want, I'm sure we could find you a cabin of your own at the camp, or we could stay together. I'll need to do things to the cabin here before I can go. You're welcome to stay and help, or you can go with Adin and Lolli. I know you have lots of questions for Lolli," Will realized he was rambling and stopped.

It took Ottum a few seconds to notice that Will was waiting for a response and that her silence was making him nervous. She had been so relieved that he wanted her to join him that she'd barely heard the rest of what he'd said. "Sure! I mean, yeah, I'd like that. Kai wanted to go to the camp again anyway."

Will beamed and she beamed back at him. "I guess that went well for two people with abandonment issues," he said with a wink.

She laughed. "Indeed!"

"So do you think you'll go with Adin and Lolli tomorrow?" he asked. "I'd prefer you stay, of course, but it might make me work faster if it meant getting to you sooner." Will smiled at her.

"No," Ottum shook her head. "I think Adin and I need a bit of time apart." She saw alarm spread across Will's face. "We'll be Okay, Will, eventually. I think it's likely that she and I will even become good friends. Avil or not and right or wrong, Adin killed my brother. Frankly, it's probably more that she killed his chances of ever changing that bothers me more than his actual death. I know that sounds awful, but it's how I feel."

"It's not awful," Will reassured her.

"For Adin, my brother killed one of her students. She seems like an intelligent woman, and I'm sure she knows that members of a family can be very different. While it's likely that she'll need to spend time with me to see who I am and to trust me, I think that some time alone with Lolli might go a long way toward helping her deal with that too," Ottum said.

"Why do you say that?" Will asked.

"When we were preparing their bodies for cremation, Lolli was the only one who looked at Leon with love. He might have looked at him with more love than even I did," Ottum said, her voice cracking with emotion.

Will pulled her close to him. "I think it's possible that Lolli looked at him as he did because, better than any of us, he understands what it means to see things from Leon's point of view."

Ottum nodded and wiped away a tear.

"By the way, I had the chance to talk to Lolli alone yesterday, and he said something really interesting. Do you remember when we talked about whether or not all of life is selfish and that maybe it sometimes just happens to benefit others?" Will asked.

"Yes, of course."

"Well, Lolli said that the only times we're being selfish is when we're not making ourselves more capable of giving back to and loving others. What do you think of that?" Will asked.

Ottum rubbed her chin as she paused to consider. "If that's true, then intent is what makes an action selfish or not. That doesn't fit with my theory that only action matters, so I'll have to think it through more. But in general, I think that might be a reasonable guideline. 'If I do this to make myself better, will it benefit other people?' seems a good question to ask if you're trying to figure out if you're being selfish or not."

"Why do you do that?" Will asked.

"Do what?" Ottum asked.

"Why do you rub your chin as though you have a beard?" he asked.

Ottum laughed softly. "That would be Oscar's influence. He never had a beard either, but he rubbed his chin when he was deep in thought. I didn't mimic that on purpose, but it's one of his habits that I acquired after spending time with him."

"I wish that I could have met him just as I wish you could have met Sasha," Will said wistfully.

"Me too," Ottum replied.

"It will be strange to be at camp without him, to never hear his laugh, to never again ask his opinion, and to see Adin with another man," he said.

"You mean like Lolli?" Ottum asked.

Will furrowed his brow. "Lolli? But," he stammered, "really?"

Ottum couldn't believe he hadn't noticed the obvious affection between the two, but then again, Will had only ever known Adin as Adin and Sasha.

"That seems a bit fast," Will said with disapproval written all over his face.

"Will, if death doesn't teach us that our time here is short and to make the best of it, what does?" she asked gently.

"Well, I suppose," he said remembering Sasha's letter. "As Sasha would say, Lolli'd be a damn fool not to want Adin."

"I don't think her enjoying Lolli's company makes her grieve for Sasha any less. We're pretty complex beings. It's possible to be happy and sad at the same time," Ottum said. She'd felt both emotions simultaneously on too many occasions lately.

"I'm glad you're not leaving tomorrow," Will said almost shyly.

"Would Sasha say I'd be a damn fool to go?" Ottum asked with a wink.

Will's deep laughter filled the air around them. "I don't know for sure. But I'm pretty sure he'd tell me I was if I hadn't tried to get you to stay."

"Well then, perhaps we should avoid his chastising and share a single cabin at camp," she said.

"Agreed," he said with a large smile. "And with that decided, I think we should head home. Adin will want to know my response to the letter, and there will be much to talk about before they leave."

"Agreed. But first I want to talk to you about Kai. I hope Kai joins us, but I'm going to offer him a termination of his pledge to be my Companion for the rest of his life," Ottum said.

"Do you really think he'll take it?" Will asked.

"I don't know. Since he was a pup, it's the only life he's ever known. That doesn't mean it should be, though. It would break my heart to see him go, but it would be wrong to not offer him the chance to. It's strange how life can seem the same for so long and then suddenly be so very different."

"Yes. I've thought the same thing more than once recently," Will agreed.

They spent the rest of their walk discussing those changes, and shortly before reaching the clearing, they talked about what would need to be done to the cabin before they could leave.

CHAPTER 31

The horses stamped impatiently. They were packed, and after being tethered for a few days, Midnight and Thunder were more than ready to stretch their legs with some real walking.

"Well, you take care, Lolli," Will said as he reached out to shake his hand. Will had spoken to Adin alone last night and assured her that Sasha would approve of her being with Lolli. Will wasn't so sure he felt the same way, but he trusted Adin. And though he hadn't seen it before Ottum pointed it out, Adin was very fond of Lolli and he of her.

Lolli grabbed Will's hand, pulled him into a hug, and thumped his back more enthusiastically than Will was prepared for. "Lolli is very happy Will and Ottum are coming to visit us!" he said while rocking Will side to side.

Ottum couldn't help but smile as she and Adin watched the exchange.

"You take care of him, Ottum. A mother is always protective of her children, and while he isn't officially mine, he is in all the ways that matter," Adin said.

Adin searched Ottum's face, and although Ottum didn't know what Adin looked for, the elder woman smiled as though she had found it. "Will seems fond of you, Lolli is quite taken with you, and something tells me that wolf would take out anyone who thought differently," Adin said with a glance Kai's direction. "So while we need to get to know each other, please know that you are welcome in our camp. And not just because Will wants you there," Adin added.

"Thank you, Adin. We're both looking forward to visiting you soon. I'll do my best to watch over Will, although he has a stubborn streak that'll make it challenging at times."

Adin and Ottum both laughed at Ottum's comment.

Ottum looked at Kai, and her heart felt like it broke into a hundred pieces. She'd talked with Kai while Will talked to Adin last night. Ottum thought that Kai would stay with her even though she offered to release him from service as her Companion. When Kai responded that he would like to leave with Adin and Lolli, Ottum hadn't known what to say. But she'd offered and Kai had accepted the offer, so there he stood by Lolli.

"He's much more than just a wolf to me," Ottum said to Adin. Her eyes watered at the thought of being away from Kai again. "Please watch over him until we get to camp."

"Lolli adores him, so I don't think you have anything to be worried about," Adin replied.

Will walked up and embraced Adin while Ottum moved to Lolli. All of the roughness of Lolli's hug with Will was gone with Ottum. Lolli held her as though she was the last good thing in the world, and it was his job to keep her safe. Such tenderness from someone who was often rambunctious in his enthusiasm pushed out the tears that had only been threatening to fall until then.

"I wasn't going to cry today!" Ottum said with a hint of frustration at herself.

"Lolli is crying too," he said, hoping it would help comfort her. "It is okay to cry. Others know how important we are to them when we cry and that we know how to love someone other than us. So crying is okay. Okay?" Lolli asked.

"Okay," Ottum said wiping away her tears and shaking her head at the wonder that was Lolli. "When we come to camp, I'd like it if you'd tell me your story."

"What story would Lolli tell Ottum?" Lolli asked, seeming genuinely confused.

"Your story, Lolli. I'd like to know about your life from when you were little to now," Ottum said. "You crossed an ocean to get from Gizmania to Nohnah, that in itself is probably quite a story."

Lolli's eyes widened. "That is a long story, Ottum. Some of Lolli's story is not good," Lolli said shaking his head fiercely from side to side. "Some of it is not good at all!"

"We all have parts of our stories that aren't good, Lolli. Some of us perhaps have worse parts than others, but your story becomes a good one. And it's even better because you made it through those parts that weren't so good. I've hoped to meet someone like you for as long as I've been a Chaser. Please, Lolli, won't you at least consider telling me?" she asked.

Lolli weaved from side to side, looked down at his feet, and then finally looked Ottum in the eyes. "Lolli will tell Ottum," he said, nodding his head. "Lolli will tell Ottum because of Leon."

Ottum shut her eyes, bit her lip, and nodded as more tears escaped down her face. "Thank you, Lolli. Thank you," she said as she hugged him close again.

Ottum stepped back and turned to Kai. She dropped to her knees and embraced him as he came forward. Tears welled and she fought them back. *I'm the one who said he could go!* she reminded herself.

"According to Lolli, crying is okay. Okay?" Kai teased softly.

That worked to change the tears to laughter. "I'm going to miss you more than tears or words can say," Ottum said. "It was hard the first time you left, but this time…" Ottum's voice trailed off, unable to put into words the intense love she felt for him.

"I know, my lady. It is no easier for me. When Oscar spoke with me on my way back here, he asked me to promise him that I would live for you. Besides finding it strange, I thought at the time that it had something to do with Leon. But now I think he meant for after things resolved. You and I have lived our lives doing what we thought we were meant to do. Neither of us really has any idea what we are doing now that we know it is almost entirely our choice of how to live. I think he knew we would both be lost and would need each other's help. If I do not leave now, you will never believe that I stay out of choice."

Ottum's heart soared. "So you are leaving to prove that you want to stay?" she asked with a laugh.

"Yes, my lady. Besides, my kind do not seem to be as abundant near the camp as in other places we have travelled," Kai said, purposely leaving out that they were being killed on sight. "I think that there is something I can do to help increase our numbers. It is my duty, you know," he said with a wolfish grin.

"Oh, really?" Ottum asked, both surprised and pleased. "Well, that somehow makes me feel better about you leaving. Just don't wear yourself out between now and when we arrive," she teased.

"I will reserve some energy if the two of you will," he quipped as Will approached. Then with a bit of reluctance he added, "My travelling companions seem ready to leave, so I am afraid I must say goodbye for now."

Ottum squeezed him close to her again. "Goodbye, dear friend. Please be safe, and I'll see you soon."

"Goodbye my lady," Kai said to Ottum as he lumbered toward the horses. Pausing for one moment to look at Will, he said, "Take care of her, and bring her to me soon."

Will and Ottum watched until their friends were out of sight.

"Shall we get started?" Ottum asked.

Will gave her a questioning look.

"I miss Kai already and am looking forward to hearing Lolli's story. The sooner we get this cabin packed up, the sooner we can join them," Ottum said.

Will laughed and shook his head. "You don't sit still for very long, do you?" he asked.

"Nope," Ottum replied with a grin.

"Before we get started, I've been thinking about something you said yesterday," Will said.

"Yes?"

"You offered Kai the chance to be something other than your Companion. Does that mean that you're no longer a Chaser?" Will asked as delicately as he could.

Ottum noticed how timidly he approached the topic. A few months ago she would have told him it was what she was born to do. Given their discussions about her being a warrior, she supposed she couldn't blame Will for being timid about asking.

"I've decide that there are other ways to make a difference, so I'll not be hunting Avils any longer," Ottum replied. "However, as Oscar once said, we're all Chasers."

# # #

.

ABOUT THE AUTHOR

Kathryn Woodall grew up exploring the timberland on her family's farm, and reading when it was too dark to be in the woods. Often there was a dog at her side and horses in the nearby pasture.

In addition to Chasing, she has started writing the story of Lolli's life. You can follow Kathryn's blog at http://www.acomfortablesoul.com to stay updated on release dates for it and future books.

www.ingramcontent.com/pod-product-compliance
Lightning Source LLC
Chambersburg PA
CBHW061139170626
46809CB00003B/918